Semper Fi ol' friend
From
Barney Quinn

THE LIGHT SIDE OF DAMNATION

10/4/06

To: Marshall,
Good friend – thank you. Hope
you enjoyed the read.

BY
WILLIAM F. LEE

Your friend – the Major
W. F. Lee

Bloomington, IN Milton Keynes, UK

authorHOUSE

AuthorHouse™
1663 Liberty Drive, Suite 200
Bloomington, IN 47403
www.authorhouse.com
Phone: 1-800-839-8640

AuthorHouse™ UK Ltd.
500 Avebury Boulevard
Central Milton Keynes, MK9 2BE
www.authorhouse.co.uk
Phone: 08001974150

This book is a work of non-fiction. Unless otherwise noted, the author and the publisher make no explicit guarantees as to the accuracy of the information contained in this book and in some cases, names of people and places have been altered to protect their privacy.

First published by AuthorHouse 7/5/2006

ISBN: 1-4259-4473-6 (sc)

Library of Congress Control Number: 2006905391

Printed in the United States of America
Bloomington, Indiana

This book is printed on acid-free paper.

In memory of

Lance Corporal Michael Baronowski

A Special Marine

Panel 12E – Row 128

8/6/46 – 11/29/66

Also by
William F. Lee

The Bottom of the List

And coming soon

The Boys in Blue White Dress

War is serious business. War is hellish.
Almost everyone claims to not like it nor want to start one,
but someone or something does.
Nevertheless, wars happen and bring tragedy.
People who have to fight in it truly despise
war for they know first hand the horror,
suffering and anguish.
However, within all the torment of
war, the strongest of bonds are created
and nurtured. Through these ties and
perhaps because of them, instances
of wit and humorous episodes breathe light
into the darkness and damnation of war.
This is a story told by Captain Barney Quinn,
a Marine captain, company commander and later
an aide-de-camp about
these precious moments and bizarre events
during the Vietnam War.
The thread that binds this story together is
the mentoring affiliation the
Commanding General has with Captain Quinn.
Barney's, at times roguish behavior, his sarcastic sense
of humor, and playfully prankish mind both
clash and support this steely-eyed,
Old Corps Marine,
Lieutenant General Walter Barto.
Through Barney's eyes and voice, you will
experience the metamorphosis between these
two, and live among a cast of loveable Marines.
Through all this, Barney tries to maintain a
budding romantic relationship with his gal.
The involuntary extension of his tour of duty,
loyalty to the Corps, and the distance between them
take a toll. Will the Mizpah medallion
Ryley gave Barney work its magic?

All the characters in this tale of
the light side of damnation have fictitious
names, with the exception of one
special Marine.

The Hollywood celebrities are real and those
events are genuine. Almost all the experiences
throughout this story are true-life.

ACKNOWLEDGMENTS

I thank Mary Elaine Hughes who assisted in the editing and proofreading during the process of writing and rewriting this fun endeavor. In addition, I thank her for her constant encouragement and countless suggestions.

Many thanks to Charles D. Melson, Chief Historian, History and Museums Division of the Marine Corps Historical Center for providing me with numerous maps of Vietnam, and for making available two historical publications on the war in Vietnam.

As usual, I relied on Colonel John G. Miller, USMC, (Ret), good friend, fellow former Marine and author in his own right, for his guidance, support, advice, and continual championing of my writing endeavors. All are sincerely appreciated. Without his urging over the past many months, this would not have been possible. John, thank you.

For my many newly found friends and co-writers at the Lesser North Texas Writers Group, a profound thanks for the hours of listening, looked-for suggestions, valuable critique, interest and moral support. All of which were a driving force.

Foremost, I dedicate this to my wife of fifty-one years, JoAnn (Jodi) E. Lee and thank her for reading and re-reading every page, listening to my readings time and time again, and for keeping me in my study hammering away. I also dedicate this to my daughter, Keely Ann Lee Helton and to my son, Michael Bernarr Lee. In reality, all three were at home waiting while "Barney Quinn" was gone.

And last, to Dave Pruet and the folks at Author House for their support.

THE LIGHT SIDE OF DAMNATION

PART ONE

THE PERFUME OF THE PADDIES

PROLOGUE

The last time I left California, heading overseas was to Korea in 1953. That was aboard a ship, an APA named the George C. Clymer, with a couple thousand other Marines. We called it the Greasy George, and it was, including the chow.

This time it is again from California and it's aboard an Air Force C-141 headed for Vietnam with a couple hundred other Marines. I don't know what they call the plane but the chow is a stale baloney sandwich, a decaying oatmeal cookie, and a carton of milk past its sell-by date. Maybe the cooks were related?

The last time I was a sergeant, had just turned nineteen and was leaving on my birthday. Nice present.

This time I'm a Captain with fifteen years service in the Corps, have just turned thirty-two, and again leaving on my birthday. Another nice present. You would think I'd stop accepting gifts.

The last time I was in love with a gal whose first name started with an R---Romy Sidler, a dark haired, dark eyed, voluptuous honey from San Fernando Valley, it didn't last. She wrote me a letter while I was gone and called me John.

I have just fallen in love again, I think anyway, with a gal whose first name also starts with R, again. . . Ryley Nolan. A fine Irish lass with brunette hair and suggestive hazel eyes. She is not from a San anything but rather from Laguna Beach, so maybe a slight break in the chain that will have a different link of luck. She says she is going to write every day, to Barney, not John, I hope.

However, this all seems too weird to me. Too many things alike. Too many coincidences. Leaving for a war again, in the same month, and on the same date, my birthday. Both gals' names start with an R and both are from California.

Bernarr Leslie Quinn doesn't like all these weird same ol', same

xv

ol' goings-on. I'm not superstitious, well maybe just a tad. I was wounded in Korea on the 15th. That bitch wrote me the Dear John on the 15th. I was injured on my 15th jump while in Recon, here in California, years ago and it was on the 15th of the month no less. Those trappings get my attention. All of this is uncanny, peculiar and I'm not liking it one bit. If one more unusual or odd event happens it is going to seriously rattle my cage.

Chapter One

THE PILOT SLAMS THE C-141 down on the runway here in Da Nang airfield, which is in the northern part of South Vietnam, in the I Corps area...the home of all Marine units in country. These are basically a reinforced Division, an enlarged Air Wing, and a bunch of supporting elements. The plane taxis over to a deplaning area near some temporary buildings where a couple hundred Marines and I, legs stiff from the long flight, stagger down the ramp onto the tarmac.

Even though it is not humid, the air is heavy with the fetidness of the country. The surrounding hills are a rich emerald green and beautiful, but the harshness of this place is punctuated by the sight of wounded Marines being loaded aboard an adjacent aircraft for evacuation to the real world.

As we stand around, anxious to get our assignments, but really in the usual military hurry up and wait mode, I notice a sedan pull up. It's a General's vehicle, with its two star plates and flag. This is out of the norm. Way, way out.

Something is up and I'm afraid it involves me.

The front right door opens and out steps an old friend. It's Major Harry Cronin, an occasional golfing partner, and former Company Commander of mine from where I just left, the Marine Barracks in D.C.

Major Cronin quickly opens the rear door and Major General Walter Barto slides out and strides from the highly polished sedan to where I am standing. He is a bull of a man, thick in the neck, shoulders and chest, squared jawed and piercing steel blue eyes. He comes up to me, returns my salute, we shake hands vigorously and while doing so he says, "Welcome to Vietnam, Barney."

"Well, thank you, sir, I think."

I'm not getting this at all. What the hell is he doing down here greeting me? I served under him in Korea where he was my Regimental Commander, and have met him on several occasions at various unit reunions while I was stationed in Washington. I admire and respect this man, even love him, but this is just a little over the top.

"Barney, throw your stuff in the trunk and get in. We're going to have lunch, meet some old friends of yours, and discuss your assignment."

Suspiciously, I get my gear and toss it in the trunk of the sedan, and slide in the back seat with the general. As I am doing this, about four or five enlisted troops from the plane watch this special treatment while pretending not to be listening. No telling what they're thinking, but as we drive off they are talking about it. My gut tells me this will somehow come back to haunt me.

While we head for the 3rd Marine Division Command Post, the general is telling me about the area and what is going on. Major Cronin is in the front seat, turned slightly to his left so he can see the two of us. He is adding his comments to the conversation. I am only half listening, however, because I'm thinking, here we go again. People from my past, popping up and influencing my career. Taking charge of my life. Mentoring. All with good intentions but I'm not happy about this and just want to be treated like everyone else. I just want a rifle company and go do my thing, what I've been trained to do.

After several minutes, we arrive at the CP and the general, with his arm around my shoulders, leads me into his office. Major Cronin excuses himself, and the general sits down behind his desk. He takes off his cap showing his dark hair, graying now, and it is as you would expect, closely cropped. However, what really strike me are his eyes. They are steely blue and he makes direct eye contact immediately. They laser right through me. If his smile, and it's a warm, lip-splitting one, isn't forthcoming, I suppose my face would feel like old plaster shattering. Fortunately, he is in good spirits.

He says, "Sit down, Barney. We'll talk a minute or so and then go get some lunch."

One thing I've learned about generals is that when they call you by your first name, you're by and large on "safe ground." If they call you by rank and name, like Captain Quinn, then it could be serious or they just don't know you very well. If they call you just by your rank, such as Captain, you're in serious trouble. Ass chewing's usually start "Captain, what the hell where you thinking?", or worse.

In any case, ass chewing's don't start on a first name basis so I must be in a sheltered cove. He asks, "How are you doing?"

"Fine, sir." .

"Not married yet?" I can't tell if this is a bona fide query or just idle banter, but it is apparent that Major Cronin clued him in to something. Hopefully not that old flame and wickedly seductive auburn-haired wench, Nancee Moreau, I was seeing in Washington.

"No, sir, not married. Did find a nice Irish lass just before leaving California."

"That's great. Where?"

"Laguna Beach area. Lives there and works in Santa Ana, at MCAS El Toro actually."

"Really?" He gets down to business with, "Barney, we've been friends for a long time."

My thoughts are captains are not really friends with generals. We know one another and I have served under him. I love this guy, but we don't go on liberty together. I'm getting uneasy.

He continues, "Did you know that Major Tony Paletta is here with me, and Brigadier General Cunningham is here with me as well, your old Battalion Commander in Korea?"

Ah, the three of them are together again, and are going to do what's best for me, bet on it.

I reply, "I knew about General Cunningham being here but not Major Paletta."

"Well, you'll see them at lunch. They are going to join us."

"That will be great, sir. In fact, lunch will be even better. I'm hungry. All I've had to eat is that box lunch they served on the aircraft." Shut up and listen, dummy, he doesn't give a crap about box lunches.

He leans forward, propping his elbows on his legs, with a serious look on his face and those steely blues locking right onto my pupils and into my brain-housing group. With a hushed voice, as if someone was listening, he asks, "Barney, where do you want to go? What do you want to do?"

"General, I just want a rifle company. Anywhere. That's what the taxpayers been paying for all these years so it's time to strap it on."

"Barney, I can't give you a company. That wouldn't be right for me to do, to interfere with a Battalion Commander's prerogative, but I will put you in a battalion and the CO will assign you, okay?"

"Yes, sir, more than fair."

"Good, I am going to send you to a tested battalion."

"What ever you think, is fine with me, sir."

"The Commanding Officer is Lieutenant Colonel James Cartwright. Do you know him, or of him?"

I think, here we go again. When are these ghosts going to stop appearing? "Yes, sir, I know him from Hawaii, the Brigade there.

4

He was a captain then. I supported him a few times when I was in Amphib Recon."

"Good, let's go to lunch."

On the way out, the general tells Major Cronin where I am to be assigned, to set up transportation for me to leave in an hour and to let the Regiment and Lieutenant Colonel Cartwright know. We leave, heading for the mess. The general has his arm around my shoulders again, telling me again how good it is to see me and generally treating me like a long-lost friend. In his mind, I guess I am.

At lunch I meet and shake hands with General Cunningham and Major Paletta. General Cunningham is tall and distinguished. He still looks very much the part of the ceremonial Marine he once was at the Barracks. General Barto trusts this man and rightfully so. He is one fine Marine.

Major Paletta, or Big Stoop as he is called only by his closest of friends, is all smiles. His nickname comes from a comic strip character in Little Orphan Annie, Daddy Warbucks sidekick or something. Stoop is huge, thick, and stands easily 6'4" and weighs a solid 260 pounds. We served together in Korea and again in Hawaii. He gives me a bear hug, then grabs me by both shoulders and shakes me saying, "Damn, Stoneface, it's good seeing you again. This is great."

General Barto looks at the major and says, "Stoop, what's this Stoneface stuff?"

"General, that's one of Barney's nicknames. Look at his face. It's made of stone, as if it's chiseled out of granite or something. Cold, hard man, General."

General Barto smiles and General Cunningham says, "Yep, one of my old Squad Leaders is going to lead a company for us."

They didn't even know me then, for Pete's sake. Met me years later, but that's how mentors are fashioned.

We sit down to eat. The food is hot, good and fills a hole. The conversation is okay, dominated by old-fashioned sea stories. We finish quickly and go back to the CP. The general shakes my hand and gives me a one-armed bear hug saying, "Take care of yourself, Barney, and my Marines. I'll be seeing you."

"Aye Aye sir." Now what the devil does that mean, I'll be seeing you. I'm beginning to hear my cage rattling.

He darts inside and I get into the jeep waiting for me. My gear is already stowed in the back, so we just head out for the Battalion Headquarters, which is in the Hill 327 area.

Bouncing along in a jeep over the dirt roads reminds me quickly that I am in the paddies again. First Korea, now here. It is dusty and it has that unmistakable smell, the "perfume" of the paddies. The good ol' honey buckets, natural fertilizer, in full use.

Shortly we bump and jar into the Battalion Headquarters. A scarlet-red sign with yellow lettering is hanging over the entrance---Camp Webb. This is after a Captain Bruce Webb who had been killed in action here with this battalion. We were in Hawaii at the same time as well. This is getting too strange, but it does serve as a reminder of how grim this can get. At any rate, I check in with Personnel and am ushered up to the CP bunker to meet the Commanding Officer. When I come in to where he's sitting in the bunker, he looks up from his field desk and has an astonished look on his face. I don't know why he was called.

"I'll be damned. It's good to see you again, Captain Quinn----ah, Barney. I just was notified you were coming, a call from General Barto's office. You were having lunch with him? Are you two friends? Do you know him well?" Ah, now it is apparent why he had an astonished look on his face. He's thinking, the general's boy. I really don't need this.

"Sir, it's good seeing you again, and yes, I know the general somewhat. Apparently he feels he knows me very well. Better than I know him."

Lieutenant Colonel Cartwright looks a little uneasy. He hasn't changed that much since Hawaii. A little older of course, more serious now that he is a senior officer, and his blond hair is thinning and graying. He still moves with a bit of a slouch and shuffle, but he is a good man and a fine Marine. In Hawaii he was a captain and I was a second lieutenant. We were acquainted and worked together several times.

He recovers and manages, "Well, good. You know Captains Rush and Evert are here in the battalion. They have companies. You knew them in Hawaii, didn't you?"

"Didn't know they were here, but yes, sir, know them both. It's getting like old home week over here."

"Yes, well, welcome aboard. I heard you want a rifle company, Barney, and I want you to have one. Right now, all of my companies have Captains as CO's, so how about you take over as the S-3 Alpha for a short while. I'll get you a company as soon as it is practicable."

"That's great, sir."

"Good, stow your personal gear. Draw your weapon and the 782 gear you need and report back here tonight. We'll put you right to work."

"Yes, sir."

As I depart the bunker I can hear the radio crackling, which is in its squawk box mode. A lot of loud and excited chatter. There is something happening. A firefight is going on and it sounds very serious. Hell, they're all serious. The voices and the noise fade as I leave the bunker.

About fifty yards from the CP, a runner from the direction

of the bunker catches up to me and gasps, "Sir, are you Captain Quinn?"

"Yes."

"The Colonel wants to see you ASAP, sir."

"Okay, Corporal, what's going on?" Before he can answer I see Cartwright jogging toward me. He says animatedly, "Barney, a change in plans. Lima Company is in a small scrape and the company commander, Captain Marsh, has been hit and is being evac'd. You are going to take the chase bird and go in and relieve him, and take command of Lima Company. They're still in contact, so get moving."

My pulse quickens rapidly. Emotions and senses are screaming for attention. I mutter, "Oh, shit." Then, "Okay, yes, sir."

"Go get your weapon and gear, and get on up to the helo pad. The chopper is inbound. Give your Willy Peter bag and Val pack to the Corporal. I'll get it to the company CP on Hill 22. The Gunny will have Marsh's map case."

My body is raging with adrenaline. It's tumblin', rumblin' and racing through me like a mountain stream cascading through a gorge. "Okay, sir, I've got the ball. No sweat."

I hand my two bags to the Corporal and break out into a dead run to the supply tent. At the same time, the colonel is hollering at me to radio him as soon as I touch down and have control.

Aw, crap. Today's the friggin' 15th.

My cage rattles loudly.

CHAPTER TWO

THE CHOPPER'S WAITING. ROTORS TURNING. I scramble up the hill to the helo pad and clamber aboard. Ol' Barney's bunghole is shut tight. That's good. Who ever says they aren't scared, needs to see a shrink. As we lift off the crew chief motions for me to pick up the headset and points to the push to talk button. When it's on I tell the pilot what I am supposed to do, and ask if he knows the location.

He responds, "That's a roger. Is just a few klicks south of Hill 22 on the south side of the village complex, in a paddy by the river."

"Do you have contact with the company?"

"Affirmative."

"Good. Call them and tell them we are inbound, and tell them to get me to the Gunny and the CP group as soon as we touch down, okay?"

"Got it. Listen in, you'll be able to hear me talking to them, but you can't transmit."

"Roger."

He calls Lima Company and informs them as I requested and they acknowledge. He comes back to me with, "Did you copy that?"

"Yes. Thanks."

"No sweat. We're coming in now. You can see the green smoke. Good luck, Captain." Green smoke, that's good. Means the zone is clear.

"Roger, and thanks. Out." My heart is pounding. It's louder than the damn helicopter.

The Huey gunship drops into the zone. The green smoke swirls around, caught up in the rotor wash. I am out, on the ground, and introduced to life as it is.

As the chopper lifts and tilts its nose, getting up quickly since its empty, I see an older, salty-looking guy running in a crouched position towards me. It's the company Gunny, "Follow me, Captain."

We head in the direction of all the antennas and a collection of several people. He is hauling ass, at the crouch again, so I follow his lead. Two or three rounds snap over our heads, quickly getting my attention. These bastards don't like me. There is other sporadic firing. It's ours, so it's not really an issue, at least not now. I just don't need to get dinged in the first thirty seconds.

The Gunny briefs me quickly, and I get on the radio to get an update from the platoon in contact. This skirmish is just about over. The CO was hit by small arms fire, but he will be okay. He was medi-evac'd and he won't be back. One other wounded, slight, and a bunch of Viet Cong (VC) were popped and dropped. Looking at my radio operator I say, "Marine, what's your name?"

"Lance Corporal Smith, sir."

"Well, Smitty, get me the Battalion Six on the hook."

"Yes, sir."

Next I hear the good Lieutenant Colonel Cartwright's voice, "Lima Six. What's up?"

"Iron Hand Six Actual, the contact is over. Charlie has crossed the river and left the area. We are headed back to the hill. Will complete the sweep as originally planned, check in upon reaching Charlie Papa with full after action report. Over."

"Roger Lima Six Actual. How are you doing?"

"Iron Hand Six Actual. Like a pig in shit. Out."

Smitty looks at me with that something-is-different look.

We complete the sweep of the village complex without further incident and make our way out of the Vill to the company CP, on Hill 22. This is southwest of Da Nang, across the river from the Battalion CP and the Tuy Loan and Cau Do Rivers. Where these two meet, the Yen River forms and it runs southward. A few klicks west of the Yen, is Hill 22, which is surrounded by rice paddies and the village complexes of Bo Ban, La Chau, and Duong Lam.

It is a nasty area and the Viet Cong roam it, mostly at night. Today they made an error and got themselves caught, in the open, in daylight. They can be made to make other mistakes.

Something that is quickly obvious is that these villages have no young men in them, just women, babies and extremely old men. Nor dogs. They are not pets, they're dinner.

I am home.

I'm where I need to be and doing what I'm trained for, commanding a Marine rifle company. Yet, a voice inside my head says, too many coincidences. Too many faces from the past showing up. General Barto. General Cunningham. Stoop. Great friends. I love them, but? Now, added to the mix are Lieutenant Colonel Cartwright, and Clint Rush and Lindell Evert, two pals, just across the river in An Trac and Cam Ne. Who's next, I wonder?

As I fiddle with the Mizpah medallion around my neck that Ryley gave me on our last night together, I think, I hope this works, because these troops and the VC are going to get a dose of ol' Barney.

Old Ra is up early and seems extra bright on my first dawn of some unknown number of sunups on Hill 22 with Lima Company. I hope that this is a positive omen. I do a map study and get a briefing from the Platoon Commanders on recent activities and the area. Then walk the hill, a tour of the trench line, fighting holes and bunkers. Besides the two rifle platoons on the hill we have our own 60mm Mortars and a Section of 81mm Mortars that is attached to us from Battalion. Also, attached are a section of Tanks and a section of ONTOS.

The tanks are M48 tanks with a four-man crew; the tank commander, the gunner, the loader, and the driver. Each carries a 90mm gun, M41, a .50Cal M2HB machine gun and a .30Cal M73 machine gun. The 90mm is an attention getter.

The M50A1 ONTOS with its three-man crew is supposed to be an anti-tank weapon, on tracks. It is light in weight and armor compared to most tracked vehicles. They are only useful here from time to time. The name ONTOS means "the thing" in Greek but Marines just call it "the pig." It has six 106mm Recoilless Rifles, with four of them having a .50Cal spotting rifle attached. The spotting rifle has about the same trajectory or path as the 106RR. The 106's can be fired one at a time or all six at once. All six are called a salvo and a salvo will wake up the neighborhood let alone the recipient.

The two tanks and the two pigs are situated in deep, protective firing slots on our hill. We really can't use them out in the paddies, but here on the hill they give us our own "artillery." Ol' Barney is going to make some careless VC's very jumpy with these.

After walking the hill, I take a squad for security and go the little over half a klick to the bridge over the Yen River. A klick is 1,000 meters and a commonly used term, a grid square on our map. We have a platoon there, along with a platoon from Clint's company to protect it for the villagers. It's one of two primary foot routes to the villages in the area, and the only bridge across the Yen. So it's important to the villagers and us as well.

Returning to the hill, it is time to set the plans for the night's activities. This means sending out the listening posts, the patrols, the ambushes, and setting the H&I fires for the night. The H&I's are the harassing and interdictory fires, meant to disrupt the VC from moving freely about during the night, and if they are out and about, maybe force them toward the ambushes.

It's also time to meet the troops, at their work, in their fighting holes, in their bunkers or wherever, and get to know my unit leaders better. I already know that this is a good cast of men, because I have briefly seen them in a skirmish and they did well. They call themselves Lethal Lima. I like it. A good aggressive name and spirit.

There is a wooden sign on the command bunker with a statement painted on it indicating what these troops think of themselves. I pause and read it a loud to myself, "A Lima Marine is a can-fed, sweat-cooled, guts-operated, more or less flat trajectory weapon that has never been known to have a stoppage." I think to myself, sounds corny but its Gospel. I'm going to love these guys.

I need to point out just what we, Lima Company, are doing each day. Set the stage for understanding what goes on almost daily, the somber side. As indicated the night activities on every night, plus the remainder of the troops are on watch on the hill.

During the day, we run MedCap patrols into the various villages that surround us. These are civic action type patrols or excursions to help the villagers, give medical aid, make friends, and win the minds and hearts as they say.

We protect the schoolhouse that had been destroyed by the VC, since rebuilt by the villagers. We provide all of the school supplies. We conduct patrols during the day, maintain OP's (Observation Posts), conduct sweeps like the one yesterday, and provide the blocking force for other units doing search and destroy type operations. These are in our tactical area of responsibility (TOAR) as well as in adjacent ones.

It has been said that the Company Commander's job is a lonely job. As a company commander moves about on an operation, he always has an entourage, the Gunny, and two or three radio operators with their radio whip antennas poking skyward attracting attention. A Forward Air Controller (FAC), and Artillery Forward Observer (FO) with their operators and radios are also in this group. This doesn't look lonely with all of these antennas sticking up in the air. This group can draw fire and there is an old saying, "Don't draw fire, it irritates the people around you." That's why it's a lonely job, the troops aren't stupid, they don't want to get too close to this group.

A road leads from our position on the hill down to the schoolhouse and the main north/south road. We have an engineer detachment, the demo guys with us, sweep the road each morning. Clear it of mines. At the times I follow them down the road, I'm reminded of another bit of gallows humor, "If you see a demo man running, try to keep up with him."

Within all of this mess, this hideousness, this madness, there ticks the clocks of humor, of lightness, of fate, of bizarre events and characters...fine Marines, but characters, nonetheless. I'm going to make it a point to get to know these folks much better. I suspect they will want to know what makes Barney tick, which ought to be interesting, as even I don't know that.

We'll see what's in the hopper.

CHAPTER THREE

THIS FIRST NIGHT IS UNEVENTFUL. This is good. It gives me time to collect my thoughts. Find my way around the hill, sometimes stumbling in the pitch-blackness of a moonless night. While touring the line, it is fortunate I don't fall into a fighting hole on top of someone. That wouldn't instill much confidence in the Skipper. I spend time in the loneliness of the night, talking in more detail with my platoon commanders, section leaders, and individual troops.

At last, shortly before daybreak, I sit in the bunker and dash off a letter to Ryley to give her my new address, tell her I miss her already, and by damn that I love her. I also remind her that the Mizpah "will work" it's magic, and we'll be together again.

After grabbing some coffee that Smitty, my radioman, has brewed and when the sun winks over the trees along the Yen, I set out to really meet my Company Gunnery Sergeant. A time that is a little more relaxed than hauling buns in the middle of a firefight. He is the second most senior NCO in the company, the first being the First Sergeant who is at the Battalion CP. The Gunny is always with the company commander in the field. Together they are the heart of the company; they must be on the same sheet of music and both in key.

My Gunnery Sergeant is a short, wiry, rawhide tough and

demanding Marine named Bobby Roe. As far as he is concerned his name is Gunny, period. He's from central Arkansas and the Corps is his mistress. The troops respect this guy and they gravitate toward him at the slightest opportunity. When he speaks, they listen. Not just hear, but listen. He knows everything that goes on inside the company, so engaging him in conversation early is essential.

He is on the way to see me so we meet just outside of the CP bunker. We sit on the sand bag entrance. He offers me some Kool Aid. Other than cocoa, Kool Aid is very often the drink of choice, especially in the heat of the day and it is hot already this morning. "Gunny, tell me something about our platoon commanders and platoon sergeants."

"Well, Skipper, they're all good men. First-rate Marines. The two First Lieutenants, Williamson and Barro, are super, been here for about six months, are experienced. Already paddy savvy. The other platoon commander is Second Lieutenant Lincoln; he's a little green, just out of Basic School and sent directly here. He's learnin' but needs help and watchin'. I put our most experienced platoon sergeant with him."

"What about the other two platoon sergeants?"

"That's the other side of the coin. They're young, just Sergeants, and haven't been here too long, but they have the experienced lieutenants, so it all works out okay,"

"Gunny, how are you doing? You okay? You've been here a while now. I can get you back to battalion, but I sure as hell want you to stay and give me a hand. It's your choice."

"Naaa, I'd rather stay out here, watch these kids, and maybe watch out for you as well." He gives me a crooked grin with the last part.

"Okay, Gunny. Great. You've got a deal."

"Skipper, mind if I say something?"

"Nope, shoot."

"Well sir, the troops notice things. Like you blowin' in here on that chopper just as cool and hard as can be, takin' charge and getting on with it. Like you ain't scared of shit. That means something to them."

"Yeah, well, that's dandy, but my asshole was up in my throat, Gunny."

"They didn't see that. They just see you walkin' around like you don't give a damn. Takin' charge and getting the job done. You know, there were several rounds snappin' around your head, Skipper. You'd do well to stay a little closer to the deck."

"Well, that's hard to do, Gunny, you know that, but, okay, I'll try to watch my butt. Listen, I appreciate you giving me the skinny."

As we start to get up I add, "And Guns, stay close. We're going to kick some zip butts and keep as many of these kids healthy as we can."

"You got it, Skipper." He strolls away taking another long slug of Kool Aid from his canteen.

Gunny Roe is a solid Marine, loyal, trustworthy and will take care of the troops, and me. But just so as not to be mistaken, he is tough. I bet he can be meaner than a rented mule. Excellent team, the rented mule and the Stoneface. We're on key and about as subtle as a rasp.

Gunny Roe does have a warm side, however. For example, he's already insured that when the beer ration was choppered in this morning, he made sure I got a can. Since we have no ice, its warm, and most folks wouldn't drink this stuff. In fact, if someone served it to you in the real world, you would raise hell. Here it's different---everything is relative. A beer is a beer.

Gunny Roe takes ours, two cans, one each, digs a hole and buries it so it can cool. Then sometime this evening, after we have dined on a fine C-Ration meal, we will sit in the CP bunker, have a cool one, and just relax. Yeah, a cool one, about 90 degrees cool. He also grabbed something for me out of the PX ration when it came. A package of *Chuckles* candy. Five flavors of gum-like candy coated with sugar. Dentist's delight. Maybe the Gunny thinks I need to sweeten my disposition.

We're going to get along just fine.

Another crucial part of our life here are C-Rations. Not bad, not good, but always interesting. There is some enjoyable stuff in C's. They are concentrated and the caloric count gives us what we need. This is vital of course. For the uninitiated, they come in a three-meal box, not unlike a cardboard lunch box. However, the most important thing about these rations is not the dietary value, but rather the bartering system they create in this closed society on Hill 22. These boxes contain some canned meals such as Ham and Lima Beans, Beans and Franks or beanie weenies, Ham and Eggs, and Beef and something or other. These are all tasty if heated, but they are concentrated. By design, they will make you constipated. This is tolerable. One doesn't want to drop drawers very often. It's a vulnerable position in these parts.

They also contain some packaged instant coffee. It is referred to as "Black Death." It's strong, will keep you awake, and will stain everything from intake to outlet. There is also the infamous John Wayne crackers and a small tin of either jam or peanut butter. The crackers are hard, but good, hence the name, John Wayne.

However, the best of all are the real treats. These are craved, bartered, paid, cursed, prayed, and begged for, and are the very basis of the "barter system." These are the canned fruits, led by fruit cocktail, one of two of the most important and valued items in the ration. The other most valued item is the packet of cocoa. The other treats, also very good and having high value as well, are the canned pears, peaches, and the pound cake.

The fun of C-Rats is in the trading. A can of fruit cocktail is of high value, and might bring two cans of a main meal but probably not beanie weenies because they also are of high value. You might get an even swap in that case. This swap would likely transpire only between the fruit cocktail freak and the beanie-weenie addict. This is serious business and an eye has to be kept on the stored C-Rat cases. There are fruit cocktail thieves about. The Gunny ensures the security of the C-Rats sanctuary.

While we are on Hill 22, we will get a hot meal choppered in maybe once a week, so we are not deprived. However, the rest of the time, and certainly whenever we are on the move, its C-Rats.

After my chat with the Gunny, and after some more meandering around the hill, I wander over to the 60mm mortar pits to visit with the Section Leader again, Sergeant Tony Parzini. He is a dark-haired Italian with an olive complexion, and a very distinct animated manner of speaking, coupled with a heavy New York City accent. He's stocky, thick in the chest, and he always seems scruffier than others do. He is also an absolute cocoa freak. I discovered this last night. In fact, he is apparently the Cocoa King of the company. He always has cocoa, stashes of it. I wonder how he stays alive on whatever C-Rat meals he has left after trading for the cocoa. I think, maybe he is running a cocoa black market ring. Naaa, but an interesting thought.

To my benefit, Sergeant Parzini will, once or twice a night, as he did last night, bring me a canteen cup of hot cocoa and one for himself. While ambling over to see him today, I remember sitting outside the CP bunker last night when he appeared out of the darkness like a ghost in an old church cemetery. I jumped at his sudden sight, saying, "Whoa, Sergeant Parzini. You scared the crap out of me. You're going to have to stop sneaking up on me. You remind me of a hustler in the city suddenly appearing out of an alley with some hot Rolexes or something."

"Sorry, Skipper, don't wanta' spill any of this stuff. Here," as he thrusts a canteen cup full of hot cocoa at me.

"Thanks Z, smells tasty." He nods in agreement.

"Sergeant Z, where do you get all this stuff? It's rumored you have more cocoa than Hershey's."

"I just make good trades Cap'n. Want a Rolex?"

"Hell, I'm afraid to answer. Sit a spell and let's just talk a while."

That's what we did. Talk, drink some cocoa. It's a treat, both the drink and the chat.

He is a hell of a solid Marine and skilled mortar man. All he wants is to talk a while each night, just the two of us. It will make my day, each and every day. I will remember these moments long after they pass.

Today, we sit and talk business. It centers on his two mortar crews, and what he and they might need. He tells me that many of the small unit leaders in the platoons are not as capable as they need to be in calling fire, and suggests we practice some during these slow days. I assure him we will, starting tomorrow. As we get up from the edge of the pit to go our separate ways, I reach in my pocket and give him a packet of cocoa saying, "Here, Sergeant, for your collection. No Rolex required."

"Not even a can of pears, Skipper?"

"Nope, nothin'. See ya tonight, Z."

"Aye Aye, sir," and he moves off, shuffling along in the dust of the hill, toward the other mortar pit.

There are additional characters in this company. The lieutenants, especially Second Lieutenant Lincoln with his youthful exuberance in every situation. I'll be spending a lot of time tonight with these three officers.

The tank and pig section sergeants are already badgering me for a chance to fire more. I make some promises that I intend to keep. They just want me to fire at something, real or imaginary. I'll go for the real. The Engineer Squad Leader, Sergeant Dave Dunlop, is our demo guy, who I'm told drools whenever he gets a chance to blow something up, down or apart.

All of these guys are first-rate. This is an exceptional team. Business-like, a little roughshod and with a sense of humor. I fit here.

Within the context of our mission, things begin to occur that just make for tales, folklore if you will, among the troops. As it turns out the troops that saw and overheard my arrival episode at Da Nang when I first landed have been assigned to Lima Company. After I arrived in the company and took command, it didn't take long for these Magpies to get the word around that I knew the general personally and must be close pals with him. We are friends, I suppose, but pals? I don't think so. Nevertheless, that's the way they see things and it appears that's the way they're telling it.

For me, my "Shanty Irish" bones tell me this is all leading somewhere unusual. I hear the rumors. The Gunny looks like he wants to ask me something but leaves it hanging. Sergeant Z is the same. Smitty's not sure what to think, but I can tell he's hoping for something. The troops, gad I love' em already, sort of stare and shake their heads when they look at me perhaps hoping the rumors are true, or maybe just in disbelief.

I guess we'll just wait and see what's in the dust on this molehill.

CHAPTER FOUR

IT DOESN'T TAKE LONG FOR my Shanty Irish bones to be right. Only a week. I am outside my bunker wandering around in the dust and heat, when my radio operator comes out of the bunker and hollers at me, "Hey Skipper, Deadlock one zero is inbound. Be here in about five. He's only a few klicks out."

Walking toward my RO, Smitty, not recognizing the call sign, I shout back, "Who the hell is Deadlock one zero?"

"I think it is some General or big shot, sir." I'm thinking the pilot probably reported a Code Six on board. Smitty makes the translation for me, in his own way. God, I love how unconcerned the troopers can be. I call them Snuffies, and in my mind, it is a term of immense endearment. Snuffies, I love 'em. On the other hand, Magpies, also a term of endearment, are Snuffies that love to mumble, mutter, and spread rumors. Smitty's yelled remark not only catches my attention but also that of several Magpies in the vicinity.

Shortly, we hear the whomp-whomp-whomp of the chopper rotor blades slicing through the heavy humid air. We can see it approaching from the northeast, coming over the river directly toward us. Gunny Roe has joined me by now.

"Pop a green smoke, Gunny."

"Okay, Skipper." He yells across the hill, "Pratt, pop that green smoke."

The green smoke is popped indicating the landing zone is clear and shows wind direction to the pilot. The chopper lands, kicking up dust all over our little hill. Actually, Hill 22 isn't really a "hill". Well, in Texas and Oklahoma it might be a hill. In Pennsylvania or Colorado it would be a mogul. It just looks larger than it really is here in the middle of these paddies.

Regardless, the rotor wash is blowing down some ponchos rigged as covers over fighting holes and hooches, and flicking and kicking small pebbles and stones in all directions. It is making a mess of our home away from home. The Snuffies usually don't consider this a good deal, unless the chopper is bringing something of real value such as a PX ration, a beer ration, or hot chow, unless it's a medivac bird.

The chopper lands, settles, but the pilot doesn't shut down the engine, which is an indication of a short stay, they don't like hot starts. As the rotor blades slow, Lieutenant General Barto climbs down from the left front seat. No co-pilot, just the general and his pilot. He heads directly for me. I salute, he returns it hurriedly, and shoves out his hand. We shake, then he grabs me around the shoulders with a one-arm bear hug, pulls me to his side and squeezes tightly. With the warmth of a friend, he shakes me vigorously. He then leads me away from the chopper and from the curious Magpies that are gathering.

When we get about twenty yards away, he says, "Just dropped in to see you on my way south, Barney. How is everything going?"

"Fine, sir." I quickly notice he is wearing three stars now, a promotion. He is now the Commanding General of III MAF. He is in command of all the troops in the I Corps area. Big job and he's the best man for it, at least in my mind. He asks, "Are you sure? Anything I can do to help?"

"Well, to be perfectly honest, sir, there is."

"What, tell me? If I can do it, I will."

"Well, that's good, because I know you can do this because you instigated it."

I pause to get a reaction. Getting nothing other than an intense look, I continue, "You can revoke your III MAF order that requires us to have a specified number of outposts, patrols, and ambushes out each night. That order takes away my prerogatives as a company commander. I know what to do out here. I know my situation each day and night. I'm way under strength and regardless of that, run very aggressive activities both day and night. The specific number of various activities you have designated is based on a full-strength company. Neither I nor anyone else out here has that. These directed numbers of activities drain my company every night which curtails what I can do during the day."

I can see that the general is a little flushed, and his jaw is taut, twitching as if his wing nuts are clamped down tight. I don't allow time for a response, and continue to pour it on. "It's a drain on the physical and mental capacity of my men. Further, and much worse, it is making liars of good Marines."

Hell, I have rattled on so fast I am almost out of breath. General Barto has bowed backward from the waist from this vocal onslaught and rumbles like a clap of thunder, "WHAT?" Then sucking in a breath of air he continues, "Barney, do you know why I had that order promulgated? Are you aware what happened to a company because they had virtually no security out one night?"

"Yes, sir, I've heard. What you should have done, if you didn't, was to discipline the company commander, not penalize me and others, and take away our prerogatives."

I go on and say, "Let me give you an example. A few nights ago I couldn't get permission to fire into another TAOR because the overlays showed a friendly ambush in that area, but it didn't exist. They would have been sitting on top of Charlie. We had four or five VC spotted and pinned down but couldn't fire. The end result, five VC's got at least another day of grace."

I further explain that the next day I went over to see the

company commander of that outfit and he admitted that he didn't have an ambush there; just on paper so he could meet the requirements of the order when he submitted his overlay.

He has been listening keenly and asks, "What company, Barney?"

"Sir, that's not important. Please, just rescind the order, and when doing so let your commanders know why you're doing it; they'll get the message. I have already taken care of the company commander in question. He won't do it again, I promise."

He stares at me with those steely blue eyes, boring a hole in my head. We are now standing facing each other, like two gun fighters. Hours seem to pass. He finally nods several times and reaches out with his arm, puts it around my shoulders again, pulls me toward him and says, "Okay, Barney, you got it. Consider it rescinded as of now. Anything else?"

I breathe a quiet sigh of relief. I'll be damned.

"No, sir, and thank you. On a more pleasant note, how are you? And congratulations."

He just smiles and says, "Thanks. I'm just fine, just fine, Barney. I've got to get going. Good seeing you, and take care of yourself, old man." He chuckles warmly at calling me an old man. "By the way, I think I will be dropping off a visitor or two down here from time to time. Okay?"

"Yes, sir. Semper Fi. Take care."

With that, he turns on his heel and heads for the chopper. As he does, the pilot revs up the old tractor so that by the time the general gets in and straps on the seat harness, he is ready to lift off. At lift off, I salute him and he returns it, and waves to the troops around the LZ. All in a matter of several minutes he is gone and off to visit other units.

Wham, bam, thank you ma'am, what a visit.

I think, not pals, but seemingly we are friends, and we do have a good relationship. This is going to stir things up at battalion since they can see choppers coming in here.

The troops are already muttering and mumbling something about their Skipper talkin', pointin' and gesturing at the general. Standing toe to toe, nose to nose. The Hill, or Mogul, is all a twitter and a dither.

No telling what is going on back at battalion about now. I can almost hear the hornets buzzing around the nest.

No sense to fret, I'll find out soon enough.

CHAPTER FIVE

I'M RIGHT, IT DOESN'T TAKE long. The dust hasn't even settled. Smitty, my blond RO, screams at me that the Battalion CO is on the radio and that he wants to talk to me "immediately, if not sooner." I surmise that Smitty is quoting the colonel, who wants to know what the hell is happening and why the general was down here visiting. The Gunny, who stood within earshot of my conversation with Lieutenant General Barto, stares at me, shakes his head slowly from side to side, and mutters, "He ain't going to believe any of this shit." Then mumbles something else.

"What's that, Gunny?"

"Nothin', sir, but I'd like to listen in on this transmission?"

"Sure, come on." We take off jogging toward the CP bunker.

The Magpies are still stirred up, and are sharing the story. They head for their bunkers, hooches and holes, some running, to get this story spread as fast as possible. "The general was here to visit the Skipper. The Captain really got into it with him about patrols or something. The Skipper knows him." In addition, whatever else they can imagine, I suppose.

I get to the radio and call the battalion CP. "Iron Hand, this is Lima Six Actual; I need to talk to the Six. Over."

In seconds, before I can take a swig of Kool Aid from my canteen, Lieutenant Colonel Cartwright is on the radio. On the air so to speak. Since he is on the battalion tactical net, that means all the other companies can hear this transmission...whoever is manning the radios.

He blurts out, "What the hell is happening down there? Why was Deadlock One zero there? Is this more of your buddy-buddy crap Lima Six?" Now, you're not suppose to curse over the radio. Grunts do from time to time, particularly when in a jam, but usually not the battalion commander. Therefore, I rightly deduce that my CO is just a little excited, and perhaps agitated.

"Six, the answers are in order. Not much. Deadlock was just visiting. And in a way, yes. Over."

"What the hell does that mean?" He is agitated. Maybe pissed.

"Iron Hand Six Actual. Deadlock was just visiting. He asked me if I needed anything so I said yes, and got him to cancel the III MAF order on night activities. He rescinded it effective immediately. You need to check that out. Other than that, I just told Deadlock that I'm okay and you are doing a grand job. Over." I love this phrase "a grand job." Just a little sophistication from the stink of the paddies.

There is a pause. When he comes back on the radio, I hear some laughing in the background. This clearly indicates that he has the transmissions on the squawk box in the CP bunker, so not only the other company radio operators can hear, and maybe the other company commanders, but everyone in the battalion CP bunker as well.

He says, "Well I'll be damned. You're somethin' else." Another slight pause followed by, "Well, good. Really good news. And Lima Six, don't be such a smartass. Out."

Now Smitty has some first hand scoop, and it won't be long

before it is fed into the Magpie network unless I say something to prevent it. I don't say anything. Some rumors are good. If the troops think I have "an in", which of course I don't, that's okay. Probably good for morale. They might think everything is going to be fine since the general and I are "pals." Further, the Captain and the battalion commander must be "really tight" because the Skipper can jerk his chain and get away with it.

It is but a few days later when we get another call from Deadlock One Zero that he is inbound. The same sequence of events occurs with Smitty, the Gunny, the green smoke and me. This time the general arrives with a stranger in tow. It is the same greeting as last time. The bear hug and the rousting. The only difference on this occasion is that there are more Snuffies out watching with the "what next" look on their faces.

After the general and I exchange pleasantries, and he releases me from his grasp, he introduces me to his guest, Richard Tregaskis, the author of several books. The most famous of these being *Guadalcanal Diary*, the best selling World War II novel, and later a movie. The general says, "Barney, what I would like to do is leave Mr. Tregaskis with you for the day. Let him see and experience what we're doing out here. Let him do whatever he wants, but keep him safe. Okay?"

"Yes sir. About what time will the general be returning?"

"We'll be back by about 1600. I will contact you to let you know if it changes. Okay?" He keeps asking me if it's okay. Of course it is, he's the general.

"That will be fine, sir. Where are you headed today?"

"South again, Chu Lai area. Got to get moving, Barney." He fixes his eyes on Mr. Tregaskis saying, "Dick, Barney here will take good care of you. Feel free to ask him anything you want and if he deems it okay, he will let you go elsewhere. If so, please be careful and do what he asks or tells you."

Tregaskis says, "Yes, and thank you. I'll be fine. It can't be worse than the Canal." He gives the general a knowing grin.

With the exchange of smiles between these two old friends, the general grasps me around the shoulder again, gives me another hard, bear-hug-like squeeze, and then he heads to the chopper. The pilot performs the same routine as before, and they are gone in a huge cloud of dust, stinging pebbles and stones. The Magpies are scurrying to share stories and sights, and some also wander up to see just who this visitor is.

I introduce Gunny and Mr. Tregaskis to one another, and tell Gunny Roe to get whatever troops are available and want to, to go into the mess tent. Then to both, "Mr. Tregaskis will be there very shortly so they can meet him."

Then quietly, out of earshot of Tregaskis, I whisper, "Gunny, tell the troops who he is, that he was at the Canal and wrote about it. They can ask him anything they want. More important, he is probably here to write a book. Tell them they might become famous. Maybe get themselves in his new one."

The Gunny chuckles, "If anybody gets in that book it's going to be me or you, not those clowns."

"Well, whatever. Seriously, you better attend so they don't go off the deep end with any wild-ass war stories."

"Aye Aye, Sir," and he leaves to carry out my order. He went the "Aye Aye" route to impress our guest, otherwise it would have been a routine, "Okay, Skipper" response.

Tregaskis follows me to the bunker where I brief him on what we are tasked to do out here on and around the hill, answer his questions, give him a quick map study and then herd him to our raggedy-ass mess tent. We put this old worn out squad tent up ourselves with makeshift poles, pegs and lines. It comes down every time a chopper lands, or we get any kind of wind. The troops have it back up again.

As Tregaskis and I are shuffling across the bare dirt and dust of this pimple of a hill, I tell him that after his session with the troops, we will, along with a squad for security, go down to the bridge at the river, but that we won't be able to go down to the school house today. The road from the hill to the school hasn't been swept for mines yet. The dinks like to mine the road in hopes that I will be coming down, willy nilly, to the schoolhouse. I don't willy nilly anywhere, and don't walk on roads or paddy dikes. You would think the VC would know that by now.

I go on to say, "The Gunny will get you a helmet, flak jacket and a weapon for the trip to the bridge. Not to worry, the odds are a thousand to one that anything will happen on the way down and back." That isn't true, but I suppose it's a comforting thought.

"Great, let's get started," and off he goes with the Gunny to the mess tent.

Just as he leaves, Smitty hollers at me again. It isn't necessary, I am just outside the bunker but he is excited once more. He probably thinks the vaudeville act, Cartwright and Quinn, is about to start again.

"Sir, battalion is on the radio."

"The whole battalion?" Oops, he doesn't get it. "Take it easy Smitty, I'm kidding, only kidding, Tiger. I get the message." I go into the bunker with a shake of my head, pick up the handset, while muttering a few choice profanities to myself. Then I say into the mike, "This is Lima Six Actual. Over."

"Six Actual, what are you up to this time? Over."

"Iron Hand Six. Nothing. Just a visitor from Deadlock...will be here for a short while. Deadlock will pick up and take him out later. Over."

"Who is the visitor and what does he want?"

I pause to think for a second, not being sure of the radio procedure requirements, then say, "Six, not sure I should say in the clear but if you read *Guadalcanal Diary* and know the author, then you know the answer. Over."

31

"WHAT?...Oh, yeah...Right...Of course I know who wrote that book. What does he want?"

"Iron Hand Six, just to know what we're doing; see the area; and talk with the troops and ask questions of them. He's probably writing another book."

Being the smart ass I am, I add, "Don't worry. The troops all love you. They won't say anything outrageous, but I might. The Gunny and I are going to ask him to put us in his new book. Over."

"You've already been outrageous, Lima Six, and for your information you're already in a book...My book. And that's not good." I hear laughter in the background again. "Let me know how the visit goes, and by the way, I'm just kidding you. You're a piece of work. Over."

"Iron Hand Six, one other thing. We're going to rig him out and take him on a patrol down to the bridge for a look-see and to chat with the troops. Out."

The colonel quickly adds, as if he hadn't finished his previous remark, "You didn't change any more orders, did you?" He starts to laugh, then stops abruptly. Apparently, a light bulb has come on, and he asks, "What was that last transmission?" Ah ha, he is listening.

"Iron Hand Six, that's a negative but I did tell Deadlock that you are still doing a grand job. We're taking our guest to the bridge. No sweat, Deadlock trusts me, but I don't know about you. Out."

As I leave the bunker, I hear him mutter something, and again hear some chuckling from the background. The squawk box is on again. I bet the next time he will use my company tact net and limit the audience.

The troops have a good time with Richard Tregaskis. He answers and asks questions for over an hour. Then we go down to the bridge and he is briefed by the Platoon Commander, Second Lieutenant Lincoln, the exuberant one, and spends time with these troops.

After about an hour, we saddle up, head back to the hill and arrive without incident. He's had his stroll in the paddies and all is well. He feels like one of us. Best of all, since we don't walk on the paddy dikes, he gets all wet and slimy, and gets to stink like the real guys. When he gets back to his clean abode in Da Nang he will possibly find a few leeches hanging on, and will maybe remember me.

Am I a prince or what?

It's around 1600. Deadlock's pilot radios us. I inform him to just land and take on his passenger unless there is something else, and tell him to let One Zero know that all went well. The response is affirmative with a thanks added. He touches down, picks up Tregaskis and is off in a bounce and a cloud of dust. Down goes the tent again. We're going to fix that damn thing today. Both the general and Mr. Tregaskis wave to me and to the troops as he lifts off. Tregaskis additionally gives the troops a "thumbs up." The Snuffies are gobbling this up.

Lieutenant Colonel Cartwright doesn't call this time. He probably can't take any more of my sarcastic comments. Later, I'll radio him and let him know that everything went well. Then I turn and say to the Gunny, "How about getting that damn tent fixed so it will stay up, or take it down and keep it down."

"I'll get it rigged so it will stay standin."

"Great, talk at ya later, Guns."

Night falls quickly this time of year. Darkness comes and it's time for some of the nastier work we do. The Listening Posts are out. A combination of patrols and ambushes go out from the units on the hill and at the bridge. I have a few less out tonight since we have a busy tomorrow. It's good having this freedom restored after my face off with the general. These tonight are all small unit activities. In my bunker, I am relegated to listening to the various units report departing, reaching check points, and other standard check-in procedures and activity reports. I'd rather be out with them, but that's not my job tonight.

The bunker is dimly lit with a Coleman lantern sitting by the radioman, and by a candle stuck in its melted wax on the edge of my wooden built-in bunk. A poncho stretches tight across the hatch keeping what light there is from escaping and providing a telltale sign to the VC.

I am sitting on my government-issued inflatable rubber lady that has a slow leak that I need to repair one day soon. Right now, it's flat again. As I sit, I hear the rushing sounds from the radio when no one is transmitting. The squelch knob is left on so that it is easy to know when someone is going to transmit. When they depress the push to talk button, the rushing noise stops. The patrol or ambush will push the button, two, three times, whatever is their indicator, to show all is well. They do this at their scheduled check-in times. This keeps things as quiet as possible. If something happens, they talk, loud and rapidly.

Also, on their end, the squelch is turned off to limit the noise. What we want is quiet, and we want the darkness to be our friend, not the VC's, as they prefer to think.

Sitting here alone in the semi-quiet and dimness of the bunker, my mind drifts back to thoughts of Ryley, back to our last evening together in Laguna when she gave me the Mizpah medallion. She told me it was a benediction from the book of Genesis. *Genesis 31:49, "God will watch over us when we are apart."* That was nice, thoughtful, and deeply meaningful. I remember her eyes welling up with tears when giving it to me. I believe it will work its magic.

My mind continues to flood with thoughts of Ryley, recalling that same evening, when later she read me the poem, Mizpah. Julia A. Baker wrote it. Ryley had found it in a poetry book she had on the coffee table, as a decorative piece, right in front of us for so many evenings. She gave me the book so I would have the poem, but I'm not going to break it out in front of anybody. Bad for my image. The Skipper reading poetry. I remember the rest of that evening. Heck of a night. Damn, she sure is a sexy wench. We're goin' to make this work.

The radio's rushing and squawking sounds suddenly stop, jolting me back from Planet Ryley, the real world, to this madness. A patrol is checking in and getting ready to set in their ambush for the evening. Good, all is well. I nod to Smitty who has turned to see if I've heard. These types of events will continue throughout the night. Mixed emotions prevail here. I want the ambush to be successful, it's our job, but I also secretly hope for peace and quiet and the safety that it brings for the troops. These guys cling to leaders who care about them, and I already love these guys.

"Hey, Skipper, got some cocoa for ya. Want it inside or outside of the bunker?" It's Sergeant Z's hulking presence in the bunker entrance.

"Ah, Z, you got me again. Snuck up and caught me daydreaming," as I tuck the Mizpah under my skivvy shirt. It will keep my dog tags company. I go on, "Sure, sounds great. Let's have it outside and get some air. Smitty, I'll be just outside the hatch."

"Okay, sir."

"Let me know each time the guys check in."

"Will do, Skipper."

Sergeant Z hands me the canteen cup of cocoa and we sit and enjoy our nightly interlude, and a moment of tranquility.

After our cocoa and chat, "Z" ambles back to his hooch. I go back inside the bunker to sit, listen, wait, worry and watch a few rats scurry along the timbers. It makes for a long night.

What will tomorrow bring?

CHAPTER SIX

I BEGIN ANOTHER DAY ON this twenty-two foot pile of semi-compacted dust. Sergeant Z. makes the hill and the morning more livable however. He brings me a canteen cup, filled to the brim with hot cocoa and a C-Rat pound cake. He has a huge grin on his face as he hands both to me. "Sergeant Parzini, are you looking for something today? Trying to get on my good side? If so, that's okay. This is great. Name your price."

"I wanna go home. Can I leave today?"

"Sure, take the next train outta here."

"I wish. Enjoy your chow, Skipper, gotta go back to the pits. See ya tonight."

"Okay. Thanks Z." I ask myself, friend or disciple? Either is fine.

As he shuffles away, I realize something for the first time. I look around, everywhere. I'm right. There isn't one blade of vegetation on this damn hill. Not one, nothing. I can understand why the upper third doesn't have any. It's nothing but bunkers, fighting holes and trench line. But why none on the remainder? Oh well, I'll ask somebody that has been here awhile, perhaps a resident.

Even with the past few visits, our normal business goes on

as usual... the sweeps, patrols, blocks, ambushes, med caps and such. I notice however that a new face is appearing near me every time I go on company size operations, or take a squad and go to the bridge or schoolhouse. His name is Lance Corporal Michael Baronowski, from the 2nd platoon. He is always just ahead of me, next to me, or never far away. He's like a twin brother. He even shows up at night to sit around the bunker and relieve the radio operator from time to time. If this keeps up I will have to share my cocoa with him and that's like going steady. I suspect a plot and set out to capture the Gunny.

I run him down coming back from the crapper, a six-holer that is uncovered and totally in the open. It's best to use it at night. Since its early morning, and the Gunny's no fool, this must have been an emergency. "Gunny, got a question. What the hell's this shadow thing, with Baronowski?"

"Oh that. Well, sir, when we leave the hill on ops, you have a habit of just goin' off places. Wander around like. Just off on your own. You can't be doin' that, so we just assigned you a bodyguard to kind of watch out for you. Keep an eye out for mines, booby traps and such. You know, just take care of you. You act like you're indestructible or something."

"You got a mouse? Who are "we", Gunny?"

"I ain't got no mouse, Skipper. We is the lieutenants and me, and the platoon sergeants."

"Oh, we have committees now?"

"No, sir. Actually I did it, but the others think it is a good idea."

"Gunny, first, I am indestructible. Second, I don't need a baby sitter. It's a waste of troops. The platoons are already short-handed."

"Not so, Skipper. Well, yeah, the platoons are short but you're short a radio operator so Ski is going to lend a hand until we get a replacement, and he's going to watch out for your ass at the same time. And you ain't indestructible, Cap'n."

I think to myself, some of me must be rubbing off on the gunny, he's becoming a smart ass.

We argue about this for several more minutes. It's not a real "argument." It's just a Skipper – Gunny thing. He continues to rave on that we are short of captains with experience. We, meaning the battalion I suppose. He isn't referring to just experience in Vietnam but rather just general combat experience. Not that those without it are not good, but experience always helps. What he's getting at is it makes the troops feel more comfortable, particularly since I'm former enlisted, one of them. He ends his plea with, "Skipper, besides I've already done it. You ain't gonna make me look bad and send him back to the platoon, are you?"

"Okay, you win. Have it your way." The shadow is going to remain, whether I like it or not. His name should be Lamont Cranston, it would be more fitting. So, I have a steady date, but, I will make it clear that he will have to strike his own deal on the cocoa. Anyway, it's nice to be loved, even by a grumpy old gunny.

As the day draws to a close, I go over our night activities and H&I fire plans. A busy night is on tap. As I look around, studying the troops, I realize many days are ending with an expectation by the Snuffies that the next day will give birth to something new or out of the ordinary. It's just a gut feeling coming from the looks, glances, them spending more time out walking around and visiting, and other little bits and pieces. They act as if they need something ripe for the rumor mill. The Snuffies, in particular the Magpies, are on the prowl for something "juicy" from the Skipper. I've got nothing planned and personally can do without the visits, but admit to myself that they are having a positive impact on morale. They are also building the chemistry of this company.

Perhaps, if the visits don't continue, I'll create something to fill the void.

This next morning begins with a quick douche in my helmet, a swift shave and a powdering down of key body spots. When I finish, there is a white cloud surrounding me, sort of hanging there, shielding me. I'm ready for the day. It's already muggy this morning and even with the scents of the paddies choking my nostrils, I can smell rain in the air. That would be good, this whole place needs a visit from Mother Nature. We are going to take a bit of a break today. I've had a lot of patrols out in the Vills the last two days, and a maximum number of ambushes out each night. As I sit on top of the CP bunker, somewhat clean and refreshed, sipping some Black Death that Smitty has made for me, I watch the OP's go out. They're carrying ponchos so others sense rain also. Good. The Gunny ambles over, plops down on the bunker top, and joins me with his coffee.

Suddenly, Smitty comes bounding out of the bunker, screaming, "Skipper...Skipper, he's comin' again. The general, he's about one klick out. Gunny, get the smoke."

"Smitty, At Ease...At Ease. We'll take care of the smoke. Damn you're gonna have a stroke at nineteen. Not good, not good at all. Take it slow."

"I'm sorry Cap'n. It's just that...Aw shoot, never mind sir."

"That's okay, spit it out."

"Well sir, when the general comes, neat stuff happens. Then the colonel always calls, and I get to hear all that shit goin' on. It makes my day, Cap'n."

"Makes your day, huh? Well then, I'll try not to disappoint you and your Magpie cronies. I know you're the Chief Magpie." Smitty grins sheepishly and returns to the radio.

The Gunny pops the smoke, the chopper lands, again turning the top of Hill 22 into an Oklahoma dust bowl. Troops are minding it less now. Too much anticipation of the surprise to worry about their hooches being blown down. The mess tent is still standing; no one has struck out yet, so all is well in Dustville.

Lieutenant General Barto, surprisingly steps out of the back of the Huey this time, along with Charlton Heston, Moses himself. They duck their heads and hold onto their caps, as they move toward me through the rotor wash. The general pats me on the back and says, "Barney, how you doing today. This is Charlton Heston." I think, no shit, General. I go to the movies.

"Yes, sir. Morning, Mr. Heston. Welcome to Hill 22 and Lima Company."

We shake hands and exchange idle comments. The general explains he is leaving Heston here for a few hours while he goes elsewhere, and that I should brief him and let him spend time with the troops. He winks and adds, "Try not wading in the paddies with the leeches." He knows I did that on purpose with Tregaskis.

"Ahhh, yes, sir. Understand."

"And no patrols. Okay last time, but not this. Stay on the hill."

"Aye Aye, Sir."

With this, the general walks toward the chopper, turns and waves goodbye saying, "Charlton, Barney will take good care of you." Then, in another cloud of dust, pebbles, stones, and lime from the piss tubes, he's gone. So much for my douche and dusting this morning. Will have to dunk myself again tonight.

Charlton Heston and I walk the hill. He stops to talk to troops at each hooch, bunker or fighting hole. At the first hole, I explain the difference in terminology between the Army and the Marine Corps. The Army calls them "foxholes"; we call them "fighting holes". I let it sit for a second or two waiting for a reaction. Getting none I add, "In Basic School, a second lieutenant in my class asked the tactics instructor, a rather crusty colonel of World War II vintage, 'If under attack, how far can we retreat'. The answer he got says it all. 'To the back of your fighting hole, and no further'. Heston, chuckles and says, "I like it. If I may, I'm going to use it if the opportunity ever presents itself."

"Great. You know Mr. Heston, the Marine Corps is a state of mind."

"I believe that. It's apparent."

We continue along. He is fully interested in what we're doing, and more importantly, in every trooper he meets. At times, he sits down on the edge of a fighting hole or trench line and talks with three or four of the men. The talk is of everything and nothing... here, home, wives, girlfriends, movies and a little about his leading ladies. Nothing indiscreet, this guy is a true gentleman. The troops love it. Hell, he looks just as he does on the screen, and he moves, strides, in the same manner. It's very distinctive.

As he is about to leave, he asks me if there is anything he can do for me when he gets back to the states, adding, "Can I call your wife and tell her you're fine?" He must figure an old guy like me ought to be married. "Well, I'm not married but you can call my gal. She lives in Laguna Beach. Would you mind?"

"Not a bit. Give me the info."

I take out my notebook, jot down Ryley's name and number, my name and outfit. I tear it out, hand it to him, and we head for the LZ as the chopper approaches.

The general's back within the few hours he had indicated. The bird lands, settles, and he gets out from his customary spot, up front. He rustles me around a bit as usual. Good thing, the troops would have been upset if he didn't give Ol' Barney a hug. Charlton Heston and I shake hands. He says, "I appreciate you taking the time to show me around. The best portion of the visit was meeting and talking to the men. I will remember the fighting hole story. Maybe it will draw some comments when I visit Army units later."

"It will, for sure. More important, I thank you for taking the time to visit, especially for the time you spent with the troops. It made their day, and they don't have many good ones."

"Well, great, and I will call your lady."

He gives me a friendly slap on the back as we reach the bird. The general and Heston step on the skid and clamber into the back of the slick. The chopper quickly lifts off as soon as they strap themselves in. The pilot banks the chopper, and circles up and away toward the river. Heston and the general lean out the open door as the chopper banks, and wave to the troops. The Snuffies wave back as if all are old friends. The mess tent is still standing, so we're two for two.

Within a minute or so, Smitty is out of the bunker, and standing before me. This time he just says in a monotone, and not meaning any disrespect, "It's him again."

"Him again?"

"The Battalion Six, sir."

"You're getting salty, Smitty. I don't know where it comes from, do you?"

"Huh." Geez, that flew right past him.

I stroll over to the bunker, jump down into the trench line and duck through the hatch. I pick up the handset, and answer the colonel before he can ask, "Iron Hand Six Actual, it was Deadlock One Zero Actual and Charlton Heston. Deadlock just wanted to see his favored one, and Charlton wants me to make a movie with him. I told him I would but only if I could be the battalion commander. I'm surprised you didn't ask sooner. Over."

"Lima Six, are you serious? I mean about who was there?"

"Affirmative. Just a visit to the troops. They had a blast. Over."

"That's great, good for the troops. I guess it pays to know people...and oh yeah, that will be the only way you'll get to be a battalion commander. Out." I'll be damned, it's rubbing off on the colonel too. I can't help myself so I throw out, "Iron Hand Six Actual, your attitude matches the color of the smoke on the LZ. Out."

Because he is on the squawk box again, I hear the muffled laughter. At least he is just on my company TAC net so the world can't hear.

"Smitty, are you happy now? Big day for you, huh? The general, a movie star, and the colonel and I jerkin' each other's chain."

"Yes, sir."

"I imagine all the platoon RO's are up on the net, right?"

"Yes, sir, it's too good to pass up...Sir."

"With the volume turned up"

"Yes, sir. Want me to stop them, sir."

"No, it's good to know that Radio is making a come back."

Based on Smitty's expression, I think this one went over his head and hit the sandbags behind him. Two for two again.

The remainder of this day passes. The Snuffies are happy, morale is high, and the Magpies busy. This evening I write Ryley telling her of the day's events and to maybe expect a call. She'll probably think I'm on some sort of vacation over here.

Near midnight, I get my usual late visit from Sergeant "Z" with the cocoa. By this time, LCpl Baronowski has wormed his way into a state of grace with "Z" and gets some cocoa as well. Sergeant Parzini is fickle, he's dating the two of us.

Heck of a day; I wonder when MGM will call?

CHAPTER SEVEN

A FEW WEEKS HAVE PASSED with no visits from Lieutenant General Barto. I feel a sense of relief or normalcy. We go out on a few search and destroy type operations in other TAORs, mostly as the blocking force.   These prove to be futile. This makes the time spent in the heat, humidity and the muck of the paddies even more unbearable. Later, operating alone, south of our hill, along the Yen River, we catch the dinks in another mistake and hurt them. I like working in our area, or wherever I'm in control.

Yesterday, the battalion commander flippantly accused me of starting World War III when one of my daylight patrols was fired on from the tree line just below our hill. The patrol had taken a valuable VC prisoner and was returning to Hill 22. The enemy engaged them and I provided supporting fire with both tanks and both pigs. It probably sounded and looked like WW III since I cut loose a salvo from both pigs at the same time. That's all six 106mm Recoilless Rifles on each ONTOS, all at once. As orgasmic as the overkill response is, they don't seem to be getting my message. Not only that, but my interpreter tells me they now have a Wanted Poster on me.

During the radio conversation with Lieutenant Colonel

Cartwright, which by the very nature of radio transmissions is stilted, he mentions something that catches me off guard. He says, "Lima Six Actual, Deadlock called me yesterday. He asked several questions about you. Do you know something I don't? Over."

"Iron Hand Six, that's a negative. What type of questions? Over."

"Lima Six, just questions regarding my insights about you. Your personal characteristics, like virtue, courage of convictions, and so forth. It struck me as somewhat strange. Over."

"Iron Hand Six, beats me. As you know, haven't had contact with him in a few weeks. Sorry, gotta go. Have Lima Two on my net. Out."

The contact from Lima Two is not hot but interesting. He discovered a fording spot on the Yen that appears to be new, and in use. I tell him not to linger there. We'll plan a surprise for later in the week.

As soon as Lieutenant Williamson, Lima Two, returns, we plan the surprise. After the meeting ends, this late spring day draws to a hushed close. I have a moment of rest at hand. The PX ration came today so I sit on top of the CP bunker, savoring my package of Chuckles. I sigh and think, simple things for simple minds. Then my thoughts drift away from the lighthearted to the colonel's remarks. What is the general up to? What's going on here? I understand we're friends, of a sort in this rank conscious society, but this alliance seems to be heading toward something beyond those bounds. Have to let it slide for now; I need to catch a catnap because we have a busy night.

A few more days pass quietly. Then, mid morning this third day after the colonel's remarks, Deadlock One-Zero unexpectedly radios he's inbound. The routine is the same, except Smitty is much calmer. He's become a veteran celebrity radioman. This time, with the general is Robert Mitchum. There is a slight difference in the seating, Mitchum is up in the left front seat and Lieutenant General Barto is in the back. They get out as soon as the chopper settles. The general comes over to me in his customary head jutting forward, charging style of resolute walk. Mitchum is rambling and rolling along at his side. Like Heston, he has a distinctive walk; this one is more natural, but it's the one you recognize from his flicks.

"Barney, Bob Mitchum. Bob, this is Captain Barney Quinn, and this is Lima Company."

We exchange hellos and shake hands. The Snuffies are surging around the LZ again, craning to see and hear what's happening. The general informs me the visit is going to be the same as the last. Then he says, "Bob, excuse us for just a minute. I need to talk with Captain Quinn."

Mitchum replies, "Sure, go ahead, General. It's your show."

Lieutenant General Barto and I slip several yards away, close to the chopper. His pilot, Captain Horner looks at me, nods, waves and smiles. It is the smile one has when they know something you don't. I hate that. I don't know him except for a few brief encounters on the radio, but I smile and wave back. The general asks, "How is everything going. Lieutenant Colonel Cartwright tells me you've been busy and having some success out here."

"I'm fine, sir. Yes, we've managed to stir things up some and got several first-rate results. Have a special daylight ambush set up for day after tomorrow. It'll work. Charlie will fall for it. Did the colonel say anything else?"

"Good. Tell me more about it."

I tell him the plan and he likes it. We chat for a few more minutes before he says, "Well, listen, Barney, I have to get moving. You take care of yourself. Keep up the good work. Give Mitchum an interesting visit but stay on the hill. I think the troops will love him, others have." The general didn't answer my question. He purposely ignored it. What the devil is going on?

"Aye Aye, Sir, an interesting visit it will be."

The general departs, blowing several inches of dust off this hill and depositing it on us inhabitants. The Pisa mess tent makes it again, and that is a wonder.

I take Mitchum on a walking tour of the positions. Most of the troops scurry back to their fighting holes and hooches, some however trail along behind us and a few others walk by his side. They love it, as he does. After the tour, Gunny will have the troops assemble in our mess tent. We end the walk-about and I take him into the tent. He remarks, "Nice," and laughs.

"It's shade," and then introduce him to the troops leaving him in the capable hands of Gunny Roe and the eager Snuffies. He receives a rousing welcome, and begins his session with a raunchy joke.

For the next few hours he talks with the men. They ask him all types of questions, but mostly about his movies and his leading ladies. Mitchum, differing from Heston, enlightens them with story after story about the ladies... and the ladies...and more ladies. Some, his leading ladies and some not, but all well celebrated. If a third of these tales are true, he'd be emaciated or dead, but who cares. The troops hang on every word, and hoot and holler their approval for each yarn. Regardless of the authenticity of the tales, the number of "Hoo-ahs" makes it clear this is one of the best days of their stay out here. Just one of the best, the unqualified best day is the day they leave for the real world.

When the time comes for him to depart and Deadlock One-Zero is inbound, a problem arises. We are taking some aggressive sniper fire. There is more than one of these jaspers dinging at us. These little pukes are really pissing me off. It's a miracle they haven't hit anyone. The Gunny pops a red smoke waving off the general's chopper. At the same time I have Smitty radio the bird, tell them what is happening, and give him an ETR. They can't wait around but will send another bird back. Suits me fine, I don't want to be critiqued when I cut loose. Now we can take care of the pesky little assholes messing up our day. A thought rambles through my mind as these sniper rounds are rattling around the hill. There is an old saying---"You don't need to worry about the round that has your name on it, it's going to get you anyway. You need to worry about the ones that say, To Whom It May Concern." These sniper rounds are in the latter category. I think Mitchum is excited and actually enjoyed being shot at. For me, it isn't fun and I take it personally.

We do what we have to do. We quiet the snipers with a few rounds from the tank's 90mm, and another salvo from the pigs. I'd take the whole village apart, but there are a lot of women and kids in there that the VC hide behind and use. I notice that Mitchum is down in a fighting hole with one of the troops. Getting inside his helmet as the saying goes. Good, smart move. The Snuffy must think its great, he and Mitchum sharing a hole. Just like the movies only these weren't blanks.

After all is quiet, Mitchum clambers out of his hole and ambles over to where I am standing, behind the tank which I had directed it's fire. He says, "Captain Quinn, or can I call you Barney?"

"Barney's fine."

"You didn't have to go to all this trouble just for me."

"Damn. I wish you'd have told me beforehand. I went to a lot of bother to stage this what with the rehearsals and all." We both grin. "Let's head for the bunker. I have to report to battalion."

"Okay, lead the way."

Once in the bunker, I radio battalion and report the activity. At the end I add, "Iron Hand Six Actual, I have another Deadlock guest here. Deadlock's long gone and we're waiting for pick-up. I will check with you after guest departure. Over."

"Lima Six Actual, roger. Out."

49

After my call, we sit in the bunker and chat. A few minutes into our conversation he asks, "Barney, you have something I can wet my whistle with?"

"Got some Kool Aid, strawberry, but it's not cold."

"You wouldn't happen to have anything stronger around here would you, Barney?"

"Sure do. Have a bottle of Jack Daniels the Gunny and I are saving for some special occasion. It was passed down from the previous unit on this hill. This is as good a time as any." Looking at Baronowski, I say, "Ski, go get the Gunny and have him come in here. Can't have any of this without him," as I reach down under my bunk and pull JD from my Willy Peter bag.

Faster than Clark Kent can change, the gunny is in the bunker. We open the almost full fifth and I pour a stiff snort into three canteen cups. Ski is looking at me forlornly, so I nod and he grabs his canteen cup from near the radio and thrusts it toward me. I give him a snort as well. Then we raise the cups in a toast. I say, "Semper Fi. And hope for tomorrow."

Mitchum says, "To you guys. Stay healthy and thanks for a great day. And one helleva show."

The gunny wants to drink, so he hastily grunts "Hear, hear."

We all take one small gulp. Mitchum takes another sip, "Barney, great toast. I know the Semper Fi bit, but what about, hope for tomorrow. It sounds vaguely familiar."

"Could be, but not as a toast. It's a take off from something from David Douglas Duncan's photo journal of the Korean War."

"What was that?"

"He shot a picture of a young Marine sitting alone, trying to chip food out of a frozen C-Ration can. It was along the road coming out of Chosin Reservoir. You know, where the First Marine Division was fighting its way out to the coast. Anyway, Duncan asked this kid, 'If you could have anything in the world right now, what would it be?' The kid says, 'Give me tomorrow.' I thought that said it all."

"Man, you've got that right, or rather, he did."

We continue to sit, sip and chat, mostly about where he is headed. The Gunny finishes and says, "Gotta go, Skipper. Mr. Mitchum, a pleasure. Thanks." They shake, and the Gunny goes outside. Ski plops down back at the radio. Mitchum and I continue to talk, mostly about my background since he has asked me some personal questions.

"Barney, can I call anyone for you when I get back. Make it someone good looking or I ain't callin."

"How about my gal? Just be nice and try to behave. I heard your stories in the mess tent. My gal makes those women look like second stringers."

"Well now, you're whetting my appetite. I'll try to behave, but no promises. Give me the scoop."

I scribble everything down on a piece of notepaper. Just as I hand it to him, Smitty says, "Chopper inbound, sir."

We get up, duck under the bunker entrance and head for the LZ. We hear the Huey as it crosses over the Yen River, its blades hacking through the heavy, humid air. . .whump. . .whump. . .whump, a great sound, especially when you need one. It's not the general, just his chase bird. The troops gather at the pad with Mitchum, shaking his hand and patting him on the back. Just trying to get one last fragment of the man. It's a good sendoff. They have really enjoyed their time with him, especially all the BS about the women. He's not in a hurry to leave so I take that as meaning he also had a great time and may have gotten a kick out of the Hill 22 sniper show. He will have something interesting to talk about when he gets back to the general, and at home.

Back inside the bunker, I call the battalion CO and tell him who was here, and how good a time the Snuffies had. He comes back with, "Lima Six Actual, I guess it's lucky for us to have the favored one in our unit. Seriously, I'm pleased for the troops. Over."

"Iron Hand Six Actual, I'm getting a little sensitive about the favored one comments. You need to be more considerate of your favorite six actual. Over."

"Lima Six, you don't have a sensitive bone in your body, and you're not my favorite. Out."

A few seconds pass, and he follows with, "Lima Six, yes, you are. Out." Our bantering hasn't missed a beat since day one. Good, it brings humor to damnation.

It's after 2400 and I've had my cocoa respite, so I spend some private moments re-reading Ryley's last letter. She relives several of our thirty plus days together. Our time in the evening at the cove as she dabbled in watercolors or at her home when she played the piano. I surprised her by also playing. She loved that I played by ear and played what she asked, or she could just hum a few bars. I believe one of the reasons we click is that we both have a creative side that's private, not many know of it. I look at the photo she sent along, of her at the cove, in a white bikini that accentuates her beach tan but mostly draws attention to her bod. This brings vivid images of another reason we click. What a gal. I need to get back to her, but for now, I need to dash off a letter.

I collect myself from the daydreams and write Ryley telling her about Robert Mitchum, and that he will be calling. I wonder what she will think of all this nonsense. I hope she gets this, and my last letter, before these guys call. She might think its some type of crank call and give them a "salty" remark or two. I also tell her of my apprehension about the general's attention and curiosity. Maybe she will have some insight or at least thoughts. I seal the letter, hand it to Ski saying, "Make sure this gets in the mail tomorrow?"

"Yes sir, Cap'n."

I lean back in my bunk propping myself up against the sand bags and listen to the rushing sounds from the radio. I think, once again, a visitor has come. The troops are ecstatic, and the rumors are wild. They are swirling around like the rotor wash from the chopper. It isn't just that the events themselves are being embellished, it's what the troops are making of them. The Skipper knows generals, writers, movie stars, just about everybody. There is even a rumor that I am going to get in touch with the President. Crazy. Just nuts. Aw hell, who cares, the morale is sky high tonight and the Magpies are crowing.

For me, I wonder what the hell is going on with this general stuff. This is way out of the norm. First, all these old friends, ghosts from my past, stirring my pot. Nevertheless, the most baffling is the general's deepening interest and his frequent appearances. Where the hell is this leading?

CHAPTER EIGHT

TODAY SOL BURNS BRIGHTLY AGAIN and this part of the world is being toasted. So much so, the dust on this hill makes the full paddies below look almost inviting. I finish the last of my morning Black Death. Baronowski is now manning the radios until replacements arrive later this week. Smitty however, is a happy camper. He is back at battalion getting ready to go home. He conned his way onto the radio early this morning to say good-bye again. Nice kid, I'll miss him, but he'll be home safe and in one piece and that's the best I can do. That's not the case all the time.

Ski turns toward me and excitedly blurts out, "He's coming again, Captain. Hot shit. Wonder who's with him this time?"

"Ski, for shame...bad language is not becoming of a guy with a Freedoms Foundation award." Ski spent his youth in orphanages and several foster homes. Along the way he did well in school and managed to win the award. He's a big, rawboned kid with dark curly hair and too-stern of a looking face most of the time for a young man, but he's a joy to be around.

"Sorry, sir, but he's only a few klicks out."

"Okay, I'll get with it."

It's not Lieutenant General Barto but his chase bird Deadlock

One-One that is going to land and drop off a Code Three. It lands making almost a touch and go so it can catch up to the general's slick. A slick is a Huey chopper with no guns. The chase bird has armament, some mounted rocket pods and machine guns.

A bird Colonel hops out and I notice he is decked out in brand-new jungle utilities and jungle boots. I'm sure the Snuffies notice this as well. He comes directly toward me, sticks out his hand and says; "Captain Quinn, I presume." Now doesn't that sort of grab you by your chinstrap? There is a great reply, but I restrain myself. I shake his hand and say, "Yes, sir, of Lima Company. And the Colonel, I presume?"

"Colonel Cunningham, FMFPac." His facial expression tells me he got my not-so-subtle barb. "Here on an advanced visit for the Commanding General. Setting up his trip." The CG, Fleet Marine Force, Pacific, is Lieutenant General Kurt Mueller. Little guy in stature with a big reputation. A tough and highly decorated Marine. Essentially, he's the boss of all Marines in the greater Pacific area.

"Well, sir, what can I do for you? Show you around the hill and tell you what's going on? Excuse me, Colonel, this is Gunnery Sergeant Roe, my Company Gunny." They greet each other appropriately.

Then the Colonel says, "Yes, a quick tour would be good for starters, but more important is what can I or the general do for you." Talk about the proverbial goose. The Colonel has choppered right into my feathered but dusty nest.

As we walk the hill I inform him of how short we are of certain items, some of which I point out he is wearing although he is not here permanently. Unwisely perhaps, I mention that it is not a good image to project to the Snuffies or good leadership to do so. He says, "Snuffies? Who are the Snuffies?" I think, arrogant prick. He knows what I mean.

"The Snuffies are my troops. A term of endearment, sir. They eyeball these things, sir." My remark is aimed directly at the jungle utilities and jungle boots. "As the Colonel can see, a hell of a lot of my troops don't have these items yet, and the ones some do have are in bad shape. Some are hand-me-downs, like mine." My jungle utility jacket has several shrapnel holes and the faded blood stains of its previous owner, since med-evac'd. I feel my anger, he senses it. "They resent, as I do, folks who are not out here, wearing them." He frowns, and his angry look tells me I am bordering on insubordination, but he just shrugs and utters, "Oh, I see, Captain."

Brashly I continue, "We are also short of bayonets and most of our flak jackets are missing plates." He has been taking notes, and I keep peeking at his notebook. He is perturbed by this, but more so by my tone of voice. The troops know what is going on by the nature of his questions and my gestures.

We complete our walk-about and retire to my bunker. I offer him some tepid Kool-Aid. It's my exclamation mark. He will be visiting other units today and I suspect he will be glad to get to them. Ski calls across the bunker, "Chopper inbound, Cap'n. It's Deadlock One-One again, sir."

"Okay Ski, thanks. Colonel, we better get up to the LZ." Once outside, I say, "Sir, thanks for the visit. I don't mean to be disrespectful, but if the Colonel doesn't mind, I don't think I will mention this chat with the troops. Don't want to get their hopes up for nothing. They have enough disappointments."

My hammer and tong subtleness is not suitable, but I feel like everything I said might have fallen on deaf ears like so much else with the pogey-baits in the rear with the gear. Some Supply Officer in the chain will get chewed out and become more disgruntled. This could be all show and the only thing that will happen is that a lot of papers will get shuffled. Wouldn't be the first time things got lost in the rear echelon two-step.

He quickly retorts, "Captain Quinn, I got your message. Okay? If I had a set of my regular utilities with me, I would take these off, to include my boots, and give them to you just to prove I got your message. Loud and clear, Captain. Do you get mine?"

"Yes, sir. Well, that's absolutely great. I'm going to count on the Colonel and his word."

I salute him as he climbs aboard the chase bird. As he does so, he frowns and shakes his head several times in obvious annoyance. I didn't make his day. He is pissed and I bet he's going to say something to my Battalion Commander, and maybe others. Well, fuck it, at least now he has to do something or really look bad.

The Gunny, who has been at my side during the visit looks at me, groans, "Skipper, you're goin to get your ass in a sling one day talking like that to senior officers. You were on the edge a couple of times, especially with that leadership remark."

"You noticed, huh? Well, you're probably right Gunny. But what are they going to do, send me to Vietnam and stick me in the paddies? Besides, sometimes you have to pound a tack with something bigger than a tack hammer."

"Yeah, but not a sledge hammer."

We grin, laugh a little and head back to the bunker where Baronowski is hollering that the battalion CO is on the horn again. I think, oh shit, I had better tell him what I did so he doesn't get blind-sided.

Lieutenant Colonel Cartwright and I exchange a few remarks before I inform him about the visit. As much as it hurts, I tell him about the general conversation and my remarks to the Colonel. I admit that it might have been a little strong on my part but I wanted to make my point. Damn, I forgot, my CO has new jungle utilities, too. Shit, oh well, so I'm not smooth.

He just ended it by replying, "Lima Six, your big mouth is going to get you in trouble one day. Not with me however, you're doing a grand job. Out."

Just before the Out, I hear chuckling in the background again. He sure loves that squawk box feature. He's enjoying my sarcastic sense of humor. Good, he'll need any kind of sense of humor when he finds out how pissed this Colonel really was when he left here.

When the mail call comes today, there are two letters from Ryley. Good, it brightens my dim beginning. Will make for some good reading later tonight. The day drags on uneventfully, and blends into evening. Finally, after some very adept trading early this morning, I enjoy a C-Rat meal of beanie weenies, fruit cocktail and pound cake. After this fine dining, and with the night activities underway, I settle in the bunker next to the radios, with a Kool Aid and Ryley's letters.

The Kool Aid is not a C-Ration item. It's sent from the real world. I need to remind Ryley in my next letter to send some more. Anything except grape. It sucks my cheeks together and turns my tongue purple. The others, especially the strawberry, quench the thirst.

She informs me that both Charlton Heston and Robert Mitchum telephoned, and mentions that my letters beat the phone calls. She writes that Heston sounded just like Moses. He was very proper and rigid sounding, but allowed that I was fine and looked "fit". Nice.

Then she tells me that several days later she got another call. This one started out with, "Hello, Ryley, this is Bob Mitchum and I just got back from Vietnam and saw that tall, lanky captain of yours. Barney is doing just great and treated me royally."

She continues that they went on to have a conversation that lasted almost an hour. Apparently, he didn't mention the sniper fire, which was considerate of him. I never mention these types of events to her. Ryley also writes that he sounds exactly as he does on the screen. It was like talking to a good friend. Then she asks, who's next? Love her sense of humor. We do have a lot in common.

It's great that they did this. You got to figure they did the same thing for one hell of a lot of guys. I appreciate it, and Ryley did as well.

For a bunch of days now, the VC activity has picked up. This is a result of our surprise several days ago at their new fording spot. It's simple, really. We made a normal looking company sweep through the Vills to the fording area, and then stopped, feinting a break for some chow and a brief rest. This gave us time and the means to drop off a squad for the ambush. They dig in and camouflaged themselves extremely well. After this, the rest of us picked up, continued on with the sweep, then across the paddies to the road and back to Hill 22. The dinks waited until almost dusk, leaving themselves some light, then came in behind us to pick up any ammo, grenades, chow and so forth that were carelessly left behind. This happens, but not in Lima Company. The ambush sprung and we hurt them very bad. They made a big mistake.

If you do nothing, or nothing different, they have you where they want you. If you do something, particularly something different, you make the rules. I believe it's my game and my rules.

Several days after the ambush, on what has started out as a quiet day we get a call on the radio that a slick and a bigger bird are inbound. It is a Deadlock call sign but not One Zero so it tells me Lieutenant General Barto has sent a Code Six, but he isn't along. I wonder what the hell this is about. That's answered in the very next transmission. Ski says, "Holy Smokes, sir, it's the CG of FMFPac...he's coming to visit you...Lieutenant General Mueller is coming in, sir." Baronowski's voice gains an octave in his excitement. He sounds better as a base.

"Yes, Ski, I know who he is."

We start the usual, now thoroughly practiced routine, at the LZ. The Gunny has a green smoke popped. Just as the green smoke starts spewing and drifting with the gentle breeze, we start getting some sniper fire again. I must be really pissing these guys off, they're doing this almost every time. Not much fire, but now that I know that Lieutenant General Mueller is in the lead bird I can't take any chances so we quickly pop a red smoke and radio them that the zone's hot, to come back later. They Roger the message. In several minutes, after the choppers are out of sight, we get things quiet again. It was just a couple of Indians pestering the Calvary in the fort.

An hour later, the other chopper returns and lands. No passengers are aboard, just a lot of boxes. The Gunny musters up some of our troops to help unload quickly so the bird can get on its way. After the helo leaves, the Gunny is busy opening the boxes. They are crammed full of jungle utilities and jungle boots of all sizes, and flak jackets. All new gear. Finally, there is one Marine green wooden locker box. It's opened and is crammed full of bayonets. There is a plain white, note-size envelope lying on top of them.

One of the troops helping unload opens the envelope and reads the note which is on Three Star personal stationary. The gunny snatches it away from the trooper saying, "What the hell is wrong with you, Burford? The letter ain't for you, it's for the Captain." It's too late, Burford's eyes are bulging out of his head and he scrambles back to his buddies in the 60mm mortar pit. Burford is a busybody, a leading Magpie. He should have been a little old lady in a crowded neighborhood leaning over the backyard fence.

The Gunny takes a quick peek at the note as he shuffles the few steps toward me. He mutters, "Damn...if this doesn't beat all."

He starts to hand it to me but I put my arm out, palm toward him gesturing him to stop,

"No, go ahead Gunny, read it…aloud. Hell, it's only my personal mail."

The Gunny hesitates with a bemused look on his face. "No, go ahead, Gunny, read it aloud so the troops can hear." Now his look tells me he gets it, and with a cunning grin reads the note, almost shouting.

> "Dear Barney,
> Here are the items you requested. Sorry
> I couldn't make it in person. Keep up
> the good work.
> Semper Fi,
> Kurt Mueller"

The Gunny hands it to me. It is handwritten and signed by the general, as if it's a personal note. Well hell, it is. I give the note back to the Gunny and tell him, "Let the troops see it. Get it back for me later." Several more troops have assembled by now. For their benefit, and the Gunny's, I turn and depart shouting over my shoulder, "About…Damn…TIME. AND IT'S A GOOD THING THEY GOT IT RIGHT." The note and signature has even the Gunny startled. Perhaps even he is becoming a believer.

About this time, Baronowski pokes his head out of the bunker and tells me, "Sir, Battalion Six for you…AGAIN, sir."

"What's this AGAIN shit, Ski?"

"Well, all I mean, sir, is that you always seem to be getting these calls after the general or his friends show up. People seem to be sweating what you're up to."

"Yeah, well, let em' sweat, Ski. It keeps you and the troops entertained and that's good for morale. Mine, too. Right?"

He shrugs, "I guess so, Skipper."

Once in the bunker, I lean back against the sandbag bulkhead and loudly sigh into the handset, "Iron Hand Six Actual, this is Lima Six Actual. Over."

"What the hell is going on down there today? You've only been back on that hill for a day or so and already it looks like the chopper base at Marble Mountain."

"Six Actual, first Pac Six Actual tried to land but we had some sniper fire. Then later he sent in a chopper loaded with all that stuff I harped about. Remember? Over."

"What stuff? Oh, that. Did I ever tell you that the Colonel you harassed jumped my bones while telling me about you. Also, he really got all over our Supply Officer, who's still ticked off at you. I told him not to worry, that you weren't happy unless you were stirring the pot. Over."

" Six Actual, that's a negative. You never mentioned that, but the gear is here now. Jungle Ute's, boots, flak jackets and bayonets, so ask your tent peg counter whose way is best; and oh yes, Pac Six Actual sent me a personal note along with the gear. Over."

"What'd he say?"

"Iron Hand Six Actual, gee whiz. It's really a personal note, but I will tell you that he didn't mention you at all. I'm going to send a message of thanks back so I will mention what a fine job you are doing and what a nice person you are."

There is a pause, the muffled laughs, and not so muffled ones, are coming through loud and clear. "Lima Six, just read me the note and stop jerking my chain."

So I do and he is happy. We sign off, and I go outside to see the reaction to all the new gear. Hell, it's like Christmas day on Hill 22. What a sight. Troops putting on their new unnies and new boots. Some look up at me with a beaming smile. Some give me a thumbs up...you know, a "way to go skipper" gesture. This is when all the bullshit pays off. When, to them the rumors are no longer rumors, but gospel. That's not true of course, but let them believe what they want.

Ah, yes, like always, the gunny takes care of me with some new gear. What a guy. I love grumpy gunny's.

Tomorrow can't possibly top this.

CHAPTER NINE

WE'RE OUT ON ANOTHER FUTILE blocking mission today. In one sense we're glad, but in another, a little testy. No one's been hurt but if we're going to go out, we'd rather be successful and knock a few heads around. At least we look good in our new jungle utilities and boots Lieutenant General Mueller sent us.

We leave the outskirts of Bo Ban (1) and head the four klicks across the paddies to Hill 22. Bo Ban is a village with two hamlets, (1) and (2), and is directly across the Yen River from the Cam Ne complex. These are two very nasty Vills. As we approach our hill a radio call crackles over the net,

"Lima Six. Have you in sight. Visitor here. Iron Fist Six Actual. Over."

"Lima Base, who is Iron Fist Six? Over." I think, that's stupid, he can't answer that in the clear.

"Lima Six, don't know, but he knows you. Another Same O, Same O. Over." Sounds like Lance Corporal Crowe, one of our two new radiomen, has picked up Smitty's and Baronowski's humor and saltiness. He's young, eighteen, with red hair and freckles, nicknamed Rooster. Okay, so it's not very original but it makes him cocky.

"Lima Base, Roger. Be there in Two Zero. Out." The other radioman, who is with me today, is Corporal Tom Beasley.

Everyone calls him Bees, what else? He's twenty, is blond with a crew cut and is a farm boy from Iowa. He's always grabbing a handful of soil, looking at it, and taking a sniff. I tell him, "Bees, looks like, smells like, it is."

"Yeah, Skipper, but this is one of the richest rice areas in this country."

"You're right, Bee's, but it still smells like shit."

We continue to slosh along as I give him the handset and say, "Let's get on back to the fort and see what's happening, Bees."

"You got it, Skipper." He has salt dripping already, but he's more formal when the situation demands. Neither one is disrespectful, just comfortable, and maybe a little like me.

We slog through the just over knee-deep paddies, with Ski walking in front of me, staying off the paddy dikes. Bad things happen on paths and dikes. Damn, I hate these paddies; smell like shit and full of leeches. We are at the barbed wire and enter North Gate. Hope Iron Fist won't mind my appearance, paddy sweet and sweat-stained.

It appears my past has caught up to me once again, in the person of Lieutenant Colonel William "Wild Bill" Donnelly. He was the Executive Officer of the Barracks in Washington when I first reported there. He was a real hard ass, probably still is, but a squared away officer. Very strict, demanding, but fair. I had absolutely no problems with him. Excellence of performance was all he demanded, and for me, that was a blessing.

He is unwisely standing on top of my CP bunker. He is surveying the area, and probably our movement through the paddies. We're in damn good tactical formation, as always. I don't get careless out here. His over six-foot frame is an inviting target for some sniper.

As soon as he sees me, he grins. "Well, well, if it isn't Captain Quinn. Far cry from the parade deck, isn't it? How are you doing, Captain?" Beyond demanding, he is also very formal. I don't think he has ever called me Barney, not even in casual conversation at the Center House bar, or dining room, at 8th and "I".

"I'm doing fine, sir. It's a bit of a change from the parade deck, in more ways than one. The colonel's lookin' good."

When I don't join him on top of the bunker, he gets the message and jumps down. We shake and I ask, "What brings the colonel out here to my area?"

He tells me his battalion is coming here, and we will be leaving. This is surprising news and a helluva way to find out. I can see my troops moving from one to the other, pointing back this way, and talking excitedly.

As usual, Burford is hanging around trying to hear, until I glare at him, and he scurries back to the mortar pits. The Magpies, who already have the drift of things, of course see the visit differently. They prefer to believe that another friend of the Skipper's, a senior officer, came to inform me personally that we're moving. Pure BS but I'll let this portion of the rumor ride. Actually, it's a minor SNAFU. I should have been informed by my own CO, but, what the hell, news is news.

After we discuss the area, and do a brief map study, he climbs aboard the chopper and leaves. I immediately radio my Battalion Commander about the visit, then get the scoop, late, but firsthand.

I call the Platoon Commanders and the Gunny into the bunker, "Here's the word, guys. We're leaving the hill, for good. We will be relieved in position early tomorrow morning by a company from another regiment. We will be going on several operations. Tonight's activities will go as planned. So get the folks ready. I will brief you in detail later this afternoon. Understand?"

A chorus of "yes sirs" rings out and the group gets up to go about their work.

Morning comes early, barely dawn. The weather is hot as usual but it's clear. Everyone is briefed and we are on our way by trucks to the Battalion CP. It's goodbye to Hill 22 and the nasty villages of Duong Lam, Bo Ban and La Chau. The women and children liked us, the guys didn't. The VC can take their stinkin' Reward Poster they put out on me and stuff it. The troops thought the poster was great. Their Skipper, Dai-uy Quinn, a Wanted Man. I wasn't as pleased, the trifling amount was an insult. Anyway, I'm out of here.

Once at the battalion CP we have a hot meal, are briefed, load up with ammo, C's and water, and wait for the choppers. We are to locate and engage the Doc Lap Battalion. The general won't be visiting me in this area, but my gut tells me he'll know where I am. Why? I still haven't figured out, but he will.

After chow we head to the LZ and don our flak jackets, packs and equipment. My unit leaders are checking their respective troops, and the radio and time checks are made again. Since we're being detached for this Op, Lieutenant Colonel Cartwright comes down to the LZ to see us off. "Barney, you look ready."

"Yes, sir. Primed and ready. Gone over everything several times. Is Kilo Company ready?" This is a two-company operation to start, controlled by another battalion.

"Yep, spoke to Evert just a few minutes ago."

"Great. Well, goin' to miss your harassing ways, Colonel, but I promise to be polite and watch my manners with this other CO."

"Well, don't change, Barney. I've already forewarned him what a joy you are to have around. He's expecting your normal obnoxious self."

"Gee, Colonel, you really do love me. Take care of yourself; see you when we get back. I hear the choppers coming. Gotta get moving."

"Okay. Barney, take care of yourself. I mean it."

"Yes, sir."

We shake; he lightly punches me on the upper arm and walks away toward the battalion CP bunker. He looks back after several steps, and waves.

I give him a "Hoo ah."

The troops, in mass, do the same. We're ready.

We'll be in CH-46's, Sea Knight choppers. Much bigger than the Huey and carry a lot more troops and equipment. We're going to land north of the Ky Lau River, advance and sweep toward Route 4 and Phu Tay (3).

The choppers arrive and land all at one time. The dust is choking. Nothing like a snoot full of dust to start the day. We board the 46's. Because of the number and size of these birds, the entire company will be landing at one time. We lift off and head for our objective.

As we land, it's obvious we have found, at least part of, the Doc Lap Battalion. We are taking a helleva' lot of small arms fire as we come out of the choppers. We are pinned down for a few minutes, until I push myself up out of the dirt, and get the company moving toward the first Vill. We're in a large area of dry paddies, and there is a cemetery-like burial mound in the middle. The paddy dikes provide us some cover from the fire.

I've got some air upstairs, so I tell my Forward Air Controller (FAC) to put some ordnance on these jaspers to let them know that Ol' Barney is in town and means business. This is going to be a nasty operation. But, we're up, moving, and takin' charge of the day and our fate.

We have a long, active, nasty day. Not a good omen, but still in all, there is some humor to be found, some in-country color.

At dusk, we set in for the night. My interpreter, an ARVN (Army of the Republic of Vietnam) Sergeant informs me that the village chief, an elderly gentleman with a well-weathered face made distinct by a scraggly and stringy, six inch white goatee wants to thank me for rescuing his village of Pham Do from the VC. He wants me to "dine" with him this evening at his home. His estate is a bamboo-thatched hut in the center of the village.

With my interpreter, Sergeant Thanh Luong in tow, we arrive at the appointed time and are warmly welcomed. We are invited in and sit on woven straw mats on the dirt floor. I leave Ski outside. He's baby-sitting me.

The Chief's wife serves us a cup of tea. She, like the Chief, is elderly and like many women here, her smile displays the blackened teeth, stained from chewing betel nut. The nut, wrapped in its leaf is narcotic in nature, and gives the person a buzz when chewed. Maybe it's just a way to say, "not tonight" to the Chief. At any rate, it turns the teeth and tongues a very deep red, almost purple. Eventually the teeth turn black. It gives new meaning to a Colgate smile.

The teacups she is using are old and slightly cracked. A thick heavy porcelain with the simple blue pattern faded from years of use. They don't match but the idea of good china is nice. The tea is tepid and I notice there are a few bugs floating, well, actually swimming in my tea. There is no diving allowed but they appear to be having fun anyway. The tea is good although I worry where the water came from. I wish she would have boiled it but then the bugs wouldn't be able to frolic. Through Sergeant Luong, we chat for a brief spell. Suddenly, without a word of warning, the old woman abruptly gets up and darts outside. I wonder if I did something to offend her. I guess not, the Chief doesn't look displeased.

She returns a few moments later, carrying a live chicken by its neck. It is squawking loudly, flapping and struggling around in her clamped hand. It has to be the scrawniest chicken in the world. It must be tubercular. Then, out of the blue, "WHOOSH" and "SNAP." The chicken has met its demise; a good ol' fashioned neck wringing has taken place right in the parlor. I'm thankful we're not having dog tonight.

She yanks out the only three, scraggily feathers this chicken has. She drops to a sitting position, slams the bird on the dirt floor and chops it up with a rusty meat cleaver. Everything, beak, head, eyes, feet, innards, everything. My mouth is still hanging open where it was when my jaw dropped at the neck wringing.

My eyes feel saucer-like with my brows still arched in surprise. Luong smirks at my expression.

She hacks this bird into nickel and dime size bites, scoops it up along with some dirt from the floor with her hands, which aren't exactly manicured. She throws everything into a pot of sizzling oil. This is going to be dinner, along with some rice, home grown from their community owned, honey bucket fertilized, paddy.

Through my interpreter, I am trying to win the mind and heart of this village chief. During this stilted conversation, I look at Luong trying to signal him this isn't all that pleasing and an excuse to leave will help my disposition and digestive tract.

He gets my message, but quietly explains to me it would be an insult to leave now. Hell, I know that but I figure he might know some ancient oriental custom to get me out of here. Oh well, patriotism calls in many voices.

Dinner is served on slightly rusted and dented tin plates, placed on a woven straw mat on the floor that is centered in the middle of the four of us. Dinner consists of some more tepid tea, rice, and the chicken, which, although very spicy, is actually rather tasty. Anything hard in the chicken I swallow whole, and try not to think what it might be. The rice is that wonderful sticky, oriental rice.

We are also having fresh lettuce from their garden, dip washed in a bucket of well water. I try not to think of drainage and all those ecological factors. It's much too late to worry now. A cup is passed among us containing something, a dressing I think, for the salad. It looks like watered down catsup but I am suspicious, so I pour just a tad on my lettuce. I politely ask Sergeant Luong, "What's this dressing? This sauce?"

He replies, running all the words together.

"Broodofaduck."

"What was that you said, Thanh?" Sergeant Luong is not my favorite person. He's lazy and doesn't like to go out in the boonies. I think he has a pale streak in him.

He repeats it very slowly, disdainfully this time, so there is no misunderstanding, and perhaps no further disruption of his friggin' dinner. I feel like twisting his pencil neck about a half turn to the starboard.

"Brood - of - a - duck." Aw, shit. Raw duck blood.

Not much I can do now. Have already eaten some, and I have this next portion, precariously clamped in my chopsticks, halfway to my mouth. I struggle and finish some of it. Enough to be polite. It is not my favorite dressing. So, to paraphrase a saying, "When in Pham Do, do as the Pham Doans do."

The meal appears to be over. I'm still alive and other than the dressing, the chow was okay. A few worms and bugs perhaps, a little protein, but, so be it. The wife pours me another cup of tea, which is free of creatures. They must have gotten tired of swimming and are lying around the saucer resting. The Chief's wife is up and moving. Oh oh, it's not over. She's going to serve a dessert. Ah, it's a bowl of pudding. Good, it's something I recognize, Tapioca. After a few mouthfuls, which are different but tasty, and only to make conversation I ask, "What is this, tapioca?"

Sergeant Luong replies, "It's good, huh? It's boiled silk worms." They can't handle the l's, so they come out sounding like r's.

I let out a long sigh, and utter weakly, "Oh yeah. Glad I stayed for dessert."

Okay, this does it for Ol' Barney. Enough of this winning the hearts and minds routine. My stomach is rumblin' and rumblin' and I figure my future holds a roaring date with a slit trench.

We leave, bowing gracefully and thanking the chief and his wife profusely. I'm not sure about the bowing protocol but it's always done in the movies.

When I come out of the hut, Ski asks, "How was it, Skipper?"

I look at him, shake my head, and say, "A fine bodyguard you are. Why weren't you in there tasting my food?"

"Huh?"

"Forget it, Ski. I'm just kidding. Let's get back to the CP."

71

We arrive back in a few minutes. I check with my unit leaders to see if everything is okay, and it is. Then check with my Chief Corpsman, Doc Eden, and tell him about dinner and ask, "Hey Doc, is there anything I can take?"

He grins slyly, grumbles a low laugh, and replies, "Yes, sir, take a shit."

"Thanks Doc. Guess you missed the bedside manners class in Corpsmen training."

"Just telling' the Skipper the way it is."

First-rate guy, great Doc, but a salty bastard. I like him a lot, and he knows it, so he gets away with some zingers from time to time. I'll be glad when Sergeant Z gets here with the cocoa. It will ease my mind and put a coating on my gut and the Hershey Highway.

It's late, the day has been long, busy and hot. The night could be long as well. Tomorrow we will be moving out to finish this Op, and then at the end of day we will get heli-lifted directly from the Phu Tay area into another operation.

Sergeant Parzini arrives in the nick of time with the cocoa. "Heard you might need this, Cap'n?" He's grinning from ear to ear.

"You heard right. Thanks. Sit a spell."

He does, takes a few sips, and says, "You're either damn good or damn lucky, Skipper. We didn't get no one hit today. You're lucky you didn't get dinged jumping up and running around that LZ this morning."

"Z, luck is when opportunity and preparation meet. We were prepared, plus we've got good troops. By the way, you did a great job this morning with that mortar fire. It was on the money, first time out."

"Thanks, Skipper. Tomorrow goin' to be as nasty as today?"

"Don't know, but we're prepared."

"And lucky." He winks.

Chapter Ten

THIS MORNING BRINGS ANOTHER HOT, blistering day. The sun looks and feels like it's only a hundred feet above us. It'd be easy to say it's the same for the other guy, but it's not. He's running around in black shorts, sandals and maybe a pith helmet. We're in steel pots, flak jackets, heavy packs, loaded down with extra ammo, our cartridge belts hanging with even more ammo, three canteens of water and a first aid packet. A mule would balk or buckle under this load, but not a Marine. We just bitch.

We finish the Op today without incident. Get to our appointed pick-up spot, secure it and wait for the choppers to take us on our next operation. This will be with another battalion. Kilo Company will not be going with us on this one, but rather back to our own unit.

This next operation takes us to yet another new area, and it is more of the same type country. Dry paddies, a few villages, and a couple of shallow rivers to wade across several times. The leeches in the rivers will be licking their chops. If we have them chunkin' on us, we'll just have to scorch their ass with a lighted cigarette so they'll drop off. Engorged, but off. We are still hunting down, engaging, and chasing Charlie, maybe elements of the Doc Lap Battalion or just individual VC units.

On this, our last portion of the operation, we work with the Vietnamese Popular Forces. Not good. Local and usually infiltrated with VC so it's hard to tell the good guys from the bad. Nonetheless, we do well, and no one hit again. Man, lucky, lucky, lucky. Nothing major or spectacular but we engage in several small firefights, and beat up some small VC units that apparently weren't alerted by the locals.

Finally, today, our part is over and we are going back to our own battalion, which has now moved to Hill 55. It is several klicks south of Hill 22 and a little deeper into Indian country. Not as many Vills in this immediate area and the paddies are dry. Nothing but dry paddies looking like peanut patches. There are some larger hard-core VC units roaming around here. We will get a night or two on the Hill before we go out again.

Later this first evening back and after I get the company set in, it's time for me to check in with my CO, Lieutenant Colonel Cartwright. We quickly re-establish our relationship. I start with, "Evening, sir, we're back as you know. When do you want a complete update briefing?"

"Well, since you're not in irons, I assume you didn't piss off any other battalion commanders."

"No, sir. I was nice."

"Why? That's way out of character." He's on a roll now.

"Because they were nice to me and didn't holler at me."

"Barney, you're so sensitive, you almost brought a tear to my eye." He laughs at his own humor. Then continues, "Seriously Barney, glad you're back safe and sound. I did get outstanding reports about you and Lima Company. Excellent work. Major Deming will be back from chow in about thirty minutes. Come back then and brief both of us. Okay?"

Major Clyde Deming is the Battalion S-3, the Operations Officer. A Naval Academy graduate. Sharp as the business end of a bayonet, and a regular guy as well.

"Oh, and another thing Barney. The general was here asking

about you. Again! I wish you would have been here, it might have saved me the ass chewing I got about the security at the water point at the base of the hill."

"Sorry to hear that Colonel. Stick close to me, sir, and you'll be fine. Get separated and you'll have to fend for yourself. Apparently that's a problem, sir."

"Also, the Regimental Commander came around and chewed me out for the same thing. Did you piss him off while you were gone?"

"Well, now that you mention it, I might have. I think he or his radio operator came up on my Company TacNet on the first Op. He was trying to play company commander from two thousand feet up. He didn't properly identify his station, so I told the operator to get the fuck off my net."

"Oh, shit, you didn't?"

"Afraid so, sir. He didn't request to come on my net and didn't ID himself. I can't allow unidentified stations on my company net. And, he never tried again, so I figured it wasn't him or he knew he was wrong."

"Jesus, Barney, you're a piece of work."

"But cute, huh?"

"Incidentally, speaking of the water point. Go get a shower, you look cruddy and smell like a cess pool."

"That's where I've been."

"Wiseass."

Although not my nature, I let him have the last word. It's okay to joke with the colonel about the general, but my brain housing group is not processing the information. Why in the hell is the general continually visiting?

On my way out of the bunker, I pass the battalion radio operator sitting by his PRC-10. He looks up at me, grins and says, "We missed your transmissions, Cap'n. Welcome back." I smile, wink and continue through the opening into the night. I pause for a few minutes to get my night vision back before walking, and stumbling a bit, back to my bunker.

Now in my hooch with a few moments of free time, I'll dash off a note to Ryley. I haven't had time to write while on these Ops, and I have seven letters from her waiting for me. I'll let her know that I've been gone, am back safe and sound, and will savor her letters later tonight when I can let my mind drift.

I finish the letter and hand it to my RO. "Get this in the mail bag for me, will ya Rooster?"

"Yes, sir. Right away."

"Thanks. As soon as Corporal Beasley gets back, go take a shower and get some chow."

"Okay, Skipper."

The brief exchange earlier with the colonel tells me everything is back to normal. After a shower and my briefing of the CO and Major Deming, I will receive my company's "marching orders." Wonder what is in store for Ol' Lethal Lima tomorrow, and beyond? One thing for sure, it appears the general knows my whereabouts, but hopefully the Regimental CO doesn't.

Two guys that do know my whereabouts are Parzini and Ski. They sit down next to me outside my CP bunker, with the cocoa. They too, like the rest of the company, have been to the water point and got respectable. Z says, "Cap'n, good to be home, or here, or whatever."

"Sure is, and I'm glad you're on to another source of cocoa. Do you ever run out?"

"Never happen, Skipper."

Gunny Roe comes up and joins us. He has his own cocoa. "Night, Skipper, guys. Look what I found sneaking around."

He's got Rooster by the arm, and is pretending to drag him along.

Bees is slinking behind, acting as if he too is being pulled along. "Think we should let them join us?"

I reply, "Sure, but they have to cut their own deal with Sergeant Z."

Rooster and Bees are all smiles as they sit with us outside the bunker.

I look at Guns and say, "Gunny, you're lookin' chipper for an old mule."

"Feel a lot younger. You know what I'm really happy about, Skipper? We didn't lose a single trooper, not even a WIA, while we were gone."

I bite my lip and grimace, slowly shaking my head, knowing we have been extremely fortunate...knowing it can't continue. I say, "Yeah, I know. Great. We got damn lucky, Gunny."

"Sure, some luck, but mostly good decisions and heads-up shit by you. Whatever, the troops are happy."

"Yeah, but they'll be disgruntled when they find out the general was here, and we weren't. They like their celebrity status."

"They like you...and hot chow, the beer ration, and bein' alive."

Chapter Eleven

Our first dawn on Hill 55, the great Sol is up, and peeking over the paddies. The brilliance of the dawn reminds me a new day begins, everywhere. In most places in the real world, it's going to be a wonderful day. Here, it's most likely going to be a crappy one, maybe more so than some others, maybe not. For my own sanity, I search for the light side of this damnation.

The troops can see the handwriting in the dust. The Magpies are mumbling and muttering for me to use my influence, to get us a plush assignment. They haven't seen the general, movie stars, authors, senior officers or any other visitors lately. They seem to forget that my influence is a figment of their rumors. There are no plush assignments for a rifle company, except in relative terms, and then few. We're not going to be indulged at this time, so the Snuffies are again disappointed and the Magpies continue to grumble.

Hill 55 is ten or so klicks south of Hill 22. It overlooks the junction of the La Tho and Thanh Quit Rivers, between the Yen River and Route 1 south. We will run several company-size operations south of the two rivers, in some real Indian Country. The terrain is pretty much the same as we've been experiencing, except it has less Vills and fewer cultivated paddies.

This area has become more treacherous because an ARVN

unit pulled out of an ammo dump, leaving all of the ordnance behind, to include a slew of anti-personnel mines. An incredibly stupid, dangerous, and unprecedented gift for the VC. We'll be feather footing in this area, but we'll still pay a price.

Even in this area, there is some humor to be found. Not much, but some. After our first one-week operation, south of these rivers, I request tank support for our next foray. The request is denied. The tanks can't get across the river, but I'm being sent two LVTH-6's (Landing Vehicle Tracked, Howitzer).

This vehicle travels on both land and water. It moves about 6 or 7 mph in the water, which is of no importance to me, and up to 30mph on smooth road. We will be using them as replacements for tanks. We won't be traveling on any roads, but it can giddy-up in the dry paddies and fields we will be covering. We won't, however, be going any faster than my troops can move on foot and the situation dictates.

The LVTH-6 is armed with a turret mounted 105mm howitzer. It also has a .30Cal M1919A4 type machine gun mounted on the turret and additionally has a .50Cal machine gun. If you have ever watched Marine amphibious landings in the movies, you have seen these bringing troops ashore.

Although not a tank, but better than nothing, I welcome these crawlers. The 105mm gives me my own artillery, and they strengthen us when we set in at night. We can use the 105mm as a direct fire weapon then, as well as when we're on the move. It's an attention getter.

This first morning out, on our second foray, I get word they will be joining me near the river junction. I move the company there, set in and wait. In a few hours the two vehicles clank, churn, and crunch into our perimeter on the riverbank. A Staff Sergeant scampers out of the lead vehicle and jogs directly toward me. He's wound up about something. However, he's not as keyed up as the monkey sitting on his shoulder, and hanging on to his collar with his little pink, spidery fingers. I'm just a little concerned. No, I'm damn concerned, however, before I can say a word or continue forming an opinion, he opens the conversation with, "Are you Captain Quinn? Are you the Cap'n that does all the shootin' and firin'? I've got two vehicles, loaded to the gunnels with ammo. We're ready to do some shootin.'"

I'm glad I'm back a few paces because he's spewing salvia with each word. I don't detect any speech impediment so I guess the more excited he gets, the damper the conversation. At the same time, the monkey is chattering, squeaking and screeching as well. I don't understand him. Maybe, in a couple more months out here I will, but not yet.

I shift my eyes to the Section Leader, than back to the monkey, which is glaring at me, and back again to the sergeant, and say, "Whoa there, sergeant. First, why don't you start by telling me your name and unit? Then explain what that fucking monkey is doing sitting on your shoulder."

"Oh, him. Yes sir. I'm Staff Sergeant Helton, sir, from Third Amtrak. The monkey is my pet, and our mascot. His name is Chet."

It looks like some type of spider monkey. "Okay. All right. Now then, where in the hell did you, and Chet, hear all these stories about me doing all this shooting? I include Chet, sergeant, because he seems more excited than you, but I prefer you answer, not Chet." I back up a few more steps.

He looks at me, somewhat puzzled. He's missed my witticism, but he is looking at me as if I've been in some other part of the world or on another planet. He hasn't missed the two steps however; he follows my retreat. "Damn, Captain, everyone knows your reputation. You like to fire the big stuff." He is still looking at me with a baffled frown on his face. Then, CLICK, a light bulb comes on, and he says, "You are THE Captain Quinn, aren't you?" His enlightened, questioning expression indicates he thinks he might have made a mistake and gone to the wrong area or unit.

"I don't know about the, THE crap, but, yeah Sergeant, I'm Captain Quinn. Why don't you get your crews out of their vehicles for a short while? Give 'em a break. Then you come back over here, and I'll brief you on what we will be doing, starting in about an hour. Okay? And, oh yeah, Sergeant Helton, leave the friggin' monkey in the vehicle, and don't let that damn thing become a nuisance. Got it?"

"Yes, sir...Sir, Chet won't be—"

"I hate fucking monkeys, especially out here."

He's taken aback and skulks away. I look at Gunny Roe and ask, "Where does all this stuff come from, Guns? Where does it get started? Who carries a monkey around on his goddamn shoulder? What is this, some kind of freakin' circus?"

"Well, you did tend to fire the tanks and Ontos a lot on the hill, and you do call a bunch of arty and air when you're out here in the paddies. You have a habit of stirring things up, or blowin' them up. Word gets around I suppose, Skipper. I don't know about the damn monkey, maybe he's the gunner."

"Real funny, Guns. Good line. Well, these guys don't have to act so damn excited."

"You mean the Sergeant or the monkey, or both?"

"I mean Helton. Ahhhh, you're jerkin my chain, Gunny. Anyway, the monkey probably has the clap or something and I'll have to explain that to the colonel like everything else."

"Maybe he just doesn't get a chance to shoot much, Skipper. You know these Hotel 6's don't get used that much over here."

"Yeah, I guess that's it. But why the monkey?"

"Beats me, Cap'n. I wonder if it's a male or female?"

"Oh, shit, Gunny. Jesus."

I leave it at that and sit back down in the dried out paddy, prop my back against the dike and continue to eat my can of cold ham and limas. These will bind me up tighter than an old corset.

The circus act does make me chuckle. Helton didn't even take the time to tell me his name first, just ran up and started rattling off how much ammo he had on board. Hell, he was drooling and slobbering, for Pete's sake.

"Hey, Gunny. Tell the troops to stay away from that silly ass monkey. Don't want them bunched up. One round and all that."

"Got it, Skipper."

"Besides, if he doesn't have the clap he probably has fleas, or mites, or some kind of vermin."

"They probably won't get on us. We smell worse than the monkey, Cap'n."

"Oh yeah, well, I look better."

"Ummm, not sure of that either...sir."

After our C-Rat break, and briefing, we head south, searching for Charlie. I'm up on the lead Amtrak, with Helton, and his monkey. I can see some of the Snuffies laughing. They know I'm not happy with this critter.

We're a few klicks along, when POP, SNAP, POP, SNAP. A zip with a carbine is trying to ding me. A couple more rounds ricochet off the turret. More than one dink. The three of us are trying to get down behind the gun turret. The monkey and I scramble for the same spot. I win, by kicking his screeching and screaming ass off the tractor. Screw him. This spot's mine.

I return the sniper fire with several rounds from the 105mm howitzer. No more snipers. Maybe a little heavy handed, but I'm in a foul mood. Between the monkey and the snipers, I'm not having a good day.

We move on, continuing south. For the remainder of the

afternoon, the monkey, now back up on the vehicle, glares at me. The little varmint is pissed. I don't think he liked me putting him in harm's way, and for damn sure didn't like the kick in the ass. The hell with him, I opt for me over the monkey. I'm not sure Sergeant Helton agrees, he's sulking, too, but at least he got to shoot.

Tonight we set in, register our artillery fires, along with our own mortars. Shortly after dark, we get probed. Bad mistake, the VC are in the middle of our registered fires. One of my patrols runs into them, on its way out. They exchange fire. I get my squad in quickly, and then we open up with small arms fire. Red and green tracers zipping back and forth, ricocheting off the two LVTH-6's, hand flares popping turning the blackness into an eerie scene of darting shadows. It looks like a traditional Fourth of July fireworks show. Unfortunately, it's not.

I have the FAC call the registered artillery fire, while I call in our own mortars. At the same time, we open up with the Amtrak's 105mm howitzers. This is direct fire, and devastating. Pretty quick, no more green tracers. It's easy pickins'.

Once again, Mizpah protects me as I dart from position to position. No one hit again. Amazing! Our luck is extended. I wonder for how long.

The monkey made it also.

Too damn bad.

We go about our mission in this area. We are alternating with the other rifle company on Hill 55. One out here and the other securing the hill. While out on an Op, and setting in for the evening I take the time to write Ryley before the light of day fades and the night brings the nasty folks out to play. I scrounge around in my pack but can't find any writing paper.

Tearing off the cardboard top of my C-Rat box, I fashion it into a postcard and write her a note telling her I am having a wonderful time, wish she could be here, and that next year I must pick a better vacation spot. I send it back with the resupply chopper for mailing. I hope it gets to her. I haven't written lately, been busy bouncing around in bandit country.

Very early this next morning, I send a completely shackled (coded) radio message to the Battalion Commander. Shackled messages are supposed to be very important, and always get everyone's attention. In addition, because they are shackled, they take longer to send and to decode when received. When you get one, you always have some anxiety. I have it transmitted to Iron Hand Six Actual, and it says, "Happy Easter, from Barney Bunny. It is Easter morning, and we are going on a hunt, just not for eggs."

He sends a reply, also shackled, saying, "Thanks, good luck. Peter." The man is continuing to develop his sense of humor. Rooster and Bees love my clowning around; it keeps their morale up and makes them a little more salty each day, although it's hard for Rooster to look very seasoned.

While out on the move this morning, we get into a scrap and take a couple of casualties. Corporal Rutherford tripped a mine, one from that ARVN ammo dump. It got him and PFC Gurno, trailing behind. Gurno should be okay, but we have to get him evac'd. Rutherford is only clinically alive. He won't make it, thank God. His face is gone, and he's a quad amputee. Damn, I would sure like to get my hands on that ARVN commander.

We continue the firefight, chase down the dinks, and call in a medivac chopper to get these kids out of here. When it arrives, the Gunny pops a green smoke and the bird lands. One Corpsman works feverishly over Gurno. Rutherford is gone, in Doc's arms. I crawl over to Gurno who is just a few yards away. "How is he?"

"Not good, Cap'n, but he'll make it."

"Hang tough, Gurno. Doc's got you patched. You'll be fine." I reach over and touch Rutherford. Good kid, married with a son. Dammit.

We're still in a small firefight. As we're about to load Gurno and Rutherford into the chopper, one of my men jumps up and gets behind the nose of the chopper. He leans across it, and bangs away with his M14 rifle, returning fire at the tree line. You gotta love the Snuffies.

The chopper pilot, strapped in his seat, rocking and jiggling with the vibration of the chopper, and with one hand on the cyclic and the other on the collective, prepared to lift off, glares at the Snuffy. His head bobs back in amazement, and his eyes are big around as saucers. His head snaps from side to side, taking in the action, while his eyes continue to widen. He glances back to see how the loading is going, then quickly turns his head to look out through the Plexiglas front of the bird at the trooper firing, then directly at me, where I've crawled back, behind the paddy dike.

My radio crackles, "Lima Six, I thought you said this zone was clear. What the hell is this guy doing leaning across my nose, firing? What the devil is goin' on?" Even in the middle of all this, there's some humor. Pilots sometimes just talk, and they don't seem to worry too much about radio procedure.

"Deadlock three dash three. I meant the zone was relatively clear. He probably feels safer behind your chopper than he did behind this paddy dike. I don't know why, you're drawing the fire. Over." He knows that, but maybe it'll warm his heart that I know, and maybe tighten his buns. Nevertheless, he's laughing.

"Yeah, well, okay Lima Six, we got your guys on board. I'm out of here. That should get this guy off my nose. Oh yeah, thanks for the green smoke." Looking directly down, and smiling, he can clearly see me behind the dike, just ten feet away, as he lifts off right over me. The rotor wash covers Ski, Rooster, Bees, the Gunny and me with dust, weeds, twigs, and whatever. Getting even, I guess.

I roll over on my back, squinting, straight up, "Deadlock three dash three Ol' buddy. Thanks for the help. Really hurry, it may be close for that one kid. You're a prince. Out." Then spit out a mouth full of dirt.

"Ahhh, that's a roger. I'm gone."

The look of shock, complete surprise on his face when that Snuffy was leaning over his chopper firing was comical. Eyes bulging, mouth draped open, moving, trying to form words, but nothing coming out. It was absolutely priceless. A flash bulb of light in the darkness of the moment.

Chopper pilots are great. They will come in anywhere to help us, day or night, hot or clear zone, makes no difference. Two breeds of folks you get to love dearly in our world, corpsmen and chopper pilots.

We continue operating south of Hill 55 for several more days, and then get notified we will be leaving. First, back to the Hill, and then straight away back to the Da Nang area, Camp Adenair, a SeaBee establishment adjacent to Marble Mountain. We all know this is better than where we've been for the past few months.

The troops are happy, and optimistic. The Magpies are suggesting a return to celebrity status is in store. The Snuffies just want out of here, even if only for a short time. Snuffies and Magpies can be interchangeable, depending on the breeze.

I know the reasons we're being pulled. One is to refit.

The other is, ill winds are blowing.

Chapter Twelve

Two features are bright today. The sun and our outlook. An hour beyond dawn, we move by truck to the SeaBee camp. The troops are upbeat, perhaps looking a little frayed around the edges, but showing some animated vitality. Leaving this area and going to where we're headed is like coming out of a sewage drain, into dazzling sunlight. It's bright and looks good, but your odor reminds you where you've been.

One platoon will be on Monkey Mountain, providing security for an Air Force communication facility, and enjoying the creature comforts that only the wing wipers can provide. The remainder of Lima Company will be at the SeaBee camp, which is in the vicinity of Marble Mountain. We will provide security for the camp and general area. Also, and here is the principal reason we're being moved, there is some strife and discord within the Vietnamese government, the ARVN commands, and with some religious factions. An uprising of sort or rebellion is in the making in the Da Nang area.

We are to refit while at these locations. We'll get a steady diet of hot chow; repair weapons as needed; and have any dental or health related issues resolved. Also, we will receive much needed troop replacements and crew-served weapons training time.

The good news is we will get a day or two at the nearby China

Beach recreational area, operated by the USO. There's nothing like sun, salt and sand to heal the body and cleanse the soul. Even better, we'll be able to get hot dogs, hamburgers, ice cream, milk shakes, fries, ice cold Cokes and other absented treasures of the real world.

The troops will ogle, gape, schmooze, and try every outdated, trite, overworked line there is to snuggle up to the gals. The Snuffies have been away for a while, so clouded eyesight is a definite liability. I think the saying is, they're having a white out.

The other news, maybe good, maybe not, is that the Magpies are muttering again. They see this as something I arranged personally. It's BS again, but I let it ride. It doesn't do any harm. It's like the difference in a lie and a fabrication. A lie is a harmful untruth. A fabrication, although it is an untruth, does no harm, and perhaps brightens the day some. These rumors by the Magpies are fabrications. They do no harm, and they do me some good.

The camp is Eden for the troops as well as me. We are living in squad-size tents that have no holes, with wood decks, wood backing, don't collapse at every whispered breeze, and come with wooden, folding canvas covered cots. We still use our rubber ladies and summer sleeping bags, but we're off the ground, dry, and relatively stress-free. These are five-star accommodations.

I live in the back of the tent used as the company office. The front two-thirds house some field desks for me, the First Sergeant and the Gunny. It also houses our on watch radiomen. Therefore, although clean and comfortable, I'm not far from reality with the rushing and crackling sounds of the radios.

We will have hot chow three times a day, and showers, hot, cold, whatever we want or need. We are actually going to look like human beings and smell respectable as well. That's important.

The stench of us in the paddies was worse than just looking or feeling grimy.

My weight has dropped significantly causing Ryley some concern when she saw the picture I sent. Hell, I thought I appeared to be a magnificent specimen, but apparently not. She said I looked like a sack of antlers. The full complement of hot chow should not only restore my spirits, but also put meat on my old, Irish bones.

I tell the First Sergeant, Gunny, and the Platoon Commanders to ensure we take advantage of this paradise, BUT to remember we have a mission to perform here and remind them of the trouble brewing. It's a high-octane mixture in a volatile environment, and can explode quickly with the strike of a single match. So, the word is, never close both eyes, keep weapons cleaner than our bodies, and think as if we're still in the paddies. In other words, keep your mental flak jacket on.

The first evening, the two Platoon Commanders and I hurriedly scamper down to the SeaBee Officers' Mess tent. We have showered, smell good for a change, and looking forward to the first hot meal in months. We have been strictly on C's lately. We enter the mess tent and take seats together, along one side of a long, fifteen-foot dining table crafted from two by fours, and one by sixes. It's not stained and varnished, but it's covered with a checkered tablecloth, with cloth napkins. It's one hell of a sight better than eating in a fighting hole or on a paddy dike.

The head of the table is reserved for the Commanding Officer of the SeaBee Battalion. The other end for the Executive Officer. As soon as we sit, the three of us plunge into one of the three huge bowls of fresh, chilled salad that sits on the table. The lettuce is loaded with slices and chunks of ripe tomatoes as red as a circus clown's nose and larger than our cavernous eyes. We can hardly get it on our plates and in our mouths fast enough. They even have real plates, no C Rat cans, mess gear or tin trays.

After a few forkfuls, I sense a strange silence. I can hear people breathing, and a few whispered mutterings. My munching of the crisp lettuce seems louder than a company of men marching down a gravel road. The burning sensation on the side of my head tells me eyes are focusing on me, boring a hole in my temple. Maybe one set in particular.

I roll my eyeballs upward and to the right, without raising my head, fork in hand with a slice of juicy tomato dripping with mayonnaise on the way into my mouth. I see the Commanding Officer staring at me with his eyebrows raised and a half smile on his face. It is not a smile of amusement. It's more a look of astonishment. No, it's clearly a smirk.

His neatly pressed and starched utilities match his sneer. His long, pointed nose makes him appear even crisper. His freshly shaven face, which reeks of Old Spice, adds to this Scrooge like scene. I think, do people still use Old Spice? I know my Granddad did, but Jesus, that was decades ago. I don't use any over here. . .don't want the dinks and mosquitoes to know I'm about.

The Commander cants his head slightly forward, and to my side of the table, and says quietly, just above a whisper, "Captain Quinn." He sounds like William Buckley. "We normally wait until after I say grace, to start eating." With that, he again leers at me, slides his eyes over to my lieutenants, and back to me. Then, unhurriedly and deliberately, folds his hands together in front of him, finger by finger, and says in a perplexed tone, "Gentlemen."

My officers and I take a deep, sniffling breath through our nostrils as we flush into a sunset crimson. I feel like spitting the friggin tomatoes back in the bowl, and see how he likes them apples, or tomatoes. We put down our forks with a clatter, choke down the salad in our mouths, and bow our heads along with the SeaBee officers that have assembled at the table. Some mayo stays on my chin. I don't think God will mind. It is fairly obvious who the gentlemen are and who are the Neanderthals.

The CO starts the blessing. I'm not listening, only because I'm thinking it's fortunate that he didn't ask me to say grace. My favorite prayer, the one I used as a boy, is, "Father, Son, and Holy Ghost. Who ever eats the fastest, gets the most." The prayer might be considered sacrilegious but would have been, spot on, mate, as they say at some tables.

With the "n" of "Amen.", we start eating. Like people turning to sit at the ballpark before the last note of the national anthem. We are polite, but quick. We want to show we have some manners, are not animals, but we intend to get our fair share, and then some. They are serving steak tonight. We stab two each, off the tray. Well, maybe not wild animals.

The Commander has seemingly capitulated and his officers watch in bewilderment. My prayer would have been prophetic. I know everyone has heard the term, paint everything that's not nailed down, well; we eat everything that isn't glass, porcelain, steel, wood or cotton. The term is, totally pig out.

After the main meal, we have dessert. It's apple pie with ice cream. What else? We eat two helpings, more laboriously since we are bordering on overload. When dinner is over, we thank the Commander, excuse ourselves and get up. My lieutenants pick up their napkins. As they do so, I wipe my mouth with the back of my sleeve. My guys, drop the napkins, do the same, and we leave to waddle back to our company area, fat, dumb and happy. We had the last word. We are Neanderthals.

At mail call tonight, a letter from Ryley arrives. I open it immediately and discover my C-Ration postcard made it. She writes that the mail carrier came to the door to deliver it personally, and to apologize. He told her that it was late in being delivered because they wanted to show it to everyone at the post office. Not only that, but the mail carrier wanted Ryley's neighbors on Cajon Street to see it as well. Ryley didn't care; it's a tightly-knit group on the block. They all thought the makeshift card was great.

The Nolan's had lived in this house for years. First Ryley's grandparents, then parents. They left it to Ryley. It's a quaint, seaside style cottage halfway up the hill. It has a picturesque view of the Pacific from its cozy living room and from the two rockers on the porch. We shared some spectacular sunsets before I left.

Anyway, she loved the card, and the humor. I want to keep it light. Let her know I'm okay, and that she can believe I'll be back. I dash a letter off, expressing my feelings, and the light side of today's experiences.

I'm snapped out of my momentary bliss by a ruckus in the front part of the tent, the company offices. As I get up, Lieutenant Williamson pops his head into my half of the tent and says, "Skipper, we have guests."

"Okay, coming out."

In the office are several SeaBee junior officers, with an ice chest of cold beer. Lieutenant Lincoln has joined Williamson. The First Sergeant and Gunny begin to leave, I say, "Hang tight. Stay put." They stop in their tracks and turn about, portraying a gleeful and thirsty grin.

One of the SeaBee officers says, "Just wanted to welcome you to the camp, Captain. Thought maybe after dinner, you guys would like a cordial, so we brought some beer, ice cold, to show you John Wayne lives."

"Sounds good to me. Top, Gunny, guys, lets crack one."

We do, raise the can, and shout, "Hoo-ah. Semper Fi."

They must like Neanderthals.

Chapter Thirteen

IT'S EARLY MAY, BUT I don't see any flowers. Sad, some things are only missed when they're gone. I'm not a flower person, but I miss having them filling the gardens and dotting the wayside. The thought brings to mind all the bright and varied colored flowers in Ryley's front garden, in particular the climbing roses on the trestle at the front of her home. There just doesn't seem to be any flowers around here. Maybe they do have feelings, and just don't want to live in an area where there are so many negative vibes. Flowers connote peace and serenity, and there is none of that here.

Our stay at Camp Adenair is going along uneventfully until the ill winds of revolt turn into a rebellious storm. The Vietnamese are having an uprising and the pot has boiled over causing a mess in the kitchen.

Our allies, the South Vietnamese Army, the ARVN, pull a bunch of their troops back into the Da Nang area and the factions' fire on one another. The Vietnamese Air Force prop-driven AD aircraft are buzzing around and diving on US troops in a menacing manner. Finally, there is some more firing, and some of it at US troops which is a real "no-no." It's a mess.

I'm ordered to bring Lima company north, up the road, to a point adjacent to the Da Nang River Bridge that connects the city to the Tiensha Peninsula.

As we approach, we are fired on by ARVN troops that are in a tree line, a hundred or so meters east of the bridge. Just a few rounds, enough to make the troops nervous and piss me off. We quickly clamber out of our trucks, and I bring the four tanks that are attached to me, up into firing positions. I have three tanks with their 90mm's and one flame tank. These are menacing creatures, especially the flame tank. The radio crackles with the voice of my battalion commander, Lieutenant Colonel Cartwright, who is across the bridge in Da Nang.

"Lima Six, what was that firing? Over."

"Iron Hand Six, this is Six Actual. Nothing much. Just a few rounds from the dinks in the tree line, east of the bridge. We didn't return fire. We're in position and ready to attack. Do you want me to jump on these guys and run them out of here. Over."

"Lima Six, No...No. Not yet. Hold your company in position. Don't fire unless fired upon."

"Iron Hand Six, I've already been fired on. How many times does it take? Once is enough for me. Over."

"Lima Six. Okay. Okay. Don't fire unless they really engage you. Now then, take a squad up to the bridge and secure that side without killing anyone for a change, at least just yet, or starting a major conflict. Over."

I think, "really engage." I know what he means but it sounds strange. Is "really, when someone is hit. One round can snuff someone. "Iron Hand, take or send? Over."

"Take. You go, and be careful. Things are getting a little dicey. I want you up there. Understand? Over."

"Iron Hand Six. Roger, out."

I grab a squad from the 2nd platoon and go, first radioing my CO. "Iron Hand Six, Lima Six moving out. Over."

"Roger Lima Six. Out."

We probe up the road toward the bridge in column formation, staggered, with one file on each side. We are primed, at the ready and a little skittish. The tree line with the ARVN is on our left, about seventy-five meters away. I can see the little jaspers in there, hunkered down. The area on either side of the road leading to the bridge is open fields.

As we move toward the bridge, the field now to my left, between the river and the tree line is occupied by a group of men. Lieutenant General Barto is there, pacing around like a caged leopard while arguing with some Vietnamese Warrant Officer who looks like a cub scout next to the general. There are other senior Marine officers and a handful of Vietnamese soldiers in the group. Looks like a Chinese fire drill. A lot of people shouting, giving orders, adding to the confusion, but no one moving and nothing apparent happening.

My orders are clear, and are coming over the radio from my battalion commander. His voice is taut and strained over the radio adding to the tension. The time line here is drawn tight and you can almost hear it creaking under the stress, like an overloaded steel cable. I think, where I am, with this squad, is not the place to be if the shit hits the fan.

We arrive at the bridge's east entrance and there are three ARVN soldiers here, and several in a 6x6-cargo truck we just passed on the road. I can feel the eyes of the ARVN in the wood line, and also the mixed group out in the middle of the field, searing into my forehead. I have one member of the squad, stand next to and cover the ARVN soldier manning a 106mm recoilless rifle. He sticks his rifle's muzzle on the soldier's temple while placing his leg in the breach of the 106 so it can't be loaded. Another of my men sits down on top of the A-4 machine gun manned by another ARVN, preventing him from closing the cover, loading and firing. He sticks his rifle on the tip of the nose of that rascal.

Then I send the remainder of the squad fifty meters back down the road to take the ARVN machine gun and its crew out of the back of the truck where it is set up in the cargo bed. My troops are more zealous than I foresee and simply toss the shocked soldiers off the tailgate like so many duffle bags in the baggage area of an airport. The ARVN soldiers are totally surprised, do nothing at first, then slink back to the tree line to join their rebellious friends.

When ordered, I have Lieutenant Williamson advance the rest of my company into the tree line, and just "sit" on the Vietnamese unit in there. As doing so, Lieutenant Colonel Cartwright comes on the radio, "Lima Six, now don't start World War III over there, damn it. Over." He knows I like to "shoot the tanks" and with this flame tank I'm probably like a dog getting the scent of a bitch in heat. Regardless of my combatant, orgasmic desires, I maintain fire discipline. " Iron Hand Six, Roger. Are these the bastards that left that ammo dump? Over."

"Lima Six, that's a negative. Do you copy? That's a negative. Over."

His voice has moved up another octave. I sense these are the same bastards. I should torch 'em. My tone will tell him I know who they are, "Iron Hand Six. Right. If you say so. Roger, Out." He doesn't want me looking for an excuse to knock these jerks around, and it wouldn't take much. I remember Rutherford and Gurno. The tension is thicker than the humid air of a Texas August. The hair on the back of my neck is feeling prickly, and I can smell fear in the air, not aftershave.

The ARVN want no part of us. The tanks make for a convincing argument, plus my troops have bayonets fixed just to make a psychological statement. I believe the message is received, five square.

Even in this stifling air, there is humor to be found, and that by a MP standing in a wooden, Marine green, sand bagged, sentry booth by the bridge. He is a young blond kid, looks about eighteen at the most. His eyes are as big around as silver dollars, and glazed over, plus he has a small string of drool hanging out of the corner of his wide-open mouth. Sweat is streaming from every pore in his forehead, dripping into his eyes, and off the end of his nose. All coupled with a deer in headlights look.

He's on a landline, EE-8, to somebody, probably MP headquarters. They apparently have asked what the hell is goin' on. His reply is simple and clear, even with his back-woods, Georgia drawl, "If'n I told ya all what was gonin' on, you wouldn't believe this shit no way, but shit's happenin' so dad gum fast I don't believe it."

Here the cherub faced blond gasps for some air before continuing, one octave higher, "Some three star General's here hollering at some dink, and there's a jackass mean Cap'n about to kick some butt or somethum."

He pauses again, listening to whoever is on the other end and nodding his head repetitively. As he does so, I glance at him, smile, wink and shrug. Then he replies to the other party, "Ye... Yes, sir, will do." He looks out of the booth at me and asks, "Um Si...Si...Sir, is the shit goin' to hit the fan?"

He's more frightened than I am, and that's skivvies-staining scared. I respond as coolly as I can muster, "Hope not, but if it does, it's going to get real messy, quick. So be ready to get out of that booth, fast, and in the ditch behind you, and cover my back. Understand?"

"I got it, sir. Should I tell somebody?"

"Only if it happens, and then only if we're still standing."

Now, eyes even larger, he drops the EE-8 so it's just dangling by it's wires and picks up his rifle which has been leaning against the inside wall of his sentry booth.

He didn't need that but it will keep him alert, and maybe save his ass. I think this is where the saying, "Shit Happens," got started. Maybe not. Just a thought that helps to relieve my anxiety. Absurdity is everywhere today, but humor is where you find it.

It looks to me that we have a checkmate here. Then, all of a sudden, the smallish ARVN Warrant Officer, in defiance of General Barto who is standing right there, gives a signal to blow the bridge. It doesn't go, his ego collapsed instead of the bridge, and his day center stage ends as a flop. It's a remarkable image. His shoulders sag and his chin drops to his chest. The general apparently had the bridge disarmed by engineers.

What no one knows is that the soldier with the detonator has his hand pinned under my boot with my .45 pistol against his forehead. He isn't going to do anything today, but continue to stare up at me with a measure of fear and uncertainty. His assessment was almost accurate, he should have been damn certain.

A platoon from my buddy Clint's company comes across the bridge and relieves us. The ARVN clear out of the bridge area with their tail twix their legs. It's over, the air smells better, and the blond MP is smiling and shouting excitedly into his EE-8, while with his free hand and arm he is animatedly waving and pointing in general to the area surrounding him. He's got a sea story to tell, and by damn, it's goin' to get told, starting now.

The general spots me on the road by the bridge. Maybe for the first time, maybe not. He comes over to where I'm standing. I salute him, he returns it, shaking his head, and grimacing, says, "Solid job, Barney. Tell your troops I said well done. Superb restraint."

"Thank you, sir. Are you okay?"

"Yes, thanks for asking."

"Excuse me, sir, but what the hell is going on around here. Who the hell are we fighting?"

"Beats me sometimes, Barney, but it's all squared away, at least for now. Thanks again, and you can get on with your business. Take care. Good seeing you again. Talk to you soon."

"Okay, sir. I've got to get back to my troops and get moving, plus check in with my battalion." He thumps me with his fist on the upper arm, turns, and leaves toward the other side of the bridge. The troops see this exchange. It's just more food for the Magpies to chew, digest, and regurgitate. On the other hand, I think, what did he mean, "talk to you soon." I'm still not sure where the hell this is heading?

I take my company and return to the camp. The day is over for us, peacefully, thank God. After all, we didn't come all the way over here to fight with these guys.

When we get back to the camp, my lieutenants and I immediately go to evening chow. We are still in our flak jackets, pistol belts held up by suspender straps, a grenade on each strap, haversacks on our backs, crammed full of mortar rounds, and helmets still on our heads. We're sweat stained, coated with a layer of dust and sand, and heavy with fatigue. We're looking pretty mean and nasty, and I suppose we're feeling that way.

We take off our helmets and packs, let them clatter on the wood decking of the SeaBee officers' mess tent. We sit down. My lieutenants allow me to sit first, then slide in on either side of me. We're hungry and ready to eat.

After the prayer, of course.

The table is abnormally quiet. The word has gotten back to these folks about the incidents at the bridge. One of their officers was apparently there and took it all in. I think the SeaBee CO, and his officers, have a little more respect for Neanderthals and a better grasp on reality tonight. He sure as hell has a more vivid image of me. It reminds me of the troops' rewording of the 23rd Psalm---"Yea though I walk through the valley of the shadow of death, I will fear no evil, because I am the meanest mother in the valley." Some edited biblical humor, of sorts.

We eat quietly and quickly. Politely excuse ourselves from the table, pick up our equipment, shoulder it back on, and leave, heading for our tents, then showers.

I hope tomorrow is a better day. This one has aged us.

Chapter Fourteen

Life is back to normal at the camp, which to us is routine security assignments and completing our refitting. We have test fired all of our weapons, replaced worn-out parts, and conducted refresher training for all crew-served weapons. We continue to fatten up on the three squares a day at the SeaBee mess. The Snuffies are healthy, equipment is in good order and morale is high. For us, in this camp, all is quiet, which is a blessing, or maybe an omen.

I'm inside the tent, sitting at my field desk doing the monotonous paper work that finds me when not out and about, or in the paddies. I'd rather be with the troops.

The Company First Sergeant enters and says, "Mail call Skipper. You've got a letter here from the Secretary of the Navy's Office, among other things."

"Damn, Top, I keep telling him not to bother me with every little detail."

"Yeah, right, sir."

"Well, I wonder what the hell I've done now."

First Sergeant Jeremy Harshman is a solid Marine, an extremely efficient administrator who would rather be out in the field than back in the company rear area. He has a smooth cover but a hard core, and he is highly respected by the troops. He and I are in the same pod, so it's more than a routine professional relationship. And as the saying goes, he keeps me out of jail.

He replies, "Hard to say with you, Skipper. Maybe your past is leaking oil again."

"Could be. Let's see."

I glance at the envelope. "It's from an old friend of mine from the Barracks, now working for the SecNav."

"Your friends just keep poppin' up Captain, like bad pennies. You must have been well liked, or notorious."

"Notorious, Top. Notorious. A legend in my own time."

"Or mind, sir."

"Yeah, that's probably more like it. Let's see what he has to say."

I read the letter from Jake Donnehy, now a major, who works as one of the aides for SecNav. When at the Barracks, Jake was a captain, and the Post Adjutant. He seemed to know everything that went on there, and best of all, he would give us, the company grade officers, a heads-up when something was hurtling our way. This letter is not a look-out, but rather a short-stop.

He has intercepted a letter to SecNav from one of my troops, complaining about the Barney Quinn form of discipline. PFC Jerry Pruitt, of the First Platoon, had fallen asleep on listening post when we were south of Hill 55, the night before we pulled out for here. This is a serious offense. It could have resulted in lost lives. I decided to handle the discipline myself and keep Pruitt's official record clean, even though he is a pain in the butt. I pointed out the gravity of his negligence in a more volatile manner than I should have, but his slackness and disregard for the importance of his job and the lives of his buddies severely pissed me off. He won't forget his laxity, and if nothing else, he'll damn sure stay awake and alert in the future.

It appears that PFC Pruitt wrote to the SecNav and complained. Could have been nasty for me. Jake has saved my ass from severe, career ending trouble.

I tell the Top about the letter. He knows about my hot-blooded handling of the matter, because he was in the office tent here at Adenair that day. "First Sergeant, how about fetching PFC Pruitt and we'll get this rascal squared away and zip this bag closed."

"Yes, sir. If you'd like, sir, I'll handle this and make it go away."

"No, Top, let's have some fun with this. Get some mileage while we shake Pruitt up a little."

"Okay, sir, be back with him in a minute."

The First Sergeant's about six foot and everything about him is square. Square jaw, square shoulders, and squared away. A meticulous man, with like I say, a hard core, and a bit of nastiness in his marrow.

PFC Jerry Pruitt is, sort of okay. The rank of PFC is probably his top rung. You wouldn't want a lot of his type around, but a few are tolerable. He's a short guy with dark hair and small, dark, shifty eyeballs, and a nose that looks like he has walked into one too many hard rights. He's from New Jersey, and thinks, like many of them, that it is the center of the universe.

The Top is back with Pruitt, who looks weighed down with an expression that tells the world, I'm caught and I'm guilty, it's just a question of which crime. He stops, snaps to attention and says, "PFC Pruitt reporting as ordered, sir."

I rise, come from behind the desk, and stand directly in front of him, close, squinting and glaring down into his eyes. He both physically and mentally caves in, wide-eyed and arching back, maybe expecting more of his first experience. He looks like a dying Jersey tomato plant craving rain. He remembers how pissed I was during our previous encounter.

"Son, you wrote the Secretary of the Navy? Not smart. I know him very well, and he sent your letter back, to me." I wave the letter in front of him, and icily continue, "He asked me to handle it. What the hell were you thinking anyway, Pruitt?"

He replies in his irritating nasal voice, "Um, ahhh, Sir, I'm sorry. I thought I could write him without you knowin', ah...you knowin' about it. Um, but you, ah,...you know...like, ahhhh—"

"Stop stammering and spit it out, God Dammit. The longer you stand here spieling your Jersey, street corner bullshit, the more irritated I'm getting."

The Top chimes in from behind Pruitt, "Speak up shithead."

This last prompting causes Pruitt to sputter rapidly, "Well, sir, it seems you know everybody else in the chain of command. So shit, sir, I wrote him. Lowery told me to do it. As soon as I mailed it, I knew I fucked up but didn't know how to get it back."

"Lowery? Private Lowery? The kid from Jersey City? Your Sea Lawyer, huh?"

"I should'na listened to him, sir."

"No shit. Well, PFC Pruitt, you're going to get lucky again. You should have just come to see me and tell me your bitch. But no, you and Lowery decide to mess with me. Right?"

"Sir, what—"

The First Sergeant leans forward, puts his mouth right in Pruitt's ear and shouts, "Shut up, dimwit. The Skipper has already given you one break and I bet he's about to give you another, which is more than you deserve, Private. So just shut up, and listen."

"Yes, sir, Top."

"Don't call me sir."

"Yes, First Sergeant." Pruitt looks like a turtle trying to shrink into his shell but can't. His eyes are setting a record for "blinks".

It's hard for me to keep a straight face, but I'm practiced. "Well, I have the letter now. I solved your problem, and got it back for you. So, you can forget that. The SecNav has sent it back to me so I can handle this for him. He and I are friends from way back." I show Pruitt the envelope so he can clearly see the SecNav return address. "Like I told you, you're lucky that someone didn't get killed because of you. Next time I'll just hand you the courts-martial you deserve and send you to Leavenworth. Then you can write a letter every day for five years. I gave you a break, Marine. I thought you learned your lesson, but maybe not?"

"Oh yes, sir. I did. I did. Won't be no next time. Goin' to get my ass squared away, Cap'n."

"And keep it squared away, right, Pruitt?"

"Yes, sir, Cap'n. Yes, sir. My mind is right."

"I doubt that, but you're gettin' the idea."

"Huh, sir? Oh, yes, sir. Yes, sir."

"Okay. Now, get back doing whatever you're supposed to be doing. And tell your sea lawyer friend, Private Lowery, and the rest of your buddies, don't be wasting any more of anybody's time writing letters up the chain. I'm your chain. I know all these guys personally."

I doubt he and Lowery have too many buddies, the little worms. Sergeant Parzini will probably visit them this evening and clarify everything for them, in a language with fewer syllables.

With that, Pruitt does a smart about face, marches quickly out the hatch, and heads for his tent, shaking his head in wonderment. The First Sergeant, who is now joined by Gunny Roe, follows him. I suspect Pruitt will wish he had run out of writing paper. Their job is to protect me, and Pruitt has offended them. His day is not over, and this one and those remaining will be long. He is going to catch a lot of shit details.

I'm sure, after he gets to his tent, the mumblings, mutterings, and rumors by the Magpies will climb off the monger chart. "The Skipper is friends with everybody, the general, even the SecNav, and probably the Commandant and the President. He knows everyone."

Some humor here I hope, but the important thing is, this kid will be okay and his record will stay clean. He didn't do any brig time and will be able to live with himself. He'll remember the unofficial discipline for a longer time, and he too will have a sea story to tell someday. And, best, no one got hurt. The Top and the Gunny come back into the tent giggling like a couple of school kids. They must have had a little fun at Pruitt's expense.

A few hours have passed, chow is over, night has draped its canopy over the camp, and Sergeant Parzini comes meandering into my tent with cocoa. He doesn't say anything specific, but his mutterings let me know that Pruitt and Lowery have a better understanding of expectations. This is not stateside, mistakes count here.

Life goes on here at Camp Adenair. It continues to be quiet and uneventful, although not elsewhere in the region. We get some more replacements, and some troops have their tour end so they get to return to the real world. At least they look a little better than they would have a few weeks back. I get a chance to write Ryley every day, and she likewise. I even get to patch a phone call to her from China Beach. This call further cements a rapidly gelling relationship. We both sense where this might be heading.

A few more weeks drift lazily by. As is routine for me, I have checked the perimeter before dawn, and then back in the office tent sipping a cup of Black Death when Gunny Roe says, "Skipper, Battalion Six on the land line. Must be important, he's up early."

"Okay, got it Guns, thanks." I pick up the EE-8 and say, "Lima Six Actual, sir. What has the colonel up so early?"

"Just knowing you're out there somewhere, plotting, is enough to do it. How are you today? Fit and ready?"

"I'm fine, and we're fit and ready, and your questions tell me we need to be."

"Good. Come over after you eat. We're moving out. Being relieved and goin' to the field again."

"When?"

"Day after tomorrow. I'll give you all the scoop here at the briefing, 1000 hours."

"Yes, sir."

"And, Barney, I'm going to need a big favor."

"Sir, a favor? My granddaddy once—"

"Barney, just be quiet and listen. It's a big favor, but it's absolutely necessary. I know I can count on you. I need you to take command of India Company. There is a problem and I need you to solve it, and damn quick. Turn Lima over to Williamson, after the briefing. I'll explain when you get here."

"Sir, I can't leave these guys—"

"Barney, you can, and you will. I need this from you. Come at 0900 and we'll talk first. Okay?"

"Yes, sir."

"And not a word, Barney, until after. Understand? I've already relieved Captain Landau. Also, bring Williamson."

"Yes, sir. See you at 0900 hours."

"Thanks, Barney."

I put the EE-8 back in its carrying case hanging on the tent pole and just sit, slumped over trying to digest the conversation. Thinking, what the hell happened in India Company? Without any warning, not even a whispered rumor that I've heard. Strange, is always some scuttlebutt. Maybe just hasn't drifted over the river to this neck of the woods yet.

The business about going back into the field is not unexpected of course, but it has a brisk sobering effect, like being pulled over by a cop. We're ready. The news that I'm being sent to India Company is a killer.

Immediately after chow, I inform all unit leaders that we will be moving out in two days, and get them busy preparing. This either stops rumors or feeds them. I'm not sure which. I will brief them immediately upon returning from battalion. The First Sergeant and the Gunny spring into action, and Lieutenant Williamson and I go to the briefing.

Lieutenant Colonel Cartwright and I meet. He explains the situation to me. It's really a request, and no matter my feelings, I can't turn him down, even if it were an option. India Company has a problem, and I am to resolve it quickly and take them to the paddies. It is not a pleasant circumstance; the company commander has been relieved and is already back at battalion headquarters.

Reluctantly, I turn Lima Company over to 1st Lt Ray Williamson. Not because he's not capable, he truly is, but rather I am deeply attached to Lethal Lima, like an IV, and want to finish my tour with these guys.

Disinclined or not, I depart. With the approval of my battalion commander I take Sergeant Parzini, hopefully along with his cocoa stash, LCpl Baronowski, and my 81mm Mortar Section Leader, Sergeant Birdwell. Actually, we just switch 81 sections between India and Lima companies. George Washington Birdwell is about six foot two, black, career Marine from Pittsburgh. He is squared away, very large, educated, and can lift a house.

Along with these three, I also take two very special and outstanding Corporals, Campbell and Bass. No one in Lima Company messes with them, and I suspect the same will be true in India. They are just big, rawboned, grizzly and a little older, seasoned. One white, one black. One a red neck, the other, not. But, they are buddies, tight as ticks, and are rarely apart when not actually on the job. When one is on patrol or out, the other is always checking the status to make sure everything is okay. As I say, cinch tight.

The troops of Lima Company are not pleased to see me go and several come by to tell me so. This is nice, heart warming, but it makes the leaving even tougher. The Gunny is pissed. He wants to come with me, but I tell him this is his company and they need him to stay, particularly now with only Williamson and Lincoln left, but I'll ask. First Sergeant Harshman is on the landline to the Battalion Sergeant Major to see if there is something he can do to get this stopped. There isn't, of course.

What is also interesting and humorous, the troops feel as if they are losing their ticket, their celebrity status, their private pass to better living. In their visits with me they all ask, in their own murmuring way, if it will continue with me gone. I say, "Sure, I don't see why not."

Not true, but it's the thought that counts. They will be just fine, and I'm sure the stories, now already hardly recognizable, will be related to India company, if they haven't been before now.

I'm going to miss these guys.

CHAPTER FIFTEEN

THE SIX OF US ARRIVE in India Company early, a few glints of sun before dawn, and we are going to catch some worms, just a different type. I dispatch Sergeants Parzini and Birdwell, and Corporals Campbell and Bell into the company area with instructions to root-out the troublemakers and bring them to me. Lance Corporal Baronowski remains, hovering around me wearing an unnecessary, menacing scowl.

While the four NCOs toss the salad, I talk to the Company Gunnery Sergeant and Executive Officer. They should not have allowed the problem to be conceived, let alone grow to birth and beyond. My mind is not necessarily open, but I meet with them, see how they carry themselves, measure their attitude, and listen to their responses to my questions. I know what I'm going to do. They failed their Company Commander, lost the pulse of the company, and more importantly, let down the troops in general.

After a few hours, I hear some commotion outside the tent. Angry voices and shouting along with the scuffling and rustling noises of groups of people moving along the gravel as they near the company office. Sergeants Parzini and Birdwell are coming toward the tent with three men skulking and stumbling in front of them. Slightly in front of this group are Corporals Campbell and Bell. They have four others in tow, being half-carried, half-dragged by the collars of their jungle utility jackets, with the soles of their boots skating across the ground. If the situation weren't so serious and infuriating, it would be comical.

My four birddogs, along with the First Sergeant, tell me this nest of rattlers started and stirred the pot of racial problems with venomous slurs and poisonous false acquisitions. I listen to the seven snakes rattle their tale of reasoning and excuses. Then say, "I'm not even going to address you as Marines, or men, because you're neither. What you are, is out of here. Now. If I had the time, I'd take care of this in another manner, but I don't. So, I'm dumping you and the charge sheets on battalion. Get on the truck, on the double." The hang-dog looks only validate their full guilt and humiliation.

The First Sergeant and the private hunting party herd these seven out of the tent and, in front of the remainder of the company, which has assembled out of curiosity, physically load them aboard the waiting truck, a 6x6. The nodding in agreement of several heads and the quiet fist-pumps of others, tell me we're center bulls-eye with these shots. I add, "Top, throw their gear on board with the rest of this crap."

"Yes, sir. Thy will be done. A-friggin-men."

The problem and the culprits are dispatched back to the battalion CP. I put the Gunny and XO in a jeep, and send them to the battalion commander. While the two vehicles are on the way, I call Lieutenant Colonel Cartwright on the landline. "Good day, sir. It pleases me to inform you, the problem is solved. The trouble makers are on a truck, to be delivered to you."

"What the devil am I suppose to do with them?"

"That's up to you, sir. Don't need or want them here and don't have time to screw with them. Remember, I'm shoving off for the boondocks at first light tomorrow."

"Okay. Okay. What was the problem?"

"There were some racial issues. They are solved. The troops clearly understand now, it's Marine green and we all bleed red.

The First Sergeant agrees with me, and he's coming in right behind them. He has the charge sheets and can fill you in on any details you need, and my methods, if you are interested."

"Okay. I'll take care of it. You're a good man, Barney. A smart ass, but a good man. Talk to you later. And, I'd rather not know your methods."

"One other thing, sir. The Gunny and the Company XO are in a jeep, following the truck. I don't want them back either. They should have prevented this from happening or snapped off its ugly head when it did."

"Barney—"

"Sir, please, just put them to work in the battalion CP somewhere. If I can't trust them to do their job back here in the rear with the gear, I don't need them out in the paddies. I'll figure out how to get along without them until you can get me some replacements. I need a few more lieutenants, and a nasty and savvy Gunny. How about Gunnery Sergeant Roe?"

"Phewwww. Okay. You're right. I'll take care of these folks. Now then, you can't have Roe. He needs to stay where he is. He's important to Lima Company. Sorry, and I know he wants to come, but, no. I'll talk to you at first light before you move out, and I'll try to scrape up some replacements."

"Sir, please, skim, as in cream. Scrape sounds like the bottom."

"Okay, skim it is."

The next day we leave the Da Nang area, without replacements, and motor southwest, to a couple of hills, not far from Hill 22. We will begin operating in this area tonight. We relieve the company in place, and they are on their way before dusk. Strangely enough, it's the company that had the map only ambush that I spoke to the general about months before. Small world, and a smelly one at that.

In this new company there is only one officer other than myself, a platoon commander, 2nd Lieutenant John Ballantine. Fresh from the Naval Academy and The Basic School, he's well trained, but it's play time training, not experience. He's shorter than me by about half a head and about zilch pounds wringing wet with sandy colored hair and pale blue eyes. His face is either reddened from razor burn, or he constantly flushes in my presence. I hope it's from shaving although, with his nearly whisker-free face it doesn't look as if that's a necessity.

Good man, I'm told by the First Sergeant, but very young and impressionable. I'll have to be careful because, for some reason, he tends to mimic what I do and say. He wears his equipment exactly as I wear mine; repeats some of my quips; imitates some of my mannerisms; has a cigar stuck in his mouth. He doesn't smoke, for Pete's sake. I tell him, "Lieutenant Ballantine, knock off this same-o, same-o stuff and just be you. That'll be fine."

"Yes, sir." He flushes, it's not razor burn. Oh well, he's a good young man, and, here, he will age quickly enough. Interestingly, none of the rattlers came from his platoon.

My other platoons are led by staff sergeants, all solid and experienced. We're going to be okay. I get the company together, and ask them to look around to see if they can locate any voting machines. They gawk at one another, mumble and mutter, look around with that What-the-hell-is-he-talkin'-about-look.

After a few minutes, I say, "There aren't any.   Listen up, there are no voting machines, and that's because this is not a friggin' democracy. This is a Marine rifle company, an ass-kicking machine, and you don't get to vote. You do as I say, when I say it, and together. A team. One heartbeat. That way we'll get the job done and more of us will stay alive. Got it?"

Some muttered "yes, sirs" follow.

I shout, "GOT IT?"

A booming, "YES, SIR," rings out.

I nod, acknowledging their reply, turn and leave. Then a roaring, "HOO AH", blows me away.

We're on solid ground now. It's nice being King, and believe me, a rifle company commander is just that.

LCpl Baronowski continues to watch me like a hawk. Aside from everything else going on, he has written to a schoolteacher friend of his, who had actually befriended him during his school years. She had her entire class of youngsters, elementary school age, write to me, about thirty letters in all.

They are in crayon with pictures drawn of the school. You know the type, red schoolhouse with a big yellow-crayoned sun, some trees with green scribbling for leaves and brown trunks and limbs, and birds, lots of birds. And flowers, love that.

Interestingly, when the Vietnamese kids in the school we started near Hill 22 drew pictures for me, they were of women and papa-sans in the paddies harvesting rice, with Water Boo's with them. Also, in each, Marines were sloshing through the paddy, but no flowers or birds. All kids, different worlds.

Baronowski apologizes but I tell him there's no need for that. We'll sit down, starting tonight, and answer every letter to each child. We do this, but not in crayon. I've advanced beyond crayons, although only slightly. We do print however. It's a pleasant break from our routine, and a nice way to pass time while sipping cocoa.

We've got a new battalion commander, Lieutenant Colonel

Arnie "Pappy" Reynolds, and although I've never served under him, we know of each other. He came out to my position to visit a few days ago, unannounced. I was gone, with a squad-size patrol to look over our new area first hand, as I have been doing for several days. There are some, not many, differences between this area and the Hill 22 area.

This is a hill, not a small pile of dust, and there are not as many villages here. A lot more paddies, stretching west into some high ground. The Vills that are here are strung out along the Tuy Loan River, several klicks north of my CP. The vegetation in the villages and along the river is thick making movement difficult and risky. We have already made several contacts there and further west along the river. It could be a nasty area.

Today, I go over to the other hill, about a half klick away, where I have a platoon emplaced. Since it isn't far, and the area is wide open and in easy view of both hills, I simply take my Chief Corpsman, Doc Ewing, and Baronowski who carries the radio. We all have M14 rifles although they're not the normal arms for us. Just a precaution should we get pestered along the way.

I spend a few hours visiting the troops, getting to know these men better, and look at the positions. We are in a similar setup as we had on Hill 22, one platoon here and two on the hill with me.

The French must have occupied both of these hills in years past. Each has one or two, eight by eight foot concrete bunkers, with firing slots on four sides. They're old, scarred and dank, but make decent CP bunkers. Not pleasant, a few dachshund size rats to evict, but better than living outside.

As the sun gets close to perching on top of the ridgeline to the west, Doc Ewing, Ski and I scurry back to my CP. As we slosh across the paddies, my other RO on the hill, PFC Henry Chang, tells me that the Battalion Commander is there and "patiently" waiting for me.

Chang is a new replacement, a kid of about nineteen and a sharp Marine. He uses proper radio procedures, and very proper English. Regardless of the latter, I understand him. Chang adds, "India Six, I do not think he is very happy. In fact, I think he is pissed that you are out there roaming around with only a radioman and a corpsman." He must be if Chang said pissed; that's a stretch for Henry.

"India Base, I take it he can see me. Is that a roger? Over."

"That is affirmative, India Six. Over."

"Base, roger. Be inside the wire shortly. Out."

We cross an ankle deep stream running between the two hills, trudge and squish out of the paddies, up the hill, through the emplaced barbed wire with the empty aluminum cans dangling and jingling, and into our position. Coming through the wire, I notice some Claymore mines are still in place. This is a careless mistake that will be fixed in short order. I need to check for other slipshod habits; don't want any leftovers. The Claymores should be put out at night, and taken in just prior to daybreak.

Lieutenant Colonel Reynolds is indeed waiting for me. He is snorting, glaring and grinning at the same time, all five feet six or seven of him. He looks like a small grizzly bear on the prowl. He asks, "What the hell are you doing out there with just the Chief Corpsman and your radio operator?" Then raising his eyebrows, and pointing his finger in a jabbing motion at me, he growls, "And what the devil are the three of you carrying rifles for? What is going on out here?"

"Sir, good afternoon. It's good to meet the battalion commander, sir."

He inhales deeply, raises his eyebrows, and with his finger still jabbing at me says, "Oh, here we go. I know all about you, Captain Quinn. You're a load and a half."

"Sir, it's really simple. It's not far from here to my other unit.

We are in sight all the way. The troops need a break, a rest, so I don't like to saddle up a fire team or a squad just to zip over there and back. We're perfectly safe out there. It's all open paddies."

"Yeah, what about mines?"

"Sir, I don't walk where they usually plant them. Besides, Ski can smell them."

"Okay, okay. But like I said, I've heard about you." Then he breaks out in a beaming smile, chuckles, puts his arm around my shoulders and leads me toward the chopper. "Don't worry, Barney. I like colorful people although in your case I may be using the term loosely. You are just a stone now, but when I get finished with you, you're going to be a gem. I'm going to polish you up, my friend."

"A gem, sir? Polish? I don't think so. I prefer to be a stone. Wouldn't look good as a gem."

He pats me on the back and says, "A gem, Captain. A gem. Now, tell me what you've got out here."

"Aye Aye sir."

We talk about the two hill positions, the village complex along the river, the area in general, and my activities and thoughts. Finished, I ask, "Will the colonel be staying for dinner? We have some excellent C's tonight, and I can probably get you a pound cake and cocoa for dessert."

"Barney, you are a thorny rose. Why would I want to dine with you? You're filthy, and smell bad."

"I just thought you might want to start by polishing my table manners."

"Barney, I like your sails, particularly when they're full of wind. We're going to get along fine. I have to get back to the CP, maybe some other time we'll spend the night together out here, okay?"

"The invitation is open, sir. But, no bundling."

"Good God! Let me out of here!"

With that, he slaps me on the back and gets into the chopper. I move away, shielding my eyes from the clutter about to start.

The pilot cranks up the bird, and away it goes. I agree. He and I are going to get along well, a   hard charger with a titanic sense of humor. This is going to keep my life balanced out here, like old times.

Chang, standing nearby with the radio, taking in the conversation, shakes his head and mutters something.

I say, "What's the problem, Henry?"

"It's true, isn't it, Captain?"

"What's that?"

"What the guys in Lima Company say."

"I don't know what they said, but you shouldn't listen to them. Believe what you see, and maybe a little of what you want, okay?"

"Yes, sir. If you say."

"I say, Henry."

Chang turns and hoofs it toward the CP bunker, and there he meets the other radiomen and Baronowski. He talks to them, pointing over his shoulder at me with his thumb. Good, it's starting. The Magpies will have it in full bloom by dawn.

I meander around the perimeter, check the positions and talk with the Snuffies, and then amble back towards the concrete CP bunker. Sergeant "Z", Ski, and Birdwell, a newcomer to the group, are sitting on top, waiting with some cocoa. New hill, new troops, but still some old friends to hang with at night. As I approach these three, I grin, wink and say, "Hey guys, let's sit and sip."

I think of Campbell and Bell, on the other hill, in the same platoon finally. Great. I ask, "What's the word on Campbell and Bell?"

Birdwell replies, "They're gettin' married."

We all burst into laughter.

We'll be just fine.

CHAPTER SIXTEEN

I'VE BEEN HERE FOR A week. This morning brings a very bright and high sky. It's early but already extremely humid. The paddies surrounding our hill are like a sauna but with their own distinct scent, and the closeness and odor rise up to greet me. We are full bore into the middle of summer.

I remind the unit leaders to ensure everyone stays hydrated. Then I walk around behind the CP bunker where Doc Ewing is set up. "Hey, Doc. I've already cautioned the guys about drinking enough water. How about telling your platoon corpsmen to keep a sharp eye on their platoons?"

"Yes, sir, I'll call the other hill first, then walk around here and do it personally."

"And Doc, tell folks to keep a cover on. I don't want any baked brains out here."

"Got it, sir."

"Thanks, Doc."

I take a long slug of Black Death and shudder. Jesus, this stuff is terrible. I need a decent cup of coffee again. Just as I am choking down this ink, Chang sticks his head out of the bunker and says, "Sir, a chopper, Deadlock one-zero, is inbound. Who is this, Captain?"

"Henry, it could be anybody but it's the CG, III MAF's bird,

Lieutenant General Barto. Might be him or someone he sent. He and I are friends, Henry, so if it's him, you better get shipshape."

"Should I do something, sir?"

"Contact them in Chinese, Henry. That will shake them up."

"Sir?"

"Just kidding, Henry. Stay loose. Contact the platoons and let them know he's inbound. Tell them to continue their routine as normal, but stay alert in case he decides to walk the hill."

"Okay, Skipper, will do. Sir, if it is the general, can I come out and see him, maybe meet him?"

"Sure, you bet, but make sure someone's on the radios, and Henry, you have to say something nice about me."

Henry grins with excitement and yells for PFC Hewgley to come up and relieve him for a short time. PFC Aaron Hewgley is my other operator. He's also very young. Hell, in this company, everyone is, except me. I see Hewgley jogging toward the bunker, so Henry is happy.

I look around for Ski, and shout, "Ski. SKI. Where the hell are...oh, okay. Go pop a green smoke, and get those troops off the LZ."

"Yes, sir."

Damn, he was right behind me. He's like a ghost sometimes. Anyway, I wonder if the general knows I'm out here, in a new company, and if so, how? Maybe he's just out and about and making a random visit.

The chopper lands, kicking up some small pebbles, some weeds, and a little dust. This hill has some vegetation on it so it's not as bad as Hill 22 when the birds drop in. As the chopper eases down and settles, I see that it is Lieutenant General Barto. He jumps down, sprightly for an old guy. He must be feeling good about something, because now he is jogging toward me. However, despite the energetic approach, he's looking more tired than I remember. A few more lines on his face.

"Barney, how are you. How's this company shaping up?" He

knows. How in the hell does he know I'm here and about this company's problems.

"The troops are fine, sir. No problems anymore. Just need a few lieutenants and a gunny sergeant. I'm sure the Battalion Six will get them for me."

"I'm a little surprised you're still here."

"Why's that, sir? Where else would I be?"

"Oh, nothing. Never mind." He pauses and has a puzzled look on his face. He immediately follows with, "Is there anything I can do for you?"

"No, sir, not really, unless you want to get your G-1 to expedite the replacements I mentioned. Otherwise, I'm cookin' with Cosmoline, sir."

"Okay, Barney. I'll say something when I get back. You're looking better than the last time I saw you, at the bridge."

"I feel better, and today is a better day than that was. If you don't mind me saying, you look a bit drawn, tired. Are you okay, sir?"

"Really? I feel fine. Maybe I'm just starting to show my age."

"It was probably just all that rebellion crap, sir. Is it pretty much a dead issue now?"

"It is, for good I hope, but you can't ever be sure in this part of the world. A lot of factions vying for power. I'd like to stay longer and talk, but I've got to get moving, Barney. I just wanted to make a quick stop. Have a lot of stops today. It's good seeing you again." He gives me his one-armed bear hug, and shakes me round again.

"Okay, sir, one quick thing, sir. This is PFC Henry Chang, my radioman. He wants to meet you. Henry, this is Lieutenant General Barto."

Henry's eyes bulge out of his head, and the color drains from his face. He is also locked into a rigid position of attention, which is probably not helping his blood flow. The general shakes Henry's hand and says, "How are you doing, Marine? Is Captain Quinn taking good care of you, and the other men?"

"Yes, sir."

"Well, good, it's a pleasure meeting you PFC Chang. Keep up your good work. I'm proud of you and all the other young men serving here. Take care of Captain Quinn for me."

"Yes, sir." Henry whips up a snappy salute. The general returns it smartly. Henry is still as rigid as the Washington Monument, and almost as tall, but he's grinning from ear to ear.

The general smiles, turns to me and says, "I've got to go, Barney. Take care. Will be seeing you soon."

"Sir?" I'm stunned by his last remark, and watch as he turns, jogs to the chopper and climbs aboard. They are off in a jiffy, heading northwest. Now what the devil was this all about? I feel like an Indian with his ear to the ground. I can hear the hoof beats, but can't see the horses yet.

"Hey, Skipper." It's Hewgley shouting from the bunker entrance, "Battalion Six Actual wants ta talk at ya, sir." PFC Hewgley's grammar suffers some, especially when compared to Chang's, but he works hard at his job and loves the corps.

"Okay, Hewg, be there in a sec." Oh, Lord, here we go again. Every one is worried about what the general and I talk about.

Inside the bunker, I pick up the handset, blow out a soft sigh, and say, "Iron Hand Six, this is India Six Actual. Over."

"Six, what was Deadlock one-zero doing there? I've been briefed that you two are buddies or something. Over."

"Six, not buddies, please. I know him from my past. We are friends, I suppose. He just stopped in to say hello. Asked if I needed anything. Over."

"What did you tell him, over?"

"Six, I told him you didn't think I was very polished. Just kidding, sir. Told him all is fine but need some replacement lieutenants and you are working on it. Over."

"You're not polished, Barney, but I love ya anyway. What'd he say about the replacements, if anything? Over." He's not supposed to mention my name over the radio. He's almost talking like this is a secure phone line. I'll probably end up on another wanted poster. If so, I hope it's for more money.

"Six, he said he would get his personnel guy on it. See, got you some high-powered help. Over."

"Okay, that's good. How's it going otherwise? Over."

"Great, except its friggin hot out here. Six, I need a Gunny out here, and a few lieutenants as well. I feel like a chaperone at a sock hop. Over."

"Okay, I'll force the issue. Over."

"Six, a strong one. No retreads. And I'm short a couple of Corpsmen. Ask your Bravo Sierra to shake some of his loose. Over."

"India Six, okay. I'll work this out for you. Stay mean and stay low. Out."

What a way to start a day. The general is hiding something, and the colonel seems clueless. Nothing for me to do but play the game and see what cards have been dealt. Maybe it's General Barto, in the bunker, with the Coleman Stove?

The day folds into night, and with that some freshening breezes drift across the hill. It slightly cools this knob, but since it is coming from the direction of the villages, it brings the odors of cooking, and yet retains the aroma of the paddies. This is like living next to a sewage disposal plant in the real world.

Chang and I listen to the reports from the night activities. At midnight, I pop outside the bunker to sit a spell. Just as I get around the corner from the hatch and sit on the bunker top, Sergeant Z is approaching, along with Ski, Bird, and Doc. The ensemble now includes Doc Ewing. That's first rate, the Cocoa

Club has taken in another new guy. If this keeps up, it'll be a Pack. Sergeant Z says, "What's goin' on, Cap'n?"

"Wish I knew Z, wish I knew."

"What'd the general want?"

"He's missin' some cocoa from his mess. Figured I might know where it is."

"You didn't rat me out, did ya, Skipper?"

"Nope. One of the guys in the neighborhood, are you kiddin'? Never hoppen, Maline."

"Well, good, here's yours then, sir. Hope it's not too hot for it tonight."

"Never. Smells great. Thanks."

Well, at least tonight is okay, hope tomorrow is as well, but since the general's visit I feel like a dog with its head up, facing into the breeze, sniffing, and not recognizing the scent.

CHAPTER SEVENTEEN

I FEEL LIKE I HAVE a hangover. My mind is cluttered with thoughts about the general. On top of this, it's another scorcher of a day, so I start the morning with a canteen cup of Kool Aid rather than my normal dose of Black Death. It doesn't give me a starting jolt but it gets the engine to turn over, and it keeps the radiator from overheating.

I get a radio call from the Battalion Surgeon, and he tells me I must go to the Da Nang Hospital, ASAP, and have a complete physical. Somehow, I have missed two annual exams in a row and have been ordered by BuMed to get one immediately. There is no argument to be offered, so as I'm about to arrange for transportation, Ski comes into the bunker and says, "Skipper, there's a jeep barreling' up the road."

"Who's in it?"

"Just a driver."

Over the radio comes the Doc's voice, "I sent a jeep to pick you up so you can't wiggle out of this."

"Iron Hand. Yeah, it's here. Thanks. It's good to know you trust me. Do I stop at your location or go direct? Over."

"Go direct. Stop here on the way back with the results."

"Iron Hand, Wilco. By the way, your radio procedure sucks,

and my physical condition, whatever it is, is a direct reflection of your care and that of the rest of your pecker-checkers. Out."

"If you would listen once—"

"Iron Hand, out means out. I rest my case. Out."

The Doc and I are buds. I like jerking his chain, particularly when I know the radio at battalion is on the speaker. He visited me several times at Camp Adenair, and always near chow time. He liked the SeaBee chow and tried to improve my Neanderthal image with the CO there.

I look at Baronowski and say, "Ski, get your gear and rifle. We're going on a trip to the hospital. I have to get an annual physical. Tell Lieutenant Ballantine I need to see him."

"Yes, sir."

Ski leaves the bunker. I put on my pistol belt which hangs on my hips like an old inner tube on a fence post. Maybe I'm not looking so good. Then slip on my flak jacket as Ballantine enters the bunker.

He says, "Sir, you wanted to see me?"

"Yes. I have to go take a physical. Be back late this afternoon. You've got the helm. Don't start WWIII while I'm gone. Well, not unless you have to, but I'd hate to miss it."

"Yes, sir."

"Seriously. Just carry out the plan of the day and do whatever makes sense for anything else. I'll have a radio with me and will check in. You've got the ship. Don't let her sink. See ya later."

"Yes, sir. I've got it. Don't worry."

"I won't. Don't you. Ski, lets move it."

The trip to the hospital is over familiar ground. As we go over the bridge near Da Nang, Ski says, "I remember this place. What a day that was. We might have gotten lucky then."

"Yep, hell of a day. Lucky we were."

"And good, sir."

"Yeah. Sometimes luck and good are the same."

After the bridge, it's only a short haul south, past the SeaBee camp to the hospital. Once there, the physical takes only a short time. All the arrangements were made by the Battalion Doc so I can get in and out quickly. I'm found to be physically fit and able to continue service in His Majesty's Marines. I do have some parasites inside my bod, gobbling up the nutrition from my C-Rats, hence my drooping pistol belt. The Doc gives me a couple of shots and some worm pills. Thank God, I'm not a horse, or him a Vet.

Physical finished, we motor back north to III MAF Headquarters so I can visit Stoop, and Ski and I can get a solid meal at their chow hall. Never want to turn down an opportunity for a hot meal. Again, this trip is over ground once covered with Lima Company and the tanks. More memories.

We arrive at III MAF, caked with dust and sweat. We're the only folks here carrying weapons, wearing helmets and flak jackets covered with grime, and smelling like an old open slit trench. I stride unannounced into Stoop's, Major Tony Paletta's, office. He leaps from behind his desk and shouts, "Stoneface, great seeing you." He grabs me with one arm around my shoulders and rousts me about, hard enough to shake my helmet loose from my head. As it clangs to the deck, he says, "You sure got here in a hurry."

He looks great. Same guy, large, white haired, big voice and a warm smile. Picking up my helmet and smiling back, I ask with a suspicious tone, "What do you mean, I got here in a hurry? How'd you know I was coming? I was down at the hospital getting a physical and decided to stop in to see you, get a hot meal, and then get back to my company. Something's not five square in your transmission, Stoop."

"What'd ya mean, what do I mean? It's five square, Snake. Hell, you were ordered here, or at least you were supposed to be ordered here, and quickly."

"Ordered to do what? Why here? What are you talking about?"

"Ol' blue eyes wants you here as his aide. You were supposed to be here a couple of days ago, yesterday at the latest. Didn't you know?"

"Hell, no, I didn't know, but a lot of things are starting to make sense. Let me make something clear, I don't want to be an aide. I don't know anything about that crap, except they all have blond hair, blue eyes, are young, polite, mild mannered and well groomed. You know me, Stoop, I don't fit that mold. They don't curse, pick their nose, or have any disgusting habits. I do all of that, and fart in elevators to boot."

He rocks back in surprise. Maybe figures he's let the cat out of the bag, so I decide to pile on, "Besides, I have another rifle company, and as far as I'm concerned I'm gonna' finish the job I was asked to do, otherwise what's the sense of me being there? And besides that, I only have three and a half months to the end of my tour, so it doesn't make any sense to transfer me."

Stoop responds in a singsong tone, "You're not listening, Stoneface. The orders have been cut. The general's had several aides, and he wants one he can keep until he leaves. He feels comfortable with you since you're older, and he knows you. Hell, he actually likes you, Stoneface, and that's not easy to do. He thinks you and he are buddies from the old days." With this last statement, he bursts into a booming laugh. Everything he does is loud, windy and full of excitement, like a Texas thunderstorm.

"This isn't funny, Stoop. I've got to get out of this. It's not fair, not right. Let's go see somebody and get it changed."

"Oh, you want to see somebody, Stoneface? Who dummy? Tell

me who. You want to see the Chief of Staff. General Cunningham and I suggested this whole deal to General Barto. So if you insist, let's go. Or, is there someone else you think has the muscle to handle this."

"Okay, let's go see him. Come on. I'll get this settled." We start across the gravel quadrangular compound to the general's office. As I pass my jeep, Baronowski stirs from his seat in the vehicle. I say, "Mike, I'll be back shortly. I've got a problem to solve. You go get some chow and meet me back here."

"Need me to help, sir?"

"Nope, I'm fine. Just eat and meet me back here."

"Yes, sir...sure?"

"Yes, and take the driver." Only then does he head toward the chow hall, looking back as he departs, checking.

Major Paletta looks at me, then back at Baronowski and to me again, saying, "Who is that? Some hired gunman or hit man?

"Just that, sort of. It's a long story. He just looks out after me. One hell of a good Marine and human being. Let's go, okay?"

"He knows I'm not the enemy, doesn't he?" Roaring laughter follows his comment. Stoop loves his own jokes, and all others.

"Yeah, but only because you're bigger than a dink and aren't wearing black pajamas. I ought to sic him on you for doing this to me."

We enter General Cunningham's office area and wait a few minutes until he's off the phone. When he's finished, he waves us in, comes around his desk, greets me, shakes my hand, and proceeds to tell me how great it is to see me and have me here on the team.

The team? I feel myself sinking, going down by the stern. "Sir, there must be some mistake. I have just taken over my second rifle company. I haven't finished the job I was asked to do. Besides, I'm an infantry officer, sir, it's where I want be, and is where I should be. I need your help, sir. I'm sure you can work this out for me, somehow, sir."

The look on his face changes from a soft, warm smile of welcome to one of hard, cold granite in less time than it takes a lightening bolt to streak to the ground. He takes a few steps back, sits down behind his desk, folds his hands in front of him, lets out a sigh of exasperation and looks up at me, "Barney, that's not the way it's going to be. You are, as of this moment, the Aide-de-Camp for Lieutenant General Barto. His Senior Aide. A Lieutenant Colonel's billet, I might add, Captain."

Each sentence is louder than the last. He rants on, "Your orders have already been cut, and that my good friend, is the way it's going to be. Now, get back to your company, pack your gear and get your bony butt up here. You're already a day late…incidentally, you look like crap. Are you okay?"

I am about to answer and plead my case, when Lieutenant General Barto walks in from his adjoining office. He looks tired, however, those steely blue eyes are the same. He doesn't look at people, he sees into them. He smiles warmly, shakes my hand and while he's doing so, General Cunningham says, "Sir, the good Captain Quinn says he doesn't want to be an aide, wants to stay where he is. I've explained to him, that's not the way things are going to be." I notice he doesn't call me Barney, but rather, Captain Quinn. That's twice in the last few minutes. Not a good sign. It's a signal in "General's speak."

Lieutenant General Barto's smile has vanished, eyes piercing like lasers, he asks sternly, "Why don't you want to be an aide, Barney?"

Ah, we're back to Barney again. This can be deceptive. I carefully phrase my response, telling the general how important it is that I keep my company. That I don't have any interest in being an aide. Further, I know nothing about place settings, menus, protocol, proper manners or whatever else aides need to know.

I pause to measure his reaction and find it to be a steel, cold stare with those damn eyes of his, boring through my soul. I say, "Besides, I'm not pretty enough to be an aide." As these last few words tumble out and I can see them hanging there in the little white cloud, I realize by the general's grimace, I should have shut up one sentence sooner.

The muscles in his jaw tighten even more. General Barto responds gruffly, "Well, first of all, there is a little more to it then you might think, Captain. Secondly, I don't want someone who, what was it you said. . .looks pretty?"

Oh shit. I knew that set him off. He continues, his index finger poking the air between us, "I want someone who is ugly and that's you." He chuckles at his remark, which causes General Cunningham and Stoop to laugh with him. They're enjoying themselves. Then he continues, "And next, none of this makes any difference because you are my aide, AS OF NOW," as he jabs his finger on his watch face for emphasis.

Actually, he doesn't need to do this. I get the point, but he's on a roll, "I need you here, and don't want to have to change aides again, so I expect you here, pronto! Get your gear. Get back up here. When you arrive, tomorrow...you understand, tomorrow, you will immediately go on R&R with Major Paletta. I'm not sure, but I suppose I can trust the two of you in a civilian environment for a week. Is all this clear?"

"Sir, but—"

"No buts, Captain."

There's that captain stuff again, and he sounds crusty. "Yes, sir."

I think, the dye is cast. No doubt about it. This topic is not open for discussion, at least not here, not today, with these three.

He smiles again. General Cunningham grins. Major Paletta beams. Actually, he's laughing under his breath, however, they hear him. Everyone seems amused. They are undoubtedly pleased with themselves, particularly Stoop. All three are grinning at one another and chuckling. I'm the only one not smiling. I am, but it's forced, like when I hear a stale joke from a senior officer.

It's time to go, so I say, "Yes, sir. I understand. I guess I better be getting back to my company, sir."

"Barney, before you leave. Listen to me. I want you on my team, and need an aide I'm comfortable with, and that will shoot straight with me. You've had your rifle company, had your time in the field, and you've done a magnificent job. Now it's time for something else. Don't take it so hard. I understand how you feel, but I need you here. Okay?"

"Yes, sir. I understand and appreciate the general's remarks."

"Good. I'm glad that we understand each other."

"Yes, I guess so, sir."

"Guess so? You don't sound convinced."

"Yes, sir. I understand, sir."

"That's better. Get moving so you can get back here, early tomorrow."

"Aye aye, sir."

"And, Barney. Don't try to get your Regimental and Battalion CO's to go to bat for you. I'm going to call them." He smiles, pleased with himself for cutting my legs out from under me. General Cunningham and Stoop grin, cheekbone to cheekbone.

As Stoop and I saunter back to where my jeep is parked, I say, "Stoop, I'm going to try anyway."

"Be smart, Barney. You were in Recon, dummy, don't swim against a rip tide."

Dummy is one of Stoop's terms of endearment. I add, "Besides, what about being extended beyond my rotation tour date? I'm due to leave in about three months."

"You're not married, what do you care? Besides, he will make it up to you later, you should realize that."

"I know I'm not married, but I'm working on a good thing and I don't want to mess it up. She might not wait. I've told you, and him, about Ryley."

"Right, and if she's as good a gal as you say, she will understand, I'll bet on it."

"Yeah, with my money. Well, I guess I'm going to find out the hard way. Seemingly, like every damn thing else I do."

With my last comment, I shake hands with Stoop, and this time I give him a one-armed bear hug and say, "Stoop, I love ya big guy, but I wish you and your two pals in there, would stop messing with my career path."

"I'm your ordained career minister."

"Yeah, right, but you screwed up. You're hereby defrocked. This isn't fair, Stoop, and you know it."

"Defrocked, you'd probably spell it with a "u", and besides the Marine Corps didn't promise you fair, Hoss. Just adventure."

We're at my jeep now, so I nod to Baronowski, and say, "Let's go, Ski."

He pops to attention and says, "Aye Aye, sir. Major, by your leave, sir." Ski gives Stoop a smart hand salute. He returns it, and I can tell by his expression that he likes the cut of Ski. He looks at me and gives me a "thumbs up", turns, heads toward his office with a fist pump and a "YEAH."

Ski and I pile into the jeep. The driver asks, "Where to Captain?"

"Battalion CP. Will this thing go faster than the speed of sound?"

"Huh?"

"Never mind. Was just thinking aloud. Get me there as fast as you can without killing us."

"Yes, sir."

Ski leans forward from the back seat and says, "Skipper, what was that fist pump and yeah all about?"

"Aw, Ski...give me a few minutes to myself, and then I'll tell you what's goin' down."

"It's not good, is it, sir?"

"No, it's not, Damnit."

As we pull out of the compound gate, I lean back in the seat, put my right foot on the outside rim of jeep by the floorboard and think, the Kool Aid this morning, screwed up my day.

Should've had the coffee.

CHAPTER EIGHTEEN

WE RIDE IN SILENCE, EATING dust and bouncing over this heavily rutted dirt road. I've lost my company, but I'm determined to run one more play before I punt. We cross the Da Nang river bridge and turn left, south, and head toward the Battalion CP. I twist to my left so I can see Ski in the back of the jeep, and say, "Not a good day, Mike."

"Something screwin' up our world, Cap'n?"

"Yeah. I've been transferred. The visit with my friend Major Paletta, then the general wasn't good."

"Is that where you went when you sent me to chow? To see the general?"

"Yes."

"The one that shows up all the time?"

"Yes. I want you to keep this under your steel pot for a while, okay?"

"Yes, sir."

I tell him what occurred at MAF and see by his constant frowning, he's not taking this well. When I finish, I say, "Not what I want to do, and I'm going to see Lieutenant Colonel Reynolds about it, but to be truthful Ski, I think I'm a goner."

"Yes, sir. I mean, no, sir, I won't, and yes, sir, it doesn't sound good. What happens to me if you leave?"

God, I hate this. I was afraid of this happening. I grit my teeth and say, "Well, Ski, I can't take you with me. You'll stay in India Company and keep doing what you have been doing. And doing damn well I might add. Just be the Marine you are, and do what you're asked. You'll be just fine, and I promise, I'll stay in touch."

"Yes, sir, but I still wish I could go with you."

"Me too, Ski, but you'll be doin' a hell of a sight more important job than me. I'll be the pogey-bait, not you. Shoot, I wish I could go with you."

"You're gonna' miss the cocoa, sir."

"Yeah, I will. But, I'll miss you guys more."

We pull into the battalion CP. I get out of the jeep, slap the dust off as best I can, spit out some mud along with a few choice words, and search out Lieutenant Colonel Reynolds. I find him in his wood-framed tent and knock on the hatch. He invites me in, tells me to sit, holds up his hand, palm out, and says, "Don't say a word. I already got a call, several calls in fact. You went for a routine physical and wound up stirring up a hornet's nest."

"Sir, can I explain to the Colonel my side of all this?"

"Yes, but let me finish, Barney. It may influence your remarks, although something tells me you have some wondrous tale."

"Aye aye, sir."

"General Barto called me. If that wasn't enough, General Cunningham also called, as did the Regimental Commander. That was followed by the Division Commander, Major General Mallory."

"Sir—"

"Should I expect calls from anyone else?"

"Maybe the Doc at the hospital, but I don't think so, I was nice to him. If you're interested, I have some bugs having chow in my system, but otherwise, everything else is okay."

"Yeah, but he didn't do a brain scan."

"Sir, let me explain. I just went to III MAF to get some hot chow, and things went downhill from there. The orders were cut days ago. All I want to do is lead a rifle company in combat. To finish the job I was ordered to do. And, I need you to help me accomplish that."

"I wish I could. I want to keep you. So do the Division and Regimental commanders. However, General Barto wants you as his aide, and that's that. It's an order from FMFPac, and as I recall from your former CO, he's another one of your buddies. Regardless, my hands are tied tighter than a flea's ass."

"Dammit, sir. It's not right."

"Maybe not, but that's the way it is. I feel for you Barney, but I can't help now."

"It doesn't make any sense. Anybody can be a damn aide."

"Not today."

"Sir, call back. How about a plea bargain deal? I stay here until the end of the year, and then I'll—"

"Not a chance. You're history here. If I make any more waves than I have, I'll be shovelin' horse dung at the Camp Pendleton stables by morning."

"Sir, if you—"

"Barney, the decision has been made. Get back to your company; pick up your gear and go. On your way, pick up Lieutenant Gallagher. He's your replacement. Give him as much scoop as you can between now and morning."

"Aye Aye, sir. You're absolutely right, and I thank you for trying. If I can get out of this, will you take me back?"

"In a New York minute. Anytime, anyplace."

"Thanks, sir. I'll see you before I leave. And sir, I'm not done trying."

"Barney, don't do anything dumb. The whistle has blown, the play is over. Don't pick up a technical foul."

Baronowski and I leave for the company, with the new company commander in tow. This tells Ski all he needs to know. I look at him and say, "Ski, I've been transferred. Like I told you. Please don't say anything, to anyone, when we get back. I'll let the unit leaders know. Understand?"

"Yes, sir. Not a word."

I turn to First Lieutenant Gallagher, "We'll be coming up on India's TAOR in a few minutes, so I'll tell you as much as I can on the way. Here, take my map."

"Yes, sir. Thanks."

First Lieutenant Gallagher has been in country for all of about a month and a few chow calls. He hangs on my every word. When we cross the Tuy Loan River, I point out the Vills on the right, to the west, the two hills where we're located, and other key terrain features as we continue south to the company CP.

Now, in the last few moments, I think, my life as a company commander is over. Tonight, I will have my last cocoa interlude with Sergeant Parzini, Ski, Bird and Doc Ewing. I will include PFC Chang so maybe the others will embrace him after I leave. Henry would like that. I'll let Sergeant Parzini set whatever tone he wants with the new Skipper. If the Lieutenant is smart, he'll join the group, sip cocoa, listen and learn.

This morning, although hot and humid once again, I have some Black Death, just so I won't forget how bad it tastes, and then walk about saying my goodbyes to the men of India Company. I introduce them to the new company commander at the same time. I can't get over to the other platoon, so I call them on the radio, and say goodbye to the platoon sergeant, and ask him to give my regards to the troops. It's done; I throw my gear into the back of the jeep, get in, and leave. Without Ski.

At the bottom of the hill and after we turn left, heading north, I say, "Driver, stop here for a second."

"Yes, sir."

"Thanks." I look back to India Company and see the normal activity going on, except for one person. He's just staring after the jeep. Then I look east, to the other side of this road, and see Hill 22, that mogul we called a hill. And here at the crossroads, the school Lima built. It's in session, and the kids are outside playing some game with a ball and sticks. The teacher looks our way; takes a few steps closer, smiles, and waves. Great, she remembers. Well, good, at least we will leave something behind of value.

"Driver, let's go."

"Yes, sir."

Life as I know it, and love it, is over. Being a rifle company commander, in combat, is the greatest job in the Corps.

What the hell is life going to be like now? No Snuffies to lead, no Magpies to listen to, and no cocoa with the guys.

It's gonna suck.

Part Two

A WARRIOR WITHOUT A WAR

CHAPTER NINETEEN

I ARRIVE AT III MAF Headquarters, smelling bad from the paddies and caked with dust from the jeep ride. I check in with Major Paletta, turn in my orders, and pick up my belongings from storage, which he has retrieved for me. Then I inaugurate the important task of getting this stench out and the grime of the paddies off. It can't be gotten out, or off, in just one wash and rinse cycle. It takes several. However, the process doesn't cleanse the mind or soul, and it for damn sure won't scrub away my respect for, and memories of, the troops of Lima and India companies.

Only after my scouring, applying Foo-foo juice, and changing into my khaki's can I be released into some form of the civilized world. Stoop and I leave for Rest and Relaxation in Hong Kong. The trip is comfortable since it's on a chartered commercial jet and not on a military aircraft. We have cushioned seats, drinks, and tall, long legged, big-breasted American women as stews. They have a few miles on them, and one in particular looks like she has been in more than a few fender benders. However, after the paddies, she still looks pretty damn good. At least none of them chew betel nut, and they all offer a ton of cleavage, sensuous smiles, and a lot of hand-to-hand touchy-feely while serving drinks. It's a chore, but I behave myself.

R&R is only five days, so, we do some mandatory shopping the first day. He, for his wife, and me for Ryley. Then we do some sightseeing and take the obligatory but cursory snapshots to prove that we're here, are cultured, and have good intentions.

We spend time on both the Hong Kong and the Kowloon side of the bay reconnoitering watering holes. We get a hotsy bath, massage and shave to start each day, then spend the remainder of our time eating and drinking at fine restaurants, and some not so fine. I fall in love with an oriental princess, or maybe something less, at every stop, but Stoop continually rescues me. A good liberty with a lot of sea stories to tell down the road.

Our time is up much too soon and we have to leave. Stoop does some last minute shopping, and we miss our flight back to Da Nang. I'm thinking, this is not good, not slick at all. An Aide-de-Camp, AWOL on his first day on the job. We finally get to the airport and manage to get ourselves on a plane to Saigon's Tan Son Nhut airfield. No problem since it's an R&R flight, but we end up in Saigon, not Da Nang, and a long way from where we need to be. Stoop tells me, "No sweat, Stoneface, no sweat."

"Easy for you to say. You're your own boss for all practical purposes. I report directly to the general, and he hasn't given me any indication that he is lackadaisical about anything, much less about any shenanigans from a captain that already gave him a hard time about becoming his aide."

At Tan Son Nhut I find out what no sweat means to Stoop. He looks at me with raised eyebrows and that okay- hot-shot-look, then declares, "Stoneface, go do some of that aide shit. Get us a flight to Da Nang."

"What do you mean, aide shit?"

"You know. Pull rank. Mention the general's name. Act really important, dummy."

"Stoop, captains can't pull rank on too many folks, and probably none that can do anything helpful. I can't use the general's name. That's not the way it works. However, it is the way you piss people off."

"Then we'll just be AWOL. That'll look good."

"Okay. Okay. Spare me the pouting routine. On you, it looks pathetic. I get the message. I'll see what I can do."

I go to Flight Operations and pull some of that aide shit Stoop talked about earlier. To my surprise, it works, and we get on a flight to Da Nang. It's an Air Force Lear jet, VIP type, that's bringing a couple of USAF non-pilot lieutenants up to Da Nang. They're going to Monkey Mountain. When I tell them I use to provide security for them there, it's like old home week. I tell them a slightly embellished version of the Da Nang bridge sea story and the rest is easy.

A few more war stories on the plane, and we get a ride in their sedan from the airfield in Da Nang to MAF headquarters. If I had my helmet, flak jacket, a couple of grenades and some dust, and had these two wing wipers at a bar, I could drink all night.

We arrive back, not too long after the flight we were suppose to be on in the first place. Stoop is pleased with himself, and I suppose, all is well.

Once back, I head out to the general's quarters that is on the beach by the South China Sea. It's part of a larger compound also occupied by Navy Seals. The general's place is called the Beach House, which to me seems out of context with the circumstances of supposedly being at war. Makes it sound like our summer home in the Hamptons. The aides and stewards live in a Quonset hut behind the main house. I already feel like an indentured servant.

Two, ten-foot-high chain link fences topped with razor wire enclose the entire area. The compound has its own security unit. Although surrounded by several villages, it's obviously in a safe area, but that's no reason to get careless. It has an asphalt helo pad within the compound, large enough for two birds. This compound is east of the III MAF headquarters on the peninsula between the Da Nang River and the China Sea.

The house has been renovated and has a good size galley with modern equipment. It has a large formal dining room with a huge round table that seats twelve. The living room is open, large, and overlooks the water and a wide, pristine, sandy beach.

It has an upright Baldwin piano, against one wall. I sit at the keyboard, play a few bars from Ellington's, *I Got it Bad and That Ain't Good.* I wonder, who here plays, besides me.

The general has a bedroom, bath, and a good size study. Outside these rooms, is an enclosed porch. A crushed white rock driveway leads to the front portico. A turn-around and parking area is in back.

Behind the house, on the northwest side is the Quonset hut. It is divided in half. One-half for the aides, and the other for the cooks, driver and stewards.

I have the lay of the land and spend the remainder of the morning unpacking and getting settled in the hut. It has its own stall shower, and standard issue steel, single racks, with springs and mattress, sheets and pillows. No more blowing up the rubber lady, which reminds me, I never did find that slow leak.

This beats the hell out of a bunker and the dachshund-size rats, and is for sure better than a hole scraped out of a dry paddy. Settled, I decide to take a shower. Another one, but by my count, I'm still at least two hundred and thirty behind.

Captain Jason Schmidt, one of two junior aides, calls me on the landline. He's been selected, along with a Lieutenant Reddick, to assist me. He tells me the general is gone for the day, somewhere up north, and won't be back until this evening. Further, he and Lieutenant Reddick will be out to the house for lunch, and before we eat, he will introduce me to the general's household staff. I say, "Okay, normally I would tell you not to waste your time, and that I'll just introduce myself, but we'll do it your way." Then I add, "When, in an hour say?"

"Yes, sir."

That's impressive, he's calling me sir. Wonder what prompted that, other than good manners. "Okay, see you then. And Jason, who plays the piano?"

"Beats me, it's just in the house, I think."

"How long have you two been here?"

"Me, three days. Lieutenant Reddick, yesterday."

"All right, thanks. See you shortly."

So far, it seems to be potluck so I guess I'll find out if it's stew or steak.

CHAPTER TWENTY

BEFORE CAPTAIN SCHMIDT AND LIEUTENANT Reddick arrive, I check out the piano again. I play three oldies, *That Lucky Old Sun, Three Coins in the Fountain,* and *Love Is A Many Splendored Thing.* It's a little out of tune but in good overall condition. I'm going to ask Ryley to send me some of my fake books and cheat sheets so I have more variety.

I slip outside before my playing draws a crowd, and walk around the perimeter of the house again. It's a beautiful day and a peaceful setting, making it hard to visualize there's a war going on in the hinterlands. The fence, and the sentry with the guard dog, draws the environment somewhat back into focus.

I see the general's sedan coming into the compound, so I head toward the front entrance of the house. Earlier I called Stoop and got some insight into the two junior aides. Captain Jason Schmidt, is an A-4 jet jockey, is soft-spoken, polite, and has a half a tour, six months, remaining. Lieutenant Walt Reddick is a Field Engineer, young, energetic and should be back in his outfit doing something constructive rather than wasting away in a nothing job as the second junior aide. They both were selected and ordered here while I was on R&R.

As they get out of the sedan, I say, "Howdy, guys, I'm Captain Barney Quinn."

Jason steps forward and says, "I'm Captain Jason Schmidt, and this is Lieutenant Walter Reddick. Welcome, sir."

"My pleasure, Jason, Walt. What's next? What's the plan?"

"I've called ahead and have the staff prepared to meet you, then we can have lunch and talk about whatever you'd like. Then we can go back to the headquarters and meet the others."

"Sounds like a plan to me; let's do it."

We step inside the house. Jason's had the staff line up in the living room. He starts with, "Captain Quinn, this is Gunnery Sergeant John Duncan. He's the Chief Steward and Cook, and has been with the general for quite some time."

The Gunny nods and I say, "Good to meet you, Gunny. Look forward to working with you."

The Gunny is black, tells me that he has almost 20 years service, all as a cook and steward, and has been with General Barto for years, ever since he was a Brigadier General. He also tells me he is the Head Cook, and the Head Steward.

I say, "Gunny, I get your point. Just make sure everything runs smoothly and I'll be a happy Marine captain. Do you get my point?"

"Yes, sir. I know what the general likes and don't like. I runs a good kitchen and house, so don't be worryin' none, sir."

"Okay, good, I won't worry, Gunny. If I have to worry, I'll resolve the problem. Now, who are these other Marines?"

"First, there's the Cook, Sergeant Cake Cartwright. His real name is Charles, but he likes bein' called Cake."

With this, Cake shuffles forward. He is fairly young, also black, late twenties I would guess. He's tall, taller than me, rangy, and lean. He slouches a bit as he stands and moves. He tells me he's been in the Corps for ten years and has been a cook for all this time. All this cooking experience, good I'm thinking, because I don't know doodly-squat about food preparation. I can cook a mean C-Rat can of beanie weenies over a heat tab, but I don't suppose we'll be serving that.

Staff Sergeant Cartwright steps forward, shakes my hand, welcomes me to the house and slides back easily to where he was standing. Other than the welcome, he says nothing. He's not sullen, just reticent.

Next is Corporal Richardo Alvarez. Before the Gunny can say a word, Alvarez steps smartly forward and introduces himself, "Sir, my name is Corporal Richardo Alvarez, and I'm a steward. I keep the general's uniforms, bedroom and study, ship shape."

"Great, Corporal Alvarez. Where you from?"

"East LA Mon...I mean, sir. Excuse me, sir, I didn't mean to... I'm sorry, sir."

My friendly tone and question must have caught him off guard to prompt an automatic East LA homespun response. "Okay, Corporal Alvarez. I understand. Incidentally, I'm familiar with the area. Been stationed at Pendleton a couple of times, so I know LA."

He's about twenty, and looks squared away. It's obvious he takes pride in his personal appearance. He restrains his natural accent and vocabulary most of the time, I'm sure. When with the guys, he probably reverts. His appearance is head and shoulders above the rest of the crew.

Next in line, and not moving smartly in any direction, is another Marine. The Gunny says, "Sir, this is Corporal Richard Sadowski, the general's driver."

I have already heard about Sadowski from Stoop. He is the son of a woman whose husband served under the general during WWII. The general is doing her a favor and keeping Sadowski under his wing. Sadowski distinguishes himself this afternoon by wearing some of his breakfast eggs on his chin and down the front of his utility jacket.

He finally shuffles forward and says, "Good mornin', I mean afternoon, sir." His attempt to do a snappy military halt causes him to kick himself in the ankle and stumble. After righting himself somewhat, he snickers and while doing so snorts a string of snot onto his upper lip, which he proceeds to wipe off with the back of his sleeve.

Aw shoot, it's all true. Behind me, I hear Jason and Walt emit a lower octave groan. I say, "Well, good afternoon, Corporal Sadowski. Hopefully you will pay more attention to your appearance from now on. You're not looking too slick at the moment."

He frowns, and says, "Huh?"

I love a conversationalist. This is a disaster waiting to happen. He's short of six feet, sandy haired, rawboned and muscular, probably nineteen or so chronologically, and certainly not the pick of the litter. I should have brought Baronowski. "Okay, Corporal, you can step back with the others. Thank you." He stumbles again trying to execute an about face. He should have just stepped directly back. Now he needs to execute another facing movement. He doesn't rise to the challenge. He simply turns around slowly.

I ask, "A question for the group, do any of you play the piano? I see we have one."

A chord of no's ring out, to include the two junior aides.

"Does the general play?"

Gunny Duncan replies, "No, suh. Sure don't."

"Well, do guests?"

"No one, so far. The general just wanted one in the house. But I know you play, Cap'n. Heard you just before we came in. Do you play much, sir?"

"I didn't have a piano where I just came from. I do at home, however. Normally, I just play for the ladies, Gunny."

"Well, we ain't got none of them around here."

I turn to Jason and say, "Incidentally, the piano is out of tune. See if you can find someone that can tune it."

"Okay. Are you going to play?"

"Not for you and Walt. Only for the ladies."

"Strange, I wouldn't thought you played."

"Well I do, and I can use a knife, fork and spoon, but I'm still working on using indoor toilets."

Jason smiles, nodding his head, and lets his eyes drift over to another member of the household staff.

Also at the house, but not staying in the compound, is the maid and laundry girl, My Lei. I'm told by the Gunny she's fourteen, is from the adjacent village, cleans the house, and does the laundry for everyone here. The house is clean; everyone's utility uniforms are starched and pressed, so it looks like she is doing a good job.

She is standing off to one side, near the door to the general's study. I look over to her and nod. She bows demurely, hands at her side. She's wearing native garb of a white loose-fitting cotton half-smock top and black pajama pants. She is a cute, petite rascal, but looks a little older than fourteen because she's wearing some makeup. I think, this is trouble brewing, or already has percolated over. My intuition tells me to fire this gal and go in the village and find some old scraggly-toothed, betel nut chewing, mama-san for the job and save myself problems.

I smile at My Lei, "Keep up the good work." She nods, and bows again.

Looking at Jason, I ask, "What's with the dog I saw outside?"

"That's the general's dog."

"General's dog? Does it come inside? Who feeds it and so forth?"

"I don't know who takes care of it, but it doesn't get to come inside."

"Good. Find out who cares for it, and tell them to keep the dog healthy, clean, outside the house but inside the compound. Since no one here volunteered an answer, I assume no one does, so appoint someone. And keep her away from the natives, so they don't eat the damn thing. What's it's name?"

"Lady."

"Jason, just make sure all that happens for Lady, so she doesn't become a tramp. I don't want to wind up in the general's doghouse over that Heinz 57 mutt."

Jason nods his understanding, and chuckles. Lady is watching me in a manner that suggests she has done something wrong, the look a dog gets when it poops indoors. Maybe it just senses I don't like her; they're good at that. They bark to holler, but speak with the eyes.

That's the staff. I say thanks to all of them, and tell them I will get around and talk to each of them individually. With that, Jason, Walt and I adjourn to the table for lunch. Man-oh-man, this is first-rate living. During lunch, I find out more about each and tell them something about myself. From their remarks, I determine that both are scared shitless of the general.

Apparently, Stoop has informed them not to worry because I'm one of the general's buddies. Plus, he has filled them with Stoneface sea stories. Wonderful! Stoop at his best, telling yarns embellished with broad-brush strokes. A couple of them are hard to recognize when Jason and Walt relate them. We finish lunch, get in the sedan, and head back to headquarters so I can meet the remaining staff.

At the office is the Stenographer, SSgt Ronald Kimmons, a prim and proper admin type, and the Vietnamese Interpreter, Captain Thanh Quy. Since Quy doesn't look me in the eye when we are introduced, I take it he is either a wimp or a VC. I give him the benefit of the doubt and assume he's just a wuss.

I ask Quy, "Have you always been here at headquarters?"

"Yes, I interpreter, and now general's aide."

"Never been in the field?   Maybe the ammo dump down south?"

"No, I staff officer."

"Well, good. Now you work for me. If you want, I can use my influence and get you transferred to a combat unit, so you can really make a contribution to your country."

"No, sir. I stay here. My wife here too."

"Yeah, okay, just asking?" I think, a "Taker," and Stoop had told me about Madame Quy. Now that I have no more questions, Quy slinks back a step, and slithers out the office door like a bamboo viper seeking shade.

Jason tells me I'm also responsible for some vehicles. We have a three-quarter-ton truck, a jeep, and a sedan for the general's use and support. The general is also assigned a helicopter and a second helicopter whenever necessary. These are Bell UH-1 Huey choppers. The general's is a slick, meaning no armament. The other, the chase bird, can be either a slick or a gunship depending on where we go.

The pilot assigned to General Barto's Huey is Captain Dick Horner. He reports to his Squadron Commander but is exclusively assigned this duty. I have seen him before on the general's visits to me in the field, but have not met him. That will come later. The chase birds, when assigned, have whatever pilot is flying that chopper.

Jason adds, "The general's call sign is Deadlock One Dash Zero, which everyone knows."

"PFC Chang didn't know it."

"Huh? Who's he."

"Aw, nothing Jason, It's a private joke. Go on with your briefing."

He tells me that the bird doesn't have a co-pilot assigned. The general sits up in the left front seat. He can fly the chopper straight and level, but that's it. I think to myself, guess we hope Horner doesn't get hit.

My duties will include a myriad of tasks, some of which I have no experience or knowledge about. Fortunately, most are primarily administrative and for that, one only needs to have common sense and some organizational skills. I have these, although my common sense has been questioned from time to time while on liberty.

I'm also answerable for the menu, about which I have absolutely no experience or knowledge, and even less interest. I simply view food as fuel for my engine. That's why I loved C's, but I guess my outlook is about to change. Also, I will be responsible for whatever protocol or seating arrangements are required. I remember my episode at the SeaBee camp and deduce that those manners will not be acceptable here.

In a nutshell, I'm a damn wife in the body of an infantry officer, so I guess we'll just see how friggin' Bernadette Quinn does as the lady of the house.

CHAPTER TWENTY-ONE

WHILE AT THE OFFICE THIS first afternoon, I find two more old friends have emerged from the shadows of my past. Lieutenant Colonel Harry Mason, the Staff Secretary, and the other is the MAF G-2, the Intelligence Officer, Colonel Roy Thomas. This place is generously full of happy people today. Major General Cunningham and Major Paletta are also present and airing the same jubilation. Makes one wonder what the hell went on in the past. Certainly are a lot of people stirring the brew in my kettle. Unfortunately, the concoction is my career path, and I prefer it be allowed to simmer on its own.

The afternoon has been educational with briefings on certain constants of this job. Some relate to my individual responsibilities, some are trip related, others are sensitive protocol topics, and a few are pet peeve type issues. I still believe this is a waste of a good infantry captain but that subject has been zipped closed, for now.

The afternoon races by and it's time to go to the quarters for dinner with the general. He'll be returning directly there from his unit visits today. Jason informs me that we will be dining in the utility uniform, not khakis, which doesn't surprise me. Having been burned once, I ask about the saying of grace before meals.

He replies, "Not so far, but I haven't been at the table when guests are present."

"Why not?"

"The prayer or at the table?"

"Why weren't you at the table?"

"He told me that he only wanted the senior aide at the table with guests, not the rest of us, unless he said so."

"Okay. Guess I'll find out what the party line is when we have guests."

The general arrives by chopper, goes directly to his room, cleans up, comes out, and calls us to join him at the table. He sees me, breaks out into a broad grin, and strides briskly toward the table. He grabs me around the shoulder, in his usual bear hug style, and says, "Welcome, Barney. Good having you here. I'm looking forward to this arrangement. Aren't you?"

Jason and Walt have stunned looks on their faces. It's as if Major Paletta's earlier remarks are just now registering. I say, "Oh, yes, sir, certainly am. How is the general this evening?"

"I'm great, now." Then he grabs me for a second time, puts his steely blues on the two junior aides, smiles once more and says, "This is my man. We served together years ago, in Korea, and we have been friends for some time now. I personally had Captain Quinn brought here to be my senior aide. You two listen to him. Do what he says, and you'll do just fine." They nod, don't say a word, and try to force a relaxed smile. Impossible, they almost seem catatonic around him. Then the general says, "Let's eat, men."

The general sits, and then we dutifully sit. I'm on his immediate right, they are on his left. A place for everyone, and everyone in their place. He is served first by the stewards. At this moment, a neon thought darts across my mind. All royalty is fleeting. Just a few days ago, I was the King of my Castle, now I've lost my moat, drawbridge and castle. Worse, I might be the Queen.

The meal is great, steak and potatoes, the conversation is

basically whatever the general and I talk about. Jason and Walt are reluctant to contribute. They answer questions of them, but only with "yes" and "no sirs." I make a mental note to ask only open ended questions to force them to speak, or at least stammer.

The meal ends. The general gruffly excuses himself and goes to his study, apparently for the evening. He seems perturbed. Jason has informed me the general likes a movie when there are no guests. His choice is always *Gunsmoke*, but Corporal Sadowski forgot to pick it up this morning. This kid is a bad dream and he is already grating on me. Captain Schmidt, Lieutenant Reddick, and I go to our quarters and await the sound of the buzzer, signaling he wants me. Something like the friggin' chicken.

It's late, about 2200. I go check to see if all is well, and if the general might want anything else this evening before retiring. He says, "No, Barney. I'm fine. Good night. And Barney, it's good having you here. We're going to get along fine. Be yourself. Just be yourself, that's why you're here."

"Yes, sir, and thanks. Good night, sir."

I return to the Quonset hut, settle down and write Ryley, letting her know my new address and that she and the Mizpah must be working their magic. Also, to create a sense of anticipation, I inform her about the packages I sent from Hong Kong. She's going to be surprised. Ol' Barney has taste, and a dab of class. I got her a Noritake China setting for twelve, and all the extra bowls, platters and such. Then added a bronze tableware set for twelve, with teakwood handles, in a velvet lined, walnut case. Sounds expensive, but in Hong Kong it was peanuts. Besides, if not these, Jack Daniels would have had some additional revenue.

I also got her a diamond pendant with matching earrings. I mailed the first two items a few days ahead of the pendant and earrings. She'll love them all, but the diamonds coming separate will be more personal and hopefully a bigger surprise. Maybe the pendant and earrings are a bit overboard, but the money was burning a hole in my pocket, and Stoop's buying spree for his wife was sucking me along.

Before turning in, I muse, "Be myself." Okay, I think he wants me to shoot straight, say what I think. I'll do that, and hope that's what he's after. Tomorrow will be my first full day. I'll just swing up in the saddle and see where the trail leads.

Dawn breaks and I'm ready for my first day as the reigning Queen, at least I think I am. It is cloud free and already hotter than a Texas barbeque pit. Worse, no breeze off the South China Sea this morning. That's a shame. I was looking forward to a sniff of salt air to start my day in lieu of the paddy perfume of my past.

Once inside the house, I sit down at the dining table for breakfast with the two junior aides and the general. We exchange morning greetings, and then it becomes quieter than a room full of cadavers. No one is speaking. Gunny Duncan serves the general first and returns, along with Corporal Alvarez, to the kitchen.

As soon as the general is served, he starts to eat, not waiting for us. No good morning, no small talk and no prayer. Duncan and Alvarez return to the table with the plates for the rest of us. This is strange, I was told protocol, manners, proper dining and such were the order of the day and that I would have to change my boondocks style and adjust to civilization. The general doesn't seem to be concerned. I guess, manners are to be observed only when guests are present. He's probably not even aware of this trait. For now, I'll adapt, Neanderthals don't care.

The aroma of the bacon and eggs drift up from the plate and register savory hot flashes in my brain-housing group. I inhale deeply through my nose to relish this moment. Life is good, even for the Queen. I politely take a piece of toast from the serving tray

Alvarez holds, butter it, and set it down on the side of my plate. Reaching slightly to my left, but not across anyone, for the salt and pepper, I begin seasoning my eggs.

As I do so, I hear repetitive metallic scraping noises and some loud clattering reverberations of silverware. This breakfast symphony of sound is joined by distinct gulping noises with a few mumbled "ummms" in between. I glance to my left and notice that the general is just finishing his breakfast. Damn, that was quick.

Before I can turn back to my plate, the general pushes back from the table, and says, "Barney, let's go. Got a busy day." With this, he is up and on the way toward the door, heading for the chopper waiting outside.

The two junior aides jump to their feet and freeze at attention. I say, "Yes, sir." As soon as the general is a few more steps away, Jason and Walt settle back in their seats and begin to eat, and unfortunately murmur a slight giggling sound in the key of G. I say to the two of them, "Hey, girls...thanks for the heads up. We'll be talking about this later. No, you two will be listening about this blindside shot."

With that, I grab two slices of bacon, cram them in my mouth, and snatch my piece of toast off the plate and hold it in my teeth. I wheel around, pick up the two brief cases against the wall, and motion for Alvarez to put my smartly starched and blocked utility cover on my head as I charge out the door, heading for the chopper.

I get to the bird just as the general is climbing in the front and the pilot is turning up the blades. Captain Horner is laughing. Apparently, he has seen this slapstick comedy act before. Another few seconds and I believe the general would have left me here. I think, okay, dummy, we got lesson number one out of the way early.

We land at the helo pad next to the Da Nang River at III MAF headquarters. I wait, allowing the general to debark first. By the time I'm out and moving, he's already bull rushing toward the headquarters building, which obliges me to run while carrying the two briefcases. The officers and enlisted men in this old, French built, one story building are watching this exhibition as if it were a spectator sport. It must be a ritual of some sort that occurs every morning. They are standing at the windows and in the doors, laughing. I'm chasing behind the general like a mouse scurrying behind the Pied Piper. Lesson two is recorded on my mental "to do" list. I'm going to get ahead of the curve on these two events, pronto. This might be a long day, or with my big mouth, a short one.

The general bursts through our outer office and barrels directly into his. I have lost a step in the final twenty yards dodging people that are on the sidewalk and frozen in salutes as the general advances. When I attempt to follow him into his office, I am clobbered with the two swinging half-doors. Fortunately, I have the briefcases in separate hands so the natural swinging motion of my arms allows the briefcases to catch the brunt of the doors, not my snot locker. Regardless, the doors cause me to recoil slightly, as if someone feinted a punch.

Once inside, I place his briefcase on the desk, open it, remove the papers and place them on the center of his desk. He nods and wearing a sly smile, says, "See you at the briefing, Barney."

"Yes, sir," I execute an about face, leaving the office at a slower and safer pace than upon entering, wondering if this is a game of some sort. Lesson three, the swinging door. Don't lose ground near the office even if it means running down people in my way.

Letting out an audible sigh, and to no one, I say aloud, "Three ambushes, but made it this far. It's been an adventure, Barney ol' boy." I suddenly realize Major Paletta, Lieutenant Colonel Mason and Major General Cunningham are present, and laughing. They have not only overheard me, but purposely were out of their offices to witness the opening act of this vaudeville show.

When the laughter subsides, I grin, and say, with a hint of humorous sarcasm, "General, sir...Colonel, sir, and Major, you three are fair-weather friends. You're supposed to help me adjust, not wallow in my distress...sirs."

Stoop responds, "Take pride, Barney. Two previous aides missed the chopper for openers and another forgot the briefcases. You're way ahead of the game."

"Really, well, things are going to change. You can count on it."

General Cunningham smiles and says, "That's what you're here for, Barney ol' boy."

Looking at my watch, I point out, "It's time for the morning meeting, and I ain't runnin' again...Sirs."

We all laugh as we depart for the briefing.

This indoctrination, on this inauguration day, is over as far as I'm concerned. I will keep my sense of humor, and endure, but I'm reminded of the general's words, "Be yourself."

Well, from here on out, I'm gonna' be me, and I'm goin' to start by tightening the jaws of my two younger cohorts, Princesses Jessica and Wanda.

CHAPTER TWENTY-TWO

THIS SECOND MORNING, I'M AHEAD of the curve. First, I eat my breakfast in the kitchen before everyone else. Then I have the stewards serve all of us at the same time, but giving me just a piece of toast and one strip of bacon. "Just put the general's plate down first," I inform Gunny Duncan.

When the general finishes inhaling his breakfast and charges to the chopper, I am alongside. He gives me a puzzled look. Something is not quite right, but it hasn't registered yet. The pilot lifts off slowly being careful not to snag the tail rotor on the chain link fence. Once clear, he banks up and out over the water, turns inland and heads for III MAF. It only takes a few minutes.

As the chopper flares to set down at the pad, I unbuckle my seat belt, grab the two briefcases under one arm, and sit on the deck with my feet on the skid. As soon as the slick settles, I'm out, and open the left front door for the general. Again, the same look, but this time something has registered. We walk up along the building, side by side, to the office. As far as I am concerned, I'm a pulling guard, and act like one. Those folks standing frozen in salutes, move out of the way. I take a couple of quick steps ahead at the door, push it open, and follow him in with ease.

Major General Cunningham is here observing the arrival and entrance, and he is grinning. Lieutenant General Barto looks at him, then me, also grins and says, "Pretty slick, Barney, pretty slick."

"Yes, sir, I'd say so. Slicker than owl shit, sir."

"It is, huh? Good, then get me my leader on the phone before the briefing."

"Who might that be, sir?"

"Don't get too slick, just get me General Mueller on the line, and don't forget, put me on the phone first." Lieutenant General Kurt Mueller is the CG, FMFPac and is senior to the general. This protocol step is important, and in this case, there seemingly are other issues at play, but I can't get involved in whatever they are.

Back in my outer office, I place the call telling the operator who I am, and that I am calling General Mueller for General Barto. While I'm waiting for the call to go through, it suddenly dawns on me that it's the middle of the night in Hawaii. This call is going to go to Mueller's home. I think, what if he answers the phone direct and not a steward? I better--

"Good evening, General Mueller."

Dadgummit, first time out of the gate. Nailed by Murphy's Law. "Good evening, sir, this is Captain Quinn, General Barto's aide."

"Captain Quinn, well, what a pleasant surprise. I was told you were being transferred. By the way, you did get all that gear I brought to you and Lima Company? And my note?" I was right, he expected me to reply.

"Oh, yes, sir. I sent the general a message, sir. I hope you got it okay."

"Oh yes, I did. I remember now. Thank you. How are you doing in your new job?"

"Just fine, sir. I'm calling for the general, sir. Please excuse me, and I will put the general on the line."

"Okay, that will be fine. Take care, Captain Quinn."

Before I can buzz the general, he pokes his head out of his office door and asks, "What's happening on that call?"

"He's on the line, sir." I jab my finger rapidly at the mouthpiece in a helpless gesture. He frowns, shakes his head, and ducks back into his office.

I listen for a second as he picks up the phone and says, "General, I'm sorry for the delay." I hang up and wait. It will only take a few minutes before I get to put my head on the kicking tee for the point after.

The conversation lasts for several minutes, which isn't long enough as far as I'm concerned. The buzzer goes off, I jump to my feet, go into his office, and say, "Yes, sir, the general buzzed?"

"Yes. I thought I told you to put me on the phone first. That was a pretty simple assignment, wasn't it? And also, what were you and he chit-chatting about?"

"Sir, its night time there. He's at home and he answered his phone. What was I suppose to do. I can't control that."

"What I want you to do is put me on the phone first, he's senior to me. You figure out how. Now, what were you two talking about like old friends?"

"Sir, we're not old friends. He brought up the subject of his visit to Lima Company. You remember, you probably sent him there, which is an interesting thought in itself."

"Well, chit-chat with your buddies on your own time, and make sure you get me on the phone first hereafter, understand? And, what do you mean by that last remark?"

"Nothing, sir. Just curious as to why you sent him to visit me."

"Humph! Probably so you could drive him crazy instead of me. You do recall my visits, don't you? Was always something you wanted, or did, or said, or... whatever."

"I thought I was business-like, and nice, polite."

"Nice and polite are not two of your strongest traits. Let's get to the briefing, Captain Quinn."

Captain Quinn, whoa, he must be pissed. "Yes, sir." And away we charge like two running backs on a dive play, out through his rear door, and head to the briefing room. As we slide into our seats, I think, ah, made it, untouched, and only the one flag down.

After the briefing, we take the chopper north and visit a few units. These go well. It's approaching twilight so we head back to the Da Nang area. We will visit the wounded at the hospital before going to the beach house.

We land and are met by the CO of the Hospital, several doctors and a few nurses. The nurses always seem prettier in the movies, but maybe they're thinking the same about aides. We head for the wards. I am carrying a Polaroid Camera, a knapsack loaded with film, and my pocket notebook. The general is directed to wherever there is a recently wounded Marine. He pins the Purple Heart Medal on the trooper if he is ambulatory, if not, he pins it on the pillow next to his head. I take a picture, let it develop, and hand it to the general so he can present it. The general says some comforting words to the trooper and asks a few personal questions. I note anything said that needs to be followed up.

We do this as we go through several wards. Photography is not in my skill set. I fumble with a few of the opening shots, but recover, and quickly get the hang of the Polaroid and its settings. The general is a little upset about my initial gaffes, allowing his impatience to show.

Our last stop today is the Intensive Care Ward. This is much more emotional for the general. As soon as we enter, the general flushes slightly, and his eyes become a little moist. Seeing these young men suffering from such traumatic injuries noticeably rattles him. He has difficulty speaking and maintaining composure. In some cases, they are not awake or conscious so we leave the medal and the picture on the pillow next to the man. In these instances, he gently pats the man's head, whispers something only he and the Marine's soul can hear, takes a deep breath and moves on. I note specifics about the man so I can check on him later for the general.

We leave the ward and are standing just outside the hospital. The general is talking with the doctors and nurses, basically thanking them for their service and the excellent work they do. I can tell by the looks on their faces that this pumps them up. He turns to leave, and the two of us head for the chopper. He stops abruptly, turns to me and says, "Barney, did you see anyone from your old outfit in there?"

"No, sir."

"If you ever do, let me know immediately. I'll want to do and say something differently. And I want to give you a few moments to say something as well. Okay?"

"Yes, sir, I will. Thank you."

"You don't have to thank me, Barney. You earned the right."

We turn, walk the few remaining steps, board the chopper, and lift off. I stow the camera and remaining film aboard the chopper as normal. Then, remind the crew chief to replenish the film.

I lean back in the seat and mutter aloud to myself, "Lets see, I beat the breakfast fiasco; the race to the chopper; ruined the day for a hell of a lot of people waiting to see the Pied Piper show; and missed the swinging door.

Lost big time on the phone call. Nevertheless, by the end of the day, we are buds again. Not bad, Barney ol' boy."

I wonder, is everyday going to be like this? Is this some form of hazing for the rookie? Maybe the general just runs hot and cold. Whatever, so far, I'm not likin' the marriage.

Chapter Twenty-Three

I DON'T FIT THE MOLD of young, blond, blue eyes and pretty but I'm off to a reasonably good start at this "Aide" job. I have managed to get the household staff to sharpen up a bit. Not razor keen, nor honed to perfection, but at least with only a few nicks in the blade. Still a way to go to measure up to the standard I would like. We'll get there, and hopefully without any casualties.

The senior staff officers, mostly bird Colonels, visit the Aide's office from time to time requesting an appointment to see the general. They test the water. Is he in a good mood or whatever? When I tell them he's fine and in good spirits, they make an appointment, and tell me what it's about so I can give the general a heads-up.

Honesty is the best approach, so if the general is a little ticked off about something that has happened, or is rushed by the schedule, I tell the senior staff officer that perhaps another time would be better. Mostly, they agree unless it's urgent, and wait for a better time. If it's important, "they pays their money and takes their chances." It isn't often that the general is in this mode, and I don't count when I piss him off, because that seems to pass quickly.

General Easton will be making a visit today. He is a four star Army general and in charge of all troops in Vietnam. I have been briefed about these visits, and blunders are not an option. I make sure the pilot, Captain Dick Horner is aware and the chopper is ready to go for the pick up at Da Nang airfield. General Easton will be flying here in an Air Force Lear jet.

The time comes and the general bursts out of his office and is, as usual, charging down the passageway toward the helo pad. I call the LZ and tell Horner to turn it up and then race after the general.

We get to the chopper, clamor aboard, and Horner snatches it off the pad, and quickly away to the airfield.

We meet General Easton who gets to sit in the left front seat of the chopper, while General Barto sits in back with me. Both of them have on radio headsets and are chatting feverishly over the helo's intercom. We head directly for the quarters. This is going to be a working luncheon, no aides or others. Vibes are good; I've got this thing wired. The six P's are the key, screw Murphy's Law.

Dick sets the bird down on the pad outside the quarters. General Barto leaps out as I do, and I'm prepared to assist General Easton descending from the bird if he needs it. When he gets out, General Barto says to General Easton, "Meet my new aide, Captain Quinn. He was one of my company commanders here, and also one of my squad leaders in Korea years ago."

General Easton shakes my hand and says, "A pleasure meeting you, Captain. Welcome to the team. I hope you have those wonderful bran muffins ready for lunch."

I nearly crap my skivvies. Bran muffins? No one told me about any bran friggin' muffins. I managed to croak out, "Yes, sir."

With that introduction, we are off to the house. I think, this is what I've been reduced to, a Marine infantry captain, worrying about Goddamn bran muffins. They go in the front entrance while I gallop through the back entrance and barge into the galley.

I look at GySgt Duncan, and say, "Gunny, you've got those bran muffins ready, right?" I give the impression that I knew about this all the time and am merely checking.

"Oh yes, sir, Captain. Cake, I mean Sergeant Cartwright, got um all ready to go. Nice and hot with real butter. Will just melt in the general's mouth."

I could have kissed the man. I just say, "Ah, good. Thanks Gunny."

They may not look as sharp sometimes as I would like, but they know their business in and around the kitchen. Thank God, for that. I don't want to be a former aide known as the bran muffin dummy, with melted butter dripping from my sawdust brain.

The luncheon goes well. General Easton is pleased with the bran muffins. As soon as he gets up from the table, he heads straight for the galley and thanks the Gunny and Cartwright. That's great. The Gunny and the cook are expecting his visit. Apparently, he does it every time, but it's still appreciated. He comes out of the kitchen, pats me on the back, and says, "Good job. Thanks, Captain Quinn."

"Thank you, sir." I think, yeah, right, as if I had anything to do with it. I wouldn't know the difference between a bran muffin and English muffin, or any other kind of roll, except hot dog and hamburger buns.

He and General Barto head for the study to continue their discussion. I thank the Gunny and the cook again. I clean up quickly, and head for the chopper to wait for the next event. They come out of the house and climb on board. Today, we won't travel anywhere as a trifecta, but rather just return General Easton to Da Nang airfield. He boards his aircraft and departs. We jump in the chopper and head out and about the area.

I'm relieved. Everything went well. I escaped unharmed. Already in this job I feel like the guy at the carnival sitting on the seat above the tank of water, waiting for the thrown baseball to hit the disc and drop me in. However, no dunking today, and we go about the normal business at hand.

We stop at the hospital again tonight. The routine is the same. Last, as usual we stop to visit the intensive care guys. We visit the first two, and then stop at our third Marine in this ward. He is awake, bright eyed, and is anxiously awaiting the general. He is a PFC, black, from Philadelphia, and he's a quad amputee. A mine was the culprit. The general, as well as myself, is shaken.

After the short private ceremony with the Purple Heart and photo, the general leans over and whispers to the young man. The Marine, about eighteen, looks up, says, "Don't worry about me, general. I'm going to be okay. As soon as I get home, I'll be fine." The general chokes up. I think, I wish I had this youngster's guts and optimism. The general spends a little longer talking with this trooper.

As we turn to leave, I wink at him and say, "Hey, I'm from your area. North Philly. Tenth and Lindley. Long time ago. Know where it is?"

"Yes, sir. Sort of."

"Well, okay. You get better, and take care of the city when you get back. I'll be in touch with you before you leave. If you need something, tell them to contact me, the general's aide."

"Yes, sir, but I'll be fine."

"Damn straight you will."

He gives me a quiet "Hoo ah" as I leave. Now I'm in the same shape as the general. I make some notes so I can check on his condition, evacuation schedule, and destination. We move along and finish our visit.

Once outside, I see the general is still visibly shaken. He looks at me, nods. We quietly get aboard the chopper and head to the beach house. We have no guests tonight, so it will just be the four of us for dinner.

At dinner, it's quiet for most part. The general gobbles up his food like a magnet sucks in straight pins. The race isn't important in the evening, because after he finishes, the general will have a cigar at the table, which gives those of us a lap behind a chance to finish our meal. After I finish, he has Gunny Duncan offer me a cigar, which I accept. Strange, he doesn't offer one to the other aides, rather he says, "Gentlemen, will you excuse Barney and me. Thanks."

They leave the table and head elsewhere, carrying their plates with some scrapes remaining. They will return in a short time because, at the general's request, we are going to watch *Gunsmoke* tonight.

He says, "Barney, heck of a day, today. That boy from Philadelphia really got to me."

"Yes, sir. He's got one hell of a fine attitude, with not much reason. He'll be okay, I hope, somehow."

"I hope so, but you follow up with him. You have all the info you need, right?"

"Yes, sir. I do, and I will." I'm learning. This is his way of telling me that if I don't have what I need, he'll make damn sure I'm able to get it.

"Another thing, Barney, check my schedule, I want to have some doctors and nurses here for dinner in the next few days. Do the hospital ship first, then later on we'll get to the Da Nang people."

"Well, sir, your schedule is clear night after next. I can get it done by then, if you'd like?"

"Good, do it." He pushes his chair back, gets up and says, "Let's watch, Chester."

"Yes, sir, let me find Sadowski and the others.

He departs for the living room which is already set up for the show. Movie projector, screen, and chairs, but no Sadowski. The general and I will sit in side-by-side easy chairs, the others in folding chairs, the cheap seats, behind us and slightly offset.

I have to find Sadowski, he's fucking off somewhere. I locate him outside, smoking a cigarette and picking his nose. I motion him inside. Trying to converse with him is like talking to an empty coconut. The good news is that "Chester" goes without a hitch, and with Sadowski, that's an unexpected blessing.

After the movie, the general says goodnight to all and then motions me to his study. "Barney, when you form the invitation list for the USS REPOSE, make sure it's not all senior doctors and nurses. Get some young people, especially nurses."

"Yes, sir. Anything else for tonight?"

"No, good night."

It's nice he treats me differently than Jason and Walt, but the table incident wasn't good. I need to find a way to broach this subject with him or some way to avoid these types of moments. It's not fair to those two.

As I walk towards the aides' hut, I think, Matt Dillion and Chester. General Barto and Barney. Not much difference except for the limp and twang. And Kitty, of course.

CHAPTER TWENTY-FOUR

TODAY THE SCHEDULE IS LIGHT, which means no guests and no traveling. This is an exception, but it will allow me plenty of time to contact the hospital ship, the *USS REPOSE*, to invite some of the doctors and nurses for tomorrow evening's dinner.

The *Repose* was commissioned in 1945, so the ship is an old lady. She served in the Korean Conflict, was decommissioned in '54, and she was recalled in '65. I suppose she is still called "The Angel of the Orient". If not, she should be. She has a crew of over 300 officers and men manning her plus a full compliment, about 370, of physicians, nurses and corpsmen. Simply put, a fully equipped floating hospital.

Thinking of the *Repose* reminds me of a fling I had as an eighteen-year-old Sergeant. I was stationed at Camp Pendleton, California, before going to Korea. On liberty one night, I met a nurse, Ensign Elaine Seitz, a fine looking, twenty-four-year old petite blond. We met at Snyder's Melody Lane, a bar in Hollywood. She apparently wanted to practice patient care on a young Marine. She was stationed at the Balboa Naval Hospital in San Diego. We were with each other often before I left for Korea. After I left, we wrote for a short time, but then I had other plans and stopped writing. She was getting too serious.

After several weeks, she wrote that she missed me and needed to be closer, so she volunteered for duty aboard the *USS REPOSE*, off the coast of Korea. I thought the fling was over so this seemed a drastic step. Fortunately, I never needed to be evacuated to the ship. When my tour was over, I went home and never heard from her again. Hopefully this gal isn't back aboard. It could be embarrassing.

My mind flips back to reality. I radio the ship and speak with the Captain of the *Repose,* and the Senior Doctor. After much haggling with these two, I resort to explaining what the general wants. That is to invite the two of them, then four junior ranking doctors, the Chief Nurse, and five nurse ensigns. I use rank as the criteria in order to get the younger ones. The two old codgers finally catch on.

They give me the names and ranks of those to be invited. Nurse Seitz is aboard; is now a lieutenant commander, about thirty-eight by now; is in charge of nurses; and worse, is on the invitation list. I give them the scenario for the evening. Pick up by chopper, social time will precede dinner with sherry or drinks of their choice, then dinner, and adjourn after for cordials. I give them an estimated time of departure and that it will be by chopper as well. The dress will be the equivalent to our utilities. No strain, no sweat, the dog and pony show is all set. It could be just that with Elaine Seitz coming. Maybe she has forgotten. I had until this moment.

I complete the remainder of my day in peace and quiet, tending to some administrative details such as the general's personal correspondence. I make sure his short, one-page scrawled handwritten letter to his wife is put in an envelope, addressed and mailed. It's the customary one letter a week. He hasn't written his kids since I arrived, nor has he spoken of them. I don't have any other clues or spoken inferences as to these relationships, but something sure seems strange. But, I'll keep my nose clear.

Today is also a non-traveling day. After the briefing, I put the menu and seating chart together as usual for the *Repose* dinner tonight. The menu will be Italian, and the chart is pretty much standard, dictated by protocol. The arrangement is by seniority; hence, the two Navy Captains are seated on either side of the general. Next to one is Lieutenant Commander Seitz, then the doctors who are senior to all of the nurses. The nurses, the young ones the general wanted me to invite, are junior to everyone.

The end result is, all of the young nurses, my harem, are sitting down at the end of the table with me, facing the general. As customary, I take the seating chart to the general for approval. Without looking at the chart he says, "Barney, let's invite everyone to go swimming before dinner."

"Sir, a good idea except we really don't have the facilities for this large a group to change, unless, of course, we put the nurses in the aides' quarters." I'm pleased with myself, and chuckle.

"You'd like that, I bet. You'd probably make Captain Schmidt and Lieutenant Reddick stay in here."

"It's a thought, and no matter the outcome I would have immediate medical help."

"Yes. Well, you're right. Too big a crowd for swimming. We'll forego that idea. Too bad."

"Yes, sir. Have a look at the chart and menu."

"Okay. In a bit."

"Yes, sir." I depart. Regardless of the humor regarding the swimming, the general doesn't like to have someone tell him no, in any fashion. Certainly not a captain, aide or not.

Less than an hour later the general buzzes me into his office. He has the seating chart in front of him, and says, "Barney, you can't do this. I want a nurse on either side of me. Then seat the others, male, female, and so forth. We can't have all the men sitting at one end, and all the gals at the other...all seated around you, I might add."

"Sir, you realize of course, that doctors and nurses are also rank conscious. The two Navy captains in particular. They definitely will want to burrow up in sniffing distance, next to the general."

Perhaps it's the phrase "burrow up in sniffing distance" which causes a drastic change in his temperament. He flushes slightly, frowns severely and fires back, "Doesn't matter. Do as I say, Barney." Regardless of how stern he has become, he still calls me Barney, indicating no bubbles in the pot yet.

"As the general wishes. I'll have it done in a jiffy, sir." I face about, return to the outer office and rearrange the seating chart. While I'm doing this, the general leaves the office to get a haircut and walk around visiting the various offices in the headquarters. I finish, place the chart back on his desk, then send a copy of the new one to Walt at the house so everything can be prepared. It's nearing dinnertime, so I walk down to the pad, re-brief the pilots and return to the office.

Just as I enter, the general buzzes me. He has the chart in front of him again. "Barney, what the hell are you thinking? You probably aren't thinking. You can't just ignore rank at this dinner, for whatever reasons you deem appropriate. These are military people. They expect to be seated by rank. Especially the two captains. It's important to them, to all of them."

"Excuse me, sir. The general's jerking my chain. Right, sir?"

"I don't jerk captains' chains. This isn't comedy hour."

"Could have fooled me, sir."

"What was that?"

"Sir. About the chart, that's the way I had it a few hours ago. You told me to change it so we would have male, female, and so forth. I specifically mentioned the rank factor to you then, sir."

His facial expression changes from one of warmth to one of cold granite. His icy-cold blue eyes are cutting into mine as he retorts, "Damn if I did, Captain."

Captain? Oh-oh. The pot is boiling. He continues, "Sometimes I wonder about you. You need to spend less time being clever.

Now get this chart correct. Seat everyone by rank. I'm leaving for the house to take a swim before dinner."

"General, as you wish. Don't forget, sir, I have to get the security troops to sweep the beach and make a check of the villages on either side first. Please don't go out on the beach until I have it cleared and sentries posted."

"So do it, Captain. Stop telling me what your job is, just do it. And be quick about it. I'm leaving."

"Yes, sir." He comes around the corner of his desk like the pulling guard he once was and blows right past me. I call the pilot, tell him to turn it up, then call the house and tell Lieutenant Reddick, "Get the beach swept, and secured. The general is on his way. He's going swimming."

"Yes, sir. Should I go swimming with him?"

"Sure, and gash yourself real good so you can draw sharks."

"Huh? What? I --"

"Forget it. The answer is no. He'll swim alone. Might cool him off, he's pissed at me again. Besides, you have work to do. The seating chart has changed again.   Captain Schmidt will bring out the updated version. Get the beach swept and sentries out, quickly. If you don't have time to sweep as far as normal, keep him in tight. Only in the area that's cleared. Understand?"

"Me, sir. Keep the general--"

"Yes, you sir. Do it."

"Yes, Cap'n. I'll try but--"

"No buts, only do's."

I change the chart back to seniority, and then give it to Jason, and tell him, "Make the table changes. You attend the dinner in my place. I've had enough of this bullshit. Besides, I smell trouble with the Chief Nurse."

Jason says, "I don't think...the Chief Nurse, what was that you--"

"Don't think, Jason. Just do as I ask and enjoy dinner with all the honeys. Maybe you'll get lucky. There are a gaggle of young chicks flying in, but be careful of the old hen. She use to like young roosters. Go, practice crowing. It's your barnyard tonight. Go. Get, now."

"What was that part about--"

"Never mind. Just go get it done."

Jason turns white and inherits a case of the jimjams. He leaves shaken when I say, "If the general asks, tell him I'm working in the office tonight and will eat here."

"He doesn't know you won't be here?"

"Nope. Go."

I feel a quake coming, but I'll let these two handle the tremors. After all, they're Marine officers.

My flimsy excuse for working late is partially correct. I do have a lot to do because the general's schedule is packed for the next several weeks to include a visit by Martha Raye. However, I have devious motives. First the return of Nurse Seitz. Second, my old battalion commander is here, and over dinner, I plan to convince him to make a case for me to return to the battalion. He'll be seeing the general in the morning on another matter, so he can present his case of having no captains in his battalion, and get me back to India Company.

Just as I sit down to eat with Lieutenant Colonel Reynolds, a messenger from the command center races in and confronts me. I'm to call the general immediately, if not sooner. I think, not another seating change, or Nurse Seitz has stuck a pin in the Barney doll. I excuse myself, hurry to a phone, call and get Lieutenant Reddick on the line. He seems almost paralyzed with fear. He's stuttering and stammering, barely coherent, but enough so that I'm able to determine that I'm to get out to the house immediately. He blurts out, "The general is pissed. He won't begin the dinner until you're here. He's really angry. He was poking his finger in my chest when he told me to get you here ASAP. He's--"

"Walt, calm down. Just tell the general that I have work to do in here regarding his schedule over the next several days. I will eat here, and be out there in forty-five minutes to an hour. Captain Schmidt will be at the table."

"Sir, I--"

"Walter, Captain Schmidt can handle dinner. Just let the general know that Jason will be at the table and can handle everything."

"Oh no, not me, sir. Captain, I'm not telling the general that. He'll kill me. I haven't seen him this angry before. He's always nice to me, but he almost bit my head off. Right in front everybody. You tell him, sir, not me."

"Lieutenant Reddick, settle down. Okay, don't you go near him... just tell Captain Schmidt to give the general this information."

"Sir, with all due respect, Captain Schmidt is basically hiding in the kitchen, staying out of sight."

"Okay, God Dammit. Crap, you two have the courage of field mice. Shoot! I will be out in five minutes or so. I have to get a ride somehow."

"No you won't, sir. The general sent the chopper. It should be there by now."

With that I hear the whump, whump, whump of the chopper blades as it makes its approach to the pad.

"Yeah, you're right. It's here. Okay, I'll be there in less than five. Let the general know...Walt, I'm sorry. I didn't mean to blow up at you."

"That's okay, sir." He sounds like a condemned man that not only just got a reprieve, but got pardoned as well.

In the chopper, Captain Horner is laughing his ass off. He asks me over the intercom, "What's happening, Slick?"

"I think I got too slick." I tell him the basics and he laughs even harder.

"Your two assistants were the color of chalk, and getting paler when I left."

"Did you call a medivac?"

"Nope, not with all that medical help so handy. Here we are. Put on your flak jacket, Slick. You're going to need it."

We set down, settle, shut down the chopper, and I stride into the house as if nothing is out of kilter. The general, all warm and fuzzy, announces that we can now be seated for dinner in that his senior aide has been kind enough to join us. I think, oh shit, it's going to hit the fan after these folks leave. The doctors and nurses look at me as if I'm a virus under a microscope. The two Navy captains are smirking, the doctors are amused, and the young nurses are tee-heeing. Nurse Seitz is staring at me as her memory gears shift, grind and drip oil, or maybe venom.

Walt now has some color back and retreats to the galley where Jason is peeking through the window in the door. They'll eat in the kitchen and slink back to the aide's quarters, not to be seen again tonight I'm sure. There they can work on their courage for breakfast in the morning.

As I sit, I notice the seating arrangement is by rank. The dinner goes well. Duncan and Cake have prepared several different pasta dishes, with accompanying sauces. The aroma of the sauces and fresh garlic bread almost make me forget where I am. The general charms everyone. The doctors and nurses hang on his every word and yarn.

Elaine Seitz is not pleased that I'm sitting among her flock of ensigns. She has been eyeing me suspiciously, but it's now obvious she clearly remembers. She smiles slyly, and mentions to the general, loud enough for all to hear, that we're old friends and use to date. There are several nods, a few looks of anticipation, but no comments. The subject is dropped and I breathe again.

I respond on cue when prompted by the general, as he delights the group with the Da Nang bridge story. His version. He's the star, as he should be. It's his war, his house, and his story. I make some small talk at the peon end of the table, and quietly answer questions from the young nurses about the bridge, enhancing my role of course. As it should be, it's my end of the table. The young nurses seem a little shocked that I was once a warrior. I don't know why. Perhaps because I am so clean and well mannered!

The general doesn't offer the usual cigars since there are ladies present. We adjourn to the living room where the stewards serve cordials. I have a triple brandy. My ambush-trained hairs on my neck tell me I'm going to need it as Nurse Seitz settles in next to me. Unfortunately, this portion of the evening drags on. Elaine, I discover, never married. I sense she would like to give me a chunk of her mind, but restrains herself in this setting. Finally, the ordeal is over.

The general bids his farewell to each, and I see them off. I slowly trudge, like a condemned man shuffling along death row, toward the general's study. The only thing missing is the priest scuffing along behind me, rattling the beads while muttering Hail Mary's and Our Fathers. As I meander back, I can almost hear the beseechments.

I approach the study gingerly, knock softly, and enter. He's at his desk. He pushes the chair away, tilts back with his hands clasped behind his head, and says, "Barney, I guess I kind of flubbed up tonight, didn't I? You had it right the first time. I apologize. Are you okay?"

I'm dumbfounded. Flabbergasted. No trap door dropping

open beneath me, nor am I strapped to a gurney. I can't get a word to come out for a few seconds. Then, finally manage, "Sir, I'm fine, I guess. It's...it's just been a long day. Is there anything the general needs before he turns in?"

"No, Barney. Good job. I think everyone had a good time this evening. Had a few laughs, even if some were at your expense. But, that's you and me, right?"

"Oh yes, sir."

"Anyway, they deserve a good time, and we gave it to them. They take good care of our Marines. We'll do a crew from the hospital real soon."

"Yes, sir, they sure do. I'll get a date set up for the next one. Anything else, sir?"

"Yes. Don't forget, Barney, I'm the general and you're the captain." At this he bursts into laughter, then adds, "By the way, what's the story on the Chief Nurse, Stitch or whatever her name is, and you?"

"Lieutenant Commander Elaine Seitz, sir. Nothing, really. A long time ago. My shadowy past is catching up with me."

"I bet there's something behind that answer. You know, my wife was a nurse when I met her."

"Yes, sir. I know. But this wasn't anything like that. This was just a fling fourteen years ago." I try to chuckle but only manage a weak grin.

"Oh, and Barney. Don't ask Lieutenant Colonel Reynolds to plead your case tomorrow. Save him the embarrassment. You're not going anywhere. You're my aide, until I leave." He laughs again, only harder and longer.

"Yes, sir. Got the picture. Good night, sir."

How the hell did he know?

Once back in the aides' hut, Jason asks, "What'd he say? Are you still here or did he shit-can you?"

"He just apologized, and thanked me. Also, he said I was doing a fine job and to keep it up. But, he's not too happy with you two. Damn, what did you two do to piss him off so bad? Well, don't worry. Good night, guys."

They both turn ashen again. I snap out the light, ignore their muttering, and let it spin dry in their brain-housing group.

As I lay here, the last several weeks flicker through my mind, along with this evening and the bridge sea story. No doubt now, I'm a warrior without a war.

Chapter Twenty-Five

THE LAST SEVERAL DAYS HAVE been both a blur and a learning experience as I live out my non-warrior existence. The general and I have been at odds. The pattern is always the same. He does or says something. I counter. He chews me out or rejoins with a harsh reply and does what he wants, which is his prerogative. Later, he abruptly apologizes or changes his ways. No further discussion, that suffices.

Some issues never change. For example, the calls to Lieutenant General Mueller. Most occur during the evening, Hawaii Time, and General Mueller usually answers in person. When I try to beat the system and put Lieutenant General Barto on the phone while it's ringing, the steward answers the friggin' phone. Every deviation I try, fails. Each time I get chewed-out or sermonized; each time I counter. Later an apology from the general and an implied understanding of my plight. Next call, more of the same.

Other examples are plentiful. The general goes to the Post Exchange without my knowledge to purchase something. Hell, at first I didn't even know we had a PX over here. I thought we were at war. Anyway, no problem, except he doesn't carry any money. I keep it for him, at his request. He shops, comes back and some time later tells me to go pay for his purchases but doesn't say what. When I ask, he tells me the PX Officer knows. When I get there, that's not the case. The only thing he knows is that I'll be along to pay for the shopping spree. I have to return, find out the items from an impatient general and start over.

After a few of these episodes, I ask the PX Officer to make a list. If I ask the general after the spree, he unintentionally forgets some items. When I ask to accompany him, he says, "No, I'm perfectly capable of doing things for myself. Don't need you dogging my trail."

"Well, sir. Take some money with you so you can pay."

"Why should I. That's what you're for." He laughs and we're back to square one. It's a mess, a real pain in the ass. The solution is simple, but mine is not to reason why, mine is...and so on.

The same holds true for his unannounced trips to get haircuts. I can make an appointment, but he doesn't keep it. He just prefers to go unannounced, and then send me scurrying to the shop later to pay. My initial resolution is to watch him when he leaves to see where he's going, but most of the time the barber isn't his first or only stop, so this is not productive. If I follow, it looks silly shadowing him. So, I tell the Vietnamese barber to come to me after the haircut to be paid. He argues saying, "No do. You come here, pay."

"No, after you cut the general's hair, you come to me at the office and I'll pay you. Come anytime, before you go home."

"No do. No cut general's hair."

"Okay. You tell the general you won't cut his hair, and why. Fine with me. We'll see what happens."

"What happen?"

"He'll close your shop and get another barber. Easy."

"Okay, I come, you pay."

"Good, and do a good job on him and me or boo-coo trouble. Con biet?. Now, di-di mau."

"Humph. Okay, no trouble. Not fair."

"Right. Tell me about it, Papa-san."

We're talking the equivalent of about five or ten cents here, but

I still enjoy the nickel and dime wins. He comes to the office to be paid, and sometimes mutters something nasty in Vietnamese. When he does, I make him wait. The muttering stops, at least until he's outside. He went to see Captain Quy once, but the wuss surprised me. He told him to Di-Di.

I get after the household staff to sharpen their personal appearance, except for Alvarez, he's an example. They don't refuse; they just don't try very hard. Worse, they have the general's ear. He tells me to lighten up some. It's always, "Barney, they're just cooks, stewards and drivers. Give them a little leeway."

I counter with, "General, they're Marines first, and they need to take more pride in their appearance. It will spill over into their duties, either way." We disagree, they win, but I keep up my insistence to get at least some improvement. It does slowly, but they still try to slip and slide and enjoy the easy life.

Every once in a while, the general will say something to them to bolster my position. I suspect he really does it so they stop pestering him about me, and so I won't take the next step. I approach the general to allow me to discipline them or get rid of them. We argue. I tell him, "Sir, this is going to come back and bite you in the ass someday."

"You mean, bite you in the ass, Barney."

"Well then, sir. Let me resolve it."

"No, we'll do it my way, for a change. You don't understand."

"Yes, sir."

"What?"

"I don't understand, sir."

I reserve these type encounters for the end of the day so Jason and Walt don't catch any stray shrapnel.

The general instructs me to vary his mode of travel so we don't create patterns. I schedule the use of the sedan in lieu of the chopper whenever practicable. He just won't do it, and always goes to the chopper.

Tonight I schedule the sedan to take us to headquarters in the morning. I tell him, he agrees. Then to force the issue, I tell the pilot not to come to the house in the morning but go directly to III MAF. I figure, if he doesn't see the chopper sitting there, he'll get in the sedan as planned.

We come out after breakfast to the sedan. He starts to walk to the chopper pad. When he doesn't see it, he turns, says, "Barney, where's the chopper?"

"It's not here, sir. We're taking the sedan this morning, remember?"

"No, I want the chopper. Get it here. I'm in a hurry today."

"Sir, by the time I do that and it gets here, we can be at the office, so why not just do what we planned last evening?"

"Get the chopper, Barney, now."

"It's not good to take the chopper everyday, sir. We need to vary how we go and when we go."

"Get the chopper, Captain."

"Yes, sir, but I fail to understand why you direct me to do something, then when I do it, you don't follow your own order. In this case, it's for your own safety."

"Captain, what you fail to understand is who is the general, and who is the captain. That's what you fail to understand. Now, get the damn chopper here, and hurry."

"Yes, sir, if the general insists."

"I am insisting. Stop always trying to get the last word."

"Yes, sir."

He turns beet red and starts to say something, but I'm on the way to the phone. I call Captain Horner, and tell him to bring the bird out here. He says, "You told me he was taking the sedan this morning."

"I did, but we're not."

"How come?"

"Dick, just bring the friggin' chopper out here, will ya...and save me a pound of flesh."

"Okay, on the way, Slick. But, I want to hear about this one."

He does, we fly, and the general doesn't speak to me all day. He grunts replies several times. That's the extent of our conversation. At least the weather is warm.

This evening, as we leave the office, he says, "Barney, lets take the sedan back to the house tonight." This is his apology. When we get to the quarters, he stops, says, "I'm rescinding my order about our transportation. I've rescinded orders before, remember, on the hill." He grins.

"Yes, sir."

"So, I'm doing it again. We'll always take the chopper, unless we just flat can't. How's that?"

"Fine, sir. Will make life easier."

This is his form of an apology, or doing what I suggest. For example, on his next trip to the PX, he has me come along, with his money. Another time, he asks me for some money to get a haircut, and continues this practice. Small victories, but they save me from riding into the valley with the six hundred. The barber is happier. He thinks he won. The PX Officer is pleased. He's at peace. Me, I just wait for another pin in the Barney doll.

The exception is calls to Lieutenant General Mueller. The rule is not the general's, its protocol. For me, it's simple. If the call is during daylight in Hawaii, it's easy to accomplish. If at night there, it's a crapshoot. Sometimes I roll a seven, and sometimes snake eyes.

I'm beginning to understand the general, and my role. I'm not to change. He likes my style. Although I maintain my style points, I just have to get accustomed to being punched around a little before we agree to agree or disagree. It reminds me of the story about the boxer that goes back to his corner after each round, and tells his handler that he is getting the crap beat out of him. The corner man says, "Naw, you're winning every round. He's not laying a glove on you." The fighter says, "Then, keep an eye on the referee, because somebody in there is hittin' me."

Buzzzzzz. . .here we go again, another round.

CHAPTER TWENTY-SIX

THIS MORNING STARTS AS ALL mornings. Breakfast is a race again. I've stopped grabbing my bacon and juice in the kitchen first since I've gotten the stewards to serve us at the same time as the general. I've tried to get the general to eat slower, for his own health, but my requests fall on indifferent ears. Someday, soon, I'll try another supplicating approach. If it fails again, then I will institute my final attack. When in a pogey-bait world, a warrior must find some war to wage, even a minuscule one.

Our day is going to be routine with the daily briefing, paper shuffling, and visiting units in the field. The latter is a favorite of both the general and me. The briefing is over, I tell Jason where the general and I will be going today and remind him that dinner tonight will have some senior staff officers dining with the general. I give him the details, the seating chart and the menu.

The phone rings, I answer, "Good morning, General Barto's office. How can I help?"

A female voice responds, "Hello, who is this?"

"This is the general's aide, Captain Quinn."

"What's your first name, Captain Quinn?"

"Why?"

"Because I want to be your friend, and want to call you by your first name. This is Martha Raye."

"Oh, Miss Raye. Great! What can I do for you?"

"I want to see the general, can you arrange that?"

"Sure, where are you, and when?"

"I'm here at Da Nang Airfield, and how about over lunch. . . but I need some time to clean up."

"Well, I don't foresee a problem but let me check with him to be sure. Do you want to speak with him?"

"No, not if you can handle it, big boy."

"I can handle most anything, but hang on for a sec, okay?"

"Yeah, but, why can't you answer a simple question."

"What's that?"

"Your first name, Captain."

"Oh geez, I'm sorry. It's Barney."

"Good, I like Barney, the name. We'll see about Barney, the person, later. Go check with Walter."

"Hang on."

The general is delighted, and snatches the phone to speak with Martha. He motions for me to sit and stay. It's the same arm and hand signal used in dog obedience training. What ticks me off is, it works. Maybe I'm being overly sensitive. Anyway, they speak for only a few moments, then he hangs up and says, "Barney, we'll cancel our plans this morning. We'll visit the units this afternoon. Take the chopper, pick her up, and get her over to the VIP quarters so she can freshen up. When she's ready, bring her to the quarters for lunch."

"Yes, sir. By chance, did she tell the general where at the airfield?"

"I forgot to ask, and she didn't say. She came up on a Lear, so I imagine she's at base ops."

"Probably. If not, I'll track her down."

I'm out the hatch to fetch Martha and arrange for the lunch. This is a fun, no sweat task. I stop on the way to the chopper and get a VIP room at the officer's quarters that are across the headquarters compound. While there, I call Captain Schmidt,

"Jason, Barney. Slight change of plans. Martha Raye is coming to lunch. Maybe swimming also, so clear the beach area."

"Okay. About noon?"

"Yep. And the general wants you and Walt to join us at lunch."

"The general said that?"

"No, but I thought it would make you two feel loved. Besides I already suspect she's a hoot, and you guys need to have some fun."

"I didn't think the-- "

"Jason, lighten up. He likes you. Try to enjoy life. You and Walt relax today. If you can't, put on some make-up so you don't look like two cadavers propped up at the table."

"He's not much fun to eat with, you know."

"Okay, okay. Enough of this. We're goin' to have some fun today. See you at noon. Don't forget the beach."

Martha Raye is a very special person to the armed forces. She joined the USO immediately after the United States entered World War II and traveled with or for the USO ever since. She visited and performed for troops during WWII, Korea, and now Vietnam. She is an honorary member of the U.S. Special Forces, or has some distinguished standing with them. She visits many of their camps. In fact, she is coming from one of them on this trip. She is a vigorous fifty years of age now, and still going strong.

Martha's not difficult to find. We get to the airfield, then air taxi to Base Ops. I look for the Lear, and then for a small crowd circled around a female in a Green Beret, jungle utes and boots.

I spy the group, and then my mean streak overrides my gentlemanly behavior. I ask Dick to set the chopper down as close as possible to the gathering. I like to watch the Air Force hats go spiraling across the concrete. The wing wipers scatter, chasing their piss cutters and soft caps. Sometimes I hate myself. Not often, and not now.

As soon as we settle, Martha comes walking toward the chopper, stops, and waits until I climb out of the bird. As I come up to her, she puts out her hand to shake. When I start to reciprocate, she pulls her hand back sharply, leaps forward into my arms, gives me a hug instead, and a kiss, full on the lips. She breaks the embrace, leans back and says, "Don't tell the general I flirted with you Barney, he might get jealous. Green Berets and Marines. Love 'em both."

"I don't kiss and tell, and he would have every reason to be jealous. I've fallen for you already."

"I'm a little too old for you Barney, but you better be careful. I'd like nothing better than to have a good lookin' captain on my arm, or elsewhere."

"Whoa, don't tempt me. I have little willpower, and these days probably only slightly more staying power."

"I like the sass. I can see already that you're a little different for an aide. Where did Walter find you?"

"Walter. That's the second time. Is that his first name? I thought it was General. Anyway, he dragged me out of the paddies, cleaned me up, but still can't take me to church."

"Probably can't take you anywhere."

"True, true. Ready to go? Climb up front. We're going to take you on a little FAM flight first, then drop you at III MAF. Have a room for you so you can freshen up, then lunch is scheduled at the beach house. Do you have a bathing suit with you?"

"Do you think I could get 'these' in a suit small enough to carry in my pocket? No, I don't have a suit. But, I am wearing panties and a bra."

"Won't do for swimming at the beach house. So, lunch it will be."

She climbs in front, I jump in the back, and we go on an air tour. We go over the city of Da Nang, out over the bay, over the *USS Repose*, back inland over Monkey Mountain, then down the coast past the beach house to the hospital, and over the USO area at China Beach. Then we head back to III MAF, land, and I stroll over with her to the VIP quarters.

The general takes the chopper to the house. Beforehand, I tell him swimming is out this trip. He hadn't thought of that, but reckons it was a good idea and tells me to keep it in mind. Sadowski and I remain behind with the sedan to bring Martha out to the beach house. I feel a little more at ease referring to it that way now instead of quarters, even though it still makes me feel like we're living in the Hamptons rather than a war zone.

We arrive and have lunch, just the five of us. The food is good of course. Nothing fancy or healthy. Just thick, juicy cheeseburgers with bacon strips and all the trimmings. I eat two; still have some missed meals to make up. We have some iced tea, which has replaced my Kool Aid. Except Martha, she has a martini, jumbo size.

She takes great pleasure in jerking the chains of the aides during the meal. As a result, Jason and Walt, the junior aides, not the general, loosen up and actually enjoy a meal for a change. Martha asks Jason, "What were you before you became an aide?"

He replies, "A jet pilot."

"A fighter pilot?"

"No, an attack pilot. A-4's."

"My, my, my. Am I safe with an attack pilot?"

Jason chokes on a large bite of cheeseburger, needs water, and is still sputtering as Martha turns her attention to Lieutenant Reddick.

After a few leading questions, then a singeing attack, the general says, "Martha, why aren't you picking on Captain Quinn?"

"He's too sensitive."

"What?"

"Well, maybe sensitive is not the right word."

"No kidding."

I mutter, "Sticks and stones."

They let it pass.

The remainder of time at the table takes on more light chatter surrounding the upcoming holidays. The general talks about his favorite subject, the troops, particularly some that he has met at the hospital. After lunch, Martha and the general adjourn to his study and chat for well over an hour. She has several more martinis; the general still has only iced tea. Never drinks during the day, and only one or two on occasion in the evenings.

By the time the session in the study is over, it's approaching mid-afternoon. She is ready to depart on incredibly hollow but remarkably steady legs. The general leaves in the chopper, and I'm delegated to take Martha back to the airfield in the sedan. She's going back to the Saigon area to visit some more Green Beret units in the hinterland. This arrangement is another telltale sign of our relationship. The general leaves to visit units, without me, and doesn't want to take either Jason or Walt with him. When I arrange for Jason to take Martha back, the general insists that I take her to the airfield and ensure she gets on her way safely. This is something else I'm going to change. I can't do this every time, with every guest.

In the sedan, she pumps me for personal information. She is genuinely interested, and I have no doubt she is storing everything I say. She will either use it beneficially, or to jerk my chain on the next trip. As we get out, she says, "Oh, I forgot to tell the general. Johnny Grant is in country and will be up here shortly, maybe tomorrow."

"Yes, we know. He'll be here tomorrow and will be having dinner with the general in the evening."

"He's brought two beautiful ladies with him, Barney. You better be good, or I'll tell Ryley when I get back home."

"Yeah, I know. Wow. He's bringing Diane McBain and Tippi Hedren. Way too rich for my allowance, but I'll enjoy just scoping them out. You know, a can look, no touch type site. Besides, I have to be well behaved."

"Why?"

"Because of you, love."

"You mean because of the general and Ryley, but I'm still flattered. You are a flirt. Goin' to get you in trouble someday, Barney."

"Yeah, I hope. Listen, I believe that's your aircraft over there. They seem anxious to get going. Take care. And next time, bring a swimsuit, and give me more notice. The first is the general's request, the latter is mine. Okay?"

"It's a deal, Barney." She gives me a hug and a kiss, then steps back and flutters her eyes in an exaggerated fashion. She climbs aboard, we wave, and then we're off on our separate ways.

The day has been fun so far. And maybe, just maybe, I have laid some groundwork for making my job easier by asking her to give me more notice. Damn, I've got a lot of people to train. . .stewards, driver, junior aides, guests, and the general. All in a day's work, but it's not over. We have the dinner tonight that shouldn't be a problem, just senior staff officers. They're predictable and sometimes stilted around the general. My job is to set a table that prompts relaxation, and to help keep conversation going at my end of the table.

After dinner, the general presents color photos of himself, inscribed with well-earned complimentary remarks and autographed. Earlier, the general was embarrassed when I suggested this in lieu of III MAF Plaques or Zippo lighters. He resisted as usual. I convinced him this would be cherished, particularly if he wrote some meaningful remarks on them. He put thought and time into this. By the reactions at the table, it paid off, big time.

After everyone leaves, he says, "Barney, good idea. The portraits."

"Thank you, sir. The remarks you inscribed were meaningful to these gents. They have a great deal of admiration and respect for you. It was a good evening."

"Yes it was. Tomorrow night should be fun."

"Hope so. You know, sir, we have a string of these dignitary luncheons and dinners coming up. It's going to cut into our boondocks time."

"Yep. Part of the job. Rather be in the field."

"Yes, sir. Me too."

"I know. Don't go there, Barney. Good night."

CHAPTER TWENTY-SEVEN

THIS MORNING IS A WONTED one, although the weather is cooler. The climate modification doesn't alter the race through mealtime. Lunch with Martha yesterday put the general in a good frame of mind, and the evening went well with the staff officers. He says, between gulps of coffee, "Barney, that portrait idea of yours was excellent. I need to do more of that, don't you think?"

I hate to answer because I'll lose ground in this great food race, but submit, "Yes, sir. With prudence. Special people doing superb jobs."

"Yes, yes. Exactly."

I only grunt so as to not lose any more ground. The collective mood today is light. As a result, the general and I are not locked in verbal combat. Jason and Walt have let their guard down, and don't need any make-up. They are more relaxed at the table. However, one snarl from the general will set their mood back a few notches, but he doesn't growl so the ambiance remains stable.

Today will be run of the mill. War Room briefing, then the general and I will be going north to visit units in the field. We will, undoubtedly, visit either the ship or hospital on the way back. I hope it's the hospital so I can steer clear of Elaine Seitz. Jason and Walt will ensure all is set up for the dinner tonight with Johnny Grant, Diane McBain and Tippi Hedren. They are excited because they will be present for the whole shindig, cocktails, dinner, cordials, music, and optimistically some dancing. They're moving uptown, hell, we all are.

The briefing is over. We chopper north for a full day in the boonies. I don't get as dirty as I would like, but at least dusty. Sometimes I feel I should react like a dog, flip on my back and roll around on the ground. The dust smells and feels good, like my old paddy home.

Johnny Grant has been around show business and the armed forces forever. He broke into broadcasting in 1939, and was in the Army Air Corps during World War II, in radio. He has done so much for the services it would take hours to cover. For example, he made fourteen trips to Korea taking with him Hollywood stars. Now, he is doing the same here with the USO, and sometimes is referred to as the poor man's Bob Hope. Johnny is also known as the Honorary Mayor of Hollywood.

Diane is probably most remembered for her role on Surfside Six, a TV show. She is also in films, is blond, beautiful and young. Tippi, also blond and an absolutely stunning woman, is a film star as well. She is best remembered for her role in the Alfred Hitchcock thriller, *Birds*. She also played in *Marnie*.

The general and I return by early evening. The day went as planned for him, but not me. We choppered north, visited units, and then stopped for a visit with the wounded aboard the *Repose*. My world shrinks again; I come upon Captain Jim Word, a friend of mine, and counterpart from the Barracks. He has been wounded, it wasn't too severe, and he is convalescing until he goes back to his unit. Regardless of my recent past, I'm embarrassed that I'm an aide, and he a warrior.

Also unfortunately for me, Lieutenant Commander Seitz tags along when we reach the ship. She manages to break through the small entourage of doctors and corpsmen that surround the general and me. She gets up in my ear as I take the snapshots. "Are we going to get a chance to talk? I'll be finishing my tour here soon."

I think, not soon enough, but say, "Well, sure, probably, but now is a bad time."

"Oh. Apparently so were the last fourteen years."

I scrunch up my face with furrowed brow and squinting eyes, and glance around to see who is listening and watching. "Look, I've got my hands full right now."

"You didn't complain when they were full before."

"Geez, Commander, this isn't the time or place. If you think it is, see the fourteen years as more than a hint. If not, I'm involved right now. Excuse me. Not here. Not now."

I deliberately move away and close up on the general. He's my security blanket today. Out of the corner of my eye I see Elaine snap around and leave. None of this goes unnoticed. Damn, fourteen years. I may need to dig a deep fightin' hole, better, maybe a sandbagged bunker. This is worse than a rocket attack.

As we arrive back at the house, I see Corporal Sadowski leaving in the sedan to pick up the guests at the USO quarters in Da Nang. I hope he can find his way, because if Sadowski either were, or acted as if he were, any dumber, he'd have to be watered twice a week.

However, Sadowski returns promptly with our guests. Johnny

Grant and the ladies sit around in the living room chatting with the general and sipping sherry. Jason, Walt and I are also participating. After my confrontation on the *Repose*, I feel astonishingly tranquil as I sit between Diane and Tippi, inhaling the fragrances of their perfumes and their very being. My hunter instincts are aroused, and although I consider no prey too large, being an aide relegates me to only imaginary stalking. It's almost as reposeful as a hot cup of cocoa with Parzini and Baronowski, although I must admit I'm not thinking of them now. Maybe later.

Jason and Walt are sitting between the general, and where I'm stashed with the gals. Their attention is focused on the two ladies. Walt looks as if he is close to a heart attack, and Jason is being assailed by anxiety.

We adjourn to the table. I've arranged a candlelight dinner tonight with the white linen in use. Prime rib, mashed potatoes, gravy, green beans and elephant boogers, meaning brussel sprouts, are on tap. For dessert, homemade apple cobbler. The chow and setting are off the page. Bernadette Quinn has done well.

This time I have seated the general between the two women, which has him beaming from ear to ear, and not to mention fumbling trying to seat both at the same time. I come to his aid, and seat Diane. Johnny Grant is next to Tippi on the general's left, and Diane to me, on the right. Jason and Walt are at the opposite end of our round table, but at least they can see the gals, and even through the aromas of the meal they can get whiffs of perfume and soap. In the candlelight, I suppose we are all fantasizing somewhat, I know I am. Next to Diane, I'm engulfed in her femininity. The gentle scent of fresh soap and delicate fragrance of perfume together with her nearness is driving my imagination to warped heights.

The cooks and stewards are exceptionally squared-away and attentive tonight. It looks like I've discovered, rather stumbled upon, their Achilles heel, but I can't arrange this guest list everyday. Sergeant Cartwright has on a fresh, clean apron, and his tall, white chef's hat.

The others are all gleaming and hovering about the table in their not-every-day black trousers and white shirts with bow ties. They take turns serving the meal, gawking at the gals and hovering over them like circling hawks. They are acting like pirates, eyeing their bounty. Corporal Alvarez slips my plate down between my silverware with the deftness of a grease-on landing. I look up and say, "Arrrg, avast matey."

"Huh...Sir?"

I whisper, "Tell the crew, enough is enough."

He flushes a pirate crimson while returning to the galley.

We adjourn after dinner. Cordials are served. I have a triple, laboring under the theory that it will dull my senses and shear my horns. When all are served, the general says, "Barney, put on some music. Maybe the ladies would like to dance."

Diane and Tippi nod and chorus, "That would be wonderful, General."

"Yes, sir. Will do."

Right, so the ladies can dance. Who's shitting whom here? I put a tape on, and the general, bless his soul, asks Tippi to dance. I ask Diane, she accepts. Hummm, does she ever feel and smell great. Whoa, it's been a long time. The closeness of our dancing. The gentle touch of her hand in mine. Her softness and the freshness of her hair as it brushes lightly on my cheek; all of this is whipping my imagination into frenzied desires. I think, Ryley, come save my butt...however, not just yet. Damn, this is tough duty.

As the night moves melodically forward, they are gracious and dance with all of us, several times, but of course, fawn over the general. He keeps looking at me and smiling, as if to say, "See, the old warhorse can still gallop." One time, while we were both up dancing, he even winks at me and grins. He's having a great time, and that means I can wallow in the joy of contentment for more than a few heartbeats.

On the other hand, Jason and Walt look like two foxes about to be let loose in the hen house. The general and I, relinquish the prey, sit with Johnny Grant, and turn the cubs loose. They are stunned into silence as their moment arrives, and can only stumble around the floor for a brief period before Diane and Tippi ask for a refill of their drinks, and sit.

We spend the remainder of the evening chatting about their upcoming tour schedule. Nonetheless, the evening is fun. Photos are taken. We all will now have something to prove the moment. When it's time to leave, the general tells me to have Walt take the guests back, indicating he wants to talk to me before he retires.

The general says his goodbyes at the door. I escort Johnny, Diane and Tippi out to the sedan. Walt is there, holding the car door open, having wrestled it away from Sadowski. I have Johnny go around to the other side, and climb in the back. Then I help Diane and Tippi in next to him. Walt looks crushed. Whatever his plan was, it just came crumbling down around his skivvie shorts. I smile, say goodnight to the guests, look at Walt and say, "I probably just saved you from the most embarrassing moment of your life, and saved your career to boot."

"Thanks, Captain. I really appreciate that. You're a real prince...sir." He doesn't smile, just gets in the front with Sadowski, and they depart.

Returning to the house, I amble to the general's study, knock softly, and enter. "The general wanted to see me, sir?"

"Yes, Barney. Superb job tonight. You're getting better at this job every day. We're on the same wave length, don't you think?"

"Well, yes, sir. Most of the time."

"Yes, well, you need to get on it, all of the time."

"Yes, sir, I'm trying. In my own way."

"Which happens to be strange."

"I admit that, sir."

"Barney, don't forget, Ambassador Buckham is coming tomorrow. I need it to go well. Pick-up by chopper and lunch here. Working lunch, only the Ambassador and I. Then chopper back to III MAF and the airfield. Right?"

"Yes, sir. Everything is locked on. I have briefed everyone twice. You approved the lunch menu this morning, so we're set."

"Good. Well then, goodnight Barney, and again, fine job this evening. I think everyone had a good time, especially you young bucks."

"Yes, sir. And I suspect some old stags as well."

He breaks out laughing, and chokes out, "You noticed. Goodnight, Barney."

"Goodnight, sir." I leave, close the door and head for the aides' hut.

Everything will be fine tomorrow as long as no one, meaning the general, throws a monkey wrench in the works at the last minute. I'll go over everything once again in the morning and then hope Murphy doesn't show up with his law books.

With something this important coming up, I suspect Madame Quy is working feverishly on the Barney doll.

Chapter Twenty-Eight

Dawn arrives not only bringing its scarlet and gold hues, but a portentous day. Ambassador Buckham is going to visit, and of course, the general wants it to go flawlessly. Before breakfast, I again brief the two junior aides about the schedule. Then follow this by going over the menu and arrangements for lunch with Gunny Duncan and the remainder of the household staff.

Breakfast is the same as always, the general inhaling his food, the rest of us chewing. Ryley once told me that her mother taught her to chew each bite twenty times; the general takes twenty mouthfuls, chewing each once. Someday, very soon, I'm going to stage a breakfast race, but this isn't the morning. The mood is too somber because of the visit.

The general asks, "Barney, is everything set for the Ambassador's visit today?"

"Yes, sir. Have gone over everything several times with the people involved. It will go well."

"Okay, good. No mistakes."

"God willing, no, sir."

"No. Captain Quinn willing."

"Yes, sir."

My mind's eye adds, and God and Murphy's Law. Then,

Shazam, we're up and away like Captain Marvel and Billy Batson Junior, racing toward the chopper. As we board, I can see that Captain Horner is not wearing his grungy flight suit but rather his best utilities and has on his game face. We exchange knowing smiles. I'm feeling confident with the game plan, especially since Sadowski is not scheduled to pitch today.

The remainder of the morning is routine. We stay at the headquarters. I check all of the arrangements for the visit one more time. I'm beginning to irritate people with my follow-up practices, but I'm going to make as many trips to the mound as I have to in order to get this inning over.

Ambassador Rodney Buckham visits infrequently, but it's a biggie when he comes. I don't think he's an Ambassador in the truest sense of the word, but it's his title over here. He's actually in the Foreign Service Branch of the CIA, and has been for quite some time. He's an Ivy Leaguer, served in the Army during WWII, and then joined the CIA in 1947.

Slightly before noon, the former pulling guard bursts out of his office and we head for the chopper. It's turning up as we get to the pad, and lifts off as soon as the general is in his seat. After I close his hatch, my foot is still on the portside skid as we bank right. The crew chief helps me scramble aboard. Horner turns, looks, shrugs and smiles.

We make the pick-up at Da Nang airfield; put the Ambassador up front as is usual with important guests, head for the beach house, and land. The general and the ambassador go inside and immediately sit down for lunch.

After the meal, as planned, they adjourn to the general's study for their discussion. While they conduct their business, I check the transportation arrangements again, and make sure the ambassador's return flight from Da Nang is ready. So far, God seems to be on my side. I don't know about Murphy, but I'm checking the tree line because he's lurking about somewhere.

They emerge from the study and head for the chopper. I have it cranking up and think, hot damn, get on board, head to the air field, and I'm home free. As we near the bird, the general says, "Barney, arrange for my launch to take Ambassador Buckham across the river to Da Nang. He has business there."

"Yes, sir."

Are you kidding me? The launch! We rarely use that damn thing. While walking toward the chopper I signal Lieutenant Reddick to get over here on the double. He lopes over and I shout to be heard over the noise of the chopper blades, "Walt, call and get the barge across the river to MAF, ASAP. No screw ups. Get those two anchor clankers movin' at flank speed."

"Flank speed?"

"Yeah, friggin' fast, Walt. Now."

"Yes, sir."

I can't hear him, but I lipread his last response. He races to the house to make the call as we lift off just as I step on the skid, causing me to hang on and be pulled in by the crew chief once again. Captain Horner looks over his shoulder and laughs at my struggle to get in the chopper. Once aboard, my hand signal lets him know that's twice today. Then I change the number of fingers to register my true feelings. The general glares at me for my inelegance. The Ambassador again sits up front. He is either looking out over the China Sea or is lost in thought, so he misses the high wire act and resulting hand and arm signals.

The launch is the Admiral's, and is available to the general. It's tied up across the Da Nang River from our helo pad at III MAF. The general has priority for its use. This is good in theory but it doesn't always work. It is manned by two Seamen. Sometimes they aren't as responsive as I would like. Thinking of this causes me to get a little apprehensive while in the chopper heading to the CP. I know I'm going to need a few minutes, maybe longer, when I get to the CP to ensure the barge is on our side, waiting dockside.

We land at the helo pad, and I don't see the launch tied up on this side. It's still on the other side of the river. Fortunately, the general and Ambassador Buckham head to the general's office. This is an unexpected "huss" for me. I race ahead, get on the phone and call the dock.

"Pier Two, Seaman Deuce Swain."

"Swain, Captain Quinn. Did Lieutenant Reddick call you?"

"Yes, sir. Sure did."

"Then how come you're not here or on the way over?"

"Sir, Seaman Roth is getting us some coffee and will be back shortly. Then we'll crank it up and come over, sir."

"Getting coffee! I don't give a damn about your coffee. Get over here. Now, dammit. With or without Roth, I don't care. Get here as fast as that scow can travel. Do you understand? Pronto, battle stations, ASAP."

"But, sir--"

"No buts, Swain. Now. The general is headed for the river. Now, damnit."

"Ye-Ye-Yes sir. On my way."

I would have felt much more secure with some strong ol' Navy parlance, like an unyielding "Aye Aye, Sir."

Waiting a few seconds, I look out the door of the building and see the barge leaving the other side. I also notice Seaman Roth running toward the dock with something in each hand. He won't be aboard; he's on shore leave this trip.

The swinging door to the general's office explodes open and the general and Ambassador Buckham barge out of the office and begin striding hurriedly toward the dock. Their heads are down in deep discussion, not glancing up at all. Just bent over, looking down or at one another as they talk and move. They are not watching where they're walking and are oblivious to their surroundings.

Troops on the walkway are scrambling to get off the path. When they do get off, they're locked at rigid attention, some saluting, others mesmerized into doing nothing. The general and ambassador hurtle past, not acknowledging the troopers presence, militarily or otherwise. I dutifully trail one pace behind, and slightly to the right. Their steps are so long and quick, I'm forced into a shallow lope. I glance at the launch several times, as it makes its way across the river.

As we near the dock, I see the barge churning against the river's current, creeping along. I mutter, "God, it's not going to make it in time." I hope He's listening and in the mood to help.

Nonetheless, this isn't my genuine fear. I mean, what's a few seconds of waiting. It would be much better for me of course if it were there and waiting for the general, not the other way around. The latter would not be good, but not as frightening as what I'm beginning to envision is about to occur.

The two of them keep steaming ahead, still in deep discussion and not looking where they're stepping. The barge, which I now christen, the *HMS*, or better yet, the *HGS Disaster*, is struggling against the current. *His Generals Ship* is getting close but not here yet. I think, okay, I hope they look up and don't just step off the dock. I'm twix and between, and think I had better say something so they realize the *Disaster* might not be here exactly on time and there will be a. . .exactly. I don't say anything. They wouldn't hear anyway. The hell with it, roll the dice. It's all a crapshoot anyway and I need a prayer answered, or a seven.

The general and Ambassador Buckham reach the dock, step off, and then look down. My head is canted to one side and I grimace in anticipation. Everything seems to be happening in slow motion. The *HGS Diaster* pulls in just as they step. Both have one foot on the dock and the other leg is hovering in mid-air. Their feet hit the deck at the same time. They both stagger as the launch rocks with their boarding. They manage to stay on their feet, grab a highly polished brass side rail, right themselves, and continue their discussion as if nothing out of the ordinary has happened.

Seaman Swain, the coxswain, reverses the props, slows the launch but doesn't stop. His mouth hangs open as if to shout a warning. Nothing comes out. He allows the launch to drift, shakes his head in disbelief, reverses props again, turns hard a starboard, guns the engine and heads back across the river like this pick-up arrangement is simply a well-oiled machine in operation.

The general is accompanying Ambassador Buckham across the river and will be returning immediately. At least that's my hope because I have nothing waiting on the other side and can only hope Ambassador Buckham has made arrangements for himself. Consequently, I just stand at the dock and wait. Inhaling deeply, I catch my breath and try not to think what would have happened if the barge would have been a second or two later. It would have been legendary. . .and my demise. . .and wet.

I mutter a loud, "Whewwww. Damn that was close." I hear foot steps behind me, turn, and see Major Phelan, the Protocol Officer, sliding in beside me.

"Captain Quinn, are you that good or are you just too lucky to believe?"

I look him in the eye, smile, and respond, "Sir, the Captain is just that damn good. You know, plan your work and work your plan. Rehearse, rehearse, rehearse."

"Bullshit." He laughs and begins to leave. After a few steps, he turns and shouts, "Pure unadulterated BS, Barney, and you are the Prince of Bullshit."

Smiling, I think, I like the title. Maybe I should carry a scepter. No, a plunger would be more suitable.

The general returns, smiles, slaps me on the back, and says, "Well done, Barney. Like clockwork. No trips today. Maybe the hospital on the way home tonight."

"Aye Aye, sir."

"Tell everyone, great job. Don't forget the two sailors."

"Yes, sir. Will do." He didn't even notice.

I will be having a word with Seamen Swain and Roth. In reality, I won't be harsh with these two Dixie Cups. It's probably too much to ask them to be ready at a moments notice, or maybe Lieutenant Reddick didn't express a strong sense of urgency issuing his order. Whatever, it was a little too close for comfort today. Swain's recollection of the scene should be enough to make them more prompt in the future and he probably painted an explicit picture for Roth.

I just have to hope that Murphy's Law doesn't get me. I'm convinced that being an aide, at least for this general, is a continual challenge of that law, not to mention Madame Quy and her pins.

God and Barney, one. Murphy, zero.

Quy, idle.

Chapter Twenty-Nine

Tonight is a routine evening after a day of traveling up north, which included stops at several units. We finish the day at the hospital to visit the wounded. Dinner tonight is just the four of us. The general wants to see a movie, so I ask Captain Schmidt to tell Corporal Sadowski to set up the projector, screen, and chairs in the living room.

Jason returns shortly, whispers in my ear, "Sadowski didn't get *Gunsmoke.* He got another film instead."

"What?...Never mind. What film?"

"*Goodbye Charlie.*"

"And?"

"It's a comedy, with Tony Curtis, Debbie Reynolds, Walter Matthau, and...someone else...a singer."

"This is goin' to be Goodbye Barney. Okay. What the hell was he thinking?"

"Thinking?"

"Yeah, you're right. Forget it."

Whatever Sadowski's insane reason for passing up *Gunsmoke,* with my counterpart, Chester, it's done. Although a little leery, I don't see any real harm since this movie could be light and humorous, and has a prominent cast. The singer Jason couldn't think of is Pat Boone.

The general says, "What's all that whispering about?"

"Corporal Sadowski didn't get *Gunsmoke*. He got a movie instead, a comedy."

"Why?"

"He just decided to, who knows why, sir."

"What was he thinking?"

"Thinking. He wasn't. He can't. When he tries, something always ends up in the crapper. Sir, please remember, he's your choice for a driver, sir."

"Hmmpf! What's the film?"

I tell him, and try to convince him it's a good film, and that he'll enjoy it. We all sit down in the living room to watch something different for a change. Jason and Walt are ecstatic. They are not into Matt, Doc and Chester. Miss Kitty holds their attention allowing their imaginations to flicker like newly lighted candles. Since Sadowski wasn't present at the table, he's not aware of the conversation, so he is pleased with himself and starts the projector.

About ten minutes into the film the general shifts around in his chair, grumbles, mutters, hems and haws. I say, "Does the general want something?"

"Matt, Chester, and Doc, not this...this...cra... stuff."

At the twenty minute mark he gets up and says, "Barney, this is stupid, don't you think?"

"Well, it's a little silly but humorous, light. A good break for a change."

"I don't want a break. Just get me Marshall Dillion and Chester in the future."

"Yes, sir. Is the general retiring for the evening?"

"Yes, and if the rest of you want to watch this junk, take it elsewhere. Goodnight, see you in the morning."

"Aye aye, sir. Good night, General."

He departs, closing the door to the study a little harder than normal.

This sounds silly, but he doesn't need this to happen. If he wants to watch *Gunsmoke* each time, so be it. I announce, "Guys, that's it for tonight. Corporal Sadwoski, take the film and equipment and show it in the stewards' hut. Before you leave I want to see you a minute. We're done for the night."

Everyone starts to get up. I get no response from Sadowski. Sensing no movement from him in his seat next to the projector, I look around. The once-pleased projectionist is asleep, so I kick his chair. He bolts upright, startled, but manages to stammer, "Huh? What?"

"The general's gone, Corporal. He didn't like your choice. Wrap this up and take it to the stewards' hut for showing."

"Yes, sir."

"Corporal, listen closely. *Gunsmoke, Gunsmoke, Gunsmoke. Gunsmoke* only for the general. Do you understand?"

"Ah, yes, sir. Cap'n, suppose there's a good--"

"No. *Gunsmoke* only. No exceptions. Not even another shit kicker. Only *Gunsmoke*. Got it?"

"Yes, sir. I guess."

"Noooo...Not I guess. *Gunsmoke*, dammit. Got it? Loud and clear, Corporal Sadowski?"

"Yes, sir."

"Good."

Geez, he's an embarrassment to all Neanderthals. He probably doesn't even know we've discovered fire.

Back in the aide's quarters, I settle at the small desk next to my bunk, and look at Ryley's picture, the one in the bikini. Doggone, she is a beautiful gal. I haven't written in a few days so I pull out some writing paper and begin. I recount some of the uneventful but interesting days that have occurred lately.

I tell her of the Jacques Sully visit. He is a Time Magazine correspondent who lunched with the general recently. He has been in Vietnam for a long time, certainly since it was Indo China and the French were fighting here. He related fascinating accounts of those times, to include the famous battle of Dien Bien Phu. An educational luncheon for all of us.

Then a few days following that visit, we were visited by Moshe Dayan, an Israeli military hero. Again, it was a luncheon with the general, key staff officers, and me. Dayan commanded the Israeli forces that won the Arab-Israeli war of 1956. He was born in Palestine, and in 1939 was imprisoned by the British for his work with a militia group. He was released in 1941 to fight with the British elsewhere against the Vichy government. He was wounded during a battle in Lebanon and lost his left eye, hence his most recognizable feature, the black eye patch.

I also tell Ryley of Captain Dick Horner's departure. His tour is over so he's headed home. He will be stationed at El Toro and will give her a call and stop by for a visit. Dick was replaced by Captain Bill Dunn. He's an Irishman, like me, but from Boston and with a great sense of humor. He likes flying for the general so far. Of course, the general hasn't thumped him on the arm yet, so he hasn't been truly tested. When it happens, and it will, then I'll know if he'll make it okay.

I close out my letter with some not so good news. The general has clearly informed me that I'm not going home at the end of my tour, but will be staying here until he leaves. He doesn't know when that will be. Ryley probably won't like this, nonetheless I believe her to be tough and think she loves me enough that she will hang in there. I assume, if I don't screw things up, we'll have a life. That's a great feeling. I enclose some snapshots Jason has taken of me so she can see that I am healthy and perhaps wise, but not wealthy.

The morning after the *Goodbye Charlie* debacle seems to start innocently enough. I'm up at O-dark-thirty, before the general. Just as I leave the hut, Corporal Alvarez confronts me. He says, "Sir, I've got a situation at the front door."

"What do you mean, situation?"

"There's a Major Bennington at the door and he wants to see the general. Says he's a long time friend."

I think, I don't know about that, but I do know he's the son of a WWII unit commander that the general served under, and greatly admired and respected.

"Okay, I'll take care of it."

By the time Corporal Alvarez and I conclude our conversation I'm at the front door, open it, and greet the major. "Good morning, Major. What can I do for you?"

"I would like to see the general. I'm the son of Colonel Bennington, and a close friend of the general."

"Well, sir, I understand, but it would be much better if you stopped by the office at headquarters a little later, perhaps after the briefing, say about 0900. In the meantime, I'll check the general's schedule again and let you know what's a good time, if not 0900."

"No, you don't understand. I'm a close friend of the general. Very close. If he knew I was here, he would want to see me."

"Is this business or is this just a personal call of some sort?"

"What difference does it make? I am a close, family friend. I want to see him."

Again, I try to dissuade the major, even though he is constantly using the phrase "family friend" and is getting his feathers ruffled. "The general never has people here for breakfast, and beside that, we really eat and run so there is never any time for small talk. We're on a tight schedule in the mornings, sir."

Now the good major, not getting or at least not listening to my message, states, "I think he will want to make an exception for me."

"Sir, I don't believe so. I think you should just come by the office at 0900, sir."

With this, the major straightens up, with a look that tells me he's about to pull rank. He stretches and twists his neck a few times, puffs up like a banty rooster, readying for the attack, and crows, "Captain Quinn, isn't it?"

"Yes, sir."

"Well, Captain Quinn. I'm ordering you to inform the general I'm here, and would like to see him. Do you understand, Captain? Is that simple enough?"

"Major Bennington, isn't it? I will do just that, and in the interest of keeping it simple, sir, I want the Major to understand that this is not a good idea, sir. In fact, it's for sure, a bad idea. I'm trying to follow what the general prefers, and save the Major an embarrassing moment."

"Captain, I just gave you an order."

"Aye Aye, Sir. Major, by your leave." I flick the door closed, hard, leaving him standing outside. At least I can spare him hearing the general's reaction.

As I approach the general's bedroom, he barrels out the door as normal heading for the breakfast table. I hop to the side, out of his way, as he gives me his good morning grunt. I think, this is going to get nasty, Barney ol' boy. I should go back to the front door and do what it takes to chase the good major off before the bloodletting. I mutter aloud, "Naw, he ordered this, so I'll serve it up."

"What's that you said?"

"General, there is a Major Bennington at the front door, insisting on seeing the general, now. I tried to discourage him and offered him an appointment at 0900, at the office. However, he's adamant about seeing you. He insists he's a close family friend. He ordered me to inform you he was here."

The general snaps, "Who? Oh yes. I admired his father. Great

Marine. Served under him, but I don't know his son very well, and actually don't think very highly of him anyway."

He frowns, shakes his head and continues with, "He's not half the Marine his father was."

I think, oh boy, here we go. This is nasty already, and headed for the ugly bin. "Okay, sir, why don't I just tell him to come to the office, or tell him you don't have time today, and to contact us later?"

He pauses for a second. Shakes his head in obvious disgust, reaches up with his left arm, scratches his head behind his right ear, and says, "Damn it, let him in."

"What about your breakfast. Do you want me to have it taken back to the kitchen and kept warm?

"No. Damnit. Just bring him in and serve him breakfast...but next time don't let this happen."

It's not the time for me and my big mouth to point out that I did everything but slam the door in the major's face. Hell, I did that too. I dutifully reply, "Yes, sir." and face about to fetch my pal, the major.

I open the door, and say, "Major, come in, please."

He mutters, "Hummp, of course." And glares at me.

I usher him into the quarters, guiding him to the table where the general is already seated. The major looks at me smugly again, as if saying, I-told-you-so,-you- dummy. Dummy isn't an endearing term to him.

My jaws clamp down tight enough to make my molars crumble. My teeth are grinding away the fillings. They must be producing sparks because I think I taste something burning. I hold my tongue and properly introduce the two, seat the Major, tell Alvarez we have one more for breakfast, and leave it at that.

The general says, "Hello. Well, what do you want?"

Ah, a nice, warm beginning. Good, I'm smiling. This should tell the major something, but it goes right over his arrogant head, rolls down his back, and off his soon to be scorched tail feathers, which are stuck skyward, but will be drooping soon.

As the major begins to answer, with some mealy-mouth monologue, the general is eating. I'm eating, and no one, including the general is listening. The two junior aides are stunned into silence, except for the clinking of their silverware on their plates. I suspect they think I should have kept the major out of this cage at all costs. However, under the circumstances, I can hardly suppress my joy watching the good major commit suicide. To be kind, I should have ensured he had something other than a butter knife.

The major finishes his under five minute monologue, which no one hears. The general gets up and says, "Very sorry, Major Bennington, I'm in a hurry. Barney, lets go." Then he looks at Lieutenant Reddick, who is still dabbling with his first strip of bacon, "Lieutenant Reddick. Host the major, do what you can for him."

"Ye...Yes sir."

I smell tail feathers burning as the general and I leave. I give the major my over the shoulder, see-asshole-what-I-was-trying-to-tell-you look. We barrel out the door and head for the chopper.

Once at III MAF, and after dashing from the helo pad to the office, the general slams on the brakes just outside his swinging door. He turns and says, "Don't let people in the house early in the morning without an appointment or invitation. For that matter, don't let them in anytime."

Ah damn, here we go again. I guess I could just say "yes, sir" and let it ride, but I don't. "Sir, that's what I tried to do, but he ordered me to tell you. I was just informing you of the situation. Besides he kept telling me he was a close family friend. Very close, was the term he used. Then, you, sir, invited him in...and for breakfast, sir."

"Close family friend. Hmmf. I hardly know him let alone like him. Your job is to screen people out, not screen them in."

I sigh, "Yes, sir."

He turns to go, stops, turns back again, and says,

"Last word. Just have to have the last word, don't you? What did I get myself into?"

He turns, enters his office through the swinging door pushing it hard behind him so it almost whacks me on the snotlocker again. I enter, place his briefcase down on the desk saying, "Your briefcase, sir."

"You did it again. Dismissed."

"Yes, sir."

He grabs the arms of his chair, knuckles turning bleach white. I execute a sharp and smart about face, and depart before he can say a word. Outside, I swear I hear him quietly laugh...naw, can't be.

After the morning briefing, and after some soul searching, I ease in to see Major General Cunningham, my friend the Chief of Staff. I tell him of the incident, and a few others, and add, "Sir, I tried to tell you I wasn't suited for this duty. How about just sending me back to my company, and get someone in here who is prettier, has more sense, can keep his mouth shut, and wants to be a war bride."

He bursts into laughter and is close to falling out of his chair he's laughing so hard. "Barney, Ol' Blue Eyes, I mean the general, told me all about this Bennington thing, and the other times you and he have crossed swords. He loves it. He thinks you're doing great and are a breath of fresh air. Just keep up the good work." He starts laughing again, more a howl.

"I take it that's a no."

"Barney, Barney, Barney. Stoop was right, you are a piece of work. Get outta here. Geez, I love your act."

I shake my head and slump back to my desk. My act? Breath of fresh air. I'm not acting, and I can't breathe.

Suddenly, wham! General Barto plunges through the office door, causing the swinging doors to crash against the bulkheads. He's heading for the chopper, and says, "Let's go, Barney."

"Aye Aye, sir."

"Get everything off your chest?" He bursts into a roaring laughter. He continues to laugh as he barrels down the walkway. I grab my cover and pistol belt, and race to catch up.

We are off and running again. People are straining and craning their necks out the windows and doors again to see the act.

Maybe I'll try vaudeville next; I seem to be well suited.

CHAPTER THIRTY

WE HAVE SEVERAL CONSECUTIVE ROUTINE days, meaning nothing of note happens to me, and I haven't pissed off the general. We did have two notable guests for lunch and I write Ryley about these gentlemen.

The first was John Steinbeck, who's nearing sixty-five now. It's not clear why he's visiting, perhaps researching another book. His last was *Travels with Charley*, a travelogue in a truck through forty states. I write Ryley the other aides and I were looking forward to the luncheon. What a huge disappointment. Steinbeck and the general either were preoccupied or maybe clashed personalities. Whatever the problem, it was the quietest lunch experienced at the quarters. Except for the munching of food and slurping of iced tea by Steinbeck and the general, it was as quiet as a morgue at midnight. On a few occasions I tried to stimulate some conversation with open-ended questions, but received only grunts for replies...so much for communication techniques. Each saying "good-bye" were the two longest sentences spoken on their part.

The other guest was Bernard Fall. Among the many books he has authored is, *Street Without Joy*. A story of the French Indo-China War and beyond. The time frame was from about 1947 until 1964. He's working on another book about Vietnam, hence his visit. He will be going up north to the Hue area after his visit with the general. Like Jacques Sully before him, it's keenly interesting to have the opportunity to probe Fall's mind about this country, the French's history here, and this long war. Again, the telling of the battle of Dien Bien Phu was attention-grabbing. The account was the same as Sully's, but Fall had much more detail, probably the result of his research. The contrast of style I suppose. One was a reporter, a journalist...the other an author.

Today, while visiting the wounded at the hospital with the general, we happen to come across a former Snuffy of mine from India Company. After the general awards him his Purple Heart, and gives him the Polaroid snapshot, the youngster motions to me. The general moves away, allowing me the few moments he earlier promised when these situations occur. I say, "Johnston, seen you looking better my man, but I'm glad you're going to be okay. The Doc tells me you'll be up and about in no time."

Lance Corporal Johnston was a rifleman, second platoon. Good kid. Had been hit once before. "Ah yeah, Skipper. I'm goin' to be fine. Might even get a chance to go back and be with the guys."

"Yeah, well, get yourself healthy first, Tiger. Have you written your folks, so they know you're okay?"

"Yes, sir...Sir, did you hear about Baronowski?"

"No, what?" My heart skips a couple of beats.

"He got hit, sir. In the chest. Small arms fire. He's dead, sir. Thought you'd want to know."

I turn away, fight for some air, and take a deep breath, regaining some composure. A tremor runs through my body. It's the same as the weak feeling you get just before you push yourself off the ground to get up in the middle of a firefight. I choke back my feelings as best I can, and turn back to Johnston. It's still hard to breathe, however I manage a, "Damn. When?"

"Same day as me, just about a week ago.

"God Dammit...Damn, I'm sorry to hear this. Real sorry. Dadgumit--"

"Sir, I didn't mean to--"

"No, no...thanks for telling me, Tiger. You had to tell me...you should have. You get yourself well, and if you need something around here, just tell one of these pecker-checkers that you know me and need to talk to me, the general's aide. They'll get in touch quickly, I promise. Okay?"

"Yes, sir, Cap'n. Good seein' ya. You sure were fun."

"Fun? That's a helluva different way to look at it, but thanks, Johnston...I guess. I've gotta catch up with the general or he'll fire me. We have others to visit."

"Would that mean you'd be back in India Company?"

"What?"

"If he fired you?"

"Yeah, I guess or the brig."

"Get fired, and come back, sir."

"God, I wish it were that easy, Johnston."

"Does the general visit here everyday?"

"Almost. He cares about you guys...a lot. Listen, I gotta go. You get well, and, Johnston, thanks for telling me about Ski. Take care."

"Ski didn't have a Mom and Dad you know."

"Yeah, I know, but he had somebody who cared. A teacher. I'll write her. Thanks."

I turn to leave, stop, move back close to Johnston, and say, "You said Ski got hit in the chest with small arms. Was he wearing a flak jacket?"

"No, sir. We didn't have to wear them if we didn't want to. Kinda dumb, huh?"

"Should be wearing them. All the time. Make sure you do when you get back. Okay?"

"Yes, sir, Cap'n."

"Semper Fi, Marine."

My eyes well-up with tears as we move along the ward and into ICU to visit. As hard as I try, my heart's not in it. I keep seeing Ski's face in each wounded Marine. He should have been wearing his flak jacket; it might have saved his life. A CO's job is to keep after that shit, and the hell with the discomfort. It's better than dead, Dammit. Aw shoot! I wish I could have brought him with me.

The general completes his visit, we leave and walk to the chopper. He stops, "Bad news, Barney?"

"Yes, sir." I tell him about Baronowski, and what he meant to me. He pats me on the back, and puts his one-arm bear hug on me as we near the bird. He says, "Let's go home, Barney. We'll eat some dinner, have a drink, and watch *Gunsmoke*. Tomorrow will be a better day."

"Ah, yes, sir. I hope so." A tear wanders down my cheek, I mumble aloud, "Aw Ski, damn it, I'm sorry."

It's early December. While at breakfast, the general tells me to set up a dinner for the Red Cross gals that are in the Da Nang area. He says, "These gals do a great job here, and it's a good way for me to thank them."

"General, how about we include some swimming, then a short cocktail period, followed by dinner. Give them a special night to remember. The aides can vacate our quarters giving them a place to change. We can use the steward's side of the hut."

"Great idea, Barney. Have Captain Dunn attend also, and invite seven so we have a full table. Okay?"

"It's done. If they can make it, I'll get it set for tonight. Your schedule is clear, and it won't be for another several days."

"Okay, good. Let's get to the CP. We're running late."

"Aye aye, Sir." This is the first breakfast that all of us finish at the same time. Maybe the secret is to get him talking during breakfast so he can't suck the plate right off the table.

The general is out and about, leaving me behind to set up the dinner with the Red Cross folks. Jason, Walt and Bill Dunn are excited. Everyone, except the general, is a bachelor. Those three have huge expectations; however, I need to be honest here. These gals do wonderful work, are very nice people, but most are not exactly pageant material. I think Jason, Walt and Bill are letting their warped imaginations go stratospheric. They're having a momentary lapse of reason, or maybe this is a classic case in point of the location of the males' brain. However, it's not my problem tonight. I've got a ticket to our Westminster show this evening... front row, center. Actually, I'm going to be the ringmaster so I will only be using the ticket occasionally.

I make the arrangements. The gals are excited and will be here tonight, hopefully with skimpy bathing suits. The seating chart will be easy. I'll put a RC gal on either side of the general, then stagger the rest of us, male-female. Every female sitting next to at least one guy. After the Navy nurse fiasco, the general trusts me in this regard.

Captain Dunn will pick them up in the chopper, put one up front, six in back and give them a FAM hop around the Da Nang area. The fly-about is Dunn's idea and a chance for The Mean Green Baron to buzz the beaches and show off his flying skills.

The beach is clear, sentries are out, the gals arrive fresh from the circus flight, and the general, along with the others, go for a romp in the surf. I stay inside to ensure all else is ready for the remainder of the evening. When the girls arrived earlier, I made a visual assessment. While the boys are at play, I devise the final seating chart. I ensure the two better-looking honeys, the French poodles, are seated on either side of the general, and intersperse the remaining women around the table. I put the English bull next to me to allow my three associates a glimmer of hope. This flicker of expectation will never be realized tonight, but why snuff out the candle before it melts to its last sputter. There is enjoyment to be had.

The swim, body surfing and salt water fore play, goes well. The general is amused with the ocean frolicking by the younger set. He is surrounded by a few Heinz fifty-sevens, as the poodles are wrestling and being dunked by the handlers. Finally, dinnertime arrives. It is a candlelit table and a dim, cozy ambiance. The general allows a nice red wine with our dinner of T-bones, sticky rice, peas and baked sweet onions. Have to hand it to a couple of these gals, they resist the urge to bury the bones. However, Lady is pleased; she'll have the opportunity to do the job herself.

Cake has whipped up some pumpkin pie since it's between holidays. The stewards are not in an all-out, pirate hovering mode since these women aren't remotely close to the same league with Diane and Tippi. I only say, "Arrg" once to Alvarez as a joke, but I think the bulldog thought I was speaking to her so she barked a reply. The cordials with music and dancing following dinner are the final tantalizing touch.

The general, wise old barn owl that he is, sees what I have been up to, and is smiling from ear to ear during the evening's activities. Jason, Walt and Bill are jostling for position, and when not, are strutting about shaking their combs and puffing up their feathers. We have three Rhode Island Reds in the coop tonight. Everyone is dancing including the general; I decline, mentally bowing to my taste. I act busy, hosting, changing the tapes and ensuring all have drinks...the ever-busy senior aide.

As I watch, it becomes vividly clear that Jason, Walt, and Bill need something other than *Gunsmoke* to occupy their leisure time and lecherous minds. I participate only in conversation with the idle gals, which always includes my dinner companion, since her dance ticket goes unpunched. Goodness and mercy are not part of my make-up tonight.

After a few hours, the general, who has been sitting, talking, for a spell, finally gives me a nod. I say, "Hey, folks, we're having so much fun, I hate to break it up, but the general has work to do and it's getting late."

The general smiles, the guys give me icy stares. The general heads for the front door, and I herd the women toward the door saying, "Ladies, say your goodnights to the general. Captain Dunn will take you back in the chopper." Since this is a full load for the bird, Jason and Walt will remain, which hits them like a bucket of cold water.

The women move toward the door and the roosters are slouching around the coop, tail feathers dragging the ground. Some gals are giggling, and a few look glum. No hanky panky tonight and Bill Dunn knows he can't park in the chopper, although that thought and of him being alone with seven gals has him smiling like the proverbial sly fox.

As the ladies and the junior aides stroll dejectedly toward the chopper, I think...sometimes I dislike myself, not often, but maybe tonight. However, it was fun!

I turn away and hustle to the general's study. "Sir, anything else for this evening?"

"Great evening. I think the gals had a good time. You have a mischievous streak in you, Barney. Maybe even mean."

"Yes, sir. Impish, like a leprechaun, but not mean."

"Oh?"

"Well, maybe a little mean."

"Yes, more than a little."

"I suppose so, sir, but you seemed to enjoy watching the

preening, crowing, and strutting. It's just as well the hopes and aspirations of our three bachelors went down in flames."

"No harm done, right?"

"No, sir, nothing that a cold shower can't cure. Anything else for tonight?"

"Yes. I want you to start thinking and planning ahead for some events coming up around Christmas. First, as you know, Bob Hope and his group will be here. I want to entertain them at lunch one day when they can spring free. In addition, I want to give a nice pre-Christmas dinner for my senior staff, and one for other selected staff members. Give me some ideas for both, and the invitation lists. Additionally, after our holiday period, it will be Tet, so long range, think about gifts I can give to my high-ranking Vietnamese friends. Last, I want to increase our visits to the hospital and the *Repose* as we near Christmas."

"Yes, sir, got it. Anything else, sir."

"No...Oh, is that nurse still aboard the *Repose*?"

"Yes, sir, I believe so...unfortunately."

"You better give her a wide berth. If looks could kill, I'd already need another aide."

"Yes, sir. I'll start wearing a flak jacket again."

"Well, do something, but don't get too close to me. I don't want to catch any stray shrapnel. Good night, Barney."

"Good night, sir." I hear him laughing behind the closed door. It's not that funny to me. He's changing.

I return to the aides' quarters. Jason and Walt are noticeably upset and sulking. Laughing I say, "Tough luck, guys. Bill Dunn has them all to himself, but then, he's had his rabies shot."

They grunt, not sharing in my humor. I ask, "Have you two taken a cold shower yet or do I need to call a Vet?"

I'll have to watch these two; they may petition Madame Quy for a séance.

CHAPTER THIRTY-ONE

CHRISTMAS AND NEW YEARS ARE fast approaching, with Tet, the Vietnamese Lunar New Year, lagging close behind. Being away from loved ones and home this time of year brings down a gray psychological curtain that matches the weather.

This Vietnamese winter day implodes upon us with the rawness of rain that comes with the season. At breakfast this morning, I test my new theory of making conversation with the general to slow down his eating habits. After my first two attempts to engage him in conversation receive only grunts, I'm discouraged. With my third, he says, "Barney, quiet. Let me eat for Pete's Sake."

"But sir, it would--"

"Quiet."

Screw it, quiet it is. Now I'm convinced I'll put my plan into action, soon.

With the general's growling, Jason and Walt have retreated into their table coma state. They ought to ignore the general and relax at these moments; they have nothing to worry about. It's just he and I bantering and jabbing at one another.

We leave for the CP in the sedan because of the rain. I'll send it back for Jason. Then he can sit up front and have the pleasure of the conk shell's company all to himself. If you stand close to Sadowski's ear, you can hear the ocean.

Since there are more units in country now, our daily trips have increased, and as the general asked, we make increased stops at the hospital and the *Repose*. However, not today. Horrible weather. Visibility is virtually zero.

With this in mind, I say, "General, you have a dinner engagement at Division Headquarters tonight. It's the CG's holiday dinner for you. No remarks required, but everyone will expect some type of holiday state of the unit comments. Otherwise, just eat and be merry. If the weather stays like this, and it is supposed to, we will be using the sedan."

"Okay, that's fine. Makes sense."

During the morning briefing the weather worsens. I remind Sadowski about tonight. I call the Military Police and inform them that we will be traveling from the quarters to the Division CP by vehicle. I want the MP's alerted along the way, and I need a couple of jeeps for security. One in front, and one trailing. Not that there is a lot to worry about in this area, but I want to err on the side of caution.

The middle of the afternoon rolls around. It's still pouring. I check all of the arrangements again, and particularly with Sadowski. I remind the general again that we will be using the sedan, and tell him the overall plan. He agrees, so I tell all concerned. It's a go.

Evening comes and all is ready. I have Captain Dunn keep the bird at the CP in case we do get a break in the weather, and the general wants to be picked up by chopper after his engagement. Everything is locked on, tight. I cannot account for Murphy, and can only hope the weather has driven Madame Quy to cover. I think she is a fair weather witch. There is, however, another fly in the ointment, and that is the general.

He is prone to do what he damn well inconveniently chooses.

However, my mental flak jacket is on and I'm prepared for his change of decision if the weather breaks. It will make me look bad if I'm forced to change at the last minute, but that can be the life of an aide. People assume it's just another dumb mistake by the aide, or something along those lines. It's embarrassing, and even grunt captains can have their feelings hurt. Not really, but it sounds good.

The rain has lessened to an unremitting drizzle, with visibility still near zero. We leave the house in the sedan with Sadowski at the wheel. Even though he's been briefed, it's wise to give him instructions once again at the last possible moment, and I do as we start to roll. As I finish, the general says, "Corporal Ski, take us to the helo pad. I've changed my mind."

The nickname, and its warmth of tone, ticks me off because it makes Sadowski think he and the general are big buddies, and he doesn't need to listen to me. Sadowski says, and smartly I might add, "Yes, sir." He glances at me smugly, starts to smile until he absorbs my sub-zero expression, then freezes into a drive and shut-up state.

My mind is racing. Oh crap, what the hell is he thinking? I say, "General, the weather is not that good. The visibility is zero. Captain Dunn can't or shouldn't take off and fly in this weather. It's not smart."

By this time, Sadowski has come to the intersection of the main road, has taken a right, thereby leaving the lead MP vehicle going left, and I'm sure the follow-up jeep driver confused. Both MP's are probably chattering madly away on the radio, trying to recover, along with a comment or two about the dumb-ass aide. This all triggers a better late than never thought. I need to get a radio installed in the sedan. I'm out of communications. How could I have not thought of this? Oh well, tomorrow, first thing. Have to handle my current plight, and quickly.

The general says, "Ah, Barney, the weather is going to change. It will be okay."

"Sir, the weather may change, but it hasn't yet. Captain Dunn will come get the general if it changes. It isn't safe to fly in this stuff."

"It's going to be fine. Stop arguing with me. I've been here a lot longer than you and Captain Dunn. I know what I'm doing."

By this time, we are pulling into the CP area, and a smiling and nodding Sadowski heads toward the helo pad. He's enjoying this.

The problems mount. My guess is that Captain Dunn is not standing by his chopper, but rather is in the III MAF mess drinking coffee and shooting the breeze with someone who is trying to get information or stories about the general. People are always sidling up to the general's pilot, junior aides, or me, trying to get some inside information or interesting repeatable General Barto stories. Some of the field grade officer's probe for humorous or spicy Barney stories so they can later, in a peculiar show of affection, jerk my chain.

The relentless drizzle has lessened to a soaking heavy mist. To me, it's raining; only weathermen would quibble over the degree and turn of phrase. I can see however that the visibility at the pad, and along the river, is still terrible. It looks like a vast gray curtain has dropped over the chopper pad.

"Sir, this is not a good idea. Look, the weather hasn't changed, at least not here. It's socked in. I think we should just turn around and take the sedan as we planned."

The MP's have now showed up with both vehicles, and will surely be asking me shortly what the hell is going on. However, if they have an ounce of common sense, they will stay in their jeeps and keep their brain-housing unit and tongue attachment inside their helmets. Whatever little degree of tactfulness I possess has washed away.

The general gets out of the sedan, and says, "Barney, where the hell is Captain Dunn? Get him and get this aircraft turned up. We're going by chopper."

Screw it, the best I can offer is a sigh and a sarcastic, "Yes, sir. As the general desires. By your leave, sir. I'll fetch Dunn."

I run to the chopper, and tell the crew chief to get Captain Dunn, and tell him we are flying to the Division CP. He looks at me in complete astonishment, eye brows arched, eyes bugging out and mouth open. He partially recovers, and says, "Sir, we can't--"

"Corporal, just go get Captain Dunn. The general says we're going to fly, and we are going to fly, crash, drown, or whatever, so get him out here. And God-damn quick."

He leaves, loping for the mess hall. Within a few minutes the two of them are racing toward the chopper where the general and I are standing in the bone chilling rain, getting soaking wet. I know why I stand out in the rain rather than getting in the chopper, but why the general does, beats the hell out of me. I say, "Sir, why doesn't the general get in the chopper, sir. Stay dry."

He growls, "No, I'll wait here for Captain Dunn. What's taking him so long? Why wasn't he waiting here?"

"My guess is that he'll wish he had, sir."

"What was that?"

"I said he probably thought we were going to follow the plan, sir. Maybe he's getting a cup of hot coffee for himself and the crew chief. Ah! Here he comes now."

When the general sees Captain Dunn's silhouette approaching out of the mist, he gets into the front seat of the chopper but not without glaring at me. He's probably pissed at my smart mouthing and arguing. While climbing in, he slips, bangs his shin, and mutters something ugly. Now, he is pissed.

Waiting until Bill gets up to me, and in my face I might add, I say, "Bill, the general has decided to fly. I have tried to convince him that we can't. That this isn't smart. He doesn't agree with me. So, get in, crank this tractor up, and let's get the first act into the ring."

"You must be crazy. Nuts. We can't fly in this shit. Hell, I can't see but a few dozen feet in front of me."

"Bill, get in and tell the general you won't fly. Argue with him, not me. Or fly. I'm getting in the back and ready for whatever you choose to do. Fly. Not fly. Crash. Screw it." I get in the chopper, look at the crew chief and say, "Where are the life jackets?"

"Huh?"

"Okay, some flippers then."

"Sir?"

"Forget it." I sit and buckle up while Corporal Christopher turns grizzly gray, the color of a mouse's fart with the thought of flying in this crap.

Captain Dunn runs around the nose of the chopper, gets in, and tells the general, "Sir, we can't fly in this weather. I can't see twenty feet. I might be able to air taxi along the river, but I won't be able to get inland to the CP, or back here if necessary. It's way below minimums, general."

"Let's go. Now. It will clear up."

"No, sir, I can't fly in this."

"Yes you can, and will. Go, now, Captain. Right now."

"Sir, the pilot is in charge of the aircraft. I won't fly in this weather, it's not safe."

"I'm in charge. Fly, now, or I'll get someone who will."

So much for pilot authority. Captain Dunn looks back at me over his shoulder with a puzzled look on his face, beseeching me to say something. About the time I'm ready to speak, the general thumps him on the upper arm with his fist, hard enough to rock Bill sideways several inches, and says, "He's not in charge, damn it, I am. Get going."

So here we go. Bill cranks up the bird. The crew chief is on the headset, hanging out the starboard door looking around, another pair of eyes. I am on the other headset, hanging out the port side, peering out as well. I think, maybe I should jump now, before we get too high. Naw, it will make me look bad if we happen to make it. I'd rather die, besides the river looks damn cold and Corporal Christopher hasn't produced a life jacket or flippers yet.

Bill carefully picks it straight up, hovers and turns slowly, then air taxis out over the middle of the river. He hovers here for several seconds, mustering some extra courage and gaining some composure. He visibly inhales deeply. Just then, the general raises his arm and points in a Moses like manner down the river, and over toward the Division CP, miles away. As he does so, the drizzle stops, the mist clears, some of the clouds part, and a ray of moonlight creeps and sparkles across the river. I cannot believe this. We're headed toward Bethlehem as the light beckons and shows the way.

The general glances at Dunn, smiles, points again, turns and looks at me with a know-it-all-posture-and-nod. Captain Dunn turns, looks at me, shakes his head, eases the collective and cyclic, and we climb out toward the guiding light, and Bethlehem. It's magic. I mumble into the headset, "Oh, man, I really need this. Am goin' to hear about this forever."

I hear Corporal Christopher utter, "I don't believe this shit."

A "Me neither" comes from Dunn.

I look at the crew chief in the dark of the rear compartment, shake my head and shrug, then laugh.

I glance out the side of the chopper, and see that Sadowski and the MP's are turning and going to follow our back-up plan. They will go to the Division CP in case the weather changes later. All is well. I'm not going to die tonight. I may get my ego bruised, but I am going to live.

We land. The general attends the dinner. I grab a bite to eat in the galley along with Captain Dunn. We laugh about this, now. The weather is continuing to clear, so I send Sadowski back to the quarters, and the MP's back to their camp. They give me that look, you-are-really-some-screwed-up-captain. I know there are perks with this job, but there are times, and these types of looks, that although they are not warranted, make me feel like an idiot. The mental flak jacket helps, but it only goes to the waist.

The dinner is over and the general comes out to the chopper, climbs in more carefully this time, and off we go to the quarters. We land, and the general and I walk to the house. He looks at me and says, "It's great being a general. The rank carries mystical powers with it, don't you think, Barney?"

"I'm sure. I mean, yes, sir, it surely does."

"Well maybe, Barney. Just maybe. If you will just do what I ask you to do and not argue with me, some of my power will rub off on you, or get to you through osmosis."

I glance at him, and since he is grinning from ear to ear, just say, "I hope not sir, it smells like bullshit to me." I start laughing, pleased with my own humor.

He smiles, shakes his head, and emits a muffled laugh, then says, "Maybe so, but the rain stopped and the skies parted. You can't deny that."

"No, sir. Blessed be the general."

"Amen, and that's the last word."

I think, for now anyway.

As we reach the house, he says, "Good night, Barney. See you in the morning."

"Night, sir." I win.

I get to the aides quarters, and tell Jason and Walt the "parting of the skies" story, with all of the biblical gestures and emphasis that I can muster. Then add from scripture, "Thy toast doesn't always fall butter side down, only when it will be the most embarrassing to thee. Barney 15, Verse 23. Thee remember this lesson."

They mumble something. Who cares what. They will surely get to Bill Dunn quickly in the morning to verify all this, and thereby become believers.

Chapter Thirty-Two

CAN'T HEAR ANY SLEIGH BELLS, but Christmas is drawing near. It means nothing to the VC, only us. It's tough on the troops in the field, so the general picks up the pace of his visits to the units. Since there are events to arrange, I accompany him on only trips to units in the field and hospital.

The two holiday dinners for his senior staff are easy. It's just a case of sorting out the invitees without bruising any egos and then seating according to seniority. I make sure General Cunningham is at both, and have a blend of the various sections at each. Add turkey and all the trimmings, plus Cake's assorted holiday pies, and success is, a "cake walk."

I have a group photo taken and the general will sign one of these for each officer. Both dinners go well. The holiday spirit engulfs the beach house and life is good.

Today is big. For all of us. Bob Hope is in country putting on shows for the troops, and he and his troupe will be here for lunch. All of us are looking forward to this. I know from first hand knowledge, these are immeasurably appreciated. Saw one in

Korea years ago. Bob Hope and his fellow show people get all the gratification they ever need from the troops. There is no better audience for him than troops overseas, and he for them.

The luncheon is a brief respite between shows for them, and a chance for his troupe to meet the general. He and the general have met many times over the years.

At lunch are Bob Hope, Phyllis Diller, Les Brown, Joey Heatherton, and Miss World. The Chief of Staff, Major General Cunningham joins the general, Jason, Walt and me at the table. Bob Hope and Phyllis Diller are on either side of the general. I sit next to Joey Heatherton. She is wearing a short mini dress with a very low cut neckline. I think it's the color of her eyes but I'm not sure since I'm not spending much time looking at either. She is oozing sensuousness that I absorb and inhale in long, deep sniffs through my once broken nose. Oh yeah, she's lookin' mighty fine and smellin' tuff. I managed to slip this seating arrangement past the general. I see him squint his eyes as he looks at the two of us at the table. He'll zap me later about this.

The lunch goes well, and the food is superb. I lose my focus on aide-like duties as soon as I sit down. The conversation after the meal lasts longer than most luncheons, which is fine with me. The time comes for their departure all too soon. I have a chopper and chase bird waiting to take them to their next show. The general and I stand at the pad, and wave them off. When the birds are gone, and the debris from the rotor wash settles, he says, "Pretty slick, Barney, pretty slick."

"What's that, general?"

"You know what. Phyllis Diller next to me, and the gorgeous blond next to you."

"Actually, I had Miss Heatherton sitting next to General Cunningham. It just happened I was on the other side of her. Besides, Miss Diller is senior."

"Senior?"

"Yes, USO rank, or age, something like that."

"That's what I said, pretty slick."

"Okay, you're right, sir. However, it was a great move, and she sure looked and smelled great. Tantalizing. At least that's what General Cunningham said."

"Sure he did. Right. I want that picture. I'm going to autograph it, not her, and send it to Ryley. We'll get this nipped in the bud." He's referring to the official photos taken that I review, pass on to him, and then on to the people in the photo.

"You win, sir. I'll shape up in the future."

"Never mind, I like you the way you are. The two dinners and this luncheon went well."

"Thanks, sir."

"Let's get to work."

"Yes, sir." He glances at me, smiles and shakes his head as we move to the chopper.

This afternoon I have another incident on the phone, with Lieutenant General Mueller, and the general. Damn, it's a real crap shoot trying to get General Barto on the phone first. Today is another example that all success is fleeting.

The general hangs up, and buzzes me. I enter, and before I can say a word, he says, "How come you can do so well with these luncheons, dinners, visits, and the seating of beautiful women next to you, but you can't get a simple phone call right?"

"Sir, I've told you before, it's a crapshoot. Most of the time General Mueller answers his own phone at home."

"Let's see, you're staying until I leave, right? So, maybe, just maybe, you will get it right one time before we go home."

"I don't think so, sir. Murphy's in total control of the phoning."

"Who's Murphy?"

"Murphy's Law. If something can go--"

"I know about Murphy's Law. It has nothing to do with it. You do everything well except this phone call...and the last word thing."

"Yes, sir."

"See?" He stares at me. This time I stay quiet. I think he's kidding, but I'm not sure. Suddenly he burst out in laughter, "Got ya."

"Yes, sir. Got me." We laugh. He's makin' progress.

"Let's go over the phone call as it relates to his visit. He's coming to check on me."

"I doubt that's the reason, sir, but, maybe it's warranted. What do I know?"

"Not much about making phone calls."

Cripes, his salt is showing and he's sharpening his quips. His sense of humor is blossoming. Good. It'll make life easier, at least for me...I think.

The news is Lieutenant General Mueller will be coming for a visit just after Christmas and before the Vietnamese TET holiday. Beside his normal touring of the area, he wants a huge luncheon set up for him with all of the generals and admirals in the I Corps area attending, along with a host of other senior commanders from the various supporting units. He wants a briefing before lunch. The III MAF G-3 will handle the briefing, and I'm to handle the luncheon which is to take place at the III MAF mess, not the beach house. The latter is out of the norm and me handling it will bruise egos, mainly the Mess Officer.

The general tells me who is being invited, and that the Chief of Staff is contacting them, as we speak, telling them the necessary info, and that I will be handling their transportation.

"General, why not just let each one handle their own transportation. Certainly make it simpler."

"No, arrange it. That's your job, plus I've already told them that."

"Well, sir, I can call their aides and tell them to ignore that, and to arrange their own. Much, much easier, less chance for a screw up, and follows a time test axiom."

"What?"

"Keep it simple--"

"Don't you dare finish that thought. Just do what I ask. That should be simple enough, even for you."

"Sir, it doesn't make any--"

"No."

I pause thinking he'll see that my idea is better in just a few seconds. "Sir, if the--"

"What is it about 'no,' you don't understand, Captain?"

"Nothing, sir."

"Stop arguing with me." Pointing to the door, he follows with, "Out."

"Yes, sir."

He grumbles something under his breath. I think, that was close. It came out wrong. I couldn't help myself, which is always a problem for a motor-mouth.

Dinner this evening is quiet. A few comments, some light conversation. Nothing harsh. After dinner, he lights a cigar, and offers three of us stogies as well. I accept mine as a peace offering, and I vow to myself that I will no longer insist on the last word, even if it's only a yes sir, which is natural. Maybe not a vow, perhaps only a mild promise.

A few more comments are exchanged, and then he says, "Barney, how about a film tonight. Do we have *Gunsmoke?*"

"Yes sir, it's all set up, sir."

"Great. Let's adjourn, gentlemen."

We sit, each in our appropriate chair of course. Sadowski

starts the projector. It runs all of fifteen minutes, and then breaks down. He fiddles with it, starts it again, and in seconds it breaks down again. This goes on for three more attempts. Next is a film breakage, so we endure the time consuming splicing and rewinding routine.

Finally, the general leans across the chair toward me, says, "I've had enough. Why don't you send him to Projectionist School? They have one in Japan, don't they?"

"Yes, sir. Don't you remember, we sent him a few months ago? He didn't finish. He was thrown in the brig for being drunk and disorderly in town. Remember, sir?"

"Well, send him again."

"Yes, sir. Can I leave him in the brig should he get drunk and locked up again."

The general turns, and says to Sadowski, "You'll behave yourself this time, won't you?"

"Oh, yes, sir. I learnt my lesson."

Turning back to me, "Send him again."

"You believed that, sir?"

"Yes, send him."

"Yes, sir."

I hope he gets thrown in the brig again. If he does, I'll just leave him there and make up some preposterous story to tell the general. If he believes Sadowski, he'll believe me.

The general says goodnight to us and goes into his study. Jason, Walt and I go to quarters.

As soon as we walk through the hatch of the Quonset hut, Jason asks, "Are you going to send him?"

"Of course, I was ordered to by the general."

"Well, you don't always do what you're told, so I wondered."

"An inspiring thought just crossed my mind." I stand, walk to the center of the hut and say, "Hopefully Sadowski will get into trouble, maybe something really serious. If not, well, at least we will have a replacement driver here. Maybe the general will see how peaceful life can be with someone else."

Jason drones, "He'll be back. He's like a dose of the clap."

"You're right, Jason. And there's not enough penicillin to get rid of him. How's this. You're a pilot. You fly him to Japan, fake an emergency, and have him eject over the ocean."

Then I turn to Walt, "Okay, I've got a more realistic idea."

"I don't think I'm going to like this."

"Trust me; you'll love it, especially as the new GBH-MOAP."

"What the devil is...what was it you said? A GBH what? Why do I have a feeling I'm not going to like this?"

"GBH-MOAP. Lieutenant Reddick, my man, you are now the General's Beach House, Movie Officer And Projectionist. The GBH-MOAP. Geez, I love military acronyms!"

"You're kidding, sir?"

"Nope, you learn to run the projector. You're an Engineer, it ought to be duck soup."

"I'm a civil...You're not kidding, are you, sir!"

"I was, but now that I've heard my own words, it's the perfect solution. You run the projector from now on. Corporal Sadowski is your assistant. He is not to touch anything, even when he returns if we are so unfortunate that he does. That's an order, Mister."

"Cap'n, this isn't fair. I'm a--"

"GBH-MOAP. You will start while Sadowski is gone. The general will realize complete movie contentment and absolute vehicular serenity during this period. You on the projector, and a different driver in the sedan. Sometimes, I love the way my mind functions. Don't you two?"

Walt responds, "You're ill, Captain. Very sick, sir."

Jason says, "Not ill, Lieutenant. Just a little warped perhaps. I think it happens to senior aides. Never see the symptoms in junior aides."

I return to my rack, snap out my table top light, lay down on my bed with a sigh, and say, "Good night guys. Don't you just love it when I get creative?"

I hear muttering from Walt and a low, bass, laugh from Jason. Then, "Sick, very ill."

Chapter Thirty-Three

CHRISTMAS IS HERE. THE LAST several days have held good news for some, bad news for others. Major Paletta is being rotated home, his tour is up. He comes to the office to see me this morning before he heads for Da Nang airfield. He tells me, "Stoneface, this makes three times we've served together. I hope we get another."

"Stoop, my friend, I'm going to miss you around here. I too hope we meet again. In some nice peaceful place, with a golf course. But, no mentoring."

He gives me a bear hug, and says, "I love ya, buddy."

"Don't get sentimental, you big ape. You got me in this spot, and I'll get even when I get back to the real world. You're going to pay for this, big time."

"Naa, you're too easy. I know you."

"Oh yeah I will, Stoop. When we get on the course, you're not getting any strokes. Never again. No matter how much you whine and cry. None. So, save your breath when the time comes."

"So, big deal. My game will be too sharp for you by the time you get back. Remember, you're staying here until ol' Blue Eyes comes home. That might be another couple of years."

"Hey, don't even kid about that. But, you remember, I can always tell Alma you never took those pictures in Hong Kong.

I did, with my camera, but you claimed you did. You were too drunk to take pictures, remember?"

"Oh Jesus, you really wouldn't do that, would you?"

"Damn straight I would."

"Alma would kill me. Okay, Hoss. You win."

We hug again, and he leaves. I'm going to miss the big lug. So will the general. They've been close since their WWII days.

In addition, Major General Cunningham will be leaving shortly, immediately after the Lieutenant General Mueller visit. He will be replaced by Major General Henry Woods. I don't know Paletta's replacement, or General Woods.

The real bad news is that unfortunately, Lieutenant Reddick got cross-wise with the general one day at the house when I wasn't around. It was surprising, since most of the time he could hardly utter a word around the general, much less argue with him. Maybe I was a poor example. Anyway, he was summarily relieved, which is unfortunate and sent back to his unit. I tried to salvage young Walter, but the general was adamant about him going. His replacement is Warrant Officer James Anders. Anders is older than Walt and Jason, but a few years younger than I am. He is not only a junior aide, but more importantly, the new GBH-MOAP.

For Christmas day dinner we have only the general, the two junior aides and me. It is a quiet dinner, reflective for all of us, and followed with cigars once again. We watch two episodes of *Gunsmoke* after dinner, without incident. Anders, being new, and unaware of the history, takes his MOAP responsibilities seriously. I like the show, but enough is enough. My only hope is that Miss Kitty will disrobe, but the chance of that happening is slim and none. The general notices my movie time personnel changes, but says nothing.

The evening passes quietly. I end the day in my corner of the aides hut, opening the present Ryley sent. It's an eight by ten, professionally done, color photograph of her, taken by the fireplace in her home. Signed, "I love you, Barney, Ryley." She's beautiful. I do believe I love her. I write, tell her so again. Put the photo on my table, and snap off the light. A good Christmas.

The day of Lieutenant General Mueller's visit is at hand. The attendees of the briefing and luncheon are two dozen or more high price help. There're more stars coming than there are in the night sky. The list includes Division and Assistant Division Commanders, Wing Commander and the Assistant Wing Commander, Force Commander, Admirals, and the one-star general who is the III MAF rep in Saigon. In addition, the two Navy captains of the hospital ships, and over a dozen senior commanders of the various supporting elements are invitees. They are coming from all over the I Corps area.

The seating arrangements at the luncheon are easy. It is pure seniority. The transportation arrangements are cumbersome, a nightmare for me. I was never able to get the general to change his mind. It isn't just dispatching choppers to make the pick-ups, it's getting them here in a correct order so that those senior don't have to wait on those junior to them. I'd rather fall face down in a paddy than go through this.

But, I've got it arranged. Huge master plan, which I monitor by radio. It's going well, when all of a sudden I realize that an admiral has been left standing at a helo pad in Da Nang. He was just missed in the shuffle of the deck. The pilot went to the wrong place, waited, got discouraged and went back to Marble Mountain, his home base. He forgot to radio me of events until after he got back.

I immediately put Jason on the general's chopper, and send him to get the vice admiral. I hate to, but I have to stay here and finish. Jason will have to apologize on my behalf, and the general's. It will help some. I will apologize personally as soon as he lands and escort him to the luncheon. I'm embarrassed. I hate to screw up. At least things are on track again.

Suddenly, General Cunningham comes storming out of his office, shouting to Lieutenant Colonel Harry Mason, the Staff Secretary, "Harry, Admiral Bohannon has been left standing on a helo pad in Da Nang. Get this squared away. We can't have a three-star admiral just overlooked. This is a major screw up. After you get it squared away, find the person that botched this up and have his ass in front of me, ASAP. Understand?"

"Yes, sir, right away." He's beet red from what he considers an ass chewing.

I say, "Sir, excuse me--"

General Cunningham says, "I don't have time right now, Barney."

"Sir, I can--"

Lieutenant Colonel Mason snaps, "Captain Quinn, the general and I are busy right now. Can't you see that?"

I raise my voice one octave and say, "Gentlemen, sirs. Listen to me. I know who made the mistake." This is the beginning of my, it-was-I-who-chopped-down-the-cherry-tree approach. Honesty always pays dividends. I hope.

The general says, "Good, Barney. Way to go. Who was it, and get him in here."

Lieutenant Colonel Mason's color returns to normal with this new information, and now looks ready to tie this person to the mizzenmast.

I say, "You don't need to look for anybody. It was me. I missed a pick-up."

The general says, "Barney, what--"

"Sir, please listen. I missed it. However, I've got a chopper on the way there now, with Jason on board to ensure we do it correctly, and apologize. Everything is back on track, and running smoothly. Sorry."

Poor General Cunningham, my mentor, my buddy, is just

crushed. His face registers his pain. His boy is the screw up. However, my undisguised admission of guilt works like a charm.

He says, "Oh, well. The hell with it. It will be okay. Good job, Barney. Great recovery. I'll cover for you, smooth it over with the boss, and soothe his nerves."

"Okay, sir. Thanks. I'll go down to the pad and help ease the pain with the admiral, and escort him over to the mess personally."

"Good, Barney. Damn you're slick. Alright, I'll meet you there and add some more oil."

It all works. The admiral is fine. The luncheon, and briefing goes well. The general is satisfied. My good friend from the past bails me out. Life is good.

I also get a bonus. A good friend from my past, Sergeant Major Nelson Kovac, is traveling with the CG, FMFPac, his top enlisted man. We served together years ago at Camps Horno and Del Mar, at Pendleton in Southern California. While the big luncheon is going on, he and I eat in the regular mess. We talk of the past, tell some sea stories, but mostly talk about the troops over here.

Everyone leaves after the briefing in a blur of chopper blades and the roar of engines. Their own aides or support people handle the departure transportation. Lieutenant General Mueller goes his own way, with his entourage. General Barto and I go ours. Their conduct towards one another is courteous, but cold. There is a definite frost in this relationship, and unfortunately I'm close enough to need a knit cap and gloves, or the very least my mental flak jacket.

Murphy's Law won today, or at least took a swing at me. Next up, the TET holidays, and whatever that brings.

CHAPTER THIRTY-FOUR

TODAY STARTS WITH GREY CLOUDS hugging this portion of mother earth, and cleansing her with a misting rain. The air is chilly and raw. The general's mood, like the clouds, is low. His close and dear friend, Major General Cunningham is leaving today. There was an enjoyable dinner for him at the III MAF officer's mess, which turned out to be a warm and robust evening. He was a well-liked and respected man by all.

The general has a small farewell ceremony in his office. After it's over, I walk General Cunningham down to the chopper. Capt Dunn has it cranked up as we approach. I climb in the back, thinking he will get up in the left front seat. He doesn't, rather he climbs in back with me, buckles up, slaps me on the knee, and nods. I motion Captain Dunn to lift off.

We land at the Da Nang airfield where the plane is loading troops for its trip back to the real world. We are standing on the tarmac. I say, "Well, General, this is it. Have a safe journey, and I hope to see you again in the future."

"Barney, thanks. Take care of the boss. Almost all of the old gang are gone, or going. You're it until he leaves. I'm counting on you to take care of the old man."

"I'll try, sir. Sir, I want you to know, I forgive you for the sneaky, underhanded way you put me in this position."

He breaks into roaring laughter. "Barney, we had you tabbed from the day you set foot in Da Nang. Stoop and I only waited until you had a company long enough, because that's what the boss wanted. So, Stoop owes you as well."

"Yes, sir, I realize that. I've already jerked his chain. Sir, take care." I step back and salute. He returns it, winks, turns about and heads for the loading ramp. I'm going to miss him too.

The new Western calendar year begins with a forty-eight hour truce. It is a twittery truce at best, with dubious feelings by the general, and all Marines. There are numerous truce violations by the enemy, at least fifty or sixty as chronicled in the morning briefings. Also, TET, the Vietnamese Lunar New Year is also at hand.

In Vietnam, the calendar is devised based on the regularly changing phases of the moon, something like my mind although it lacks the symmetry. Most Vietnamese have a lunar calendar in their homes to consult for festivals and auspicious dates. This ought to tell me it's seemingly difficult to determine what is when, and when is what. Because of the use of the lunar calendar, the actual days of the New Year vary from year to year. I'm not knowledgeable in this area, and rely solely on our Vietnamese interpreter, and I guess, aide, Captain Thanh Quy.

Banking on Quy puts me on tenterhooks. The good Captain Quy seems more interested in being known as the "General's Aide" among his contemporaries. He piddles away his time trying to impress his wife, the "Dragon Lady", Madame Quy, who is as political as one can be. She owns and operates the laundry business at the III MAF compound, and I think a few other businesses on the side as well.

She has Captain Quy by the nose, and constantly leads him

down her path. He would look good with a ring in his nose, like a small Water Boo. On occasion, she comes to the office and wants, actually demands, to see the general about something or other. I don't let her get comfortable, or stay long, much less see the general. I told her wimpy husband, Quy, to tell her to stay out of the office. He won't of course, he is much too sheepish, so I have to toss her out, and tell her to stay out. The last time I did this, she muttered something nasty in Vietnamese, probably something about my ancestry or my lineage. She might have called me a "dog", since that would be my sign in the Vietnamese zodiac. Maybe she put a curse on me. Based on my experiences so far as an aide, it's a toss-up between Murphy's Law and the Dragon Lady's curse. Or maybe, it's Quinn's Law, not Murphy's.

One of the twelve animals of the Vietnamese zodiac sponsors each Tet, or year, sequentially. Of these animals, one is mythical (the Dragon), and four (the Rat, Tiger, Snake and Monkey) are wild, shunning contact with humans. Seven (the Buffalo, Cat, Horse, Goat, Cock, Dog and Pig) are domesticated. Every twelve years, the sponsorship reverts to the same animal. What year it is, turns out to be a little confusing, for not only me but also it seems for the Vietnamese as well.

The general wants me to go to Hong Kong, as we discussed weeks ago, to purchase gifts, silver, that will be engraved with something signifying the New Year. I consulted with Captain Quy weeks ago, regarding which year it will be. He tells me it is the year of the Monkey.

Not trusting Quy, I ask the other interpreters at the Headquarters. The two of them also tell me it's the year of the Monkey. The mere mention of a monkey gets me to wondering how Sergeant Helton and Chet will celebrate their year. Anyway, after all this checking, I feel confident I've got it wired. After all, these three are educated Vietnamese officers, and it's their country, their customs, their history, so I reason they should know.

Captain Quy helps me with a short, appropriate saying or statement to have engraved on each piece of silver, along with the name of the recipient. Something along the lines of Happy New Year, or Happy Year of the Monkey or some such crap. All in Vietnamese of course. I like the ring of that. Reminds me of the saying about monkeys and footballs, and this thought rekindles memories of Chet and me again, on top of that tracked vehicle.

I go with it and have it typed so when I purchase the silver and leave it with an engraver, it will be easy for him to follow. No mistakes. Having done all this, and aware of Murphy's Law, Quinn's Law or the curse of the Dragon Lady, I have a third interpreter at the Headquarters check the inscription and year again for accuracy. He does and agrees it's correct. Feeling good about this, it's time to embark on my shopping trip to Hong Kong.

Upon arriving in Hong Kong, and after getting settled in a hotel, I immediately get in touch with V. C. Cong, a middle man I met through Stoop while here the first time. He comes immediately to the hotel, we meet in the lobby, go to the bar, and I tell him what is needed and why. I ask V.C. for his thoughts, an Asian, since these gifts are going to leaders within the country, like Premier Ky, Major General Lam who commands all Vietnamese forces in I Corps, the Mayor of Da Nang, and many other Vietnamese officials and dignitaries.

V.C., with me in tow, shop, barter, badger, haggle and finally purchase the various pieces of silver. Striking trays, bowls, serving dishes, and so forth. Not a bad job of selection for a grunt. A wife couldn't have done any better, but of course, I am the woman of the house.

Having completed the purchasing, I get V.C. to find a trustworthy engraver. He does, and we give him the slips of paper with the typed Vietnamese inscription and recipient's name for each gift. I scotch tape these to each gift.

It will take a few days so I relax and do some unwinding. A hotsy bath, massage, and steam cleaning each day is in order. I try to get the stench of Vietnam out of my system, my pores. Even though not in the paddies anymore, the dirt, dust, grime and stink of the country just seem to permeate my body. It goes all the way to the soul, and only time cleanses that deep.

Some R&R is in order as well. If Ryley were here, it would be perfect. Maybe not much rest, but certainly the best of relaxation. However, she's not, so the hotsy bath routine along with a quiet dinner and a snort or two of the ol' barleycorn will have to do.

My nervousness about Captain Schmidt and WO Anders being alone with the general dulls my R&R mood. The general will be just fine, but those two get a little twitchy around him, particularly if he barks at them.

Four days pass and finally the silver is back. It looks good. I check each piece against the typed copy attached. All is well. Time to check my transportation arrangements; pack everything up, head for the airport and my flight back, which will be into Saigon. From there, arrangements are for an Air Force Lear jet to take me to Da Nang.

As soon as I land in Saigon, I call Captain Schmidt. As soon as he hears my voice, I can tell something is wrong. He mutters some guttural sound of despair. I probe him with a touch of a singsong tone, "Jason, you don't sound like a happy camper. You don't seem ecstatic to hear from me. What's wrong?"

"You're...ummmm...you're, umm, not going to like this."

"Of course not, when you begin stammering and sputtering like this. Spit it out, Jason."

"Captain Quy just skulked into the office and informed me that he and the others got the year wrong. It's not the Year of the Monkey but rather, it's the Year of the Goat."

This is a left hook out of the cheap seats! A staggering, breathtaking blow. Maybe I should have seen it coming, but I didn't. My utterance to Jason is a rhetorical question that leaks out of my stunned brain-housing group, "How can those three assholes, not know the correct year of their own friggin' New Year!"

"I guess--"

"Don't bother. I can guess the answer. Jason, do you think that little foul smelling SOB did this on purpose?"

"No, I can't--"

"Naw, he doesn't have the guts. Okay, okay."

At this moment, I remember an old story a former crusty and wise Company Commander of mine, Captain Hugh Davis, told me when I was a second lieutenant. He said,

"Barney, someday when you're a Company Commander, something is going to happen that could send you over the edge. You'll be prone to over react... want to blow up."

He continued, "Someday you'll be sitting in your office, peacefully, everything is going well, and life is good. Then, out of nowhere, the Supply Sergeant will burst into your office and jar you loose from your moorings by saying, "Sir, twenty rifles are missing from the armory."

Before you blow up, take a minute, catch your breath, and tell the Sergeant to "go back down to the armory and count the rifles again." While he is doing that you can pray that he is wrong, and just in case he is correct, take the time to think exactly what you're going to say and do when he returns and reports, "Sir, there are twenty rifles missing from the armory."

This is a twenty rifles situation, so with my pulse now having slowed, I say, "Jason, tell Captain Quy and his two cohorts, who also had rectal cranial inversions, to check again...and then, again. Understand?"

"Yes, but--"

"Quiet. While they're checking, call that dink in the admiral's office, he's a good guy, and ask him the year. Okay? See what he gives us."

"Then what?"

"Well, if Quy is wrong once again. Not to worry. If he has made this mistake, then bring him with you when you meet me at the airfield. Also tell him that before I get there, he better find the best little ol' engraver in Da Nang or wherever, and have him standing by so we can determine if we can get this buffed off somehow, and re-engraved."

"Barney, that's a tall order. Suppose he can't?"

"Tell him I'll kill him with my bare hands if he can't get me some damn good help in resolving this mess he made. I may just bat him around a little bit anyway."

"If I tell him that, he may not come."

"Then kill him yourself. If you don't have the stomach for it, just cold cock him, I'll do it later."

"Ahhh--"

"No wonder the Dragon Lady leads him around by his muzzle, the stupid little shit. I should have asked her the year. She's a pain in the ass but at least she probably could have told me correctly."

"Do you want me to check with her?"

"Hell no, it would make her day. She put a curse on me, do you know that?"

"Huh? A curse?"

"Yeah, she's a witch or something. Never mind. Got to go. The Lear is getting ready to depart. Meet me at the airfield and don't forget, bring that little wimp with you."

"Yes, sir."

He doesn't have to say sir, we're both captains. He's simply being respectful because of my position, and he knows that I'm fuming. Besides it's a way to let me know that it will be done, for sure.

I hang up and head for the aircraft in a state of near rage or panic. I'm not sure which, but I do know, I'm one pissed off Marine captain.

The trip from Saigon to Da Nang is taken up by some relatively sane thoughts of how and why I became an aide. These views are clouded by my imagination, which seems to suggest I just leave, go over the hill as an aide. Just show up in some infantry battalion asking for diplomatic immunity or maybe an Aideomatic sanctuary. Perhaps there is possibly an Aide-de-Camp Protection Society somewhere that will hide me in exile.

As we descend into Da Nang, I compose myself, and mentally set my course of action. If there is a mistake, and I can find an engraver, we will get it all changed in time. If not, I'll approach the general and take my lumps. I might be dismissed as an aide, but that's what I want anyway, so it can't be all bad. Of course, my career might then be a tad slow in progressing over the next several years, but I'm sure duty in Adak, Alaska can't be all that bad...cold, and perhaps I could forge a comeback.

The Lear greases down on the runway and taxis to the tarmac where our vehicles are parked and waiting. After deplaning and directing the unloading of my hopefully not worthless cargo, it's time to see what progress has been made. Jason is here to greet me, along with the worm, Captain Quy. I should stuff him in a bottle of Tequila.

Captain Quy immediately starts to prattle on, trying to apologize. Listening to him is a chore. What I really want to do is reach over and just knock him on his ass, but my training as an officer and a gentleman prevails. Besides, he's hiding behind Captain Schmidt. Finally, my patience wears thin. I step to the side so I can better see the little shit and growl, "You have the wrong fucking year, that's about it, right?"

He whimpers, "Yes, sir."

It's a damn good thing he said sir. It probably saved his life. "Okay, did you find an engraver, and can we get this salvaged somehow?"

"Yes, sir. I find engraver, sir."

By this time, he has inched back closer and slightly behind Captain Schmidt again. He is squinting over Jason's shoulder, cowering like a little rat, and incidentally, that's his Vietnamese Zodiac sign,. I ask, "Where?"

"Da Nang. He can do tomorrow. No sweat."

"No sweat! You little shit, I should-- "

He gets even closer to Jason, who is looking over his shoulder at Quy, and trying to move away but Quy stays with him like a shadow. Taking in a breath, pausing for control, I lean over somewhat, and nudge Jason to the side slightly, and calmly ask, "Quy, are you sure it's the year of the Goat? No mistake?"

"Yes, sir. I check. For sure now."

I look at Jason for confirmation. He says, "I double checked. It's the Year of the Goat."

Quy adds, "It's Year of the Goat. I'm sure now."

I pull Quy by the arm, from behind Jason, up nose to nose with me, and hiss, "Now, you little shit! Well, you better pray this engraver can do the job. Until then, I'm goin' to let you live another day. Think of life only in twenty-four hour segments." I let go of Quy's arm, and he sidles over behind Captain Schmidt again.

Jason sighs, Quy breathes in deeply. He looks like a guy that was just pardoned. I'd rather he pissed his pants.

I think, not yet asshole. "All right. Now, this is what we are going to do. We are going to return to the house. If the general wants to see what I have purchased, and I'm sure he will, we will show it all to him. I don't plan on telling him about the mistake unless it becomes a problem, meaning we can't get it salvaged. Understand? Not a peep."

They both say, "Yes, sir."

"Good, now then, tomorrow, Captain Quy and I will go to Da Nang and visit with the engraver to see if we can get this fixed somehow. Quy, you're paying for this so you better sharpen your negotiating skills."

"I pay?"

"You pay, and guess what? The engraver can practice on your gift, and if necessary, the gifts for your two comrades in crime. I think that's fair, don't you?"

He vigorously nods his approval and understanding. Everything is loaded, so we get in the sedan and head for the house. Sadowski has been busy loading everything, so he is not privy to the screw-up, thank God.

We arrive at the beach house. It's near dinner time, and as I suspect, the general wants to see everything, so we unwrap the gifts, and show the general each item. Then I explain that I will re-pack and re-wrap everything with appropriate gift paper, have the stenographer letter their names on the general's card, and attach these to each box.

The general smiles. He is pleased and comments,

"Well done, Barney, well done."

Jason is still extremely uneasy. Quy is so nervous he is shuddering. His feet are doing some sort of involuntary movement, like a tormented cat trying to crap large fish bones on a marble floor.

For some strange reason, I'm as calm as a small lake on a windless day. Nary a ripple. I figure, with the curse and all, it's the uneasy calm in the eye of the hurricane. I do however feel a pin prick in my butt. I suspect Mrs. Quy is jabbing a pin in her "Barney doll".

The following day, in Da Nang, Quy and I work with the engraver. He is able to buff off the word Monkey and replace it with Goat. It's not perfect, but passable. There is a gap in the craftsmanship between this fella and the gent in Hong Kong, but since its good silver, I think we'll get away with it.

After inspecting the last piece of silver, I turn to Captain Quy, "Captain, you're going to take these to the various recipients and you will ensure that nothing becomes of this mistake of yours. Nothing, and I mean not a sniff, is to get back to the general to embarrass him. Do you understand?"

"Yes, I will do, sir." Once again the, sir, saves him some grief, and the fact that he's standing at rigid attention in a freshly pressed uniform also helps.

In my mind the oriental psyche will grasp this. They seem to be very status conscious and extremely polite. I go on with Quy, "You get to their aides and make sure this works. Tell them you made the mistake, and if it leaks out somehow, you'll be humping ammo in the paddies with the Popular Forces. This is not an idle threat my friend."

Quy nods his agreement. His pale complexion, his

odor, and the look in his eyes cause me to believe he does understand.

Today is Captain Quy's day to shine or select the dimmer switch. The gifts are delivered and all goes well. Time will tell for certain, but it looks good at this point. The general is happy and the recipients are seemingly pleased and appreciative.

The war goes on; Captain Quy gets to live; and my life continues, until the next pin in the Barney doll.

Chapter Thirty-Five

Colonel Roy Thomas, my old friend, has left. Everyone who had a hand in squeezing me into this job is now gone, except of course the general. Captain Schmidt is also leaving. His tour is complete, and he is not only going back to the real world but also will be getting out of the Corps and entering civilian life. He's going to fly for one of the major's.

His replacement is already here and has joined us at breakfast this morning. The general is being congenial today, lulling Captain Jerry Olney into a false sense of well-being. On the other hand, maybe the general has learned a minor lesson, not to scare the crap out of the two new junior aides...at least not yet anyway.

Olney is a recently promoted captain. An infantry officer, not an aviator like Jason. This is a slight change in concept, but not so important as to affect anything. He's young, bright-eyed, and his captains tracks are still shiny. He exudes enthusiasm, which needs to be channeled in the right direction. I will dampen, but not soak, his spirits somewhat by informing him that he is not the general and will not wear his stars when dealing with people. I sense he is prone to do this. This is a common fault of young aides. Admittedly, occasionally, it is necessary in order to get done what the general has requested. Then, I'll do it, but not often.

It's important to have a good relationship with the senior staff. Regardless, if it needs to be done, I'll do it, not Olney.

The general grins, says, "Well, well, Barney. We have a mostly rookie group now, except for us old guys." He's referring to Olney and Anders. They force a smile.

"Not exactly, sir. We could make it an all rookie team if we let some of the enlisted staff go. Perhaps to start, maybe Gunny Duncan and Corporal Sadowski."

"Barney, not again. Drop it, okay?"

"Yes, sir." It was worth the try. "Ready to go, General?"

"Yep, let's get moving." With that we get up and head for the chopper, leaving Olney and Anders to finish their breakfast. They too, like their predecessors are not up to the race. They weren't even close this morning, and the pace was way off the eggs, bacon, toast and juice record.

After the briefing, we head north again. The general wants to visit a CAC unit. This Combined ACtion unit is essentially a Marine rifle squad set in a Vietnamese village. They are there to protect the villagers, live among them, be a part of everyday life, and win the hearts and minds of these folks.

We land at an Army encampment, unannounced I might add, commandeer a jeep with driver and then the general tells me his plan. We are going to head down the road, a good five or six miles, to the Vill. Just the three of us. I say, "Sir, this isn't smart. Going out to a village in the boondocks, in a jeep along a road we don't know much about, with just the driver and me for security. "

"Don't worry, Barney, nothing is going on out here. This will be a walk in the park."

"Sir, I hate to count the number of people that said that over here."

"But they didn't know what I know."

"We don't even have a radio. We need to at least have radio contact with somebody. People here or in the village, or somewhere."

"So, go get a radio, but hurry because I want to get moving."

I go over to the chopper, tell Captain Dunn what's happening, and tell him that as soon as we leave, lift off, and keep us in sight, along with the chase bird. When I return, I tell the jeep driver, "Corporal, go get me a radio, and call signs, so I can keep in touch with the base here in case we need some help. Ensure our pilots know our frequency and call sign."

He says, "Where we going, Captain?"

"Down to the CAC village and visit the Marine unit there. You and I are the security for the general, so get a weapon also, a rifle."

"Dumb. . .real dumb, Captain."

"That's me Corporal. My middle name. Now get yourself a rifle, some ammo, the radio and get back here, ASAP. The general is anxious to leave."

"Yes, sir, but this is dumb."

"Okay, I heard you. Go. Think of this as an adventure."

I go to the chopper and get the AR-15 rifle and four magazines out of the back. This along with my sidearm, the .45 pistol, is as much of an arsenal as I can muster. I think, I should add a grenade launcher. I will have the choppers overhead, but only one is a gun ship. I don't intend to tell the general I'm putting them on station. He will see them soon enough. Hopefully, others will see them too. Ol' Barney may be an asshole, but not a fool.

The Army corporal returns with a radio jeep, and a rifle. I send him back for a couple of bandoleers of ammo. I think that's important; you would think he would have thought of that since he was so intent on advising and cautioning me. While waiting for the driver to return, I give the pilots our frequency and call sign. The corporal's back. I say to the general, "Sir, we're set."

The general gets in front; I jump in back with the radio and my AR-15. We lurch into motion, grinding gears as we zip out the compound, and bounce down the dirt road in a cloud of dust toward the village. He turns in the seat and says, "What, no tanks?"

"No tanks, sir."

"But we have air on station, huh?"

"Yes, sir, and trigger happy."

"Like you."

"I'm not perfect, sir."

"Tell me."

The man has a budding sarcastic sense of humor.

Geez, it sure does smell good to be in the paddies again. Nothing like the tang of the natural fertilization program drifting under my sniffer once more. We pass a peasant woman in the ditch along the road. She just lifts up her dress, cops a squat, looks up and grins at us with those betel nut teeth. Ahhh, home again, just a rural boy at heart.

The village is about five miles down this road, in the middle of nowhere. To be honest, I don't expect to be overrun with any sort of enemy force, but it would not surprise me to have some local VC's start dinging at us. Maybe even get extra brave if they found out some three- star general was out for a Sunday drive in the country.

As usual, the general is right, and this is fine with me. There are no problems, and the troops in the village are ecstatic about the general coming all the way out here to visit. The sergeant, squad leader looks at me and asks, "Sir, is there anyone else with you?"

The idea that he pulls me aside and as others have, questions my judgment, is making me prickly irritable. I just shrug and say, "Nope, just me, the general and the doggie. No big deal, the general likes to travel light."

"Not real smart, sir. Not smart. And you should know better, sir."

That does it...over the line...tripped the nasty switch. I squint my eyes, and give this young, well meaning, fine Marine a hard stare and say, "Sergeant, there ain't nothing out here I can't handle, or haven't handled before. We do this all the time, and as you can see, the general is fine and is safe in my friggin' hands."

I pat the sergeant on the shoulder a few times to lessen the blow, nod and nudge him along next to the general so he can lead him around the village.

The trip goes well, of course, what else. The general decreed it. If he can part the skies, this is a piece of cake. We visit, and drive back to the Army compound, board our chopper, which has returned, and off we go, safe again.

Once airborne, Captain Dunn and I just look at each other, shrug, and smile. The general is sitting in the left front seat, smiling, pleased as punch. He's seen us reacting and has probably read our minds.

A good day. We didn't change the weather or multiply any loaves, but a nice, peaceful day. Gotta love these.

CHAPTER THIRTY-SIX

BREAKFAST IS GOING AS USUAL this morning. I've eaten in the kitchen and have only a piece of toast at the table. Captain Olney and WO Anders are no match for the general. They start late, have too much food on their plates, and have prissy table manners. The general leaves them in his dust, or crumbs as it were. Another win for him; I scratch.

Today is going to be a good day. Nothing planned this morning other than the normal briefing, a PX run, and the Barber Shop routine. Piece of cake. The general is going to a function given by Ambassador Buckham this afternoon, without me. He will go over and back on the *HGS Disaster.* Sadowski will meet him on the other side, and drive him to the event in Da Nang. I will send Anders along to get him out of the house, keep an eye on Corporal Sadowski, and Seamen Swain and Roth who haven't fully recovered from the dockside calamity.

The day across the river goes like clockwork. I meet the general at the helo pad when he returns, and we go to the quarters. There will be no guests for dinner tonight. There is nothing to fear. I have *Gunsmoke* on hand and a highly efficient GBH-MOAP.

Dinner is fine. We eat in quiet, punctuated only occasionally by some idle chatter from the junior aides. They're becoming more courageous with each meal. However, the next time the general growls they will crawl under their helmets again. When we finish, he lights his nightly cigar. He takes a few puffs, then a more leisurely one. He leans back and blows the smoke out and up, unsuccessfully trying for a floating blue ring. He shrugs off his failure and says, "Barney, I met a truly unique woman today at the Ambassador's function. Lucy Caldwell, working here for the USO. She's the wife of Charlie Caldwell, the famous football coach at Princeton years ago. Invite her to dinner tomorrow evening. Do we have anything on the schedule?"

"No, sir. Nothing. I'll contact her in the morning and set it up."

"Good. Barney, you're going to like her. She's a nice person, and is over here on her own. . .paid her way. She's come here to serve the country. To do something for the troops. Just that simple. Amazing, really something, isn't it?"

"Yes, sir. Damn sure is. I'll get on it first thing, and I look forward to meeting her."

We get up, go watch Matt, Doc, Chester and Kitty. No problems, Anders is doing a great job as the GBH-MOAP. Sadowski, school trained or not, is only a spectator and can do no harm except for his snoring.

After I get into the office this morning, I visit Major Phelan in the Protocol Office and do some quick research on Lucy Caldwell, adding to what I already know. She is indeed the wife of the former Princeton football coach. He passed away, however Lucy still resides in the Caldwell house at Princeton. As anyone who closely follows football knows, he was not only the former

Head Coach of Princeton, but also one hell of a person...highly successful as a coach, loved by his players, and highly respected within and outside of the Ivy League and sports community.

I know this because I grew up across the river, and followed a Princeton football rival, the Quakers of the University of Pennsylvania, among others. In 1950, Princeton won the national championship and he was selected the Coach of the Year. He coached at Princeton for some twelve years and had a Heisman Trophy winner, Dick Kazmaier, in 1951. They ran the single wing in those days, so Kaz was a triple threat tailback.

Ambassador Buckham knows her from the past. Lucy is something more than just a former football coach's wife working for the USO.

I track Lucy down in the USO Center at China Beach. I get her on the phone and introduce myself. "Mrs. Caldwell, I'm Captain Barney Quinn, General Barto's aide, and--"

"You can call me, Lucy."

"Okay, Lucy, as I said, I'm General Barto's aide and the general would like you to come to dinner this evening if your schedule permits."

"Don't you want me to come to dinner, Captain Quinn?"

"Ma'am, ahhh, sure, but the general offers the invitations."

"Got ya, huh?"

"Yes, ma'am. You sure did. Well. . . can you make it this evening, about 1800 hours?"

"What time is 1800 hours? I'm not a Marine."

"Ma'am, that's six in the evening."

"Got you again, didn't I?"

"Yes, ma'am, and you will probably continue to, but if you would just give me a yes or no at this time, you'll make my life much simpler."

She laughs and says, "You're still calling me Ma'am. But yes, I'd love to. What should I wear?"

"Ma'am, I mean Lucy, whatever. Meaning, whatever you

wear at work during the day; what you normally wear to meals; or a dress if you choose. The general will be wearing his utility uniform, as I will be. It will be the general, you and the aides for dinner."

"Aides, meaning more than just you?"

She's really jerking my chain, nonetheless, she is charming.

"Yes. The two junior aides, Captain Olney and Warrant Officer Anders will be joining us."

"My, my, my. All those men, and just little ol' me."

"Yeah, I sure hope we'll be safe."

"Ahhhh, a comedian for an aide. Well, good. I'll wear a dress."

"Fine, Ma'am. Now I will-- "

"Barney, may I call you Barney, or should I call you, captain? Or should I call you, Captain Quinn? I suppose, since you're the aide to a three star general, I should call you captain, but, I would prefer Barney. However, more important, you need to call me, Lucy and not Ma'am. Okay?"

"Yes, ma'am, I will call you Lucy from here on out, and you can call me Barney, captain, or whatever you choose, if you will just please allow me to finish my job here. I will be down to pick you up in the chopper."

"Chopper. You mean helicopter?"

"Yes, Lucy, the general's helicopter, his chopper, whirly-bird, his Slick."

"Slick? It's named after you?"

"Geez, Lucy. Give me a break. But, that was good."

"Thought so too. Can you pick me up at the hospital because that's where I'll be late this afternoon?"

"Sure. I will be there at 1745, quarter to six, promptly, and we will chopper back to the general's quarters, up the beach. We will chat first for a spell, and then dinner will be served around 1830 or 1900 hours. Will that be okay?"

"Do you have to use those numbers all the time?"

"Six-thirty or seven o'clock. How's that?"

"Better."

"So?"

"Yes, that will be lovely, Barney. Are you my date, or what?"

"No, ma'am. I'm just the escort. Just the general's aide."

"What a shame, just an aide. Well, okay. I'm looking forward to tonight. Please tell the general I will be there with bells on. My goodness, all these men just for me."

"Yes, ma'am, I mean, Lucy."

I hang up; look over to Captain Olney who has just arrived in the office, and say, "This is going to be something else. This woman is a load."

"How's that?"

"You'll see first hand tonight. I suggest you wear a flak jacket and helmet."

"Huh?"

"And tell Anders to do the same."

It is a beautiful seaside evening. A slight breeze has come up, it's clear, the sunset hues are fading and will, I'm sure, give way to a profusion of stars. Hard to fathom there's a war going on.

Captain Dunn and I chopper to the Da Nang hospital. He radios ahead so they won't confuse us with an evacuation chopper, and also so they realize the general is not coming for a visit. Just two Marine captains, coming to pick up Lucy. Listening to the reply on the radio, they seem to know Lucy. Wonder why? Interesting.

We land, and I jump out to meet Mrs. Caldwell,

"Good evening, Lucy. I'm Captain Quinn, the general's aide. I'm pleased to meet you."

"Hello, Barney, and I you. Do I look okay?"

"You look just fine; just beautiful, Lucy."

"Captain, are you flirting?"

I laugh. She's in good form early. Lucy is well into her sixties, not too tall, sort of grandmother size, and although bright and chipper, the not-so-recent passing of her husband has probably helped to age her more than Mother Nature alone. Her hair is gray, almost white, and worn short for the climate here, I'm sure. She wears wire frame glasses and is ever so slightly round shouldered.

"No, Lucy, I'm not, but if I didn't have a gal back in the real world, I would."

She feigns embarrassment and shyness. I help her climb into the front left seat of the chopper. She'll have a better view there and will probably enjoy it more than just riding in the back like cargo. She does have to pull her skirt up a tad because of the cyclic between her legs. She pretends mortification again, flutters her eyelids, coyly smiles, blushing. This lady is a piece of work.

Bill Dunn lifts off, and we give her a ride up and down the coastline so she can see the hospital, Marble Mountain air base, the USO at China Beach and the general's quarters north of these locations. She's having a ball.

We land, and the general is outside waiting for her. Nice touch. We three enter the quarters and before sitting down, introduce the other aides to Lucy. The general offers some Sherry and we all imbibe. After chatting for a few moments, I get up and move to the piano. The general doesn't look astonished, so I figure Gunny Duncan told him I play.

I bang out three lively tunes, and then finish with *"Ebb Tide"*. I get up and slide back into my seat on the couch next to Lucy. She says, "My goodness, gracious, Barney, who'd ever thunk? That was wonderful."

"Thanks, don't get much chance, or rather, don't take the opportunity much around here."

The general says, "He can play anytime he wants. It's his choice, but he's surprised I know he plays."

"Yes, sir. I am surprised. I only play on special occasions, and this is one of those, Lucy."

The general says, "It is that."

Lucy blushes slightly and says, "Thank you, and to you too, Barney. Very nice."

The general stands and says, "Let's eat, shall we?"

We adjourn to the dinner table. I guide Lucy to the guest book and ask, "Will you please sign the general's guest book before dinner, and at the same time you can glance at the seating chart next to it."

It's my standard pitch to all guests, and one that has never encountered any resistance or remarks. Not so this evening.

Lucy stares for a second, signs her name, then says,

"I have a problem."

"What's that?"

"The book has a column for rank. I don't have one. What should I do?"

Just a little antsy, I whisper, "Lucy, it really doesn't matter. Leave it blank, or put USO down, or anything. You've signed it and that's what's important."

She offers a cunning smile, like a cat that is about to paw at and play with a cowering mouse. "Nooo, it asks for a rank, and it should be completed."

"Lucy, please just put anything in there, and let's get to the table before--"

The general calls out from the table, "Barney, what's going on? Why the delay? Is something wrong?"

"No, sir. Not really. Lucy doesn't know what to put in the guest log for rank. I'm just trying to explain that she doesn't need to complete it, but she is insisting."

The general comes around the corner, looks at the book, then Lucy, and says, "You must have some position there?"

"No, I just help. There are 33 of us, so maybe I'm 33. Is that a rank?"

I say, "Yes, in a way that's a rank, not an age."

Her head snaps around to me and with a grin says,

"Now, Barney, you retaliated, didn't you. Good, you have spunk and a sense of humor. I was beginning to wonder."

The general leaps into the fray with, "Barney what was that about?

"Nothing, sir. Mrs. Caldwell and I went round and round this afternoon."

She says, "Lucy--"

"Okay, Lucy it is...forever."

Lucy finally leans over the guest log and signs in as Number 33. Geez, I just want to sit down and eat. Give me a break here. Captain Dunn has joined us, and the six of us sit, and have a wonderful time.

Some of the time is spent talking about Charlie Caldwell and his record, however most of the time we listen in awe to Lucy telling us how she got here, at her own expense, to serve her country. Refreshing, absolutely uplifting. She goes on about what she is doing at China Beach USO, but more important is what she's involved in at the Da Nang hospital during the evenings.

She visits the seriously wounded in ICU everyday and evening, doing whatever she can to bring them comfort and peace of mind. Just listening to them, writing letters for those incapable of doing so, and often sitting giving them a sense of presence...of caring. She does whatever is possible to alleviate their suffering and ease their mind. She is an angel drifting and hovering among them. She found her niche, her means to serve, or as she says, "I need to repay country, and these Marines that serve her."

The evening ends and it's time for her to return. Not to her quarters in Da Nang, but the hospital for her last good night tour of her wounded Marines. Normally I have one of the junior aides take guests back to their quarters these days, but not tonight, not this woman.

We get back to the hospital; Bill Dunn sets the bird down, and Lucy and I get out of the back where we have been sitting together. She says, "Good night, Barney, and thanks for playing. It was beautiful. You're full of surprises. It's been a pleasure. Do I get invited back?"

"My guess is that you will, and frequently. Good night, Lucy." I turn to leave, then over my shoulder I add, "As long as you behave."

"Barney, I--?

"Gotcha."

She laughs as she walks away, and steps into the Quonset huts serving as the hospital. I think, days like this and a person like this is worth all the pins in the Barney doll.

Lucy Caldwell, one. The rest of civilization, zero.

CHAPTER THIRTY-SEVEN

I GOT CROSSWISE WITH THE general over a request he made one evening at dinner several days ago. He told me to have the engineers build a tennis court on our asphalt helo pad outside the quarters. We argued about this, but the discussion ended with him ordering me to have it done.

I thought it over, and right or wrong, decided to ignore the order. He will never play tennis out there. Just building it would look bad, let alone the general and his aide playing tennis as if they are members of a country club. Besides, the Engineer Battalion has more important things to do. Last, I figured the general would forget the idea.

At lunch today, he raises the subject, "Barney, how's the tennis court coming along?"

"It's not, sir. I never asked the Engineering Officer to start."

"Why not?"

"It's not a good idea. The general will never play tennis. You haven't the time, and if you did, it would look bad...you and I playing tennis when a war is going on. I just decided not do it, sir, and not bother the general about it."

He doesn't buy my logic. He gets angry and we argue some more. Fed-up, he leaves the lunch table abruptly, slams his chair into the wall behind him, knocking down a painting Major

General Lam, the Vietnamese I Corps commander, gave him. A unit plaque some Vietnamese leader had given him also hits the deck and rattles to a halt. The general doesn't seem concerned about these, which is no surprise to me.

We have so damn many of these things displayed around the quarters, and beaucoup more in a storage closet it's hard to account for all of them. It can get comical at times. When guests revisit, I have to scurry about and ensure their gift is on display, and then remind the general to say something to them about it. I don't think he cares much about any of these bounties.

Once again, we don't speak to one another for the remainder of the day. Then, before dinner, while having a drink in exiled silence, and waiting for Martha Raye to arrive, he breaks the quietude, "Barney, you were right, not to build the tennis court. However, you should have found a better way to discourage me."

"Sir, you don't discourage well, so I don't try."

"I guess you're right. Well, forget it...and also disregard converting my launch into a fishing boat."

"I did. It's not your launch anyway, sir, it's the admirals."

"What am I suppose to do with you? You don't follow orders, you're argumentative, and you have to have the last word."

"General, I do follow orders, just not a few of the goofy ones. The arguing and last word thing are character flaws of mine. I'll try to correct them, sir."

"Goofy? Goofy orders! I give goofy orders?"

"Sir, those two were. Perhaps goofy is a poor word choice. Inappropriate might be better."

"Inappropriate is a little better, but there's still the last word thing." He stares at me, pauses, and since I haven't answered, says, "Did you hear me?"

"Yes, sir, but I was trying not to have the last word."

"Fine, be quiet now."

"Yes, sir."

"See?"

"Habit, sir."

"I give up." He leaves the couch while shaking his head, and goes into the study to await Martha. She arrives within minutes, and his mood improves immediately. A dinner of pork chops, sauerkraut and potatoes goes well, and then they retire to his study with drinks in hand.

I return to the hut along with Olney and Anders. As I sit here, waiting for Martha to conclude her visit, I reflect on another recent incident which angered the general, and rightfully so.

Two days ago, we had a luncheon for some dignitaries. Just so happened, we had a different chase bird pilot assigned. Before lunch, as the chase bird was leaving to get fuel, I cautioned the new pilot to be careful setting down at the Beach House because of the chain-linked fence and the LZ being a tight fit. I told him to land in spot two, and once in, just sit, don't try to move the bird around. I reminded him he had a full load of people after lunch so don't take on too much fuel.

He wasn't paying attention to me, a grunt, telling him anything about flying choppers. This was accentuated by several telltale indicators; the tugging at his gloves with his head down, flinging his white scarf back over his shoulder, and his bored look when nodding as I spoke.

Well, Andy the Ace, came back and landed. Apparently, he didn't like the way he positioned the bird on the pad, so he tried to reset it. He strayed slightly in the hover and caught the tail rotor on the chain link fence.

I was at lunch with the general and a full table of congressmen on a junket when we heard the explosion. That boom was followed by a loud clunk on the roof. This was closely followed by the clanging of silverware being dropped by several guests, along with a few cups of coffee splashing and clattering to the table. My first thought was, we're being mortared, and luckily the one on the roof was a dud.

The general looked at me and without missing a bite said, "See what that's about," and went on with the luncheon.

I went outside, found black smoke billowing, and flames still shooting skyward. What remained of the chopper was scattered over the pad, outside the fence line, in the Seal compound, and one piece of a tail rotor on the beach house roof. The biggest pieces intact were the engine and main rotor blades. The pilot, co-pilot, and crew chief were standing off to the side. The sound of sirens told me that fire trucks and emergency vehicles were on the way. How they knew was anybody's guess. Probably Anders or Olney called them from the hut.

I went up to the pilot, and asked him, "Is everyone okay? Anyone injured?"

"No one hurt, Captain."

"That's good news. Now, tell me, Ace, what happened."

He did, and all I could think to say was, "You just couldn't listen, could you, hotshot?"

"Captain, I figured I could--"

"Please, spare me, Lieutenant. Get this mess cleaned up and do what you're suppose to when you have an accident."

"Cap'n, you --"

"Did you follow my instructions?"

"Well, sir, I was just--"

"I bet. Tell it to your CO, and the crash investigators. Did you have a full load of fuel? And did you try to move after you luckily got in here?"

"Yes, but I--"

"Stop, don't say anymore. Enough."

We got some vehicles out to the house, took the general and his group to the CP, met Captain Dunn and another bird there. The trip went on as scheduled. Fortunately, Bill Dunn wasn't sitting at the pad when this occurred so the general's bird was okay. I told Dunn about my earlier conversation with Andy the Ace. He was furious and said he'd take care of the situation back at the squadron.

The general was not pleased with this incident, and chewed me down to the bone. He deemed it my fault. We argued, he got angry, and we weren't speaking again until that evening. The ending was the same. Later he told me that I was right, forget it, keep up the good job, and disappeared into his study. Dinner guests arrived, it went fine, and we were buddies again. The cycle seems constant, but my scars are increasing, and the bites on my ass are leaving me skittish.

My reflective mood is cut short by the sound of the buzzer going off in the aide's hut. It sounds like some giant, prehistoric insect. I snap up, straighten my unnie, and head for the general's study. Either Martha is ready to leave, or he needs something.

I tap lightly on the study door, the general says, "Come in, Barney." He turns to Martha who is sitting in one of the easy chairs and says, slightly slurred, "Don't worry, Martha, Barney can do anything."

My mind is racing with this ominous statement, trying to decide whether to bob, weave, or both. He turns to me and says, "Barney, Martha has a problem. I told her you can solve it. Go ahead, tell him, Martha."

Martha waves a drink around in one hand and with the other, reaches in the top pocket of her jungle utilities and pulls out a crumpled, soggy, paper napkin. "Barney, dear. I was visiting a Special Forces Camp earlier today, down south, somewhere." She is slurring every word. I love her; however, she's half in the bag, maybe further. She continues, "I met an Army Specialist First

Class today. His wife is pregnant and in the hospital delivering a child. As we speak, I think. I want to find out how she's doing, and how the child is, or what it is, or...you know, whatever. Can you find out?"

The general chimes in, "Of course he can. Barney can do anything, and find out anything. He'll just call."

I ask, "Martha, what is the man's name, and his wife's name?"

"I forget, but I wrote it down on this napkin." She hands it to me. It is not only crumpled and soggy, but the name, which was written in ink, has now run into enough blots and streaks to look like an aerial photo of the Mississippi Delta.

I look at this mess, close my eyes for a second, and inhale deeply. Martha adds, "I remember now, his name is Smith. . .Specialist First Class Smith." She smiles with great pride with this piece of enlightening information.

"Where were you visiting today, Ma'am?"

"I forget."

"Do you remember about where it was?"

"No...Yes, down south...I think...maybe."

"What's his wife's name, Martha?" I realize this is a bad question as soon as I see the words hanging in the little white cloud in front of my mouth.

"Mrs. Smith."

"That's it? Where is she? What hospital, where?"

"She's in New York City. I don't know the hospital."

"Let's see if I have this correct. He is SFC Smith, his wife's name is Mrs. Smith, she is in New York City, in an unnamed hospital, and you want me to find out how she and the child are doing. Is that pretty much it? Anything else?"

"Nope, honey. Please find out for me."

The general beams, says, "Don't worry, Martha, Barney can do anything." Then looks at me, "Get on it, Barney. Let us know as soon as you've got something."

I'm about to make one of my smartass remarks, when an aide

inspired thought bludgeons its way into my brain housing group. I believe the general knows this is impossible, and just wants me to solve the immediate problem. That's gotta be it. At least I hope so.

Returning to the aides' hut, I sit down, look at my watch, note the time, and open a can of pop. Olney and Anders want to know what's going on, so I tell them. Their faces pale, mouths drop open, and finally Captain Olney says, "What the hell are you going to do?"

"Nothing. Absolutely nothing, except sit here for thirty minutes, drink my Coke, work on the script and polish my lines."

"The script? Lines? I don't follow."

"And that's why you're the junior aide and will go to heaven. When I'm done mentally rehearsing, I intend to go back, give Martha an answer, and solve the problem."

"How?"

"Its better you not know until it's over, that way you won't have to lie to anyone. You can honestly plead ignorance."

"What?"

"Jerry, who knows? You may be the senior aide by midnight. A Cinderella story."

"Huh?"

"Forget it. Quiet, a Maestro is at work."

Thirty minutes drag by. My devious, pea size brain is working overtime on my lines and the script. Finally, I drain the coke, crinkle the can, get up and flip the can over my shoulder into the trash basket and look at Olney and Anders, and say, "Hell of a shot. Give me yours, Jerry, I'll do it again." I wink at Olney and Anders, and head to the study.

Tap, tap.

"Come in, Barney. What's up?"

Martha chimes in, "Did you find out anything, sweetheart?"

"Ah, Yes, ma'am, General. It's not much. I patched a call through to the hospital in New York. The connection wasn't very good, but I was able to get through to her room. Mrs. Smith is doing fine. She gave birth to an eight pound, four ounce baby boy earlier today. The child is absolutely fine. Then I lost the connection, and couldn't get it back. Sorry, Sir. . . Martha. That's all I was able to find out."

The general leaps out of his chair, smacks his open palm with his fist and says, "See, Martha, Barney can do anything. Best damn aide a general can have. Great job, Barney."

"Thank you, sir."

Martha is up and moving unsteadily toward me. When she arrives, she drapes herself over me, arms around my neck, splashing some of her gin on my ear, and gives me a huge, wet, *London Dry* kiss on the lips. Leans back, almost toppling over, and says, "Barney, you're a dear. A dear, dear man. Thank you so much. My God, I feel better."

"Not a problem, Martha. Glad to help. Will there be anything else, sir?"

The general says, "Not just now. However, Martha will be ready to go shortly. Have one of the junior aides take her home."

"Aye, aye, sir."

Martha asks, "Barney, do you have the napkin?"

"No, ma'am. It fell apart, so I just threw it away."

"Okay, I guess. Good night, Barney, and thanks again. Oh, what hospital?"

"Bronx General. Night, Martha." I turn quickly, close the door and leave for the aide's hut.

Once back in the hut, I tell Captain Olney that he will be taking Martha home tonight. Then add, "If she asks you any questions, just tell her you don't know anything. I didn't say anything to you.

I was busy on the phone and couldn't talk to you, or Anders. Got it?"

"What's goin on? Shouldn't I know something?"

"Yeah, you should know something and I hope you do, but not this. I'll tell you someday, when it's safe. Now go, there's the buzzer."

"Safe?"

"Go."

Captain Olney and Martha leave via the sedan, with Corporal Sadowski at the wheel. Jerry will take his task seriously, but it will be an experience. If he knows nothing, he'll be harmless.

I go to the study, knock, and enter. "Sir, anything else for tonight?"

"No, Barney. Fine job. Don't know how the hell you did it, but you did. Great."

"Was just lucky, sir. Made a couple of good guesses. Good night, sir."

"Good night."

Damn, he thinks I really made that call. Or, does he know and is just playing out the game with me. I'll just wait to see if the other shoe drops.

"Barney."

Clump!

CHAPTER THIRTY-EIGHT

THE GENERAL IS CHIPPER THIS morning at breakfast. Last night has him pleased with himself. Both the general and I are hoping Martha will forget the incident last night, although it would be interesting to see what he would do if confronted. Another reason he's "up" is because Lucy is joining us for dinner this evening. Although he's pleased, the other aides are on edge over her needling. I think it's great sport. We will pick her up at ICU on our way back from wherever we go today.

As we leave the table, the general says, "Barney, lets take the sedan today, okay?"

"Yes sir, it's out front and ready." I say this with some degree of trepidation.

We get outside only to find Sadowski dozing in the front seat of the car. He hears our footsteps on the gravel driveway, leaps up, and clunks his head on the door. He slides out, unsteadily staggers around the front of the car to open the right rear door for the general. I've already done this, along with the front right for me. I look at him and say, "Corporal, just get yourself squared away. Wipe the drool off your chin and the boogers off your nose. Get in and drive us to the CP."

"Huh? Oh, yes, sir." With that, he turns and collides into the open front door, staggers back, and regroups. The impact has at least shaken the cobwebs out of his pea-size brain. Anything else it does is a blessing.

The general laughs at this slapstick comedy act. Maybe this is why he prefers taking the chopper all the time. After a few minutes he says, "Barney, I'm going to the states on two weeks leave. Make my flight arrangements."

"Yes, sir. As soon as the briefing's over. Sir, does this mean we'll be staying here for awhile longer?"

"Yes, for how long I don't know. Major General Mallory will fill in while I'm gone. He'll bring his aide. They won't be staying at the beach house."

"Aye aye, sir."

"You take care of the routine office admin, handle my personal correspondence, and give the aide a hand if he needs it."

"Yes, sir."

As we continue the drive to MAF I think, I need to write to Ryley tonight. Let her know I'll probably be staying here and that I don't have a clue how much longer.

I've already been gone fifteen months. Twelve is the normal tour. I hope she understands, but she sure has been doggin' my trail about this issue the last few months. This is the same thing that happened to me in Korea years ago. It caused severe problems with Nancee in D.C. It's life in the Corps. It's not an easy one, but I love it.

At the CP we attend the War Room briefing as usual. As soon as it's over, I make the flight arrangements for the general. Then we head north to Khe Sanh, a Fire Support Base not far from the Laotian border. This is followed by a trip to a similar base at Con Thien, and then to an outpost at Gia Linh. The latter two are northeast of Khe Sanh, right on the southern boundary of the

Demilitarized Zone, adjacent to North Vietnam. This is truly Indian country and we've taken some fire previously getting into these places. Not a place for the general to be flitting about, but this is his leadership style and it's appreciated from what I observe of the troops when he is walking about at the positions. The Snuffies always try to get close to the general, try to get a comment or a handshake. This is good in one respect, being bunched up isn't, it draws fire, and that makes me nervous.

We break out a box of cold C-Rats and eat on the way from Khe Sanh to Con Thien. The can of Ham and Limas serve as a reminder for me. I miss my company, the Snuffies, and the Magpies. Damn I wish I were back. At Gia Linh we draw some small arms fire as we drop quickly into the position. No harm done, this time. We only stay for a short period, and damn if we don't draw some more fire on the way out.

On our return, we visit the hospital ship, *USS Sanctuary* that is also here now along with her sister ship, the *Repose*. We leave and fly south for a stop at the hospital to visit the wounded and meet Lucy.

We join Lucy in ICU, and she accompanies us through the ward as the general awards Purple Hearts. She adds whatever comments are appropriate because of her nightly visits with these men. A few troops ask me to include her in the snapshot, so I do. We leave and chopper back to the beach house. I ride up front, the general sits in back with Lucy.

After lift off, Bill Dunn continues my flying lessons. He wants me to be able to fly this machine in case of an emergency. If so, it'll be a crisis just getting up front.

I'm okay at the straight and level, but can't make a normal landing. At a critical point while flaring out, I lose it and start sliding backward. All I can manage is a run-on landing along the beach or some other long, flat strip, like Marble Mountain or Da Nang.

This evening I take it up the beach, turn into the wind near the house, and turn it over to Dunn for the landing at the pad, which is a tight squeeze. The general has been glancing back and forth between Lucy and what is happening in the cockpit. He's obviously worried and becomes anxious as we near the house. He's relieved when he sees that my hands are free, and Dunn has the controls as we land. "O Ye of little faith," has real meaning, and merit in this case.

As we leave the chopper and walk toward the house, Lady, the mongrel dog that is supposed to be the general's pet, greets us. She looks like a German shepherd with the conformation of an obese coyote. Why she shows up tonight, leaves me clueless. It's a first, which leads me to believe it's an omen...that witch, Madame Quy is at work.

Lady greets us, tail wagging, and jumps up on the general. He pretends this happens all the time. Lucy says, "Who's this?"

The general continues to pat Lady, and says, "She's my dog, however she's not a house dog, except on special occasions. We keep her in the compound."

I think, what's this "we" stuff? That mutt has never been in the house, but I have a feeling we are about to have one of these "special occasions."

We enter, with Lady at the general's heels. He says, "Barney, watch Lady for a few minutes while I show Lucy where she can freshen up."

"Sir, and put the dog out, like normal, right?"

"No, let her stay in for a short while, just until we sit down to dinner."

"Like normal, sir?"

He ignores my sarcasm. Lucy has heard the remark and catches the drift. She heads for his bathroom, he waits in his study, I get the mutt. I like dogs, just not this one.

Captain Olney and WO Anders stroll in from the aides hut. I say, "Mister Anders, using some ol' naval parlance, you've got the dog watch."

"What's that mean?"

"Usually it means you've got the last watch before morning, but tonight it means you watch this dog. Which reminds me, aren't you guys suppose to clean it up occasionally?"

"Yes, but no one ever goes near this mutt, so I figure it's not a big deal."

"Well, you're almost right, except that Madame Quy has stuck her pins in the Barney Doll again and it's a big deal tonight. The general wants it in here with him until we eat."

"What for?"

"Who knows? To show he's warm hearted and family oriented, maybe. Doesn't make any difference. You just keep her next to you, off the furniture, and away from people, especially me. When we go to dinner, put it out and tell Sadowski to give it a bath, tonight...the mutt stinks, and is probably carrying a record flea population."

"Okay, Cap'n."

Lucy and the general return to the living room. The stewards serve a glass of sherry to each of us. Lady is not drinking, but does roll over on her side and starts licking herself, slurping, industriously and loudly. At least it's not a male.

Lucy says, "Barney, so this is Lady?"

"Yes, ma'am."

"Lucy."

"Ah yes, Lucy."

"And she stays in the house or the compound all the time?"

"Well, yes and no. It stays in the compound, all of the time, and stays in the steward's hut if the weather is bad."

"But, not in the house, or the aide's hut. In the compound, always?"

"Yes, that's correct."

I think, where the hell is she going with this? I feel like one of those targets in the arcade shooting gallery, moving back and forth, going "ding" every time the shooter gets a hit. I think I heard the first ding.

Fortunately, the general isn't interested in Lady and changes the subject. We chat for a short time, then adjourn to the dinner table.

As we head to the table, Lucy says, "Barney, do I get to sign the guest book again?"

"Yes, please do. And your rank is 33, remember? Give me a break here."

"Why are you so nervous?"

"Because you're up to something. I smell an ambush."

"Maybe it's the dog."

"No, I know the difference."

From the table, the general says, "Come on everyone, let's sit down and eat. What's the delay?"

"Lucy is being Lucy, again."

"What?"

"On the way, sir." She signs the book, which is good, but I sense she has larger prey in mind. I escort her to the table. The general seats her, and then we all sit. Lucy grins. The others unfold their napkins, lean over and smell the addictive aroma of the steaming minestrone soup.

Only I hear the guillotine creaking slowly to the top, and look around for an appropriate head.

We finish the minestrone. The stewards serve the chow, sorry, the entrée. As a grunt, I'm still struggling with the uptown terminology. Anyway, it's spaghetti and meatballs, which accounts for the checkered tablecloth, napkins and red candles. Nice setting, pleasant, family oriented. Very warm, until Lucy grabs the chain on the guillotine, "Barney, you say that Lady stays in the compound all of the time?"

"Yes...And normally it's better cared for."

"Really?" Ding.

"What I mean is it's normally a lot cleaner."

"Oh, of course, and she's cared for, and kept safe?" Ding. Ding.

"Yes, ma'am."

"Lucy."

"Lucy, yes, I keep forgetting."

"If Lady never leaves the compound, how do you account for the fact that she's pregnant?"

Ding. Ding. Ding. Where is my flak jacket and helmet when I need it? "It's what?"

Now the general shows some interest in what he thought was a meaningless conversation, though I know it was a purposeful interrogation.

Lucy announces, "She's with pups. Been bred. Has had an affair. Going to have a litter, and soon I would guess." She cants her head, raises her eyebrows, and displays a sardonic smile that only a woman can conjure up. "Are you blind? And, by the way, she's not an it. Its don't have pups."

"Really?" I reply. "Well, good. A family after all. Wow, this pasta is good."

Lucy shakes her head slowly, closes her eyes and raises her eyebrows, indicating no way am I getting out of this. "Barney, if she never leaves the compound, how did she get this way?"

The general burst out laughing. Lucy also laughs, pleased with herself.

I say, "Beats me, but I can account for all of my time." And, I laugh, pleased with myself.

They continue laughing. Olney and Anders join in as well. Lucy is on a roll and looking to continue the attack. So, I look around and find the head for the guillotine, "Mister Anders, why are you laughing? You're here all day. You're in charge of the quarters, which includes the dog."

Lucy turns to him, says, "Yes, James, who accounts for your time? What's your story?"

The general adds, "Yes, Mister Anders, what's going on here?"

Anders first flushes into a pinkish color, which slowly turns into a deep scarlet, accompanied by tiny droplets of perspiration forming on his furrowed forehead. He looks like the man in a police lineup when they say, number three, step forward. He's struggling between answering or remaining mute.

Having flung him on the block, I'm faintly overcome with compassion and say, "Well, it appears that Lady has gotten out, and had a wild liberty for herself. Has gone into the village and met a beau. Doesn't say much for our security, or her morals, does it?"

Anders recovers some, "No sir, I'll check and find out what happened."

Lucy, not letting up, says, "James, we know what happened; what Captain Quinn wants to know is how."

I quip, "I believe I know how, Lucy." And laugh again. "What I want Anders to find out is why she got out. Maybe we should just drop the subject for now? He can let me know later."

Anders sighs and says, "Thank you, sir."

Lucy does not let go. She asks, "Well, what are we going to name them, once they blissfully arrive, which I might add will be in about a week?"

"How about we call them, 34, 35, 36, and so forth, since she also has no rank, and since you discovered her apparent merrymaking."

"You win, Barney, but only for poor James' sake." Then she adds, "Great meal, Walter, a real treat. Thank you."

We all have to think for a second. We only know him as General or sir.

The general smiles, "Thank you for gracing our table this evening. I've had fun. How about a movie tonight? Do we have my favorite, Barney?"

"Yes, sir. Doc and Chester for you, Matt for Lucy, and Kitty for me."

Lucy says, "You wish."

"Perhaps we both wish."

The general injects, "What is it with you two?"

Lucy says, "We're sparring. He won this round. Also."

We get up and head for the living room, and hopefully the end of the Inquisition.

Chapter Thirty-Nine

THE GENERAL HAS BEEN GONE for a week and a half. Life is peaceful, orderly, and admittedly dull. The aide for Major General Mallory doesn't want my help, and that's okay. The two of them stay at the III MAF compound. I go in each day to check the mail, do a few administrative chores and essentially stay out of the way.

Today, I receive another letter from Ryley, and this one has startling news. She tells me the general paid an unannounced visit to her, but she wasn't home. He left a note on his personal three star stationary in her mailbox. He invited her to attend a dinner as his guest at a nearby Commanding General's home. Further, that he would send a sedan to pick her up if she could attend. Ryley enthusiastically accepted.

She said that there were several generals and their wives in attendance, and that General Barto spent a great deal of time telling everyone what a wonderful aide he had, and how close they were, plus several other accolades.

She went on to tell me that she didn't understand how I could be so unhappy as an aide when I worked for a person that had so much admiration for me. Further, she thought he was cuddly, and had the most intense, beautiful, pale blue eyes she had ever seen.

In addition, he told her to write or call him anytime. She indicates this means they're buddies.

I wouldn't go so far as to describe him as cuddly, and his eyes are more like an eagle's laser-like stare, but that's my perspective. What do I know? They're buddies!

Apparently, he also mentioned he would be remaining in country longer, and that I would be staying along with him. This did not appeal to Ryley. She writes that sitting around this long not knowing when I would be back or if I would be, is not what she expected. Her remark sets me back. Until the general gets back there's not much I can say in return, she knows more than I do. Based on her last several letters, this isn't sounding good. I wish he hadn't said anything.

Regardless, visiting with Ryley was one hell of a thoughtful thing to do. I bet she looked great, and the general has an eye for pretty ladies.

This morning I take the chopper over to the Da Nang airfield to meet the general. He debarks, and looks rested. His walk seems even more invigorated as he charges toward me. I pop smartly to attention and salute. He returns it, and then gives me one of his patented one-arm bear hugs. "Barney, good to see you. How is everything?"

"Everything is five-square. You've got a busy day ahead with briefings and updates. I planned a casual dinner tonight with your senior staff. It's tentative, so I can cancel if you want. I just thought you might want some informal time with them after all the briefings and such."

"Sounds great. Good thinking." Then smiling he says,

"Saw your gal. Nice, nice woman. She was my date, did she tell you?"

"Yes, sir. I appreciate you taking the time to see her, and treat her so nice. She really had a good time."

"Well, not meaning any disrespect to the other generals, but I had the prettiest gal there."

"Thank you, sir. She told me you mentioned you'll be staying here longer."

"Well, yes I did. Probably shouldn't have said anything. Cause any problems?"

"Not sure, sir. We'll see. Let's get on the chopper, and don't forget to give Captain Dunn a friendly punch in the arm. He hasn't been abused since you left."

"I can see that my absence and some rest hasn't changed you any. Let's go."

"Aye aye, sir."

"Last word again, huh?"

"Yes, sir."

We get on board the chopper. He gives Dunn a solid punch on the arm, then smiles, points to me, and says, "He told me to do it, and you know I always do what Captain Quinn says."

Dunn replies, "Right, sir. Welcome back."

"Thanks. Good to see you again, William. Let's go."

The day and evening go as planned. The only minor change, which isn't a surprise, is a visit to the hospital on the way back to quarters this evening. It's lucid evidence of his character, he truly cares. He missed his troops.

A few days have passed. We do a lot of traveling, all up north. Activity is increasing up there. This third day back, we have a celebrity for lunch with the general. She is, *These Boots Are Made For Walkin',* Nancy Sinatra. This woman is extraordinarily beautiful and gracious, and she has a smile that truly lightens the heart and brightens the room. When she beams, her eyes sparkle like fireworks and she radiates overwhelming warmth. Her grin muffles all ailing. In conversation, her voice is a melody. She has all of us under her spell at the lunch table. Bill Dunn, our debonair chopper pilot, our team wit, is completely smitten. For the first time his tongue is tied in knots. He can only sit and ogle Nancy, stammering when he does try to speak.

The general breaks Dunn's trance, "Nancy, are you enjoying your visit?"

"Yes. I feel good about what I'm doing. The men have been fantastic."

"Good."

"However, I'd like to see a little more of this area."

"Okay, we can do that. When we go back to the CP we'll put you up front in my chopper, and Captain Dunn will take you on an air-tour of the Da Nang area. How's that?"

"That would be wonderful, General. Thank you."

"Done deal, right, Barney?"

"Yes, sir. Think you can handle this, Bill?"

Captain Dunn comes out of his reverie and manages an answer, and in our native language. "Huh...oh yes, can do. No sweat."

Nancy replies, "Thank you, Captain Dunn."

He doesn't answer, only responds with a goofy grin and returns to his swooning state.

I lean over to my left and whisper to the general, "I think he can still fly, but not certain."

The general quietly laughs.

After lunch, we board the chopper and the general puts Nancy up in the left front seat, where he usually sits. The general joins me in the back. Bill takes Nancy on a brief sightseeing trip around the area, skirting the coastline north from the beach house, around Monkey Mountain and the Da Nang harbor before going to the CP. Dunn is in hog heaven. He is no longer just smitten, he's in love. A puppy sitting on her lap couldn't look any happier.

I can't tell whether Nancy knows what she has done to him. She exhibits no outward sign. I suspect she can sense it. She pours it on poor William by chatting over the intercom with him, smiling, and laughing at his stabs at humor.

We stay at the CP this evening to see Nancy's show. The general eats with the Chief of Staff and the senior staff at the regular mess, but first walks around and visits with the troops. We attend the show after dinner, and it's fantastic, particularly when she sings her hit song to end the show. Bill Dunn isn't the only one smitten. All of us are swallowed up by her charm and grace. Hell, I'm in love with her too.

The general and I catch the ending as we walk to the chopper, so that we aren't immersed with the crowd of troops when the show breaks. When we get to the pad, Bill Dunn is nowhere in sight. I ask the crew chief, "Where's Captain Dunn?"

He looks sheepish, hesitant to answer, so I say, "Come on, where is he?" Since the general is standing along side, he is still reluctant to answer. "Corporal, it's not that tough. Answer the question."

The general laughs and says, "Corporal, at least give us a clue."

He points in the direction of a tree near the make- shift stage, "Up there, sir."

The general says, "In the tree. What in the world is he doing up there?"

"He wants a better look at Nancy."

"Nancy, is it?"

"Yes, sir, I guess."

I say, "General, I'll go get him...be back in a minute."

"No, lets both go. I want to see his face. You always have all the fun."

Damn, the general's joining my circus. We walk over to the tree, look up, and there, perched on the first branch is our pilot.

The general calls up, "Captain Dunn, could I bother you for a ride home?"

Dunn looks down. An expression of surprise mixed with stark terror races across his face. He quickly but clumsily swings down, clipping his jaw on a branch in his rush, and stammers, "Sir, I'm sorry. Um...I...I, didn't know that--"

"How about just getting my chopper turned-up, Captain. That is if you're capable, and not in some over-sexed trance." I break out laughing. I'm lovin' this. The general sees and hears me; it prompts him into some of the same.

Even with the poor lighting in this area, we see that Dunn is flushed, a bright red. He finally answers, "I'll get the bird wound up, sir." He salutes, and jogs to the chopper, screaming at his crew chief, who is now alongside, as they head to the pad. The corporal is bearing the brunt of Dunn's embarrassment, while the general continues to roar in laughter.

I mutter aloud, "Geez, I love it when someone else is in the barrel."

The general says, "What's that?"

"Nothing, sir. Just thinking out loud."

"Oh."

We walk to the pad, "Barney, this is fun. You should include me more often in some of your dealings."

"Not too often, sir. You're having way too much fun."

"Well, at least tell me more about them."

"Okay, sir. But not all of them. I have to be selective, to protect your reputation."

"Any portion of my reputation in your hands is a scary thought, but I'll settle for a few anecdotes occasionally."

We board the chopper. Dunn continues to apologize to the general, and gets himself in deeper. I say over the intercom, "Bill, shut up and concentrate on flying. You haven't been worth a crap since lunch."

The general chimes in, "Hear, hear."

Dunn turns and mutters something to me, two words I think, and we lift off. The general adds to the sideshow by giving Dunn the parting of the clouds point, and laughs. He turns and looks at me to make sure I caught his humor. We zip through the moonlight for the beach house. Nancy will never know she turned one of the best chopper pilots in the Corps into silly putty.

The next day, Martha Raye calls. Again, she is somewhere down south, and wants me to have her picked up and brought here to see the general. I let him know, and he gives me the go-ahead. I take all kinds of abuse while making the calls to get an aircraft down to get her. From snide remarks about general's aides to lengthy monologues about a war going on. These are obviously not the perks of the job, but rather the drawbacks. Abuse of an aide seems to be a rite of passage for some.

We pick Martha up and get her to dinner at the beach house. It's a fine meal with pleasant banter from Martha. She too enjoys jerking the chain of an aide now and then, but she isn't as barbed as Lucy. After dinner, she and the general adjourn to the study to chat and have a few drinks. She doesn't mention the last visit, so it appears the general and I are off the hook. I certainly hope she doesn't have any more soggy paper napkins with her.

After a few hours, I take her back in the sedan to the USO quarters where she's staying. I take on this chore in case she brings up the baby story. I don't want Olney or Anders blurting out a giveaway answer. When we arrive, she says, "Barney, come on in for a drink."

"Better not, it's late."

"Oh, come on in, just for a short while. Plenty of folks here."

"Okay, just one." Famous last words. If not the most famous, certainly the most often spoken. I have more than one, but since I don't, or can't drink much over here, it doesn't take many. I stay too long at the fair.

I wake up groggy and with a fuzzy tongue. I'm a tad hung over. I mumble aloud, "Whoa, easy does it. Can't make it this early."

Captain Olney who is up and hopping around like a damn Jack Rabbit says, "What'd ya say?"

"Jerry, you and Anders do breakfast, and you take the general to III MAF. I'll be in later."

"What should I tell him?"

"Tell him I'm a little sick this morning. Have a bug or something, a touch of the flu. Anything. Just let me know what you come up with. And let him know I'll be in later."

"Okay, but what if--"

"Jerry, just do it, and try not to panic."

"Right. How long will you—-"

"Captain Olney, surely you can last until mid-morning. My God man, you're a Marine captain. Suck it up."

"Yes, sir."

A few hours later, I come into the office. Captain Olney has the look of a condemned man on his face. Before he can confess anything, the buzzer goes off, signaling the general wants to see me. He's angry, I can tell by the buzzer sound. If he just wants me for something, it's a short burst. When he is upset, he really leans on it, hard and long, making it sound like an angry bee in an attack mode.

I go into the general's office, and before I get to his desk, he says, "Where were you this morning? I understand from Captain Olney you were hung over." Then he motions me with his hand, from where I'm standing at the corner of his desk, to get around front. This and the buzzer are clear signals. If he calls me captain, it'll be the toilet flushing.

"Well, yes, sir. A bit under the weather. Had a few drinks with Martha and the USO folks last night."

"You can't do that Barney. You're my aide. My senior aide. It looks bad. I can't have that. I won't have that. My aide, drunk and carousing around at night. Good God!"

"Sir, I wouldn't say drunk, maybe a little shaky, light in the head perhaps…and I certainly wasn't carousing around, sir, although I must admit the thought crossed my mind since there were some good lookin' honeys there"

"This is not a joke, Captain. You were carousing around if I say so, and you were incapacitated this morning."

"Sir, not incapacitated. Perhaps a little less spry than usual."

"No, not capable of doing your job."

"Aye aye, sir. I'm not going to argue with the general."

"Why not. You always do. Must mean I've got you dead to rights this time."

"I suppose. Yes, sir."

"Well, what do you think I should do?"

"I don't know, sir. Be merciful, sir, and fire me. Send me back to a rifle company."

"Oh, here we go again. Up to your old tricks. Well, I am not going to fire you, and you are not going back to your company. I'm going to put you in unofficial hack, for two weeks."

"Hack, what's that, sir?"

"It means you can't go anywhere except the house, the office, or with me, wherever I go."

"That's hack? I've been in hack for months then, sir."

"Get out of here. You're in hack. And don't you dare say another word."

"Yes, sir."

"Dammit, Captain."

There's that captain business again. Time to shut up and leave. When I get outside his office, I lock my jaws, shake my head, and glare at Jerry Olney, "What did you tell him this morning?"

"I told him what you told me to say, then he started grilling me, and I panicked. It slipped out."

"What slipped out?"

"That you were hung-over."

"Great job. So much for the toughness of an infantry officer. We had better hope you never get captured. Well, don't worry about it, you didn't get lucky, or unlucky, or whichever. You're not the senior aide yet. He only put me in hack."

"Hack, what's that?"

"Don't sweat it. We're all in hack."

"Huh? He put me in hack too? And Anders?"

"No, no, no. It was a joke, Jerry. Forget it. Let's get on with what's left of the day. Take some time to read the *Code of Conduct.*

"What?"

"You're only required to give your name, rank and service number. Not spill all the beans."

"Oh...I didn't mean--"

"Yeah, sure, and he didn't even pull out your fingernails with pliers or attach electrical wires to your... ah, never mind, Jerry."

"Come on, you know how he--"

"Jerry, forget it. Let's get to work."

The day takes its usual course, except the general tells every senior staff officer in the headquarters that he has thrown his senior aide in hack. I have visitors all day, asking, giggling and poking fun.

The Protocol Officer, Major Phelan makes at least five visits, and each time he makes a wise-ass remark, then leaves laughing before I can reply. There will be a payback.

Tonight after dinner, just before being dismissed for the

evening, I say to the general, "Sir, you're pleased with yourself, aren't you?"

"Yes, very much so. I'm having my day in court."

"Ah, yes, sir. Goodnight, sir."

"Don't go far."

"Ouch."

"What's wrong?"

"Thought I felt a pin prick. Maybe Madame Quy gave you a Barney Doll to stick."

"What?"

"Nothing, sir. It was an attempt at some humor."

"Oh, right. And the last word. Goodnight, Barney."

I leave and head for the aide's hut. Outside I see Lady standing by the hut with a strange look on its face. Maybe laughing at me, or at the very least, smiling.

It knows I'm in the doghouse. Probably thinks we'll be sleeping together for a spell.

Everyone's a comedian today, even the damn dog.

CHAPTER FORTY

AFTER THE HACK EPISODE, BREAKFAST this morning should be interesting. While shaving I decide, however childlike, I'm going to stage my eating race. I've got to get the general to slow down. It's unhealthy the way he eats, and I've mentioned this to him several times. He promises to change, and doesn't...or he just dismisses the subject. Oh hell, this is all bull. I'm rationalizing. He's just had too much fun putting me in hack. I'm gonna get even.

We sit, and as the general is being served, first as usual, he unintentionally gives me a leg up with a chuckle, "Barney. Made it this morning, huh? Ha-ha-ha-ha."

"Yes, sir. Bright-eyed and bushy-tailed. Now that's a hackneyed saying. Isn't it, sir?" I laugh softly, pleased with myself.

"Well, it's a novel start. Don't you think, Captain Olney?"

Olney replies, "Oh, yes, sir. I--"

The general interrupts him and starts telling how the senior staff is enjoying the hack episode. As the general is speaking, Alvarez serves me, and I start eating immediately, just as fast as I can shovel the eggs and sausage in my mouth. I don't even cut the link sausage, just stuff 'em in, two at a time. Captain Olney responds to the general, but he ignores the remark and starts to eat, causing Jerry's voice to trail off, not completing his sentence. It's too late. I'm way ahead.

Olney and Anders are stunned into silence by my antics. Deer in the headlights syndrome! They don't believe I'm doing this. When I told them earlier, I guess they just thought it was Barney blab. My fork sounds like an automatic weapon firing as it hits the plate while it shovels in the ammo. The general glances over, and realizes what's going on. He stops, says, "Okay, Barney, you win. You made your point."

Now finished, I push the plate back, wipe my mouth with the napkin and say, "Sir?"

"Let it go. As I said, I get the point. You win. I'll slow down." He laughs, then asks, "Don't we have a luncheon scheduled today?"

The junior aides sigh, and begin eating.

"Yes, sir, but I don't think you should entertain this gal, celebrity or not. Her reputation is not good. Other places she's been have had some problems. Ugly incidents and I don't think the general should subject himself to any of this."

Olney and Anders stop eating again. They're wearing those here-we-go-again looks. I think, I need to tell these two to stop worrying about the bantering between the general and myself.

"Barney, you don't know her. I've had lunch with her before. Some time ago, with Cardinal Spellman in attendance as a matter of fact. Wasn't a problem."

Olney and Anders start eating.

"Well, sir. That might have been then, but now, it's different, for sure. Besides, you're not a cardinal, just a general."

The general's eyebrows raise, "Just a general! You're off and running again, Barney."

Jerry and James stop once more. Alvarez tries to pour me a second cup of coffee but spills most of it since he's shaking, or maybe bobbing and weaving trying to miss the verbal jabs.

I look at both of them and say, "Eat. Eat. You two are making me nervous, and look what you've done to Alvarez."

They look at Alvarez, then the general who flicks his hand at them, "Eat. Ignore us."

They start eating. Good. The freeze frames of these two are comical, but enough is enough.

The general turns back toward me, gives me a smug look, and ask, "Just a general. Hmmm. With all of your vast insight, exactly how would you describe her?"

"Let me see, sir. How about, a light-haired detour off the autobahn of knowledge. How about, sexually extroverted...one step out of the Texas Chicken Ranch."

"What does that gibberish mean?"

"She's a tramp...a slut! Worse, she's been practicing her skill set in country. In particular, on board the Lear she's traveling in."

"Oh God, you're overreacting again. Way overboard. Specifically, what do you base your opinion on?"

"You don't want to know specifics. It's better you not know. Please, just trust me, sir."

"Okay, don't tell me, but I know what I'm doing. I know her. Just set up lunch."

"Not smart."

"Do it."

"Okay, if you insist, sir."

"I insist."

For once, everyone is finished breakfast when the general and I depart for the CP. He notices this, looks at me and says, "See, I can heel, sit, and walk on a leash." We leave and he laughs all the way to the chopper. On board, he repeats our conversation to Dunn, highlighting his one-liner. Bill dutifully laughs, and glances back at me with his eyebrows raised. The general is still laughing.

I look at Dunn, give him my "general's" hand flick and say, "Fly."

We get to headquarters and start the morning as normal. Shortly after the briefing, the Chief of Staff calls me into his office. "Barney, the general is going to be away during lunch, so how about I shift the luncheon to the III MAF mess? You can stand down."

"Yes, sir. Good move. Must have been one hell of a morning briefing. How did you swing this?"

"I didn't, you did. This is just his way of letting you know you were right again."

"Sir, if I were you, I wouldn't host this one either. Let the Protocol Officer and the Press Officer handle it. You can grab a bite in your office, or something. Stay out of sight."

"Is she that bad?"

"Worse. Give her a wide berth, sir. Trust me."

"What's the world coming to, Barney?"

"A better place, not just here, today...sir."

"Okay, Barney. How about you letting Major Phelan know. Tell him it's an order."

"Aye aye, sir. It will be a distinct pleasure. It's payback time. I better get moving, Captain Dunn is inbound with her. He just picked her up at Da Nang. Sir, please tell the general to stay put until I get her away from the pad."

He ignores my payback comment and says, "Okay, good. Will do. Go." I think, the Chief is a gentle man.

He gives me a look of relief, and I dart out of the office to meet Dunn at the helo pad.

I get there just as he is landing. It's a sight to behold. Our platinum blond bimbo is sitting in the left front seat of the chopper. She's in a see through, wide gapped, knit, micro-mini dress. Absolutely nothing is left to the imagination, from her twin forties to her front lawn that is not the color of dormant Bermuda. She has no undergarments on. Bill Dunn is excitedly jerking and nodding his head, trying to get my attention. I don't need his help. I can see a gnat crawling in a cornfield at five hundred yards, so I can certainly see this, or that, or those, or whatever. She has my attention. Dunn is all eyes, drool and lust.

When the chopper settles, she feigns difficulty with the shoulder harness and seat belt, causing Dunn to lean over and assist her. When he finishes this one-second job, in three or so minutes, she puts her hands on each side of his flight helmet and gives him a kiss. A quick one so he can't respond; he just sits there with his mouth hanging open, and his eyes glazed over. Dunn is done.

Having rendered Bill Dunn useless, she drops her left leg out of the chopper and at the same time lifts up her right leg, swings it over and across the cyclic, so she can slide down to the skid. This gives the now several dozen troops that have assembled at the pad, a sight to remember and record. The cuffs don't match the collar. The camera bugs are going crazy. This picture is going to show up time and again...bet the ranch on it, even the chicken one.

I meet her at the chopper door, and help her down and out onto the dockside LZ. Then I advise her that she will be staying in the VIP quarters, and of her luncheon at the mess, with the men. She smiles and says, "Groovy", not disappointing me with her command of the language. She waves to the gathered troops. The Snuffies are smiling and waving back, the Magpies are murmuring and drooling, and all still snapping pictures. I escort her, and her entourage of three guys, or three something's, to the quarters where Major Phelan is standing. "Major, thank you, sir. Ma'am, this is Major Phelan, your escort and host."

"Groovy."

"Sir, by your leave." He glares at me and starts to speak but I cut him off with, "Sir, I'm in hack, I've got to get back. Can't be away, you know."

"Du-Dit. Di Di Mau."

"Love your command of the local language, sir. Is it true, sir, that you also speak French?"

"Foxtrot Yankee, Captain."

"You do, sir."

The bimbo says, "What was that?"

"He speaks French."

"Groovy."

I salute the major, smile, face about, and leave. Paybacks are sweet.

Ten minutes later, guest clearly out of sight, the general and I board the chopper and head south. A rifle company had been in a serious skirmish the day before. Just before we leave, he told me the name of the Company Commander, and asked if I knew him. The general seemed displeased about something and wanted my opinion of this officer. I told him I knew the man well, and that I thought extremely highly of him, giving him all of the reasons for my judgment. He listened intently, calmed a bit, and didn't say anymore. We continued flying south.

Several minutes pass. He asks me if I really feel that strongly. I reply, "Yes, sir. I do. He's a damn fine Marine."

That was the end of it. However, on the way back we stop at the hospital as usual. While there he awards the captain the Purple Heart, I take the Polaroid as usual, and leave it with my friend. He's going to recover and be okay.

We visit several more wards and meet Lucy who is wandering about visiting her Marines. The general invites her to dinner, and we all return to the beach house for a quiet meal and a movie. Lucy leaves the subject of today's celebrity visit alone, thank God. She could have a field day with this one.

When all is done, Olney takes Lucy back to Da Nang. When saying goodnight to me at the study door, the general adds, "You were right." I leave it at that, for a change.

Chapter Forty-One

I GET UP EARLIER THAN normal this morning and hold reveille on the household staff. We have the beginning of a busy two days. *Life Magazine* folks will be here to do a story about the Marines in the I Corps area. I need to check and make sure everything is a "go" for these two. A writer and a photographer, free-lancers, I think. Should be interesting. Media guys can be a load. No, a first class pain in the ass is more like it.

The plan is simple. They will be brought here for breakfast by the general's chopper. We will go to the morning briefing, from there to the same CAC unit we visited several weeks ago, and then on to one of the Fire Support Bases. Then back here for the evening and a working dinner. I've double-checked arrangements. Everything is set. I hope for no surprises, but suspect Murphy is lurking about as usual.

The writer and photographer from *Life* arrive and we sit down for breakfast. The article is supposed to be about what the Marines are doing in I Corps. However, the conversation at the table this morning seems to be more about the general than what is going on in our area. The general keeps trying to steer it in that direction, but the writer keeps asking questions about him. I suppose they need it for background but I'm suspicious. I sense Murphy close by, or worse, Madame Quy is poised with pin in hand.

In the middle of a question by the writer, the general interrupts and says, "Barney, we're going to the airfield before the briefing this morning. There's a planeload of casualties leaving for the U.S. We'll visit with them first."

"Yes, sir."

"And Barney, we'll present some Purple Hearts while there."

"Yes, sir. Not a problem. Have everything we need."

The writer leans toward me and asks, "Does the general do this often?"

I respond, "Yes, whenever possible, plus he visits the *Repose* and *Sanctuary* frequently and the hospital down here several times a week. Perhaps you would like to come along later today?"

The general senses my intolerance and says, "Excellent idea, Barney. You fellas like to come along?"

The writer responds, "That's great."

General Barto nods and says, "Barney, there is a young wounded corporal going out today on that plane. I'm told he has been recommended for a Bronze Star. See what that's about. Get the info and get the medal, and we'll present it at the airfield."

"Okay, sir. Do you have a name or unit, or something, for me to go on?"

He does and adds, "And Barney, get a citation, or if not, get some info and write one. We can't present the award without reading the citation."

"Yes, sir."

Now it's getting sticky, and time is of the essence. I leave the table, go into the general's study and get on the phone. Shortly, I have some of what I need. Full name, rank, unit, date and some sketchy information on the event. I start writing the citation while the group is eating. In addition, I send Captain Olney to the CP to get a Bronze Star medal and meet me at the MAF helo pad. We'll stop on the way to the airfield. Although this is a surprise, I don't consider this a Murphy strike.

As I hurriedly write, the general shouts from the table,

"Barney, lets go." I grab my notes, and head for the chopper. We board, and I continue to write as we lift off and head for the pad, then the airfield. The chopper is lurching, bouncing and vibrating during takeoff and flight. My writing looks either like a second grader doing his first essay without lined paper or a seismograph recording during an earthquake.

We land, Olney hands me the dark navy blue leather box with the medal, and we are off, almost like a touch and go aboard a carrier. I peek inside the box to ensure we've got the correct award, and continue to scribble the finishing touches on the citation as we land at the airfield.

We find the corporal, I read the citation, adding words and phrases as I read, and stumbling through this hoping the young man somewhat recognizes the actual event. It will be a miracle because I can hardly make out my handwriting; however, I've always been a good BS'er so this is just on a higher plain. The general presents the Bronze Star, and the photographer gets a great picture. All is well. The Marine is deserving and even though a litter case his chest swells with pride. It is enhanced by his wide beaming smile as the general shakes his hand. Both men are proud and pleased...and the young man is goin' home.

Then we start moving about the litters that are lined up waiting for loading, as others are being taken aboard the aircraft. We award Purple Hearts along with the Polaroid snapshot as appropriate. The photographer takes some pictures of the awards and overall scene as we continue to move from Marine to Marine. We approach a trooper who has been wounded in the head. He's covered with bandages, including his eyes. Only his nose and mouth are visible. His hands are also heavily bandaged. The general presents the Heart, I put the Polaroid picture on his chest and say, "Here, hang on to this. It's a snapshot of the general presenting your Purple Heart. Show it to your folks when you get home. It's lying on your chest."

The trooper pushes himself up on his elbows and says, "Captain Quinn, is that you, sir?"

"Yes." I hurriedly glance around to find his name but before I can, he says, "Sir, its Lance Corporal Crowe. Rooster, sir."

"Rooster, sure. Of course. How you doin' son? You've got your freckles covered. Didn't recognize you without your dots showing. The folks here tell me you're going to be okay."

"I'm goin' to be okay, sir. I can't see now, but the Docs say I should get most of my sight back in a few months."

My eyes tear up some. I think, Rooster, he's so young. Damn, they're all young. "Hell, you're going to get more than most back, Rooster. Might have to wear specs, but shoot, you'll look good in them."

The general has moved on, and is calling, "Captain Quinn, what's going on over there."

"Sir, one of my old troopers. Just saying goodbye to him. Be right there."

"Oh, okay, Barney." He waves his hand indicating for me to take what time I need. He talks with the two *Life* people while waiting for me to finish up. It's part of that early pact he made with me.

"Listen, Rooster, I've got to go. When you get back, write me and let me know where you are, okay?"

"Yes, sir."

"Promise?"

"Never break my word to you, Skipper. I've missed you, so have the rest of the guys."

I'm struggling to speak, so I give him a pat on the arm and choke out, "See ya, Rooster. Have a safe trip. Leave the nurses alone. Gotta go. Lima Six, out."

He gives me a "Hoo ah." The *Life* guys missed all this and that's a shame. They would have learned something about the Corps, about these men, and get a feel for it in their bones. Maybe even touch their souls, however that may be a stretch for the media types.

I walk over to the general. He looks at me, square in the eyes, and doesn't say a word. He knows I'm hurting. He nods, pats me on the back, and we move off to present several more Purple Hearts. We finish, watch the final loading of the plane, and then head to the chopper to go back for the morning briefing. As we lift off, I glance at the C-141 starting to taxi and think, I hope Rooster will be okay.

When we get to the office, the general stops, turns to me and says, "You okay, Barney?"

"Yes, sir. I'm fine, but I've had better mornings."

"Understand. The boy will be fine. Nice job with the Bronze Star. Let's take these two to the briefing."

After the briefing, the general, the two media guys and I take the chopper and head north. We are going to visit that same CAC unit first, then on to Khe Sanh.

We land at the same Army compound, again unannounced, and I scratch up a radio jeep and another stock jeep for us. As luck would have it, I get the same driver. His first words are, "Not this again, Captain?"

"You bet. But, I've got reinforcements this time."

"I don't think a cameraman and this other guy count as reinforcements, sir."

"Okay, so I exaggerated. Go get the call sign and a weapon for yourself."

"Already have everything. When I saw you get off that chopper, I figured it would be something dumb again."

"Better than last time. We're going to take pictures. You might become famous."

"I don't want to be famous. I want to be alive."

"Oh, come on. Nothing happened last time and won't this time either. We're armed to the teeth."

"Yes, sir. A camera and a whole lot of BS, sir."

"Well, it's something."

We load up, head out of the compound, up the road toward the village and its CAC unit. I figure, it will be more of the same when we get to the village and that sergeant sees us.

I radio ahead and let him know we're coming. He asks, "Do you have armed support with you this time? Over."

"That's a roger. Out."

It's not a lie. I have the general, the two *Life* guys, two drivers and me, plus the two choppers overhead. It might be a fabrication, but not a lie.

We arrive in the village. The sergeant salutes the general, and welcomes him. He looks around, eyes the two media gents, then me, and says, "Morning, Captain. This is your support?"

"More than last time. . .a reinforced fire team."

"Armed?"

"Sure. Camera, paper, pen, and maybe some poison." He misses it, so I give him a gentle nudge toward the general, and we move out. The writer caught it, but didn't laugh. I thought it was funny. Hard to fathom but maybe I'm too subtle.

The general tells the writer about the concept of a CAC, and then turns it over to the sergeant to explain what is happening in this particular village. We spend the better part of two hours here, plus eat some C's with the troops. A little bit of real life for the *Life* gents. I actually believe the correspondents see it as a treat.

For me, it's a little bit of home. I sit away from the general, and next to a couple of Snuffies. I get a fruit cocktail in my box, so I trade it to one of them. He deserves it. I give my cocoa away, with a tear, to another Marine. I keep the pound cake I traded for.

Want to keep my hand in the business. The leftover main meals we'll keep and store in the chopper for future use.

We leave here, go back to the compound, and board the chopper. Then we head north, and visit the FSB at Khe Sanh. Here, more briefings, and a walk about. After this, we board the chopper and head south, to the beach house, with a stop at the hospital beforehand. While enroute the writer again asks me, "Does the general do this a lot, or is this just for show?"

This pisses me off. I nose up to this rascal and respond, "Like I said earlier. He does this several times a week, every week. He does it for the troops. Because he cares. Each visit takes days off his life. Has nothing to do with you, just them. Got it?"

He leans back, shifts away as much as his seat belt will allow, and looks at me with a guarded look. He shrugs and says, "Okay, okay." He knows which way my gate swings, for sure.

After our visit at the hospital and as we head to the chopper, the general springs another one of his patented surprises. "Barney, when we get to the house, I'm going for my nightly run. Clear the beach. Then we'll swim."

"Your nightly run?"

"Yes."

"Oh, sure, sir. Okay." Hell, I can't argue with him now. Not in front of these folks, but first chance I get, I'll remind him, he never jogs, and if he does now, he had better be careful and not go far, fast or for long. Now this is a Murphy strike. Oh well, at least it's not a Madame Quy hit.

As soon as we get in the chopper, I tell Bill Dunn to radio Anders at the house, and tell him to clear the beach and post sentries a half klick in both directions.

When we land, I gently pull the general aside and say, "Sir, you don't run, for Pete's sake. Never. Forget it. Just go for a nice swim with these guys."

"Nope. Gonna go for a run, and so are you. We're going to show these guys what we're made of."

"Snips and snails, and puppy dog tails."

"What was that?"

"Nothing sir. Nothing. Let's get changed. I've got some trunks in the aides hut for these two."

"Good, see you on the beach...Snip."

He's catching on much too quick. I'll have to change my MO.

In about ten minutes, we all assemble on the beach. I take a moment to try again to dissuade the general, but he will not hear of it. Therefore, off we go, thank goodness at only a jog. The "we" however, includes only the general and me. The other aides and the two gents from the magazine leave their egos on the beach, go for a refreshing swim in the ocean. Actually, this works out fine because they don't see the general stumble after a few hundred yards, and apparently pull a muscle in his calf causing him to half-jog and half-limp back to the others. Madame Quy might be getting into the act, but at the general?

When we get back, he looks at me. I can't tell by his expression whether he wants me to say something merciful or sarcastic. So, I just give him my best "I-told-you-so look." He puts his index finger to his lips, and shakes his head slowly back and forth. This is okay. My look counts as the last word...at least as far as I'm concerned.

He carefully wades out in the surf and swims a while with the others. At least this is therapeutic, both physically and mentally. I go in, change, and check to ensure all is ready for dinner tonight. This will be a working dinner in that they will be asking questions of the general. Our job, the aides, will be to speak when spoken to, and only then. Not a problem for Olney and Anders, only me.

The night ends well. The general bids them goodnight and says, "See you two in the morning, here, for breakfast."

The writer responds, "Okay, sounds great."

This is a change in schedule, but that's okay. It's easier to keep track of them if they're in sight. After today I still haven't developed a high degree of trust of the media. These two leave in the sedan with Anders and Sadowski. This is good. They'll try to pump Sadowski for info. When they do, they'll find out he's not wired to code...it'll leave them shaking their heads in wonderment, or better, dazed.

The general looks at me, grins and says, "Why did you let me do it?"

"I assume that's a rhetorical question, sir?"

"Not originally, but now it is...be humble for a change. Let me have the last word tonight."

He's already had it once tonight, so I just nod.

The general starts to turn away, and then says, "You're going to let me have it, aren't you. Don't answer."

"Nods and looks count the same as the last word, sir."

"There, you did it again. Good night, Barney."

I nod.

He laughs, and closes the study door.

Chapter Forty-Two

Morning breaks clear, warm and with not even a sniff of a breeze off the ocean. The general up first, buzzes me to his study and informs me Con Thien was attacked last night, and once again less than an hour ago. He says, "As soon as the correspondents get here, we'll eat and get on up there. See if you can hurry them along somehow."

"Yes, sir."

I call the Ops Center at III MAF; have them send someone over to the VIP quarters and get the two of them to the helo pad, ASAP. Then I call Captain Dunn; get him moving to make the pick up and tell him to make sure we have a gun ship for a chase bird. It all happens quickly. That's fortunate because the general is waiting at the table, drumming his fingers and anxiously sipping a cup of coffee.

We eat in a hurry, reverting to old form. The general updates the two *Life* folks. We will pick up the MAF Intelligence and Operations officers at the CP on the way.

We finish breakfast lickity-split and scurry to the waiting chopper which Bill Dunn already has turning up. We climb in, lift off, and go get Colonel Bob Rice and Colonel Dan Bartlett, the G2 and G3. They, along with the crew chief and a full load of fuel make us too heavy. I jump out and get aboard the gun ship dragging the photographer with me. He's savvy enough to know what's happening and is easily led. We head north for Con Thien.

Everyone carries a side arm. Although this is normal, the checking to ensure they're loaded and the safety on make the two correspondents nervous. I hope so, because I am. I don't like the general going into an area so soon after it's been attacked. In fact, I don't like him going into any of these areas up around the DMZ. The NVA are probably still lurking about since it's so soon after the last attack. Anything could happen, from the chopper taking fire, us being dinged, or worse, rocket or mortar fire.

We arrive, take no fire as the two birds set down. We scamper out and they take off almost like a touch and go. Both will stay aloft, keeping an eye on us. As soon as we get out, it's apparent an attack has taken place recently. There are dead NVA soldiers about, along with a dozen or so unexploded mortar rounds, plus the usual battle debris of expended ammo, a helmet here and there, and some blood-stained unnies. There is the still pungent odor of the fight, burnt powder, destruction, coppery smell of blood, and the slowly ripening fetor of the dead thickens the humid air.

We are down in an area on the perimeter, and not at the CP. No one seems to be around. We don't belong here, especially the general.

I look around, get oriented and shout, "What the hell are we doing in this area? This isn't the CP."

The general yells, "I know. I know. I pointed to the wrong area."

Suddenly, Wump......Wump......Wump.

"Aw shit!" Mortar rounds being fired, from outside the perimeter. The gut wrenching sound is all too familiar to me. I shout, "Incoming! Get Down! Incoming!"

I snap around to ensure that everyone is scurrying for cover, and to make sure the general has found cover. He has, in an abandoned bunker. Good. He hasn't lost any of his agility under these circumstances, pulled muscle or not. Then I dive for a trench line only a few feet away. It's a typical, hastily dug, unfinished, Marine trench line, only a few feet deep and barely shoulder width wide.

The first mortar round lands on the parapet of the trench line. I see and hear the explosion, and I feel myself lift and flop and rattle around like a pinball. I hear but don't see the other two rounds hit and explode.

I'm dazed, eyes out of focus and my nose is drooling blood. I suddenly have no sense of time, other than some has passed. The ringing in my ears is piercing. My head pulsates with sharp jabs of pain, much worse than a giant migraine. I feel stinging sensations on my face and chest, but I know I'm alive and maybe okay. Everything for the moment is in slow motion and vivid color. I'm on top of someone. It's Colonel Bartlett. He must have been in the trench when I leaped in.

I smell copper again...blood. I feel warm, sticky moisture on my clammy face and an acidy taste in my mouth. Blood is dripping off my face, onto Colonel Bartlett. I feel my head, get smears of blood on my hands, but don't find any gashes or rips. Then I see a ragged, quarter dollar size hole in the colonel's cheek. Blood is gurgling out. I stick my thumb into the wound and put pressure on where it's spewing. Some of his blood must have spurted on me when he was first hit.

He's hit pretty bad and starting to go into shock. I reach back and pull my pistol belt around my belly so I can more easily reach my first aid packet. I've got one arm cradled under his head. With the other hand, I get the packaged bandage out. I place it over the wound, compress it, and apply pressure, while holding his head up.

I look around, see that the general is okay, and Colonel Rice is up and not hit. The two correspondents are out and moving, the photographer snapping pictures. Again, it's all in slow motion, but I know less than a minute has passed. I look around and shout, "Corpsman...Corpsman!" But none are around or at least not within shouting distance.

I look up, see Captain Dunn overhead in a tight orbit, peering at us through the window on his side of the chopper. I take my hand off the bandage and with hurried motions of my arm, signal him down. He drops out of the sky like a Texas twister into our original landing spot. The general and Colonel Rice help me carry and load Colonel Bartlett into the chopper. They climb in as well. I get the two *Life* folks on the bird and wave Captain Dunn to get out of here. Dunn lifts off, and heads for a Battalion Aid Station.

I take cover again, check myself over. Knocked silly but at least acting and moving instinctively. Could be a concussion since my vision is blurred and my brain-housing group hurts. I have some scratches, but nothing serious. My hand comes across the Mizpah, and I think, lucked out again. The damn thing works! That round went off just a few feet from my head.

I get up and wave the chase bird down to pick me up. He does, and I tell him to follow Deadlock One-Zero. We catch up just as the general's bird is leaving the Aid Station and heading back to Con Thien. We turn and follow.

We land, one at a time, near the CP, at the designated LZ. Everyone there is all in a dither about the general almost being dinged. He's calm as usual, but intense. The general, Colonel Rice and the two correspondents meet the commander, get briefed, and walk the area. Still dizzy and slightly out of focus, I straggle along behind the general. Where is ol' Doc Eden with his Cheshire cat grin, bandages and sarcasm when I need him?

After about an hour we leave and head back to III MAF. As we flare out to land, I see a number of folks gathered at the pad. The

Chief of Staff, Protocol Officer, Press Officer, and several other senior staff officers wait to meet the general.

The Chief of Staff quickly gets to the front of the bird to greet the general, along with Major Phelan. Lieutenant Colonel Pressley, the Press Officer, scurries over to the *Life* people. They all walk from the pad toward the headquarters. I trail behind. Major Phelan breaks from the herd and drifts back to slide into step with me. He says, "Your face and jacket are covered with blood. Are you okay?"

"Yeah, okay, I guess. Got my bell rung...a damn...ummm...close call. How's the...ah, the Colonel?"

"He's on the way to the hospital ship, and will probably be evac'd sometime soon. He's going to be okay, but he's goin' back to the real world."

"Damn, I was hoping he wasn't that...uh...that bad. The wo... ah...hole, the hole was pretty damn big. If he's goin' to be okay, that's what...umm, that's all that counts. It was a close one."

"Are you okay? You don't sound so hot."

"Huh? Oh, sure. I think, ah...landed in the wrong area."

"Well, for damn sure, a bad one. Probably lucky they didn't blow the friggin' chopper out of the air."

"Yeah."

"Are you sure you're okay? Why all the blood?"

"Mostly from Bartlett, maybe some is mine. Not sure. He was under me...some damn how. Can't figure out how that piece of shrapnel got under me, and in his cheek. Weird."

By this time we are at the office. The general stops, turns toward me, looks straight into my eyes for a few seconds. I frown and mutter, "What?"

He turns and says to Major Phelan, "Get him to the hospital. He's not looking so good."

"I'm fine, sir."

"You're screwed up, Barney. Better get your oil checked. Get him down the road, Major."

Major Phelan or someone has already taken action. Within a moment or two, I'm on my back, on a litter, and being loaded in the cracker box ambulance. A small crowd of the curious has now gathered around the doors of the meat wagon. I'm going for a ride, with a Corpsman at my side. I look up and say, "Hey Doc, I'm okay, really. Ummm... my damn head is killing me. Helluva headache. How about...ah, an aspirin...or somethin'?"

"I got your aspirin, Captain."

I got what I wished, another Doc Eden. I get the grin, and he gives me a shot. I mumble something else, then it's good night Barney.

I wake up. Look up. Lucy is staring at me, and she is talking a mile a minute and playing Mom or nurse, tucking in the sheet. I look around, gather my dimmed wits, and realize I am in a bed in the Da Nang hospital, in one of their funny blue PJ suits. A Corpsman asks me, "How you feel, Captain? You've been out awhile."

"Feel fine, Doc. Hi, Lucy."

"Hello, Barney. I suppose I have to be nice to you for awhile."

"Yeah, do you know how?"

"I'll work at it."

The Corpsman interrupts and says, "You're okay, Captain. A bad concussion. Some small cuts, scrapes and minor punctures from the debris. Nothing serious. Do you want to notify someone?"

"About what?"

"Your status."

"Naw, not important. I'll take care of it later."

"Okay, sir, but you should let me see to it."

"Nope, forget it. Don't want to worry anyone. All in due time."

I spend two days here. My lucky break is a result of the mortar round being a ChiCom 60mm., which unlike ours, breaks up in an irregular pattern, and is not as effective or dependable. If it had been one of ours, I'd be a dead man. Maybe the Mizpah protected me.

Everyone leaves so I write a note to Ryley to let her know what happened without going into any details, and that I'm fine, cute as ever, and haven't lost anything important. I think, to be perfectly honest, I'm surprised I'm alive.

Sadowski waits for me with the sedan when I am discharged. We return to the beach house in time for dinner. The general is in jovial spirits because all turned out okay. Colonel Bartlett is on the way stateside. He will be fine although he will have some problems with his right eye, plus some nerve damage on that side of his face. I'm okay, fully recovered and back on the job. The general believes the article will be great and tell the story of what the Marines are doing over here.

The general says, "Barney, I spoke to the Commandant, and he had a representative from his office call Ryley to let her know you're okay."

"What for, sir. I wrote to her. I don't want to scare her to death."

"Well, yes, that's good. I was told that you didn't want anyone notified, but there was, or is, a slight problem with your logic."

"What's that, sir?"

"The photographer took a picture at Con Thien that shows you in the trench line tending Colonel Bartlett. You didn't look so good either. Unfortunately, it went out on the AP wire and wound up on the front page of most major newspapers in the country. Forty-three to be exact, to include the *LA Times*. A lengthy article accompanied the photo. So, your remark about the notification, however admirable, was at the worse ill timed, and at best, entertaining."

"Was my name under the picture?"

"Of course. And in the article. Why?"

"I don't know. How clear was the picture? If it wasn't clear, no one would know it was me, but then those jerks put my name in the paper. Never mind, sir, stupid thought process. Not thinking clearly. Well, I guess I owe you and the Commandant's office a thanks."

"Yep, you owe me one. Actually when I think of it, you owe me a lot. But then, I probably owe you something as well. So, how about a movie? Nothing like a good western to pep you up."

"Let me guess, Bob Steele and Frontier Playhouse?"

"Nope, but close. Chester and I are going to humor you. Barney, let's have a drink to welcome you home."

"Now that sounds great, General, unless you're going to throw me in hack again?"

"It's an idea, but not tonight. It made you too popular with the staff. Tonight, you get some slack. Just enough to--"

"Yes, sir. I get it."

So, it's off to the living room for a drink, and some *Gunsmoke.* Life is good. Tomorrow we continue our journey as if nothing happened, and wait for another pin in the Barney doll. None of this bothers me.

What does bother me however is, he said welcome home, and I agreed. Home! One of us, or perhaps both, has been here way too long.

Chapter Forty-Three

A FEW DAYS PASS AND life as I know it goes on. Enemy activity picks up throughout the I Corps area, especially up north. The NVA engage us in larger numbers around the Khe Sanh firebase.

The calls to Lieutenant General Mueller increase, but Murphy's Law doesn't allow me to win, not even once. It would be my Achilles heel except that General Barto no longer chews me out, or even pretends to do so. It must not be entertaining anymore.

At the briefing this morning, the Intelligence Officer indicates there is an expectation that sapper attacks will pick up. The general's beach house in particular is a prime target. I don't want to hear this, but realistically while it may be an inviting target, it's not an easy one.

The Seal compound is next door, so that takes care of one side. The ocean is on another, with a white sand beach not easily crossed undetected. The other two sides would mean scaling two chain link fences with razor wire on top, or cutting through them. Then the open area of the helo pad to be traversed, and another fence line. Sentries with dogs patrol the entire area. Ah ha! The guard dogs...Lady, it's all clear now. I don't need to worry about sappers, just the guard dogs, and maybe Sadowski.

Nonetheless, we do heed the alert and increase security. I go over our plan with the household staff should anyone breach the fence line and get at or into the house. I have their undivided attention. Even Sadowski is alert; well, conscious.

Today, the general has scheduled a luncheon for all the Marine Corps generals in country plus the admiral from Da Nang. This is nine two and one-star generals and one admiral. Including General Barto, this is a lot of brass, and one chunk of chrome, me, attending the luncheon.

After the morning briefing, the general buzzes me into his office and says, "Barney, I'm going up north this morning. You stay here. Make sure everything is set for the luncheon. I want this done right."

"Okay, sir. You know, Anders can handle this just fine. I don't need to stay here."

"Yes, that's probably so, but I want you here to make absolutely sure."

"Sir,--"

"Barney."

"Aye aye, sir. Here's the seating chart and menu. The chart's easy...just seniority. I was the easiest to place."

"That's true, but you won't always be a captain."

"Well, if you put me in hack a few more times, I won't even be that."

"Now that's a tempting thought. See you later."

"Later?"

"Yes."

"Aye aye, sir."

The general slams his cap on his head and charges out of the office. I'm uneasy. I feel a pinprick, or smell an ambush. Maybe my senses are working overtime. I think, leaving me behind, and then he said, "See you later", not "See you at lunch". I'm probably just getting punchy.

Speaking of pinpricks, I see the pin, Madame Quy, and the... never mind, Captain Quy, hurrying toward the office in short, choppy steps that are caused in part because the Dragon Lady is wearing an Ao Dai. Strange, that's a bit formal for this time of day. She's up to something. Wonder what? I don't care and not going to find out. Since the general is gone, this will be easy and quick. However, I need to be careful. I don't want a curse on top of the pinprick.

They enter; I greet them in a warm tone of voice, "Ah, Captain Quy and Madame Quy. Good to see you. The general's gone, and I'm leaving."

She says, "He no here?"

"You got it. And, I'm soon no here. Bye."

"Me need--"

"Me don't. Captain Quy, take care of this...as I've told you before. I'm outta' here." I put on my cap, head for the lesser of the three evils. Corporal Sadowski is waiting in the sedan. I should have been nicer. Could be a mistake. She could put a curse on me!

Noontime arrives, and I'm waiting at the house. Everything is in order, except the general has not shown up yet, nor have I heard from him. The first of the generals land.

One by one, each in their own chopper, they arrive, until all are present, with one exception, General Barto. I still haven't heard from him, and can't raise him on the radio. I tell the stewards to serve some sherry, and I play aide and host, pretending that everything is hunky-dory. Just about the time a few of the generals begin to grumble and start to get peeved at me, the steward tells me there is a call on the general's line.

I take the call in the study. It's the general. He says, "Barney, I'm not going to make it back. I'm still up north. You take charge of the show. Ask General Wayne to sit at my spot at the table as the official host."

"Sir, I don't think this is going to go over very well. Everyone is already ticked off."

"No, no. They'll understand. Just do it. I'll see you later tonight. Oh yes, another thing, Martha needs to be picked up this afternoon. She's in Saigon and is coming for dinner. She'll call you. Take care of it. Got to go." The line goes dead...so will I in about thirty seconds.

I return to the living room to find the tight-jawed generals glaring at me. They probably think when I issued the invitations, I got the date mixed up. No one ever, ever, thinks the general screwed up. Has to be the dumbass aide. I sidle up to Major General Wayne and whisper the situation. He takes a step back and loud enough for all to hear, says, "What! Are you sure?"

"Yes, sir. Positive. I just got off the hook with the general."

"Why didn't you let me speak to him?"

"I couldn't. He hung up."

"Well, this is a helluva mess. Okay, tell the others and let's sit down and eat."

"Yes, sir."

The others are obviously already alerted. They are frowning and staring at me. I feel like I'm tied to a post in the middle of a courtyard waiting for the crack of the rifles. Madame Quy, damn her!

I inform the others by making a brief announcement, starting with a smooth opening, "Sirs, I mean, Generals, no, I mean, Gentlemen. General Barto will be unable to attend, and has asked General Wayne to host the luncheon on his behalf. Sirs, lunch is served." There is some mumbling, a few grunts and some more glaring at me. Then, like a good Border Collie, I gently herd them toward the seating chart and table.

Just as I'm about to reach the table, Major General Nichols pulls me aside and says, "Captain Quinn, I am senior to General Wayne, so I should sit in as the host. Let General Wayne know, and change the seating cards accordingly. I'll wait out here until you do so."

"Sir, wouldn't it be better if you informed General Wayne, and just sort of quietly switched chairs?"

"No, you're in charge here."

I think, that's highly unlikely today, but I ease over to General Wayne, who is already seated in the host spot. I lean over and whisper the message from General Nichols. He rakes back his chair nearly clipping me on the jaw, leans back in his seat, jutting his chin up and forward toward me, and says, "What did General Barto tell you to do?" Everyone hears his question, probably even General Nichols in the other room.

"Well, sir. He told me to have you sit here and host the luncheon on his behalf."

"Then, that's what I'm going to do, and I suggest you also follow his orders. You tell General Nichols what General Barto said, and let's get on with this luncheon. We're all hungry, busy and have places to go."

"Sir, wouldn't it be better if you informed General Nichols of this, sir?"

"No, you do it."

Damn, now I feel like the steel ball in a pinball machine. First one general, then the other pulls the spring-loaded knob back. The I go ding...ding...flip...ding, ding. I back away from the table, go around the screen at the end, and confront General Nichols, who is waiting in the living room with his hands on both hips. "Sir, General Wayne asked that I inform you that General Barto specifically asked him to host the luncheon today, and that he is going to do so, sir."

"Well, is that exactly what General Barto said?"

"Pretty much, sir."

"Is that exactly...exactly what he said, Captain?"

"Yes, sir. Exactly. Sir."

"Humpf. Tell my deputy, General Gallagher, I'm leaving. Is my chopper here?"

"No, sir."

"Well, get it here, quickly."

"Yes, sir. It'll take several minutes. Can I get the general anything, sir?"

"You can get my Deputy, and you can get my damn chopper. And quick, is that clear?"

"Yes, sir. Clear as...Very clear, sir."

Things are going to hell in a hand basket. I may not forgive the general for this one. Wow, big threat!

I quickly call for the two generals' chopper. The voice on the other end says, "Sir, all the pilots went to chow at the mess."

"Listen carefully! Go get him immediately, and tell him to get his aviator ass out here quicker than a duck on a June bug. Understand? A-Friggin-SAP."

"Damn, yes, sir! Aye aye, sir. Right away, sir."

I return from the study with 'sirs' ringing in my ear, fix myself at attention in front of General Nichols, "Sir, the choppers are on the way, I hope." I wince. I wish I could suck back in the "I hope."

"Hope, bullshit! Get 'em here."

"Yes, sir. On the way, sir. By your leave, sir."

With my own 'sirs' dancing in my ears, I stride into the dining room, whisper to General Wayne what has occurred, then quickly side-step over to Brigadier General Gallagher snapping my heels together with each step. I whisper to him his commander's wishes. He gets up, excuses himself with a sheepish grin and leaves. I sit down at the table, and say, "Gentlemen, I'm very sorry for the delay, and the confusion. Lunch is served. Thank you, sirs." I nod to Alvarez and the others who are frozen at parade rest, watching with bulging eyes this verbal sumo-wrestling match.

I hear the chopper arrive. The two generals leave the house without a word to the others. The lunch goes on, rather quietly. I attempt to start a few conversations, but get the "shut-up-dummy" look, so I do. There is some small talk, but it is clipped in nature thereby setting a new speed record for a guest luncheon at the quarters.

The meal ends without further casualties. I call in the choppers in the proper order so not to bruise any more egos. The admiral came by sedan, so he isn't subjected to any delay. The time between choppers is not very long. It only seems like an eternity as the waiting generals glare at me, glance at their watches, then at the sky, and then back at me. I shrug and scan the sky, as if I'm also concerned. However good my act, it's probably apparent I don't give a crap.

As each chopper lands, and the appropriate general boards and takes off, I stand and dutifully get pelted with debris while saluting the departing general. I hope they can't read my lips.

I take for granted Captain Olney and WO Anders are hiding. They won't come out until after I confront General Barto this evening, and an "all clear" is sounded. I tell the stewards, who are huddled around the stove in the galley that Martha is coming for dinner tonight. I also tell them the lunch was great, and they did a good job. This relieves their stress although they are looking me over for any telltale battle damage. There isn't any, unless the pinhole is apparent. Madame Quy not only pricked the Barney doll but perhaps rewarded my rudeness with a curse.

I head to the general's study to take Martha's call and arrange an aircraft to bring her here this evening. All I need is one person to give me some crap on the phone and I'll assume the general's three stars, and chew some ass. No one utters a word, which makes a statement for mental telepathy.

Evening comes, the general is not back yet, but Martha is already here, at the house. She says, "Where's Walter, Barney. He invited me, and he's not here?"

I still struggle with the first name bit but manage, "Please, Martha, don't start, even jokingly."

"Why?"

"Trust me, you don't want to know."

"Tell me. I won't say anything. Really!"

I do and the good woman that she is, understands, says no more about it, and sits. Corporal Alvarez gets her a drink. The other aides have come out of hiding and join us in the living room. I have Alvarez get me a drink, and Olney and Anders follow suit.

While we are sipping refills, I hear the chopper approach and land. Everyone looks at me. I don't move, just continue to sit and sip.

The general walks in, looks around, then back to me and says, "Oh, started without me, huh?"

"Which time, sir?"

He laughs, and says, "Good line, Barney. Been an entertaining day, I guess. Martha, I'm sorry for being late."

She nods, smiles, and says, "Not a problem, Walter. Barney has been entertaining me."

"Again, huh? Good. Barney, come into the study for a moment."

"Yes, sir."

We go into his study. He closes the door behind us, looks at me, grins, and says, "Got kicked around a little today, I suppose? I've heard from just about everyone."

"Yes, sir, I'd say as luncheons go, today was pretty much a flop. We did set the guest luncheon speed record, however."

"Well, Barney, you did just great. Everyone told me to tell you that. They are all sorry they put you through the wringer. So am I."

"Do I get to put you in hack, sir?"

"Not likely, but you won't have to watch *Gunsmoke* tonight. How's that?"

"What a deal."

"And you won't have to take Martha back tonight. Someone else can."

"That'll keep me out of trouble for a change."

"Yep. Okay. Why don't you go back out and host the group while I clean up. Consider it some additional general officer training." He laughs. I smile, along with a muffled laugh. He's taking my place as the team comedian.

I turn, go back to the living room, and say, "Let's have another drink. I don't feel like dinner just yet. Mister Anders, tell Sergeant Cartwright I'll let him know when I want to eat."

Anders gets up smartly, and starts walking toward the galley. I say, "Mister Anders, it's a joke. Sit down. Finish your drink. The general will be out in a minute."

"Yes, sir."

"And Mister Anders, stop having the last word all the time."

Damn, I feel good. I think I can be a general.

Chapter Forty-Four

I RECEIVE A LETTER FROM Ryley tonight. I expected one sooner after the incident at Con Thien. When it didn't come I was concerned and now the reason is apparent. She writes she did get a call from the Commandant's office, and it was very timely to say the least. The CMC's rep called early, ten minutes to seven in the morning, west coast time. He explained what happened.

After the call, she turned on the TV for the morning news and within a few moments, there was the trench line picture of Colonel Bartlett and me, and the story. She was most thankful for the call, particularly under the circumstances, but the picture still shocked her.

She tells me she got my "scribbled" note after the incident. Her callous manner of referring to it sounds as if she is upset with me for taking so long to write and for scratching out a brief, almost indecipherable note on pocket notebook paper. Damn, that was all I had.

She continues about being unable to cope with not knowing when I will be home. Further, she writes women friends at work tell her not to expect me home very soon and not to expect me to care. She writes some said, "Marines only care about the Corps." This is gossipy and not true of course. She is in a selective listening mode.

I thought I had detected some discontent in her last letter but I let it slide. This letter rambles on about me staying longer not being fair. She wants to date and not just sit around wondering if I'm okay, or when I'll be home. Hell, it was her decision not to date. She adds she wants to move ahead with her life. This remark pisses me off. To start dating is no big deal, but the last line says much more. I believe it's a reflection of some previously hidden or unseen character flaw.

I write back telling her I can't influence what happens to me here and have little control over events. Additionally, it's highly unlikely any great harm will come to me. That time has probably passed. Further, I have no idea when I will be coming home. The general wants me here until he leaves. I'll stay. It's my duty. It's life in the Corps...or as I know and love it. Nancee saw it.

I let Ryley know that my feelings toward her haven't changed. She should remember the words of the Mizpah, and listen to her heart and me, not disgruntled gossipmongers and witches. I'm devoted to the Corps. That's different than lovin' a person. Helluva difference. I tell her if she is truly unhappy, and wants to move on, so be it. It's her choice, but give it serious thought first because I will be returning. My final words are, "If I hear back I'll know you're still on board. If not, you've jumped ship." After I seal the letter, I think, maybe I should have phrased it differently but that's me...my lingo.

I'm not pleased about this. It hurts, but it's the ebb and flow of life. At least it's life, and that's more than Baronowski and others have.

Breakfast this next morning is as normal. I don't feel much like talking, and don't. We eat, in silence except for the occasional, "Salt down," or the "On the way" response. Olney and Anders speak only when spoken to at the table. The good news is that the general has slowed down his eating so we all finish at the same time. When done, the general and I head for the chopper.

When we get to the office the general tells me to follow him inside. He asks, "What's wrong with you this morning?"

"Nothing, sir. Just a bit preoccupied."

"What's wrong?"

"Aw, nothing important, sir."

"Tell me."

I tell him, at least some of it, and end by saying,

"No sweat, I'll be back on track before the briefing is over, sir."

"She's important. I just don't have a date, Barney. Don't even have a clue when we will be leaving."

"That's okay, sir. I understand. Not to worry."

"Good. Let's get to work. However, if there's something I can do, you'll be sure to ask. Won't you?"

"Yes, sir. Moving on, sir. Has the general rehearsed that speech I wrote? The luncheon with the Koreans is today."

"No, but I looked at it. It's fine."

"Sir, you should have rehearsed it. You need to take time after the briefing to do so. I can sit in and listen if you want."

"No, not necessary. I've given speeches before. Let's get to the briefing."

"Yes, sir."

He and the Chief of Staff charge through the back door of his office. I go out the front and head for the chopper to make sure Bill is ready for the trip to the Blue Dragon Brigade. The Koreans are leaving Vietnam and going home, hence the luncheon.

The thought of that just rubs more salt in my mental gash and gets me to thinking. Ryley should remember there are three categories of people leaving here. The dead, the seriously wounded, and those whose tour date is completed. Right now, I'll be in the latter group at some point in time, and I would think that should be enough.

After the briefing, with my mind on business again, the general and I head south to the luncheon. He is their guest of honor. He still hasn't rehearsed the speech. I'm worried about this but helpless at this point.

We land at the Blue Dragon Brigade headquarters, and are met by their Commanding General, and instantly overrun by his entourage. There is something about Asians; they react like disturbed Texas fire ants, crawling and scurrying about, surrounding their generals. Today is no exception. I'm nearly trampled into the dust of the LZ, and quickly separated from the general. He's okay, and oblivious to all the hoopla. I'm not invited to the luncheon, so will simply stand just inside the door of the large general mess to watch and listen.

The luncheon goes well, except for the native Korean dishes that will, I'm sure, give the general heartburn and probably the Seoul, kimchi quick steps. The traditional toasts follow lunch. Their CG presents General Barto with several mementos and follows with the introductory remarks. I will have to carry the mementos and find a place for them at the beach house, along with the hundreds of others he's received in the past. If I can't find a spot for display, they go into the storage closet until a Korean guest arrives. Then they come out, are put on display so as not to hurt feelings and bruise egos.

Every unit has a plaque, and they present one to the general. The other popular gift is *Zippo* cigarette lighters with the unit emblem. We have enough of these to supply a battalion of arsonists. We get another.

After being introduced, General Barto rises slowly to

resounding applause and a tumultuous Korean Marine version of "Hoo Ah." He breaks out in a broad grin, absorbing the moment and then thanks the gathering. He acknowledges the CG, and then the other dignitaries, some press, and commences his remarks.

It doesn't go well. At the end, the Koreans, on cue from the CG, politely applaud, loud enough but there is a noticeable contrast to earlier. He and the CG shake hands and start moving to leave. The entourage rumbles toward me like a stampede of water buffalos. A Korean lieutenant laterals me the three or four mementos. The entourage or more accurate, the herd shoves me aside, and in a cloud of dust and the smell of lighter fluid and Kimchiba, head for the chopper. I ride drag.

Unknown to me, the general has offered a ride to some of the press. Consequently, when we get to the helo pad he is busy personally directing traffic and loading the chopper. I try to take over and get him on board, but he pushes me toward the chopper, motioning me to get in. He's busy being an aide, so I jump in and leave him to his folly. Screw it, in this turmoil if not careful, I could be left here, and wind up back in Korea.

He has put a correspondent, Jim Lucas, up front in his seat. We have almost a full load in the bird. Captain Dunn, looking into the back of the chopper, sees me, and assumes everyone must be aboard since I'm always in last. He turns up the rotors, picks up slightly in a hover, and is preparing to leave when I tap him on the shoulder and point to the general standing outside, glaring into the cockpit. He is partially obscured in the swirling dust, but Captain Dunn can easily see the look on his face since the general's cap is cartwheeling across the LZ.

He scowls at Dunn with those steely blue eyes. Some Korean Marine lieutenant is chasing the general's cap around in the swirling rotor wash like a guy running down a decapitated chicken. He finally captures the cover and hands it to the general, while losing his. The chase starts anew. Meanwhile, the general is yelling something but no one can hear him above the whine of the engines and the whomping of the rotor blades. He is also eating a lot of dust so every several words he has to stop and spit out some mud. I should take out the Polaroid and snap a picture, but I don't dare. He is one pissed off three-star general.

Bill Dunn settles the bird back down on its skids and the general climbs in back, scowling and muttering. He sits, puts on his seat belt, and with a snarling look, glances over to me on the far side of the chopper. I shrug my shoulders and give him my best "you-were-in-charge" look.

We drop the hitchhikers off at their various locations, and continue on to III MAF. The general and I debark, walk up the pathway to the building. Halfway there, he stops and asks, "Well, Barney, what did you think of my speech?"

"Sir, the speech was very good." He smiles as I pause gathering courage. "The delivery was terrible. You didn't rehearse." His smile vanishes.

"What do you mean, terrible? What was wrong?"

"Well, sir. First, you mispronounced several words, some more than once. Then, twice, you referred to the South Koreans as North Koreans. Then you 'renamed' their unit the Green Dragon Brigade. Last, you called the Brigade a Division. Overall, not good. Rehearsal would have been good."

"It was a poorly written speech. Hard to follow. Awkward phrases. I'm not going have you do this anymore. I'll get someone with more experience."

"That's fine, sir. I can accept that, but it won't make any difference if you don't take the time to rehearse."

"As usual, you don't know what you're talking about and worse, won't shut up." He turns abruptly, takes several more charging steps toward the office. He suddenly stops again causing me to ram into him. He snaps around facing me and says, "If it was so poorly done, why did they applaud, and tell me afterwards what a wonderful speech it was?"

"Sir, you really don't think they would boo, and tell you it was a terrible speech, do you? Of course they told you it was wonderful. You're a three star general."

"What's that got to do with it?"

"Everything, sir."

"Hogwash! You just can't admit you're wrong, can you?"

"Not this time, sir."

"You're doing it again."

"What, sir?"

"Last word."

"I was just answering the general's questions, sir."

He shakes his head in frustration, turns, and charges the last several steps to his office. The Protocol Officer, Major Phelan, who was with us today, and has been trailing behind, has overheard both exchanges.

"Jesus, Quinn! Does this go on all the time?"

"Until death do us part, Major, and an annulment or divorce is not possible, not an option. We're catholic."

He looks at me, shakes his head, and gives me the sign of the cross as if he were a priest. He strolls toward his office, laughing aloud, and shouts over his shoulder,

"You're priceless...just priceless, Barney." He has another aide story to tell at the bar.

The general and I continue the afternoon in silence. At 1800 hours, Jim Lucas returns. He's a correspondent and author of the book, *Dateline: Vietnam.* He's coming to dinner tonight, so the general has invited him to ride with us on the chopper out to the quarters. He sits down, makes some small talk with me, and then finally asks, "Captain Quinn, when do you think the general is going home?"

I expect this from most of the media people, but not Jim. He is a favorite of the general, has been a guest at the house often, and the general gives him preferential treatment. I say, "Jim, I'm really surprised you would ask me. Not only surprised, but also irritated. You know better, dammit."

"Just asking. If anyone has a clue, it would be you."

"Well, I don't have a clue, and if I did, I couldn't, and wouldn't, say a word."

"Sorry, just askin."

"No, you were probing, digging. Looking for an edge. There's a big difference. There is no date. Ask the general tonight if you'd like. I should drop a flag. You're hitting late, and out of bounds to boot."

"Okay. Okay, I'm sorry. Jeez, you're sensitive today."

"I'm sensitive all the time. Today, I'm pissed."

He shakes his head back and forth, sighs, and slouches back in the chair. This has not been a good day for me, and looks as if it is continuing to barrel downhill. I probably need to be put in isolation or get a rabies shot.

After a few minutes, Jim asks, "Hey, Barney. When are you going home?"

"Un-friggin-believable! Jim, kiss my ass. That's a cheap shot. What is it about 'no date' you don't get?"

Before he can reply and the situation gets any uglier, the general bursts out of his office, grabs Lucas around the shoulders, and they beat a hasty path toward the chopper. I call Dunn, tell him to turn up the Huey, and then jog after the two of them, drafting along as usual.

It's just the general, Lucas, and the aides at the table tonight. Dinner is congenial, mostly because before dinner I hang my mouth over a glass and drain the venom. The conversation at dinner is mostly about the war and on-going ops. No remarks about going home.

After dinner, the general and Jim Lucas go into the study, and spend a few hours talking. The other aides and I go to the hut. I think all hands would like to put me in a cage for the night. I tell Olney that he's the duty rider tonight and will take Lucas back to Da Nang. Then I sit, and re-read Ryley's letter. It hasn't changed. The outcome is the same.

I'm jolted out of my gloom by the buzzer. The general wants to see me, or Jim Lucas is leaving, or both. Because of the hour, I assume both, and tell Captain Olney to saddle up and come with me. He scurries after me. My personal entourage.

The general and Lucas are waiting at the front door. Jerry escorts Jim to the waiting sedan manned by Corporal Sadowski. Sadowski looks relieved it's not me taking Lucas back. In fact, all of the household staff has been giving me a wide berth since I stormed into the quarters tonight. They can be perceptive on occasion. Even Lady is not poking around the door as usual, looking to sneak in or to snag a handout.

The sedan pulls out, and the general and I return to the study. I ask, "Is there anything else tonight, sir?"

"Jim and I had a good evening. He apologized for asking about our departure date."

"Sir, he didn't ask, he probed. Was digging, like a nickel and dime reporter."

"Barney, you're a hard man. Okay! Whatever. He apologized. You need to lighten up. I told him I don't have a date and am not anticipating leaving anytime soon. Happy?"

"Yes, sir. I'm sorry I jumped his bones but, he was acting like an ordinary press puke."

"Whoa, you are angry."

"Sorry. I'm over it. Anything else for tonight, sir?"

"No, I don't think...Ah, yes, there is something. Barney, you were right about the speech. It was well written. It was me. Next time, make me rehearse."

"Make you? Don't think so. Maybe, insist."

"Insist?"

"Urge, sir."

"No, insist...and be resolute."

"Yes, sir. Good night. See you in the morning, sir."

He nods.

I say, "Remember, nods count, General."

He shakes his head, mutters, "Hard man. Hard, hard man. But you're like a...never mind. Good night, Barney." He smiles and closes the door.

I nod, even if only at the closed door.

Chapter Forty-Five

THE BUZZER IN THE AIDES hut goes off, startling me out of a comatose-like sleep. I've been sleeping like this ever since leaving the paddies. No need for one eye open and an ear listening for patrol reports. Olney and Anders are up as well, and like me are trying to guess what the hell is happening. I jump into my utilities, slip on my boots and dash to the general's room to see what's cookin' at this hour. It's 0517, so whatever it is, can't be good.

I arrive at the study, slide to a halt on the tile to find the general in his skivvies, on the phone. He's listening intently, nodding his head, emitting grunts and groans, and asking a question every so often. Something has occurred, probably in the last thirty minutes or less. Possibilities race through my mind as to what might be going on or has happened. By the general's facial expressions and his replies, I know this is an ugly start to a day. In this part of the world, one doesn't need words, just the senses. After what seems like an eternity, he's off the phone. "Barney, the Nam O Bridge has been blown. We're going there as soon as it gets light. Have the cook rustle up something and get the chopper."

"Yes, sir, will do."

"How soon can we go?"

"First light will be in about forty minutes. Everything will be set so we can leave right then."

"Okay, get on it. And send Alvarez in here."

"Yes, sir."

I leave, get Alvarez up first and on his way letting him know what is happening. At the same time, I roust SSgt Cartwright up to cook, and the others as well, to start their day. I tell Cake, "We don't have a lot of time so just make some egg sandwiches that we can eat here, or on the run. Plus some coffee and juice." Then I call Captain Dunn, brief him, and tell him to come directly here and bring along a loaded chase bird. I'll have feed bags for him and his guys.

Checking my watch, I realize I have already used up fifteen minutes. I hurriedly shave, get squared away, and take off my boots so I can now put on some socks, which I hadn't taken the time to do earlier. I head to the kitchen and check Cartwright's progress. Everything is about ready. I hear two birds landing outside. Captain Dunn is a good man.

The Nam O Bridge across the Cu De River is just northwest of Da Nang, and connects the area to the Hai Van Peninsula and points north. It is the main train and road artery. It's important, and the general is more than perturbed.

As I get to the study, the general is on the phone again. When he's off, he tells me the III MAF Engineering Officer went out to the bridge immediately after the incident, and while there inspecting the damage, either slipped, or the part he was inspecting, collapsed. He was killed in this mishap. The general is visibly upset, distressed, and now angrier than previously. This is not a pleasant dawn, and Barney's Law suggests it's going to be downhill from here, straight to the crapper.

We go to the table, don't sit, just chug-a-lug the juice, take a few gulps of coffee scalding our tongues and throats. We grab the fried egg sandwiches and run for the chopper. Cake has thrown several more in bags. I bring these for the pilots and crews. The general and I get on board; we lift off and head for the bridge.

We land inside the rifle company's perimeter at the bridge, get out, and the general says, "Barney, go find the Company Commander and tell him to get over here. I'm going to take a look at the bridge."

"Aye aye. Sir, be damn careful around the bridge."

"Right. And Barney, look around the area, tell me what you see here and what you think. How prepared is this company? Be your company commander self again, okay?"

"Yes, sir. And be careful, Dadgummit."

"Okay, okay. Don't soft peddle the answer. Tell me like you see it. Be you."

"As always, sir."

The general leaves, stomping briskly toward the bridge with short, angry steps and fists clenched. I locate what looks like a company CP tent and head that direction. As I approach, a captain is ambling toward me. I say, "Captain, I'm Captain Quinn. General Barto's Aide. He just landed, as you can tell, and is over by the bridge."

He nods and grunts, "Huh?"

"Are you the Company Commander?"

"Yeah."

"Okay. The general wants to see you." Pointing to the bridge, I add, "Over there."

"Ah, who are you again?"

"Captain Quinn, General Barto's Aide. You need to get moving.

He is not a happy camper this morning. But, first, what the hell happened here last night?"

"Oh, sappers I guess, came in and blew the bridge. We just got here last night. Relieved the company that was here. They left late, after midnight, so we were just sort of getting into our positions."

"How many sappers? Just them or with a unit?"

"Not sure."

"Did you have LP's out? Patrols? Any activities out?"

"Whoa, is this any of your business?"

"Captain, if it's the general's business, it's mine. Now just answer my questions. Any ambushes or patrols out last night?"

"No, didn't have time by the time we got set in. Will tonight."

"A little late, Skipper. Okay, get over to the general, ASAP. He's pissed, so be careful."

"Yeah, yeah, right."

"Hey, Captain, I'm giving you a heads up here. You had better take advantage of it, because things could get ugly for you real quick. And oh yeah, shoot straight with the general."

"Hey, I heard you."

"Good, then you won't have any complaints when the shit hits the fan, right?"

He smirks, raises his eyebrows shaking his head as he shuffles off toward the bridge and the general. I walk around, eyeballing the area and the troops. They look tired, and probably are, but they have another look about them. They're not alert, sloppy, have the look of an undisciplined unit; don't seem concerned. Sometimes, units get that way. Tired, worn down, then careless. It takes attention with positive and stringent leadership to preclude this. The general will see this in a New York minute if he already hasn't. He won't have to ask me.

I work my way back to where the general is standing, talking to the Company Commander. When I get there, I have no way of knowing what has transpired to this point, but I can tell it hasn't gone well as far as the general is concerned. He is flushed, hands at his side, clenched into fists again. His lips are jammed closed and sealed white. Just as I come up to them, I hear the general say, "Captain, you stand at attention when I talk to you, regardless how damn tired you may be."

I think, oh shit, I don't know where this conversation has been, but it's going downhill faster than a California mudslide. Just after the captain slovenly eases to a position of attention, the general asks, "Captain, why isn't your name stenciled on your utility jacket?"

"Sorry, sir. I haven't had time to do that yet."

"How long have you been here?"

"Here, sir, at the bridge?"

"No, Damnit, in country, Captain."

"Five months, sir."

"And you haven't had time? It's a III MAF order! My order! What other orders do you ignore?"

The captain doesn't reply because he doesn't have time, which is fortunate. The general quickly follows with, "Captain Sanders, do all your troops have their names on their uniforms?"

I'm standing behind the general, slightly offset, and looking the captain square in the eyes. I have his attention, and in the few precious seconds before he conjures up an answer, I violently shake my head back and forth, indicating, say no. No! No! I've been around the area and didn't see one troop that did.

The captain, for whatever reason, probably thinking I'm some sort of pompous, real-echelon asshole, decides to roll the dice. He says, "Yes, sir, they do."

The general turns around, and says, "Captain Quinn, go get me a trooper...Any Marine, do you understand? Any!"

"Yes, sir. Affirmative. Comin' up."

I move a few feet away, look out into the now brightening sunlight since dawn has slipped away, toward what appears to be the main area of activity. I shout, "Give me one Marine over here.

On the double." Getting no response and only seeing some Snuffies staring but not moving, it pisses me off. My earlier observations seem correct. I take a few steps toward some activity, point to a Marine strolling along some twenty yards away, and bark, "You, Marine, come here, right now. Over here. Pronto."

The trooper sees my captain's tracks, sees the general's three stars, and his CO, standing at attention. His eyes get wide and bright. He goes from his shuffle to a lope in one step, and leaps to a halt in front of me. "Sir, Lance Corporal Webster, reporting as ordered, sir."

"Good Webster, now go over to your captain and the general. They want to talk to you."

"Me, sir. I didn't do nuthin'"

"Yes, you, Webster. That might be the problem, no one did nuthin' except the dinks. He just wants to see you."

"Huh?"

"Go, now. Di-di Mau."

"Yes, sir." He darts several steps, slams to a stop kicking up some dust, and repeats his reporting procedure.

Lance Corporal Webster is priceless, vintage Magpie. He's young, unshaven, and looking a bit salty. His jungle utilities are stained and mud splattered which is to be expected under the circumstances. He's holding a can of half-eaten Beanie-Weenies, some of which are on his chin and a glob on the front of his jacket. Unfortunately, he has no name on his utility jacket. He looks like the proverbial Joe Shit the Ragman. Perhaps all can be forgiven this time of day, even the missing name under different circumstances, but not now. I hear a death rattle.

The general looks at him. Raises his eyebrows and shakes his head. Turns to the captain, and says, "Where's his name?"

"Sir, I guess he forgot to put it on the jacket."

The general looks at Webster and asks, "Why don't you have your name stamped on your jacket, Marine?"

"Out here? Am I supposed to, sir?"

"Yes. You're dismissed Marine, and get your name stenciled on your jacket."

"Yes, sir." He salutes, faces about and jogs off to finish his now cold beanie-weenies, and is probably thinking, "Why me? I was just eatin' my friggin beans."

The general continues with the captain, "Why did you lie to me, Captain, or try to BS me?"

"I don't know, sir. I wasn't trying to B--"

"Stow it. I'll tell you why, Captain. You're a gambler. Well, you gambled and lost, which is almost meaningless to me. What is meaningful, however, is that you gambled and lost last night by getting careless because you moved into this area late, and thought it was a rear area, so you could rest easy. You got slipshod. You had no LP's or patrols out. Well, you can't get lackadaisical. Now God-Dammit, I've lost one hell of a fine Marine, a Colonel on my staff, because of your negligence. I can have the bridge rebuilt, but not him."

"Yes, sir. I'm sorry, sir."

"Sorry doesn't hack it, Captain."

The general turns again, says, "Captain Quinn, call this captain's regimental commander, as soon as we get back. Have the captain relieved of his command."

"Sir, I--"

"Barney, just do it."

"Aye aye, sir."

The general turns and heads toward the chopper. Before turning to leave, I look the captain square on and mouth the words, "I told you. Friggin' dumb." I scowl at him and shake my head in disgust. He's still at attention, brows up, eyes wide, and mouth hanging open in disbelief. I jog a few steps to catch up with the general, and we board the chopper and head directly back to the CP.

We land at the III MAF pad and stride briskly toward the office in silence. When we get there, I say, "General, don't you think you should reconsider. I mean, the captain has probably learned a lesson. Relieving him and an official reprimand will be devastating."

"No. You may be right, but I do not want liars, and careless ones at that, commanding my Marines. Do you?"

"Put that way, I would say, no."

"Exactly, so call his regimental commander and have him relieved."

"Sir, don't you think it would be better if you called. You really should in a situation such as this."

"Perhaps, but you can do it. He will be more prone to ask you questions than me, so think of it as you're doing him a favor."

"Well, once again, put that way, I guess you're right. Although, if I were you, I would make the call myself."

"You're not me, and if you keep arguing with me, I'm going to throw you in hack again."

"Yes, sir."

"Barney!"

"Sir."

"Stop."

I nod. He takes a step toward his office, stops, turns, returns my nod trying to lighten the moment. At least we're on the same page this emotionally overcast morning.

I call the Regimental Commander, explain the purpose of the call, what happened at the bridge, and what I saw that I'm sure the general did as well. He listens patiently and says, "You were a company commander before your current assignment, weren't you?

"Yes, sir."

"I've heard of you. You had Lima-three-three, didn't you?"

"Yes, sir."

"Thought so. Do you think the incident could have been avoided, Captain Quinn?"

"Sir, the bridge or the relief?"

"Well, both."

"Sir, not sure about the bridge. My guess is there was an excellent chance it could have been if all the proper activities had been out...although it was a perfect time for sappers to try, what with the change."

"And?"

"The relief. Absolutely. All he had to do was be one hell of a lot more alert, and respectful. And not lie, particularly when I was giving him an obvious signal to say no. It was the straw."

"You gave him a signal. The answer?"

"Yes, sir."

"Did he see it?"

"Five square, sir."

"Okay, Captain. You've done your job, I'll do mine. Good day. Give the general my regards. And Captain, I understand your position and I appreciate your tact."

"Thank you, sir. That's not normally my strong suit. I will pass on the Colonel's regards to the general, sir."

"On second thought. Don't pass on anything. The less he thinks about me today, the better. Thanks again, Captain."

Right or wrong, I quickly give the captain's battalion commander a call. It's a heads up type. When I explain what has happened, he's appreciative. He also knows me, from an operation months ago. I was attached to his battalion.

The remainder of the day is uneventful, which is fine with me, and somber, which is not. If truth be told, I don't feel good about myself, and on top of everything else, no letter from Ryley again today. She's probably jumped ship and left the Mizpah on deck.

My life seems to have a lot of Irish pennants lately. I need to get my sewing kit out and mend my mind.

CHAPTER FORTY-SIX

WEEKS HAVE PASSED SINCE THE bridge incident. We go north again today, visit several positions, are briefed and walk about at each. Then we head back and visit the wounded on first the *Sanctuary,* then the *Repose.*

While aboard the *Repose,* my past catches up to me once again. Chief Nurse Seitz dogs my heels the entire visit. It's awkward. I try to work the Polaroid, pass the snapshots, and take notes but she is trying to get my ear. Finally, formality called for, I say, "Ma'am, I'm busy with the general. Whatever's on your mind, it has to wait. I don't have time for this." Her face floods bright red with anger, her eyes are green pools of hate, and she spins on her heels, mumbling something threatening. I catch enough to know it's an oral nasty gram. This woman is nuts!

The general and I complete our rounds in an uneasy silence. As we depart the ward, he looks at me and says, "What was that all about?"

"Just a skeleton rattling around in my closet, sir."

"Oh? Sounds like a lot more than bones rattling to me. You must have done something ugly. It was quite some time ago as I recall you telling me, wasn't it?"

"Sir, if the general doesn't--?

"Never mind. I don't want to know...anything. Not my business, and want to keep it that way."

"Absolutely, sir. Shouldn't we be leaving, sir?"

"Yes. Don't worry. I don't think she's armed."

"Very funny, sir. Not your business, right, sir?"

"Not unless she shoots."

"The general's become a regular Henny Youngman."

"Good."

"Last word again, sir."

"Finally, the way it's supposed to be."

He laughs aloud as we climb aboard the chopper and head to III MAF even though its early evening.

As we charge up the path toward the office, the general abruptly halts, as he has done so many times before. I'm getting better anticipating these sliding quarter-horse stops. Nonetheless, I almost collide with him. He reins about and says, "Barney, the Commandant called this morning. He told me he thought the *Life Magazine* story was superb. He liked the slant. I agree, I think they did a good job. Have you seen it?"

"Yes, sir. First thing this morning."

"Well, what did you think?"

"They didn't do what they said. It was supposed to be about what we, the Marines, are doing here in I Corps. However, it was really a character study of you and some of that questionable. Not true. Misleading, at best."

"Not true? Misleading? What?"

"The running on the beach. You never ran before that day, not once. It was just bull, sir."

"No, it was a little color."

"And the C-Rats eating routine. That was color too? And you know what they do. I had to get the Doc again."

"How come you always disagree with the Commandant?"

"That was a helleva leap, sir. I don't always disagree with the Commandant."

"You just did."

"Well, sort of, yes, sir, just now. That's not always, sir."

"Damn, you must just like to argue, or rile me."

"No sir. I didn't say I didn't like the article. I just said what they told us they were going to do, they didn't do. It was all about you. In that sense, it was interesting, except for the 'color', sir."

"Forget it. I'm sorry I asked...as usual." He turns about, and stomps the last two steps into his office. He got the last word, at least that's positive. I decide to read the article again. I sense this will come up later, as usual.

In about an hour, the general comes out and says, "Barney, lets go to the hospital, visit the men, pick up Lucy, and head home."

"Yes, sir. Can I have a minute to call the house and let them know that Lucy is coming for dinner?"

"Sure. I'll just stroll down to the chopper."

"Stroll, sir. You've never strolled in your life. If you even have a stroll, it's probably a normal person's trot. And sir, don't leave me here, however great the temptation."

"I should."

He leaves, walking slowly, a nice leisurely stroll. It will do him some good. After several steps, he turns and grins as if to say, "See, I can do it," and wanders on his way. I call the house, alert them, and also call Bill Dunn and let him know the plan. Then, jog down the pathway toward the chopper. I don't have far to lope.

The general has stopped to talk to a few headquarters troops out in the open area of the quadrangle.

As I'm jogging, I see Captain Quy's wife, the Dragon Lady, advancing on the general. This seems to be my day for the older gals. She thinks she has caught him alone, without her mortal enemy protecting him. For her, a target-rich environment, and a chance to get to him with some wild illegal scheme, I'm sure, let alone an opportunity to chastise me.

I change pace to a dash and get to him before she can make contact. He's surprised when I grab his arm, but surrenders to the pressure. As I lead him toward the helo pad he says, "What's this about?"

"The Dragon Lady cometh."

"Oh. Right. Let's get moving."

"Yes, sir, and not at a stroll."

We shift gears into his normal brisk, head down, charge toward the bird, leaving the Dragon Lady behind, frowning with her arms folded across her chest. She will be back at work on the Barney doll this evening. I can feel the daggers from her eyes on my neck. The pins will come later.

We get to the bird and lift off. I look out the chopper door at Mrs. Quy, giving her a sarcastic smile, more a sneer, and wave. I need to work on my behavioral patterns.

The visit at the hospital goes as normal. Lucy meets and accompanies us. We leave, come back to the beach house, have a sherry before dinner, steak and twice-baked potatoes tonight. Their aroma is floating through the galley door as we sip the sherry. The general is quieter than normal so Lucy takes over the conversation, good-naturedly jerking my chain and poking fun at the other aides. She brings up Lady and the pups, which have arrived. She's pressing for names. Anders is in a cold sweat because Lucy pushes him again for some explanation how Lady got into her condition in the first place. Initially I let it slide, he's a better target. However, he appears helpless so I inject, "It was one of the guard dogs."

Lucy's eyebrows rise in mock disbelief, "How so?"

"The usual way, right, Mr. Anders?"

"Huh?"

"Stay alert, Mr. Anders or you'll continue to be easy verbal prey."

Lucy laughs. The general ignores the sparring. After dinner, she and the general go into the study to chat, and Olney, Anders and I return to our hut.

About 2200 hours the general buzzes me, which means Lucy is leaving. I tell Anders he has the guest watch tonight so we head to the house. She is at the door, and Sadowski is waiting with the sedan outside. As she leaves, Lucy looks at me, winks, smiles, then whispers, "Surprise, Barney. Good night." She's gone before I can reply.

The general says, "Barney, come in the study for a few minutes, okay?"

"Yes, sir."

We get inside, he sits down at his desk, rolls the chair away from the desk, leans back slightly clasping both his hands behind his head, and trying not to smile, says, "Barney, I read that magazine article again. You're right. It's mostly about me, and they didn't really do what they said they would. I'm glad I have you around to set me straight."

"I wouldn't go that far, sir."

"Yes you would, and usually do."

"It's my nature, unfortunately."

"Never mind Barney, I'm just kidding with you some."

"You mean about the article, sir?"

"No, not about that. I do have a message for you from the Commandant."

"The Commandant asked you to pass on a message to me, sir? I bet this is a classic. I know for sure he never agrees with me."

"No, no, no...to both of us. We're going home, Barney. I'm going to be relieved in a week. Great news, huh?"

"Well, yes and no."

"What's that mean."

"Good that we're going home, but you're going to be missed over here. You're a fixture. Provide stability, and you really care about the troops."

"Barney, that's the best compliment I've had. Thank you. We made a good team, didn't we?"

"Well, we had our moments. Some great. Some not so great. Some knock-down drag-outs."

"You shouldn't worry; you won almost all of them."

We laugh. Then he says, "Barney, don't say anything to anyone until I notify the major commanders and my senior staff. Tomorrow after the SeaBee Change of Command, you can tell the other aides. They will be going back to their units. Also, I will give you the details of the change of command and of our trip back."

"Yes, sir. Is that all for the night, sir?"

"Isn't that enough. I bet Ryley will be glad to know."

"I don't know, sir. I haven't heard from her in over a month. I believe we're history."

"Really? Are you sure?"

"Pretty much, sir."

"Anything I can do?"

"Naw, not really, sir. Thanks for asking. Goodnight, General."
I close the door, and head for the hut.

Hot damn! I've made it. Well, almost.

Once in the hut, I change out of my utilities and into a sweat suit. I've been sleeping outside on the general's back porch adjacent to his bedroom ever since the threat of a sapper attack. Probably not necessary, but there is a cot out there with a mattress, and the patio is screened so it's pleasant sleeping. It makes me feel better in case something should happen. I keep a pump action shotgun with me. It's my pacifier, and good in close quarters.

The fresh ocean air and sounds of the gentle spilling surf put me asleep quickly while fantasizing about going back to the real world. A loud rushing noise jars my reverie. It sounds like steam gushing out of a huge pipe, but that can't be the case. I leap off the cot, thinking, oh shit, sappers. I grab the shotgun, chamber a round, and with my heart pounding, dart outside around the back of the house toward the noise. I'm expecting to see dinks in black pajamas, but instead there stands Sadowski with a fire extinguisher, putting out the flames in the back of the general's sedan.

There are a few of our sentries also out here, watching the act in the center ring. I unload, sling the shotgun over my shoulder, and approach the ringmaster. "Corporal Sadowski, what the hell happened?"

"The car is on fire."

"No kidding. I see that. How?"

"Not sure, sir. I think maybe I flicked a cigarette out the front window on my way back from Da Nang, and it must have blown in the back. Started the seat on fire."

"Great, it's a nice way to end the day. I thought the general told you he didn't want you smoking in the car? Not to stink it up. Or as it turns out, burn it up."

"Yes, sir. That's why I had the front window open."

"That's why you had the window open?"

"Yes, sir."

"What's the window open have to do...forget it."

"Huh?"

"Yeah, that's another helluva good answer. Great thinking, Corporal."

"Huh?"

"Huh, sir', Corporal."

"Huh?"

"Oh God, never mind. Make sure it's entirely out, clean up the mess out here, and take it in to the motor pool in the morning, if it still runs. They'll be happy to see you."

"Yes, sir."

"Now we're really making progress. Get it done...and get a replacement." I turn and leave. I don't see any lights on in the general's room, so maybe he didn't hear the commotion. I'll tell him in the morning.

Olney and Anders are standing, wide-eyed, outside the aides' hut, with their weapons in hand. I say, "Mister Anders, your boy was smoking in the car. He's not supposed to do that. You were with him. Didn't you see him smoking?"

"Yes, sir."

"You didn't stop him?"

"No, sir."

"Nice, go see your mess. Good night, and don't miss breakfast tomorrow. It should be fun. Oh yes, put your forty-five away. Sadowski might think you're going to execute him. Actually, it might...never mind."

As I enter the hut, I mutter, "The sappers don't have to come here. Sadowski is more dangerous. He'll destroy us piecemeal before we can get out of this place."

Olney says, "Did you say something?"

"No, just mumbling a not so comforting thought. I think I'll spend the remainder of my time here in comfort and sleep inside."

"Yes, sir."

As I stretch out on my bunk, I think about what life will be like without Sadowski everyday. Boring, but blissful. I close my eyes and try to recapture my pre-Sadowski mood. Life in the real world and I'm going to make it.

Fan-friggin-tastic!

CHAPTER FORTY-SEVEN

AT THE BREAKFAST TABLE THE general starts my day by asking, "Barney, what was all that commotion last night?"

"It was Sadowski and the fire extinguisher, sir."

"Fire extinguisher? What was he doing? Was there a fire?"

"Yes, sir. The general's sedan caught fire. He was putting it out."

"Sedan caught fire? What the devil happened? He got it out, I take it?"

"Yes, sir."

"That was quick thinking."

"Not quick enough, nor good enough."

"Why's that?"

"It's pretty much ruined. He flicked a cigarette out the front window on the way back from taking Lucy home. It flew in the back seat, smoldered, and eventually burst into flames."

"I asked him not to smoke in the sedan. What was he thinking? Why did he do it?"

"Well, sir. In the order you asked. You did ask him, but that wasn't an order in his one-cell brain-housing group. Next, he is incapable of rational thought. And, third, because of the first two."

"Don't answer me in your Aide-de-Camp gibberish. When a general asks, it's the same as an order."

"Not to him, sir."

"What do you think we should do about this?"

"Execution is one thought I've had, but I seriously doubt we could get away with it. You could charge him with disobeying a direct order and destruction of government property, plus throw in conduct unbecoming for all the pain he has caused me. If he's lucky, he'll just be busted to private, and we can transfer him to the guard unit and let him walk post in the Motor Pool. The least administrative work would be to transfer him to a rifle company but I wouldn't wish that on anyone. He would get someone hurt. Perhaps best, charge him and let him do some brig time. Then perhaps, we can have a few sane months. And, of course, you would make me immeasurably happy."

The general is quiet momentarily. Captain Olney can't decide to nod in agreement or stick his head in the proverbial sand. He sees himself clear of any culpability, but he probably thinks it's possible to be hit with a stray arrow. Poor WO Anders is squirming in his seat like a man with a bad case of hemorrhoids. He remembers my comment last night. The general takes another sip of coffee, puts down the cup, shakes his head and says, "Barney, what else can go wrong?"

"A lot but we don't have much time left, so perhaps, mercifully, very little."

"Let's go. What's on for today?"

"Briefing as normal, then at 1100, you will be the guest of honor at the SeaBee Change of Command Ceremony. It is followed by a luncheon there at Camp Adenair. Nothing after that."

"Ah yes, you wrote some remarks for me."

"Yes, sir. Did you--"

"Yes, I did. Everything will be fine. At least there's no north and south Seabees." He laughs at his own joke again, and adds, "Let's go."

"Yes, sir."

The general gets up and leaves. I stall for a few seconds, then ask, "Mister Anders, enjoy breakfast this morning?"

"Not really, Captain."

"Good. Just making a bunghole pucker check. You got lucky again. The general is getting mellow."

"Sir, it's tight. Mellow isn't either of you, sir."

"Enough, everyone is trying to be a comedian around here. Get Sadowski and the sedan into the motor pool and explain what happened, and tell the MTO we won't be pressing any charges."

"Sir, the general didn't say--"

"He will. See you guys later. Let's see if we can at least keep the house standing for a while longer. If the sappers come, offer up Sadowski. If they don't take him, surrender the house, but only if they'll take Sadowski too. If not, fight to the death."

I jog out to the chopper. The general is patiently waiting, which is another indicator that our relationship has blossomed into a solid friendship. There was a time when he would have left me. As soon as I get aboard, we lift off for the CP.

We arrive, and walk, not charge, up to the office. As normal, he stops before we get to the office and says, "Barney, you almost let the cat out of the bag."

"Yes, sir. Sorry. I couldn't resist the line."

"Well, don't press charges. I can't do that to his mother."

"It might be a blessing."

"Barney, be kind. He's an okay kid, just a little slow."

"Slow! He's almost comatose."

He raises his eyebrows and slowly shakes his head back and forth several times until he stops, says, "Hard man." The issue is dead and we'll see what the remainder of the day has in store. The Change of Command should be interesting. Commander

Knowles is my SeaBee friend from the dining table. I wonder if he'll remember me?

The general makes the announcement at the briefing about his going home, which is the biggest stir of the morning, hell, the year...no, years. Then he calls all of his major commanders and gives them the news and time frame. This is a courtesy issue because certainly there will be an official communiqué. He looks like he has mixed emotions. He knows he should go home, turn over the job to another, and move forward. However, I believe he would like to stay just a little longer. For me, it doesn't seem to make much difference anymore. Ryley still hasn't written, but then when I seriously think about it, I know I want to get back to the real world, and a life. I'm tired of my role as a glorified house mouse. This conflict is going to last and I'll probably have a second tour here.

When all the calls are made, it's time to leave for the Change of Command. The general charges out of the office and I say, "Sir, do you have your remarks with you?"

"Yes, and I went over them again, Captain." He smiles, and we make our way to the chopper, load up, lift off and head to the show.

We arrive and Commander Knowles greets the general. The general introduces him to me, causing a strange look to creep across the commander's face. In seconds, TPRS, the problem recognition syndrome begins to register. A look of dreadfulness flows down from his forehead to mouth. He greets me pleasantly however, and then leads us to the Reviewing Stand. He takes one last glance back at me. Ding! His eyebrows raise and eyes widen as his head snaps back imperceptibly. Identification, he's certain.

The ceremony takes place and it goes fine. The general makes the first of his remarks to the formation of SeaBees. Then we head to the Officers' Mess Tent for lunch. The general and commander sit at the head of the table. General Barto is sandwiched between the outgoing CO and the incoming one. The XO is next to Knowles. At one point, I see Commander Knowles nod toward me as he converses with the general. The general smiles, then laughs. The XO leans forward and adds to the conversation, chuckling as he does so. This happens two or three times during the course of the meal. I become paranoid. I'm sure it's about the Neanderthal era.

All goes well. The general makes the second set of remarks. When done, he receives a nice round of applause. While this is going on, he glances my way, smiles, and winks. He is developing one helluva sense of humor. I mock applause and nod.

We jump in the chopper and return to the CP. On the walk up, he stops once again and says, "Barney, Commander Knowles remembers you quite well."

"That's nice, sir. I was in his camp for only a short period."

"Yes, and distinguished yourself I might add."

"Well, sir. I had my moments."

"Yes, he used the term 'Neanderthalic individual." Is that a word?"

"Don't have a clue, sir. I've never heard it used before. Was he referring to me?"

"Yes."

"Hummm. Strange, I don't know what--"

"Yes, you do."

"Sir, that was when I was but a wretched ruffian and rowdy. Before you selected me to be your Aide-de-Camp, at which time I became Polite, Refined, and Clean.

The general paused for a few seconds, then laughed and said, "That's you. The Acronym, and I don't mean the radio." With that, he turns and laughs his way into his office, very pleased with himself.

I mutter, "He got it pretty quick. We're going to have to settle who's the comedian and who's the straight man. Barto and Quinn? Sounds okay, however Quinn and Barto has a catchier ring."

"I heard that."

"Yes, sir."

Our days beyond the ceremony are like so many of the others lately. He visits as many areas up north as possible. Khe Sanh, Dong Ha, Gio Linh and a return to Con Thien. We get dinged at by small arms going in to Gio Linh. No hits; I hope we're not pressing our luck.

Today our return to the CP is punctuated by a visit to the hospital in the Marble Mountain area although it's late. I'm going to miss visiting these wounded Marines, and I know the general damn sure will. It's never really pleasant, but their positive attitudes are always infectious. After our brief stay, it's home to dinner with just the aides in attendance.

Dinner starts quietly. Actually, the general entertains us with some sherry before dinner. He informs Captain Olney and WO Anders that he's leaving, and that they will be completing their tours of duty in country with their original units. They seem happy about getting back to their units and real jobs. I don't blame them. All said and be done, they did fine here.

The actual chow time goes quietly and quickly, and after dinner we take in one of the last of the *Gunsmoke* showings we will have. The general will be busy from here on out with farewells at the various units, so we won't have time for Matt, Chester, and the gang.

After dinner, he calls me to the study. It's apparent he's pleased with himself about something. He opens with, "Barney, did you figure it out?"

"Yes, sir. Not too difficult, but it was a dandy zinger. You should be proud of yourself. The general made a joke."

"Who said it was a joke."

"That's two, sir."

"It's a joke, Barney. Just kidding. Let me just tell you briefly that we will be leaving next Saturday and will be going to Korea first. Seoul, landing at Kimpo. We will visit several units during the day. Some locations will be old times for us. The Korean Marines are going to honor me and have a big to do that night. Next, we will go to Atsugi to put on some fuel, then on to Guam for refueling. From there, to FMFPac on Oahu. I will be debriefed and we'll stay over night. Then we'll head home to California, Marine Corps Air Station, El Toro. From there we will go our separate ways."

"I understand. Does the Chief of Staff have all the details?"

"Yes."

"Okay, got it, sir. I'll start coordinating the trip."

"One other thing, our household staff will be going with us."

"All of them? I can understand one."

"Well, we'll be taking the CG FMFPac's specially rigged out C-130 so we'll need SSgt Cartwright in its galley. And, I'll need Alvarez in Korea and Hawaii for the uniforms, so we might as well take the others."

"That means I have to put up with Sadowski for this entire flight, and he and the others will be getting liberty in Korea and Hawaii?"

"Yes, they can go on liberty there."

"I don't think it's a good idea to turn those guys, especially Sadowski, loose in Korea and Hawaii, or any place for that matter."

"You just watch them, and lay down the law. They'll be all right."

"Sadowski and Cartwright wouldn't be all right in a cage."

"Well, they're going, so make the best of it."

"Aye, aye, sir."

"Barney, have you given any thought about where you would

like to be stationed. If it's reasonable and right for you, I'll have it done."

I think, the career monitoring just won't stop. The tour started in this mode, and apparently is going to finish in the same manner. But, what the hey. I say, "Yes, sir. San Diego would be fine. At the Recruit Depot there."

"Consider it done. Plan on it."

"Thank you, sir. Will that be all for tonight?"

"Think this will change Ryley's mind?"

"What? Oh. I don't think so, sir."

"Well, we'll see. You never can tell."

With that the evening is over. I return to quarters to the waiting questions from Captain Olney and WO Anders, and the cook, stewards, and candlestick makers that I have to take with us.

Maybe I could just leave Sadowski in Korea. He probably wouldn't be missed, except maybe by his mother. There is a possibility however that leaving him there would be doing her a huge favor. Not nice, but a thought. I need to be kind. The general has asked, and that's an order.

It reminds me of a line from a poem I once read. "There is one love, even greater than the love of a mother. And that is the love of one dead drunk for another." I don't have a clue how this applies, it just came to my mind.

Maybe I'm losing it, or have lost it.

CHAPTER FORTY-EIGHT

FINALLY, DEPARTURE DAY IS HERE. All the visits are over, the Change of Command is complete, ceremonies are history, and we are choppering over to Da Nang airfield for boarding, and eventually, the real world. I'm still not having any evocative feelings about leaving, but from what I observe the general is suffering a few departure pangs. It's his turn to give up a command. He isn't any more willing to do so than I was. It's not easy. He looks at me, shakes his head. He knows what I'm thinking.

Captain Dunn flares out the Huey, lands and settles. The senior staff is standing in a line leading to the C-130 awaiting the general. The household staff has already arrived, loaded the aircraft with our personal belongings, basically, uniforms so long ago worn in the land of the round eyes. I quickly say goodbye to the gathered III MAF staff, friends indeed. Major Phelan, the Protocol Officer leans forward, shakes my hand, pulls me close and says, "You're a piece of work, Stoneface. You made life a lot easier and more pleasant around here. Good luck."

"Thanks, Major. What are you going to do for belly laughs now that ol' Barney is history?"

"Just think of your travails."

"Travails. That's a ten dollar word for SNAFU's, isn't it?"

"Barney, my friend, you wear travails better."

"Major, thanks...for everything, and go get yourself a real job in a rifle battalion."

"I wish, Barney, I wish. Take care."

I nod, and hurry aboard the aircraft. The general follows in several minutes after the handshakes and comments with those seeing him off. The crew closes the hatch and our tour is over. A simple slamming and securing of a door. Not exactly, but that's what it feels like.

This C-130 of Lieutenant General Mueller's is a thing of beauty. It has a capsule that slides into the cargo bay. The forward section has a small galley, followed aft by a small crew compartment with six bunks. Then it flows back into a staff section with three bunks and a worktable with cushioned bench seats on either side. The last compartment aft is the general's. It has a large bunk, desk and chair, lounge chair, intercom and phone. This may be slower than going home on an Air Force C-141 with its stale box lunch or a chartered commercial flight with its washed out stews, but it will be much more comfortable.

We taxi out, go through the run-up, then the pilot gives full throttle, releases the brakes and we lurch forward. Wheels are up and bang into the wells, and we head north for Seoul, South Korea. It's on the west side of that peninsula, south of the DMZ, the 38th Parallel. We will go over the South China Sea, giving mainland China a generously wide berth, and north over the East China Sea, cross over Inchon, and into Kimpo Airfield, near Seoul.

My first task on board is to write the several dozen thank you notes for the mementos the general has received at the various ceremonies, luncheons, and dinners given by the different units in country honoring him upon his departure. Write the memo, tag it with the gift, and leave it for the next aide to be typed, signed, and mailed when the general gets to his next assignment in Washington, D.C.

About an hour after being airborne, the general buzzes me

back to his quarters and says, "Barney, what are you doing up there?"

"Starting on all those thank you notes. Will have them done before you get back so your new aide can take care of them without any mix-ups."

"Okay. That's great. What's the uniform in Korea when we land?"

"They told me it would be Summer Service "C"... Khaki's, short sleeves and ribbons. Small ceremony at landing, then off for the visits."

"Good. Comfortable. Then, for tonight?"

"Whites, ribbons. Big dinner. Have some remarks ready but you'll probably have to ad-lib some."

"Fine. Oh, and I'll rehearse. Is Alvarez aware?"

"Of course, sir. I haven't quit yet."

"Nor your habit either."

"No, sir, but that was a question and a legitimate response, although a bit caustic."

"You win."

I smile, say nothing. He chuckles softly.

I'm going to check about the uniforms and schedule again before we land. I don't trust the Koreans. They like to go bonkers, and this sounds too easy. With this in mind, I go up to the cockpit, ask the pilot to raise the Koreans on the horn so I can check one more time. This isn't any problem for these pilots, they're accustomed to this. The word comes back, nothing has changed. I should be at peace, but I'm not.

The aircraft groans on for hours, seemingly forever. Finally, we're in the pattern, and the pilot puts this beauty down softer than a virgin's kiss. As we are taxiing to our parking spot, I look out of a porthole size window, straining to see if all is as I am expecting. "Oh crap, it's not! Damn these guys."

The friggin' Korean Marines are out in formation, in their entire splendor! Dress uniforms and medals. The full blower.

The general sees this at about the same time, comes rumbling into my area and says, "I thought you said Summer Service, with short sleeves?"

"That is what I said, and more importantly what those little assholes told me, twice."

"Are you sure that's what they said?"

"General, come on, sir. You know me better than that. Of course it is. You know what these jaspers have a tendency to do. Besides, it's only those in formation in full dress. Their generals are in the same as you, for the subsequent visits I assume. We're okay."

"Not all the senior officers are the same."

"Well, maybe they're not in the group goin' on the tour. If they are, they're going to be uncomfortable. We're fine. Trust me."

"You're right. Let's get this show on the road. Stay close, Barney."

"General, I'll try, but you know that will be a task. I'll be lucky these fire ants don't trample me to death in the stampede of the entourage. Might never get home."

"Well, that's your problem. I'm the general, and you're just a captain. Better you than me." He breaks out laughing. Another joke. He's having a good time. I guess I'm the straight man from here on out.

We debark. Ruffles and Flourishes are sounded, the gun salute follows, and the arrival ceremony is in full orbit. The general troops the line, standing in a jeep, with the host and the formation commander. It's a helluva show. It ends and we are ready to move on. The fire ants are out and scurrying again.

The entourage is gigantic, and I'm so far back in the herd I can't see the lead steer...I'm riding drag once again. The only thing behind me is the chuck wagon, which is in the form of an open jeep carrying the general's household staff.

The host and the general get in the lead vehicle, a sedan. The entourage scurry to the others. I'm relegated to one of the trailing jeeps, along with the remaining underlings. We are off in a blare of sirens and a blaze of flashing emergency lights. The sedans just grease along while the jeeps make most turns on two wheels. While on the base at Kimpo, everyone heeds the sirens and lights. We get the right of passage as we weave in and out of traffic. Once outside the base it's a madhouse. It resembles one huge over-crowded roundabout with half the vehicles going the wrong way. It's a death-defying ride toward the city of Seoul.

We head north to visit several different Korean Marine units. We pass through the Capitol, Seoul, which I remember as a dirty, bombed out city, with buildings full of shell holes and bullet pockmarks. Of course that was some fourteen years ago. Now, it's a modern city with all of the normal hustle and bustle you would expect. It teems with pedestrians jamming the walks, taxis careening wildly about, cars honking, buses polluting, scooters ducking in and out, and other transportation to include bikes over-laden with the riders' wares. The contrast is incredible. A modern city flurry, but with many of the merchants clad in traditional white pajama-like clothes with a wide brimmed straw hat perched on their heads, pedaling their bikes. Even a few ox carts are about. However, it's difficult to appreciate this contrast since we continue to hurtle along with sirens blaring. It's every citizen for themselves.

The trip to the Korean Marine units takes us into the hinterland and is clearly punctuated with the familiar smells of the Korean countryside. Out here, not much has changed. Villages, people along the roads in native garb, walking and pedaling bikes, some carrying honey buckets, many more ox carts, and occasionally a rice-paddy momasan squatting, relieving herself in a roadside ditch...the binji ditch as I recall. Nevertheless, best is the sight of the rich, green fertile land and the smell of home, the paddies. Of all the senses, smell is the one that etches the most clearly. I could close my eyes and know where I am.

At each of the units we visit there is a ceremony, and gifts. Gifts, gifts, and more gifts. Everything from crystal, to silver, to highly finished, walnut stained, wooden unit plaques, and lighters of course. All of which I collect, make some sort of note so I don't forget who gave what, and then load them up with the help of our household staff. I'm given several Zippo lighters, with the various unit emblems. Perks of my job. They're overfilled with lighter fluid so I smell like a Louisiana oil refinery. I give one to the fire bug, Sadowski, and say, "Be careful, don't set the plane on fire." He giggles and snorts. The others go to the remaining gang.

I try not to count on Sadowski to assist me. Alvarez is my first choice. I have not been close to the general since we debarked from the aircraft. Every once in a while, he breaks decorum, turns and looks back at me, smiles, nods, and continues on his way. It's a long, dusty, tiring day. These people are allies, and I have to hold that thought closely because I'm building up a hatred for them as I'm jostled about eating dust back here in drag. For the remainder of my life I will make it a point to step on all ants!

We get back to quarters at Kimpo. I make sure the general is settled. I will be several rooms away in the visitor quarters. Aide or not, I'm only a captain, so I don't get one of the nicer VIP rooms, but since these are Air Force accommodations, they're pretty much upscale, as usual. If they were Marine facilities, I'd be in a tent with a pee tube and four-holer outside. The general looks at me and says, "Barney, you look bedraggled. I'm surprised you didn't shove and claw your way to the front like you usually do."

"I was hopelessly outnumbered and apparently well scouted. I think the Green Dragon folks gave them some advance info. How are you doing, sir?"

"Fine, but tired, and I caught the Dragon quip. Very good."

"Couldn't help myself, sir. Do you want me to check your uniforms for tonight and tomorrow morning?"

"No, Alvarez is here. He'll take care of everything."

"Sure?"

"Yes, stop treating me like--"

"I'm not, sir. It's just best to double-check."

"I can do it."

"Yes, sir."

"What do you have on tap tonight since they have excluded you from this shindig? I could insist you be invited, but it's not worth the effort dealing with them."

"Yes, sir. I know. You're right. Not worth it, and frankly, I might turn into my acronym self with any more exposure to these folks."

"It wouldn't be much of a change from what I noticed today when glancing back at you."

"Now General, I was good. Didn't offend anyone."

"For a change."

"Anyway, I had a pleasant surprise today. My former platoon commander from Korea is stationed here. Lieutenant Colonel William Batten, you should remember him. He invited me to dinner at the Officers Mess. We're going to tell sea stories and lies about the good ol' days, and maybe the general."

"Oh yes. I remember him well. Navy Cross winner. Heck of an officer."

"Yes, sir. Sure was, or is, or whatever. Well, have a good

evening, sir, and stay at the head of the herd with the Trail Boss. See you at first light, or before."

"Good night, Barney, and you two be kind to the old man tonight."

"We'll try...Night, sir."

It's just before first light when I meet the general at his room. The general's wing nuts are clamped down. Lip-whitening tight. He's perturbed to say the least. I ask, "Sir, something wrong? You look ticked."

"I am. My whites didn't fit too good last night. The seam in the seat of the trousers split open. Just before dinner. My jacket covered it, but I was worried all night it would split more and I would show my butt to the Korean brass. To everyone."

"I should have checked everything. I'm sorry."

"I know, I know...don't remind me what I said when you asked. Drop it. Let's get out of here. And leave Alvarez alone. I already chewed on him."

"Aye aye, sir. Not even one little shot of venom?"

"No, not a drop."

We are escaping here without any more pomp and ceremony. Just the Korean Marine general, some senior staff members, and the former Blue Dragon Brigade Commander, and of course a thin string of ants, insignificant lieutenants, trailing after the Korean general.

We board the C-130, and leave this land of enchantment and its many memories, past and present. The general's night was, well, a nervous one, I suspect. Mine was a pleasant walk along memory trail, with no dust, just ghosts and shadows from 1953.

On to Atsugi, Guam, Hawaii and home. I can almost smell a different perfume, the smog.

CHAPTER FORTY-NINE

THE TRIP TO THE BASE at Atsugi, Japan won't take long. It's only about 800 miles. Atsugi is close to Yomoto, and also near Camp Fuji. The well-known city of Tokyo is only twenty miles distant. What's important about all this? We'll be flying eastward, toward home.

We eat breakfast on the plane. Shortly after this moment of pleasure, I start on the thank you notes again. The pile of gifts resting on the lower bunk is waist high; I'll be taxed to finish the notes before arriving on the west coast. I keep the letters gracious, brief and most important, accurate.

Soon after starting my administrative chore, the general beckons me back to his compartment, with a buzzer of course. Those and generals go hand in glove. I think, I wonder what life will be like without buzzers? As I poke my head into his compartment, he says, "Barney, when we get to Atsugi, I want to shop at the Post Exchange. Need to find some gifts for my kids, and Mrs. Barto."

"Sir, it's Sunday. I don't think the PX will be open, maybe Hawaii would be better."

"I don't want to stay in Hawaii any longer than I have to, so arrange this and if necessary, open the PX."

"Open the PX, sir?"

"Yes, find who's in charge, call him on the phone, and have him open it so I can get some gifts for my family. Should be a piece of cake for you. You got the info on that mother and child for Martha, didn't you?"

"Right, sir, and this will be equally as fun."

"For whom?"

"Not me, sir."

He laughs and waves me out with a flick of his wrist. I sure hope whomever I get on the horn has a sense of humor because I don't think this is going to rate very high on the Sunday morning entertainment barometer.

I work my way up to the cockpit again and approach the pilot with this assignment. He tells me he will get the gent on the horn and call me up front when he does.

It takes the better part of a half hour, but I'm talking with Major Trevor Haddock, the Exchange Officer, who since the pilot gave him a slight heads-up, is already pissed and screaming at me, a lowly aide. "Captain, who the hell do you think you are, ordering the Post Exchange opened?"

"Sir, I didn't order it opened. General Barto did. I'm just following his directive and trying to make this as painless as possible. Is that do-able, sir?"

"To be painless, or to open the PX?"

"Both, sir?"

"Hell, no, it's not painless. I'll have to do it myself. I can't bring in workers. I have no cash on hand. Can't open the registers, and probably for half a dozen other reasons it doesn't make sense. However, it can be done. I just don't like the idea."

"Sorry, sir, nor do I, but thank you. We'll be there in about two hours I'm told, so if the Major can meet the general at the plane, and escort him to the PX, it will be appreciated, sir."

"I have to meet him, and take him to the exchange?"

"Yes, sir. We don't have any transportation."

"Very well, Captain. And what is your name again? I want to remember it."

"Captain Quinn, sir. A fine Irish name."

"Yes, I'm sure. See you when you land, Captain Guinn."

"Quinn, sir. Q as in Quintessence."

"Quintessence? What happened to the phonetic alphabet?"

"Originally it was Queen, now its Quebec, sir. One's embarrassing and the other, un-American. I prefer Quintessence, the essence of a thing in its purest and most concentrated form, sir. That's me. Aide, Barney Quinn."

"Jesus, I can't wait to meet you...Captain Quintessence."

"Quinn, sir, as in--"

"Never mind."

"Aye aye, sir."

I knew it. Can still get in the last word. With that prevalent in my mind, I wander back to the general's compartment and say, "Sir, the PX will be opened. The Exchange Officer will accompany the general. He will need a check or credit card; he has no cash, sir, among other problems."

"What other problems?"

"No help, sales clerks and so forth."

"You won't need them."

"Me?"

"Yes, I'll just give you a signed blank check and you can fill in the rest."

"I'm not following your trend of thought, sir...or worse, I am. Why do I need a check? Isn't the General going shopping alone, as usual?"

"In your own brief, sarcastic form... because you're going, and no. Now, for clarity, I won't be going with him. You will. I want you to call ahead again and get me scheduled for a hotsy bath and massage, while you shop."

"What? Sir, the general's kidding? Right?"

"Yes...I mean no. I'm fatigued. It will be just what the doctor ordered. You can shop for me. Select something special for Mrs. Barto, and whatever you think is right for each of my kids."

"General, surely you jest? You need to shop for your family, not me. Particularly your wife. I don't know their tastes and what's right for them. Plus, that major will run a lance through my chest for drill. He'll hemorrhage when I tell him this, let alone getting another vehicle arranged."

"Barney, hospital in New York...remember? You can do anything."

"I knew the moment I did that it would come back to haunt me, but I didn't think a three star general would stoop this low to call in the chips."

"It hurts me, deeply, but what can a general do?"

"Yes, sir. I'm sure it does." Geez, this is going to be painful.

"I'll need about an hour and a half there. Tell the pilots they can refuel while I'm gone."

"Yes, sir. They won't mind. The entertainment in the cockpit on this next call will make their day."

"Outstanding! Great! I'm going to contribute to the morale of the crew."

"Yes, sir. Wonderful. Just wonderful, sir. The General does have money in the bank, don't you? This major would probably love to get me some brig time."

"Now there's a tempting thought. Yes in deedy."

Dadgummit, he's getting adept at getting the last word and he's bustin' his gut laughing again, and my chops.

I trudge my way to the cockpit. Tell the pilots what the general wants. They burst into laughter. I have a sinking, putrid feeling rumbling around in my gut and gurgling up into my throat while waiting for the call to go through. Medically, it's called heartburn; however, in my acronym world it's called AAR, aides' anticipatory reaction.

The co-pilot gets the major back on the radio. I start, "Sir, good day again. This is Captain Quinn."

"I know who it is. What do you want now, Captain? Open the Officers Club early? Perhaps some music in the store while the general shops? Just what is it now?"

"No, sir, not exactly, but it's a thought." I can't resist the comment. He deserves it. He knows this isn't me wanting anything, other than just to get home.

"Well, what is it?"

"Sir, we will need another vehicle. The general wants to get a hotsy bath and a massage while he's here. So if the Major could make an appointment for that, I will be doing the shopping for the general at the Exchange."

There are several moments of silence. Well, not total silence. There are some sighs and groans, maybe a few other sounds that are not distinguishable, and some mutterings, which I believe refer to my family history. Finally, he says, "Okay, Captain. Anything else. Do you know what he or rather you, want at the PX, so maybe we can speed up the process?"

"No, sir. He wants me to use my own judgment, and I don't have a clue so I will just have to sort of shop around."

"Wonderful. Are you a married man?"

"No, sir."

"Great, I bet you're just full of ideas."

"Sir, is the Major married?"

"Yes. And no, I'm not going to help."

"Thank you, sir. See you shortly."

Once again, I plod back to the general's area, "Sir, all is arranged. And I want to thank the general for this wonderful opportunity."

"Great, I knew you could handle it. After all, you can do anything, right?"

"Sir, even three star generals have to face judgment day. This is cruel and unusual punishment. The Aide's Benevolent Society and Saint Peter will remember this. He will dole out more than a few Hail Mary's."

"Whatever the penance he administers will be worth it, and the ABS has no disciplinary authority over generals."

Damn, the general has gotten good at this. He's dishing it out in stronger doses. It's all coming back to haunt me.

We land at Atsugi. The general greets the major, thanks him, slips into the waiting sedan and heads for his hotsy bath. Of course, the major is all smiles when speaking to the general. Then he turns to me, and snaps, "Let's go shopping, Captain, God Dammit."

"Yes, sir. Major, I don't enjoy this you know. I'm an infantry officer, a company commander, trapped in the body of an aide, and after eighteen months in Vietnam, I'm just trying to get home."

"I know, Captain. Sorry. Let's go, so we both can go home."

"Yes, sir." I think, actually this is an easy manipulation. The major is really a good guy.

All goes well. I shop, spend the general's money freely. I get a number of items for Mrs. Barto, and get portable radios and some souvenir type items for the kids. No clothes; don't know sizes. Mrs. Barto gets some jewelry, a necklace and matching earrings plus scarves, and a selection of bath soaps and scents. The general is pleased with the selection and says, "Looks like you're trying to influence my homecoming."

"Just trying to give you a head start, sir."

"Hmmm. With my writing record, I might need it."

I also purchase cards for the general to sign to accompany the presents...a warm personal touch; certainly better than a one page scribbled letter on three-star stationery, and apparently he knows that I know.

We are off and flying a long leg to Guam, which is the largest island of the Mariana's. It's still a long way from home, about 5800 miles from the West Coast, but we're movin' east. There is both an Air Force and Naval Air Station on the island. We will be stopping only to refuel so we'll get off, stretch our legs and get some fresh air. It's the rainy season so we may get wet. Native Guamanians, called Chamarros, remind me of one of my BAR-men so long ago in Korea, Pfc Guatamalamalamala. Since his name was a tongue-twister, and it took too long to say, we just called him Squat. He was short, and one "tuff" Snuffy.

The refueling is accomplished; we are onboard and continue to chug east. The household staff has been good through all this. No need to leave Sadowski or anyone else in Korea, or here.

However, at the rate the general and I are going we are losing ground in the popularity polls. Me in Korea, him in Japan. Probably won't get any flower leis in Hawaii, but he and I are now tighter than ticks.

Chapter Fifty

We leave Guam in darkness, not exactly sneaking out of town, but we didn't make much noise. A little shut-eye will be the first order of business, followed by a light, quick breakfast. Then, for me, the continued writing of "Thank You" notes. I'm making progress but, the lower and middle bunks in my section are cluttered with gifts so my place of haven is the top rack. The climb up is steep; the trip down could be treacherous in a bumpy aircraft.

On this leg, we'll be crossing the International Date Line. In essence, until we cross, we're one day ahead of the date in the western hemisphere. This is too technical for a grunt. This simply means we will be getting to Hawaii on Sunday. Fine. All I know, and all I care about is, I'm getting closer to the real world.

Time drags on while I write and tag, write and tag, seemingly without end. The general goes over his debriefing comments, checks his 3x5 cards, places a few calls from his compartment, and occasionally naps.

Finally, after an eternity, we start letting down, and smoothly hug the runway at Hickam Air Force Base on the southern side of Oahu. This is part of the several historical major military installations clustered together in the area. It is adjacent to Pearl

Harbor, and in the neighborhood of Camp Smith, the FMFPac Headquarters where the general will be going for his debriefing.

There isn't a reception committee. None! No troop formation, no ceremony or any form of acknowledgment. I was correct, we must have worn out our welcome...no flower leis. Just a few sedans and drivers. One vehicle will carry the general and me to Camp Smith, another will take the household staff to a barracks for the night, and yet another, the general's and my overnight baggage to our quarters. I would have thought there would be some form of a warm greeting, maybe the CG, FMFPac, Lieutenant General Mueller and senior staff, or perhaps friends. However, not the case. Just an icy cold reception in a literally warm ambiance. The greeting for the general sucks, but purely from an aide's point of view, it's nice not to have the scrambling and shoving entourage to contend with again. No ants, not even a solitary bug.

The trip to Camp Smith is short, a hop, skip and sedan ride. The debriefing, or briefing, or whatever one wants to use to describe this session, is concise in content and short in duration. Again, chilly, cold. It's late afternoon when the general and I emerge into the slowly fading, tropical sunlight. There is a warm breeze drifting up from the harbor which is truly a Godsend considering the icy atmosphere of the welcome and debriefing. This gentle wind rustles the palms, and the sounds of the leaves rasping upon each other at least warms the soul. We both stop, take deep breaths, and the general says, "Barney, what do you have on tap for tonight? Want to come with me to visit an old friend in Kaneohe Bay?"

"Oh hell, General. I would love to do that, but the FMFPac Sergeant Major, Neil Kovac, an old friend from my past is picking me up and taking me to his home for dinner. Sorry, sir."

"General Mueller's Sergeant Major?"

"Yes, sir. I saw him a few times when they visited us in country and promised I would stop to visit on the way home if the opportunity presented itself. We go back a long way."

"Oh, I knew you liked to chat with my leader, but wasn't aware you were so deeply imbedded in the command structure here."

"Sir, you're jerking my chain again. That's not nice to do to such a loyal and faithful servant."

"Servant? Hell, I wondered at times who was the general and who was the aide."

He has another laugh for himself over his witticism, and then goes on, "Just kidding. It's okay. Have a good time. It's too bad, we would have had fun talking about our tour. My old Raider friend lives right on Kaneohe Bay, a nice swim before drinks and dinner, like old times."

"Yes, sir. That would be great. I'm really disappointed, but I can't renege. If I would've known sooner--"

"I know, and I wouldn't want you to back out. Have a good evening. See you bright and early in the morning at the plane. We're leaving at dawn. Don't want to stay any longer than I have to...we'll eat on the plane."

"Okay, sir. See you in the morning. Have a good evening, and be careful driving over the Pali. Go just before it gets dark. The sunsets are magnificent from there, and be sure to stop for a moment to see the upside-down water fall."

"Sounds like a plan."

"And sir, watch for hammerheads in K-bay."

"Hammerheads? Sharks?"

"Yes, sir. There's a slew of them in there."

"Oh! Sure you won't come? You'll be right at home."

"That's cruel, very cruel. Still it's tempting, but I just can't back out of this other invite."

Dawn comes early, especially when I stayed up too late drinking cold beers and swapping stories with my good friend and his wife. We must have told the Case Springs jump story a dozen times. Each time, we looked better in the telling. Still, a sad story, three of our fellow jumpers were killed in the accident, and the rest of us injured, most seriously, from being dragged over the countryside. This tour is probably his twilight cruise before retiring, and heading east to Civil War country where he can pursue his battleground hobbies and interests.

Early or not, hung-over or not, I'm at the plane waiting for the general. As he arrives, so does Lieutenant General Mueller and his wife. They are here to say goodbye to the general, and present each of us with a farewell flower lei. How about that? Can't trust the polls. They look great around our necks, and for damn sure smell good, at least mine does. And, thank God, no trays, plaques or Zippos, however, still a note to write.

We board, the general last. Each of us settle in our compartments. The hatches are closed, and we taxi out for take off. The final leg to the actual real world. We'll be landing at Marine Corps Air Station, El Toro, in Santa Ana, Southern California, a little south of LA. It is suspiciously close to Laguna Beach which sets my mind to wondering.

The props pitch whine with the urgency to bite into the air. Then they are changed and that and the brakes releasing send us leaping forward. As I look at the general's lei, which he flung on my desktop as he passed, I think, what a strange reception here. There was always something extraordinarily chilly about the relationship between these two generals, but this was artic icy. Frigid! Didn't meet the general when he arrived, not present at the debrief, and spent all of five minutes planeside when we left. Well, not my business, I'm just a captain, and a damn tired one at that. We're airborne, and Diamond Head on the southeastern end of Oahu, passes under our wing. We're on our way home. Final leg, Hot damn!

As soon as breakfast is over, I start to work again on these doggone letters. The good news is, I'm going to finish, and leave things in good order. No Irish pennants.

I hear a rustling in my section of the capsule, and look up to see the general standing at my worktable. He's staring down at me with hands in his trouser pockets, rocking back and forth, smiling warmly. He says, "What's up, Barney?"

I place the pen on the table, wave a finger at the writing tablet and say, "Just finishing the last of these notes, sir."

"Well, forget it. You've worked hard enough, and long enough. Get some coffee for us, and come on back to my cabin so we can chat."

"Sounds like a deal to me, sir, but I have just one more to do, General and Mrs. Mueller. Okay if I just finish the note, and then I'll close up shop. All right?"

"If you must. Hurry, I want to talk."

"Want anything besides coffee? Cartwright has some tasty looking Danish up front."

"Now, that sounds good. You know, I don't remember us having any of those treats at breakfast in country."

"No, sir. We didn't. And if we would have, you wouldn't remember it anyway, you ate so fast."

"Another dagger in the heart. You're out to regain control, huh? Well, let me tell you something, I'm going to get the last laugh, and the last word. Count on it."

"Yes, sir. Be back there in a jiffy."

"Okay, hurry with that last one, it's not important." He returns to his compartment, laughing to himself. Frisky and very pleased, indeed. He is up to something.

I knock and enter his compartment with SSgt Cartwright trailing behind with the coffee and a tray of Danish. The general offers me the lounge chair since he is leaning back in the high back, leather executive chair with his feet propped up on the desk. Cartwright pours us a cup of coffee, offers the general then me a Danish, and says, "Anything else General? Captain?"

The general replies, "No thanks. Leave us alone for a while."

"Yes, suh, General. Cap'n?"

I reply, "Okay, thanks Sergeant Cartwright, and please check to make sure everything is set for us to get off quickly when we arrive."

"Yes, suh, Cap'n."

"All the stuff on my two lower bunks needs to be boxed and sent with the general."

"Me and Ski will get it done while the Cap'n is in with the general, suh."

"Okay, but no Sadowski, he'll...never mind. Thanks."

Cartwright leaves smiling. The general rocks back and forth in the desk chair, squinting his eyes, grimacing some, and I suppose contemplating his choice of words. I'm busy chowing down on the Danish, with plans for another, when he says, "Barney, I want to tell you a story. Personal. Just between the two of us. Never repeat it."

"Yes, sir. Want another Danish?"

I'm in a total free fall here. When the general said, hang it up, I felt every muscle, nerve, fiber in my body release from the hooks they have been hanging on for over a year.

"No, you eat 'em. I just want to talk."

"Fine, sir. I'm listening."

I'm not even sure of this. I may hear, but my body and mind have gone into a total vegetative state. If a rung-out sponge has feelings, this is it.

He takes a few more sips of coffee, frowns, and says, "Barney, I have been in competition with that little man my entire career."

I don't need to ask anymore, I know exactly about whom he is talking. All the icy moments make this clear.

Then after a short pause, "He's planning on becoming the Commandant of the Marine Corps. That's not going to happen. Not if I can--" His voice trails off.

"Humm? Sure you don't want another Danish, sir?"

"Do you know, one time when we were Second lieutenants we were at a party. He stood on a table and proclaimed that he was going to be the Commandant someday. I knew, right at that moment, I was going to prevent that from happening, maybe become CMC myself. However, now, if not myself, at least ensure through some form of actions that he won't. Nothing has changed my mind over the years."

I'm now stunned out of my sponge state, senses screaming with alarms, but locked into an eerie silence. This is not the time for my sarcastic sense of humor or any witty remarks. Just sit, sip coffee, eat the last Danish, listen and shut up. For the next few hours the general outlines his plans. He tells me what he believes will happen and gives me a homily in military politics, or at least his envisionment. I am spellbound, and haven't touched another roll.

When he finishes, he gets on the intercom and orders some more hot coffee. Within a few minutes, Cartwright brings in a fresh pot with clean cups, and says to me, "Cap'n, everything is ready. Items packed. Uniforms pressed and hangin' up. The generals unnie is up front. I'll bring it back when you're done. Anything else, suh?"

"No, thanks a lot, Sergeant Cartwright, and thank the others. Especially for my uniform. You didn't need to do that."

"That's all right, Cap'n. You're a good man, suh."

"Well, thanks Sergeant Cartwright."

We sit in silence until the coffee is served once more and Cartwright leaves, then the general says, "See, I knew they liked you. Well, anyway, what'd you think?"

"General, this is way out of my league. I'm speechless. To be honest, I can't think of anything helpful to say, or that I should say. Way, waaay out of my league. Not appropriate for me to comment, sir."

I'm flustered. In a way I feel compelled to say something, anything, but hesitate. The general doesn't say anything for several moments. Like everyone, I feel that overwhelming compulsion to speak when silence falls. I don't. I despise politics, so best I let things pass.

Finally, he says, "Why don't you say something. You've never been at a loss for words before."

"Sir, this is different. However, if you truly believe this is what needs to happen, then do it. I think I understand. I'll always support you, and whatever is right for the Corps. Always the Corps, sir. The troops."

"You're right, Barney. I'm being unfair. It's not your place to comment. Just to listen. But I thank you for what you did say, and I will be mindful of the intent of your last remark. After all, that's what's most important, isn't it? What's best for the Corps."

He continues to talk some more, mostly about how he sees this all playing out. I again relegate myself to silence, being a good listener, not a sounding board. This is not only a three star general talking, or rather sermonizing, but also someone who has become a good friend. A close one at that. I said all that I needed.

Our session is ended by the voice of the pilot over the intercom system. "General, we're about forty five minutes out of El Toro. If you need to freshen up some, now's the time. And General, that request of yours is not there yet, but on the way I'm told."

"Thank you. Captain Quinn is in here with me so he can hear you."

"Roger, sir. Understand. Out."

I love the abbreviated replies, "Roger. Understand. Out." Sounds like old times, in the paddies. The general and I get up, and he says, "Let's get ready to land. It's a great day, Barney. We're home."

"Almost."

"Almost? Don't be so pessimistic, we could swim from here if necessary."

"Yes, sir, but bear in mind your beach jogging escapade."

"And the fishing boat, and the tennis courts, and the nurses, and the C-Rations, and the...I know, I know."

He breaks into a roaring belly laugh. He is still laughing as I leave the cabin to clean up.

I can feel the aircraft beginning to emit the groans, thumps, creaks and whines of letting down. Have to hurry with a quick birdbath, but not in a helmet anymore. I'm going to miss those douches and dustings. Anyway, a few scrapes with the razor, put on some Foo Foo Juice, and a fresh, pressed unnie, thanks to Cake and the guys and I'm ready. Man, am I ever.

The wheels kiss down, the engines reverse pitch, brakes sporadically grab, and we slow, turn and begin to taxi.

We're back...at last...the real world.

God, I love America...home!

Chapter Fifty-One

WE TAXI TO THE APRON, and the final few feet of our trip. These turns of the wheels seem to take longer than the rest of the journey. Everyone in the aircraft is in a dither. The household staff is jabbering away, boasting what they're going to do first. Of course, it's never first, but damn close. I'm excited, anxious to plant my feet on mother earth in the real world.

The general is acting strange, fidgeting nervously. He's up front in the cockpit, looking out the windshield, talking with the pilot and co-pilot, and then straining to see outside again, looking around.

We pull up, lurch to a stop, and the pilot shuts down the engines, however, the crew isn't opening the hatch. We can't deplane. I go to the cockpit and say to no one in particular, "What's happening? Let's open up, set our feet on the good ol' US of A, and smell the sweetness of home."

The general replies, "No, we can't get off yet. Have to wait."

"Sir? Wait for what?"

"None of your business. I'm in charge here."

"You've always been in charge, but you're getting more involved than normal and seem edgy. Can I help, sir?"

"Don't need your help right now, Barney. Just be quiet, and enjoy the moment."

"What moment, sir?"

"Dammit, Barney. Shut up."

Whoa, he's excited, nervous. As I suspected, he's up to something. Best be quiet...for now.

The pilot breaks this next moment of silence, and says, "Okay General, it's here. Everything is ready. We'll open the hatch."

"Ah, good. Thanks."

The crew chief opens the hatch. It's a sunny, summer day. The air is...well, its air. There is no smell of the paddies, only the normal odor of gasoline and aircraft fluids, and of course a whiff of good ol' Southern California smog. The general grabs me by the arm and says, "I've got a surprise for you. Look." He points to a sedan parked at the edge of the operations hangar. The back door is opening and Ryley slides out, waves, and then clasps one hand over her mouth, jumps up and down, and waves again.

I look at the general and say, "What's going on here, sir? Looks as if you've been busy playing Cupid. My, my, my, sir! Idle hands truly do get into mischief...Sir."

"Well, get over there and say hello. Give her a hug and a kiss." He gives me a gentle shove in her direction and adds, "You're home, my friend."

I jog, hesitantly at first, over to the shadows at the corner of the hangar where Ryley is standing. I'm a grab bag of emotions, irritated and happy, cautious and anxious, perplexed and wondering. I'm not sure I know what to make of this. Her expression is changing from a sheepish grin, to a broad, gleaming smile with eyes sparkling, and then back to the awkward beaming again. I slow to a walk as I get to her and say, "Hello, Ryley. . .you're lookin' more beautiful than ever. This is one helluva surprise. I take it the general set this up?"

"Yes, he did. I tried to tell...but..." Her voice slips off into the hushed stillness that engulfs the two of us.

We stand and stare for a split second more, then we hug, release, hug again, grasping each other tightly, rocking back and forth. I bend back slightly, look into her eyes, lean forward, and we kiss. Hesitantly at first, then into a long, deep kiss that is not only steeped in raw emotion but one that is searching for answers. I can't help myself, she's lookin' fine, and I'm, well, me.

The general comes over, and says, "Hello, Ryley. Good to see you again. You gave me a scare. I thought something had gone wrong."

She colors into a pale blush, smiles coyly, gives the general a hug, and a kiss on the cheek. "No, everything was fine. I was a little late, or rather hesitant, but the driver did all he could to get me here on time. Thank you, Walter."

I frown and say, "Walter. Walter is it?"

"We're pals, buddies. He told me to stop calling him general and use Walt or Walter."

"Stop, you two. Glad to do it, Ryley. It's my pleasure. This is great. Just great! Well, what'd ya think, Barney?"

"Helleva surprise, General. Well orchestrated. You'll make a decent aide in your next life. You have a larger soft spot than I imagined, excluding the hospital."

"Just trying my hand at a form of social work in case things don't work out."

I laugh. "You're also getting to be quite the comedian, sir."

"Yes, you're right, however belatedly. My aide stifled my development...or forced me into the role. Not sure which. We made a good team, Barto and Quinn."

"Quinn and Barto."

"Barney, for Pete's sake! But, what'd ya think?"

"Well, we were a good team. No, a great one, but I don't think you're aide material. However, I do believe everything else will work out for you. It always does, and rightfully so."

"Thanks, but I mean of this," pointing to Ryley. "General, I know. I was just...it's thoughtful, and you finally got in the last word, or last something."

"Sure did. Feels good. Now I understand." He gives me a slight push, and we chuckle. I say nothing, not even a nod.

The household staff has unloaded and placed everything in the waiting sedans. The general says, "Barney, this is it. What can I say that I already haven't? Job well done. Superbly done. I'm going to miss you. An aide and friend, in a grunts body. Damn good combination. I have a flight to catch. Ryley, give me a hug and a kiss. Got to go."

She does, and I reply, "Sir, what can I say? Thanks for everything, but most of all, for your friendship."

We shake hands, he pulls me close one more time and gives me his rustling, one-armed bear hug. He steps away, smiles, and raps me on my upper arm with his fist, and says, "That's for old time's sake...and for Bill Dunn. He asked me once why I never punched you, only him. I told him I would, when the time was right."

"Well, to be honest, sir, I probably deserved several thumps over the months."

We look at each other directly in the eyes. The moment takes me all the way back in time to Hill 22, and beyond. I suck up some much needed air, and step back.

I pop to attention, snap up a solid Marine Barracks, 8th and "I" parade ground salute. He responds in kind, turns and slides into the back of his waiting sedan.

It's over, much too quickly. Doesn't seem possible. We've been jousting and locked in verbal combat for over a year, and now we're thick as target paste, perhaps forever. The sedan slowly pulls away; he turns and waves through the rear window. I return it, with a low, growling, "Hoo ah." Who knows, we both may be on our twilight tours. His obviously with greater consequences.

The household staff confronts me. They pop to attention, smartly, and salute. I'll be damned, they look like Marines. In unison they say, "Bye, sir. Good luck. You're a hard man, but fair, sir." Sadowski grins, no saliva. The others smile as well. Sadowski and I shake. Cake and the others give me a mystic, ethnic five of sorts.

I say, "Thanks. Semper Fi. Lookin' sharp, men. Stay this way. Wherever."

I step back, turn, take Ryley by the arm, and head for the sedan, not knowing what is in store for our relationship. I think I know, but always a Marine, like the troops, first things first, or damn close.

At the car, I stop, and look at the general's disappearing sedan, and say to Ryley, "You know, at first the general and I were in the same orbital path without realizing it. Then we crossed without colliding, and later we joined paths. A relationship smoldered in our...our own solar system. It grew, a solid team evolved, and finally a close and probably a lifelong friendship developed."

Ryley says, "What was that?"

"I was just thinking out loud. Anyway, a hell of a show and ride. The general and me."

"Barney, I'm still not..."

"Never mind. Let's see what the Mizpah has in store."

CHAPTER FIFTY-TWO

My THIRTY-DAY LEAVE IS OVER. Ryley and I are unable to resolve our problem. I suppose it was just not made to work. She wanted out, got it, and then wanted back but only on her terms. Happened to me before. She wants me to leave the Corps now, and then tuck myself away, safe and sound in her beach cottage home in Laguna, doing something drowsy with my life in a sleepy town. No adventure, no surprises, no excitement. Isn't me, and as a result can't be us. In one of my rare mellow moments somewhere in the past, I read a line that is apropos. "True love can't be found where it doesn't exist, and can't be hidden where it does." I looked, maybe not long enough, but I didn't find that gift. So be it. I've had worse patrols.

After we say our goodbyes at the cottage, I stop at the beach in the center of Laguna, where Ryley and I first met. I find a bench near the beach volleyball area, and sit for a spell in the warm sunshine. I gaze out over the ocean listening to the hushed, soothing sounds of the rolling surf and the harsh squawking of the gulls. V-ball players flash in front of me as blurs. Time passes slowly, or quickly, I'm not sure which, but enough of it ebbs by to allow me to ensure I've made a good decision. I know I have...I'm positive I have. It's time for a kick restart.

I stand, take the Mizpah medallion from around my neck,

walk the few steps to the beach, scrape a small hole in the sand with my foot next to the mini boardwalk, and drop it in. It did its job, kept me safe and got me home. Now maybe some guy or gal, or better a couple, will stumble upon it and allow its magic to spin a special web for them.

I check into my new duty station in San Diego, the Recruit Depot, and as I'm handing over my orders, the personnel clerk says, "Sir, we're holding a message for you. Been here several days. Actually over a week." He reaches under the counter top and hands me a sealed, plain white envelope with "CAPTAIN BERNARR (BARNEY) QUINN" typed on the outside. It almost looks official. However, it has no return address and no postage marks. I feel like a mouse sniffing the cheese, knowing something's not right but too hungry to stop. I'll take a bite.

First, I say, "Thanks, sergeant." While he is processing my orders by pounding away with several different rubber stamps, I start to open the envelope. The thump...thump...thump of the rubber stamp and the rustling of papers distracts me enough to cause me to fumble with the envelope flap. "Awwg. Damn!" I snap my hand away and mouth the paper cut, then return to the chore at hand. I get it open; unfold the note leaving a tiny smudge of blood on the top edge.

I take a quick glance, then step back in astonishment. It reads,

> "Dear Barney,
> Call me at Balboa Naval Hospital.
> I've been assigned here. We need to talk.
> SOON. DAMN SOON.
> > > > Elaine."

The note stuns me. The blood smear must be symbolic. I think, are you kidding me? No way. I'm not messin' with this any longer. She's nuts! Maybe the bloodstain on the note is an omen. Whatever, I'm going to let this die a natural death, if it will.

I'm snapped out of my thoughts by the sergeant clearing his throat. He has finished thumping, stapling, shuffling, and initialing. He says, "Sir, you're all checked in. Here are your copies...and sir, the Commanding General and the Chief of Staff want to see you immediately, sir. It's just across the passageway and two hatches up on the port side."

"Thanks, Sergeant." Pretty salty Marine. Must be a product of the Sea School.

Then I mutter aloud, "Dadgumit, the skeletons are rattling around again. It never stops. They're in every closet."

The sergeant says, "What's that, sir. Can I do something else?"

"No, sergeant. Everything is fine. I was just mumbling."

"Don't worry, sir. It'll pass."

"I'm not so sure. Yeah, I guess it will." He must think I have some sort of paddy hangover. Oh well, got to go up the passageway, see the general and chief of staff, and start this tour the same way all the others have started. Someone telling me what's best for me...dadgum mentors.

Epilogue

STANDING NEXT TO THE COMMANDING General in the Reviewing Stand, I think, four years here at the Depot have zipped by much too fast. I stare out across the asphalt of the parade deck here at MCRD, San Diego, at the mass formation of Recruits, formed for the weekly Friday parade. The difference today is that I'm retiring from the Corps. I've taken a job in the civilian world and will be starting a new career. This parade is for me. It's my epilogue. No more Snuffies and Magpies...at least not Marine ones.

The General commands, "Pass in Review."

The Parade Commander salutes, faces about, and with a booming voice, repeats, "PASS IN REVIEW."

With this comes the other bellowed commands from troop leaders, and with these, and the music, the regimental formation of recruits commences to march.

I stand at my best parade deck attention. Tall, shoulders squared, back straight, arms naturally at my side with thumbs along the seam of my trousers, and heels locked. My eyes are focused and straight to the front, but my mind drifts along with the music, and I wonder how this past four years in San Diego got away so swiftly.

I reported in and it was de ja vu. I knew the Commanding

General from the Basic School so many years before, then from serving in his division in Vietnam, and while an aide to General Barto. The Chief of Staff here is Colonel Roy Thomas, an old friend from Hawaii and Vietnam. My boss here, the G-3, was the Press Officer in Vietnam. The warm, friendly but crotchety Colonel Arnie Carter, the helicopter squadron commander where we got the general's pilots, is here as well. All here, and all ensuring that I was assigned doing what they thought was best, in the Depot G-3 Section as an Assistant Operations Officer.

I wanted to go to the Recruit Training Regiment, and work with the recruits, the future of the Corps...the Snuffies and Magpies. However, no one asked what I wanted. I belong with the troops, not papers and perforator droppings. Unlike me, I didn't say anything at the time. I regret that now. I suppose General Barto and all my mentors, past and present, unwittingly wore me down.

The lead troops flash by, bringing me back to the present, with the sun beating down on my back and bouncing off the asphalt grinder making it feel warmer than the ocean cooled seventy-two degrees. However, once again my mind quickly retreats to flickering images of other people and other times.

Lucy Caldwell, my dear and prankish friend had visited me on several occasions here in San Diego. She had written a book of her experiences in Vietnam, *Sin/One Way/Economy Class*. 'Sin', the acronym for Saigon on an airline ticket, allows Lucy to poke some fun through the title. She came to San Diego a few times to visit her wounded Marines recovering in the Naval Hospital here. She would always call me, and we would spend the evenings dining and talking about our times together. Even then, she was Lucy, making me order from the menu for her. She insisted she was keeping me in training as an aide so I would not slip back into my revolting Neanderthal habits.

The only downside of her time here was bumping into Commander Seitz while visiting the wounded at Balboa Naval Hospital. This gave my nemesis, Elaine, another opportunity to raise her back, bare her claws, and hiss and spit at me. Damn, she is one angry woman. She must have missed her distemper shot. If looks could kill, I would already be in Arlington.

Later, Lucy dropped off the radar. Then one day I received a letter from her attorney. He informed me that Lucy had fallen ill, passed away, and had left her estate to be divided among her wounded Marines. Rightfully, the most substantial amounts went to the most severely wounded and still recovering men. She left me a token amount, with love, and her book. The book would have been more than enough. She had signed it,

> "To Barney,
>
> Who was part of every word.
>
> Love, Lucy."

To paraphrase a remark, she put her Will where her heart was. She was a perfect example of the meshing of thought, word, deed and love. I will never, ever forget this lady, nor do I suspect will many others. She left a lot of footprints on the pages of life of many Marines.

She also left me something else. On one of her trips, she introduced me to Toni Leonetti. A tall, long legged, dark-haired Italian gal, my age, who is wonderfully attractive and adventuresome. She lives and works in San Francisco but is entertaining a move to this area. Besides her stunning beauty, she has character stronger than Kryptonite. I don't know where this is headed, but she's not hesitant about peeking around the corners of life.

This introduction is a blessing in many ways. One, it lessens my forays to animal night after Happy Hour on Friday nights at the MCRD Officers Club. This was the ultimate jungle. Hunters and prey mixed together without any cover other than the cigarette smoke of the bar. It was difficult telling one from the other. However, both had a sporting chance, and I hunted well.

Again, I snap out of my daydream. The Color Guard is passing the Reviewing Stand. The CG and I salute the colors, and I again lapse into the past.

My mind focuses on General Barto, now a four-star general. He's not the CMC, but he is the Assistant Commandant, and I guess he at least accomplished his secondary objective. General Mueller's retired. Obviously, neither are nor will be the Commandant. There is what I suppose is a compromise CMC... And if that's so, he is for sure a solid Marine and the Corps is in accomplished hands.

The general visits out here on occasion, always contacting me. He also calls from time to time to ensure I am okay. Recently he was here and we met in Long Beach, a few towns north of Laguna, where he was the Grand Marshall of a Fourth of July parade. He tried to talk me out of retiring, but after a three-hour conversation in his hotel room where he had me cornered, he finally went with my flow. Our parting was the same. A bear hug, a jostling, a thump on my arm...and the warm smile with his steely blue eyes boring into my soul.

Others come out of the shadows of my past, or call, all trying to get me to change my mind. It isn't to be. Too many mentors and too much politics for my taste. It was one helluva ride, and I would take it over again in a heartbeat, but I'm leaving. No more mentors, just merit.

The last of the troop formation has passed, and the Depot Band is formed in the center of the parade deck. They are playing the "Hymn." I feel the CG's presence, standing next to me. I sense my sister and her family, friends, new and old, seated behind me in the Reviewing Stand. My mind fades away once again, and I see the ghostly silhouettes of Generals Barto and Cunningham, of Stoop and Dunn, of Gunny Roe, Doc Eden, Beasely, Crowe, Chang, Rutherford and all the Snuffies and Magpies in my life pass before my eyes. Last and lingering, Ski, LCpl Baronowski. Faintly, I hear their voices..."Hey, Skipper".."Stoneface".."Cap'n "..."Lima Six Actual, over".."Fire Mission"...and of course, Parzini uttering..."Cocoa, Skipper?"

I suck in some much needed air as the Band Director, a friend of mine from many ceremonies together here at the Depot, catches my eye from the parade deck, gives me a barely noticeable wink, and strikes up my favorite, *"Men of Harlech"*, as the Depot Band marches off. I mouth the words, "Men of Harlech, Spear tips gleaming..." I love the music of the parade deck. It reminds me of the boys in blue, white dress. Love it...always have, always will.

The Commanding General, turns, shakes my hand and says, "Major Quinn...Barney, damn, the Corps is going to miss you. And you'll miss the Corps. Good Luck."

I nod, imperceptibly, remembering its definition. I think, the Corps is, a state of mind. Then I say, "Thank you, sir. You're absolutely right, sir. I will miss it."

We salute, it's over, and again much too soon.

I know where I'm headed. I hope it's as good as where I've been. I feel the hairs on the back of my neck bristle. Is it the music? The moment? Or do I smell an ambush?

Whatever, Barney's goin' on patrol, just in a different kind of paddy.

THE END